PASSPORT TO CRIME

PASSPORT TO CRIME

the FINEST MYSTERY STORIES *from* INTERNATIONAL CRIME WRITERS

Edited by
JANET HUTCHINGS

CARROLL & GRAF PUBLISHERS
NEW YORK

PASSPORT TO CRIME
The Finest Mystery Stories from International Crime Writers

Carroll & Graf Publishers
An Imprint of Avalon Publishing Group, Inc.
245 West 17th Street, 11th Floor
New York, NY 10011

AVALON
publishing group incorporated

Library of Congress Cataloging-in-Publication Data is available.

ISBN-13: 978-0-78671-916-7
ISBN-10: 0-7867-1916-8

9 8 7 6 5 4 3 2 1

Book design by Maria Fernandez
Printed in the United States of America
Distributed by Publishers Group West

CONTENTS

INTRODUCTION

Sometime in early 2002, *Ellery Queen's Mystery Magazine* began making plans to launch a new monthly department devoted to stories in translation. For years American mystery writers had been finding lucrative markets for their work in other parts of the world, without there being a reciprocal flow of foreign mystery and crime fiction into the American market. By 2002, thanks partly to the efforts of the International Association of Crime Writers (IACW), the direction of the current was starting to change. A few crime novels in English translation were not only finding American publishers but getting review attention in American journals. *EQMM* felt the time was right to throw in its oar.

It wasn't the first time *EQMM* had put out a call to writers outside the United States: The "worldwide short story contests" the magazine ran yearly between 1946 and 1957 and again in 1962 were advertised across the globe and brought in submissions from at least a dozen non-English-speaking countries. Subsequent decades saw *EQMM* translating into English for the first time the work of Jorge Luis Borges and other internationally renowned writers. Our perspective has always been global; what was different this time was that we intended to take a very active role in securing the translations. We would do some real-life detective work and identify authors unknown to American readers. We would commission our own translations. We would investigate the state of mystery fiction in countries few Americans associated with the genre.

Finding the right literary agents, first-readers, and translators in each of the countries we targeted was a sometimes-daunting task. A few years earlier—before members of the international mystery community began actively networking through organizations such as IACW—the same searches would have been far too time-consuming to be practical for a magazine with a staff the size of ours. As it was, the first issue with the department we christened "Passport to Crime" appeared only after nearly eighteen months' gestation. It has run continuously ever since. What you have in your hand is a selection of stories from the first three and a half years of the series—twenty-six tales from fifteen countries and eleven languages.

In these stories, beneath differences in mood, tone, and customs, readers will find much that echoes the themes and conventions of American and British crime and mystery writing. Indeed, the book opens and closes with tales that pay direct homage to immortals of the American pantheon: Poe and Queen, respectively. In between are stories that run the gamut from hardboiled to historical, humorous to psychological, private eye to police procedural, sociological to supernatural. All the forms of English-language crime fiction are represented, but rendered in ways that reveal profound differences from the American or British sensibility. To accent the effect of nationality on perspective, the stories have been ordered in globe-hopping sequence, never allowing the reader to stay in one place for long.

In the five years since the first translations for our Passport series were commissioned, several of its authors who had not previously seen print in the United States have obtained book contracts with American publishers. We are right on the cusp now of what promises to be an explosion of interest in the United States in translated fiction. In the UK translations have already claimed some of the most prestigious mystery prizes and awards. The introduction to each story in this volume includes a reference to the author's available work in English, and, for readers of other languages, some indication of what the author has published in his or her native land.

Nearly sixty years ago, when *EQMM* published a special "United Nations Issue" composed of the foreign submissions to its worldwide contests, then editor Fred Dannay said that the magazine's receipt of submissions from so many different corners of the world showed that "while we still have a long way to go politically, the planet Earth is truly One World detective-storywise." May the fast-unifying world of crime fiction we see today prove to be a harbinger of the political unity that has eluded us for so long. We offer this book in that spirit.

—Janet Hutchings

Fred Kassak

Who's Afraid of Ed Garpo?

Translated from the French by Peter Schulman

A tale about a French writer obsessed with Edgar Allan Poe is irresistible, from an editorial standpoint, for the start of a book of mysteries in English translation from around the world. After all, though it was penned by an American, the first detective story ever written, Poe's "The Murders in the Rue Morgue," was set in Paris and employed a French detective. The author of "Who's Afraid of Ed Garpo?" Fred Kassak (a.k.a. Pierre Humblot), burst onto the French mystery scene in the 1950s when he won the Grand prix de Littérature policière for his first novel. His reputation increased when his books—whose witty style earned the attention of French filmmakers— began to be adapted for film. To date, only one of Fred Kassak's many novels, all so popular in France, has been translated for publication in the United States: Come Kill With Me *(Bobbs Merrill, 1976).*

W hen my first cousin's son (my first cousin, a.k.a. the third-rate actor who got himself killed along with his wife, a third-rate actress, when they were both on the road in a third-rate play and riding in a third-rate bus that crashed) asked me if I could help him find a job and a place to live in Paris, I happily offered him (at a modest rent that I didn't feel the need to declare on my taxes) the sixth-floor maid's room turned *studette*[1] in the

---

1. *studette*, a tiny studio without a bathroom

building I owned, in which my wife and I lived on the third floor. And it was just as happily that I got him a job warehousing books at my publisher's.

When the boy was born, his parents had asked me to be his godfather, an honor I felt I couldn't refuse even though I was slightly peeved that they hadn't named my own godson after me (Alain) but preferred to name him Edgar instead.

To be perfectly honest, I had been a somewhat inattentive godfather for quite some time. I had never had any children of my own (nor had my wife) and I had little interest in other people's children, as I couldn't bear the thought of anything distracting me from my work. A writer's first duty is to devote himself exclusively to his work. Everything else is superficial.

As for my work, I don't think this is the most appropriate time to talk about it. I would simply remind those who might not be familiar with it that, in a style which, I dare to flatter myself in saying, upholds the purity and clarity of the French language and which is in keeping with the rules dictated by our great literary tradition, I endeavored to portray a certain high-minded, self-centered, hypocritical, and vain bourgeoisie.

At an early age, Edgar had distinguished himself by his stunning lack of studiousness, which was exacerbated by his propensity for violent sports. With no help from his parents (with whom he had all too often shared an itinerant lifestyle) and with no diploma whatsoever, he was hard-pressed to find either a job or an apartment once he had completed his military service, and was quite relieved when I provided him with both.

As such, Edgar was indebted to me, but life and the study of the human soul have taught me that we always find good reasons to be ungrateful, and, as I have blithely written in one of my novels: "Indebtedness has never been grounds for gratitude."

I have to say, however, that the boy was not completely unlikable in my eyes. Despite our difference in age (I was pushing sixty) and in a society where soon-to-be senior citizens spend all their time scorning young people, he seemed to have a certain respect for me.

In the studette, my wife had installed a little shower near the kitchenette. But rare are those in our day and age who are satisfied with the bare essentials, and Edgar wasted no time in asking us if he could use our bathroom from time to time. I attach no importance to the material world and the idea of ownership is practically a foreign concept to me. I therefore barely criticized my wife for having granted him permission to do so once a week.

When he was either going to or coming from the bathroom, we would sometimes meet and exchange a few words. Besides the fact that I have no prejudices in terms of class, an author owes it to himself to be curious about everything and I asked him succinct questions about the warehousing of books before going on to explain to him (in great detail) what was wrong with those who had written them.

One day, he was emboldened enough to ask me if he could read one of my own books and I cheerfully lent him several of my most accessible novels. He returned them to me a week later and told me how impressed he was with the subtlety of their narratives and their stylistic craftsmanship.

I immediately had him over for dinner, much to the shock of my wife, who had somehow come to the conclusion that I looked down upon him. I quickly explained to her that the boy was no mediocre thinker, and for a writer my age, the approval of young people is a strong indication that one's work will withstand the test of time.

Over dessert, when we had finished talking about my books, I asked Edgar about his other literary tastes, half out of courteousness, half out of curiosity. He had hardly read anything my living colleagues had written (I was able to reassure him that he was not missing much) and he had a predilection for *B.D.*s.[2] He was familiar with all the great authors of *that* genre, the deceased as well as the living. He thought that he had a particular talent for that kind of artistic expression and had even completed several comic-book layouts. And, while we were on the subject, since we both worked for the same company, which, coincidentally, also had a comic-book division, could I please slip in a few words of introduction to my editor on his behalf . . . ?

I smothered the words "subculture," "para-literature," and "some nerve" that were lining up on my tongue. Why not, after all? I owed it to my reputation to encourage the young ones, especially those whose "means of expression" were in no danger of competing with mine. Nonetheless, just to be sure of what I was about to support, I asked Edgar to fill me in on the kinds of comic books he designed: humor, satire, science fiction, or sado-masochistic porn?

"I'm adapting Edgar Allan Poe's *Tales of the Grotesque and Arabesque.*"

I recoiled in my chair and my wife dropped her little spoon onto her dessert plate. There was a silence before I forced a smile.

"Are you doing it because you share the same first name?"

"Because I think he's awesome!" Edgar said, looking at us incredulously. "Don't you agree?" he said, using the familiar "*tu*" form of address.

(I suddenly realized that I found it jarring that he used the *tu* form with me and that he referred to me as his uncle, and by my first name to boot. But he was my godson and I couldn't stop him from doing that. I also noticed that there was something

2. *B.D.*, for "*Bande dessinée,*" can be translated as "comic book," but in France they're taken seriously; published in hardcover, for both adults and children

about him that I found repugnant: his gelatinous lips clashed with his athletic bearing. Those thick, viscous, and undulating lips resembled two snails caught in the act of endless copulation and disentanglement.)

"For me," I said, articulating each of my words with great precision, "Edgar Poe is a literary histrionic who is solely interested in shocking his reader. He is a mere manufacturer of bloody and morbid phantasmagoria, the pretentious—even pontificating—form of which barely masks an incoherent essence. A grab bag of cheap thrills! Even as a child, I had an instinctive, visceral aversion to him, from the first time I picked up one of his books, and this continued with all subsequent readings—which, I can assure you, were few and far between. Your aunt knows that he is the author I hate the most. So, you see—"

"That's strange," Edgar said. "It's as though you had a personal vendetta against him."

"I hate false glory, that's all. And what 'masterpiece' are you adapting at the moment?"

"'The Tell-Tale Heart.'"

I couldn't help springing to my feet and shivering with disgust: "THAT ONE!"

"Why not?"

"Come now! It's . . .THE WORST!"

"Honestly, I don't think so . . ."

"If I remember correctly, an individual tells us that he is seized, gradually, with an urge to murder his old neighbor not out of any hatred towards him, nor to steal his gold, but because one of his eyes 'resembled that of a vulture—a pale blue eye, with a film over it' which 'makes his blood run cold.' He becomes so obsessed with this 'vulture's eye' that he believes that only the old man's death could permanently free him from it. That's about right, isn't it?"

"That's the right one, all right," Edgar said as he looked me over, slightly perplexed.

"One night, as he creeps into the old man's bedroom, the old man, who was sleeping, suddenly jumps up in terror with his vulture eye wide open. And suddenly, the crazed narrator begins to hear 'a low, dull, quick sound . . . It was the beating of the old man's heart.' And the heartbeat, which becomes 'louder and louder,' begins to make so much noise in the silent night that the narrator fears it will wake his neighbors up. 'With a loud yell,' he lunges towards the old man and proceeds to strangle him until the infernal heart finally ceases to beat and until that abominable eye is finally closed once and for all. After which, he cuts the body into pieces which he skillfully hides under the floor. . . . Am I still on track?"

"Yes, that's pretty much the gist of it."

"Nevertheless, alarmed by the screaming, the neighbors decide to call the police. The policemen interrogate the narrator about the old man's disappearance. He tells them that he went away on vacation, escorts them to the room in order to show them that the gold has not been stolen, and, in a euphoria induced by having committed the perfect crime, invites them to sit and rest awhile. He laughs and jokes with them, and feels quite at ease . . . when suddenly, he begins to hear 'a low, dull, quick sound' . . . which grows 'louder—louder—*louder*' . . . to the point where he is at the end of his rope and blurts out to the police (who, curiously, did not seem to hear a thing): 'I admit the deed!—tear up the planks!—here, here!—it is the beating of his hideous heart!' . . . Did I do a good job in summarizing it?"

Edgar sized me up with accrued confusion.

"Man, for someone who purports to have read the least amount of Poe possible, you seem to know him pretty well, Uncle Alain!"

"Such a masterpiece doesn't need to be read very often to be remembered! It's a condensed bit of blather."

"Poe's subtitle was 'A Madman's Defense.'"

"That's the easiest trick in the book! You can make a madman say and do anything! But even for a story about a madman, it's filled with completely implausible details. Come on, it doesn't hold up at all! I never would have dared to hand it in to my editor; I wouldn't even have dared to put such drivel down on paper."

"That may be, Uncle Alain," said the viscous lips as they splashed lightly, "but we're talking about the great Edgar Allan Poe! . . ."

After that, I would have been completely justified in letting Edgar fend for himself with his beloved artistic expression. But, as my wife finally convinced me, I would have been guilty of a meanness that was beneath me, and might have had imputed to me an offense equal to his. I also have to say that my wife thought of Edgar as the son we never had, and was sometimes excessive in her kindness towards him. I had enough trust in her conjugal loyalty to be sure that she would not have recommended just anything to me, however: When Edgar volunteered to show me his little bubble drawings, I felt perfectly comfortable passing this chore on to her. And when she assured me that they were accurate representations of Poe's incoherent rambling, I took her word for it, sight unseen. Mind you, my thoughts were decidedly elsewhere, as I was on the verge of finishing my own novel.

I took advantage of my handing in my manuscript to the main editor of my publisher's literary division to talk to him about Edgar—while making sure I let him know that I wouldn't be upset in the least if he did not want to pursue this matter, and would drop the whole thing if my efforts on Edgar's behalf were the slightest bother to anyone he worked with. Nevertheless, and to my dismay, he felt compelled to call his equivalent in the B.D. division, and I was able to tell Edgar that very night that I had succeeded in getting him an interview for the following week. For which he thanked me to the point where his sluglike lips trembled with delight. I forgot all about it after that, as I became solely preoccupied with how my manuscript was about to be received. Even an author of my stature (as my dear old deceased colleague, the author Henri de Montherlant,[3] once remarked with such subtlety) is always a little bit nervous right after handing in a manuscript to his editor. I still hadn't heard anything by the time the cocktail party rolled around.

It was the annual reception for the "Pain Prize," the prize awarded to the most moving account of the loss of a loved one. This year's laureate was the mother of a soap-opera actress who, with the help of a journalist who was a specialist in that sort of thing, managed to describe the agony of her eighteen-year-old daughter's death of leukemia in just 380 pages.

The happy winner was quickly dropped in favor of the buffet, which everyone swarmed—and where I came face to face with my editor. In truth, I was expecting to see him there, and that was even why I had decided to attend the party: Would he mention my manuscript? I wondered. As soon as he saw me, a giant smile spread across his long face. "My dear friend! I was just about to call you, in fact!" He downed a glass of champagne, fattened up his plate with foie gras, took me by the arm, and led me to a window recess. "I had to thank you for that little masterpiece you gave me!"

"Really?" I said as a wave of relief and joy rushed through my body (despite his rather restrictive use of the word "little").

3. 1930s author known for morality plays and preachy narratives. Committed suicide.

"Absolutely fantastic, my dear friend!"

"You're too kind, dear friend."

"So rich in its descriptive power! And what virtuosity!"

"You're too kin—Excuse me? What virtuosity?"

"In the sense that it was both faithful to the spirit of Edgar Allan Poe, and yet completely unique as well! I'm not a big fan of the comic-book genre, but this! I can't tell you how grateful we are to you for having recommended that boy to us, my dear friend! I understand he's related to you in some way?"

"He's my . . . godson."

"A real thoroughbred! What I also appreciated is his talent for expressing so much in so few words. By the way, old boy, I hope you won't mind my saying it, but I found your latest book a trifle verbose. I think a few cuts here and there would do it some good. You seem a little pale all of a sudden. How about joining me for a shot of whisky at the bar?"

Normally, my novel should have come out well before my godson's comic book. It had been scheduled a long time ago, while—thanks to me—his comic book had appeared to them all of a sudden—like the Virgin Mary to Bernadette. Moreover, it takes a long time to manufacture a hardcover comic book with color drawings. And yet, in the end, various scheduling glitches delayed my novel's publication date, while miraculous technological innovations hastened his. As a result of all this, his comic book came out before my novel:

PHANTASMA-GORE

by Ed Garpo

The jacket cover had a drawing of a heart (dripping blood) erupting from between the planks (which were also doused in blood) of a greenish floor. It was all quite alarming, but, after all, Poe deserved no less.

• • •

After having given me an autographed copy of his magnum opus, Edgar, as it turns out, took off for Angoulême for the opening of a festival dedicated to his fine art form. Needless to say, I wasted no time forgetting him so that I could concentrate on the publication of my own book.

A few evenings later, I was having dinner with my wife, happily watching the evening news, which featured an inter-European massacre chock-full of bloody images, when, brutally and without warning, they cut to a report on the closing ceremonies of the Angoulême Festival, with a closeup of the bloody heart from the cover of *Phantasma-Gore*, which had won first prize. This was followed by the obligatory interview with Edgar, who, smiling with all his lips (which were as sluglike as ever), spoke about his unwavering admiration for Edgar Allan Poe, about how he had always dreamt of adapting Poe, about the strategies involved in adapting Poe's work, and about all the words of encouragement his editor had given him. Not one word about me. It was enough to make one throw up. Which, of course, I did.

In response to the thinly disguised criticisms with which I greeted him upon his return, he could only muster a mealy-mouthed explanation of how he was afraid I would have been offended were he to have attached my prestigious name to his humble little comic book—as though he were still so naive as to think that any author would mind hearing his name mentioned no matter what the context might be.

In any case, *his* name was certainly mentioned all over the place. And his face was equally ubiquitous. With his slug-lips, Ed Garpo was invited to every possible "arty" talk show on television and on the radio. As for the newspapers, there were entire pages devoted to the "aesthetic ramifications" of *Phantasma-Gore*—along with the requisite pictures of Ed Garpo and his slug-lips. They all declared that he had brought some badly needed new blood to the anemic world of French comic-book writers. *Phantasma-Gore* was prominently displayed in all the bookshops and in every supermarket under huge signs that boasted: "As seen on TV," accompanied by pictures of Ed Garpo and those omnipresent slug-lips. Predictably, *Phantasma-Gore* was an enormous success, proof positive that mass media produces mediocre masses.

As though by chance, Edgar never missed an opportunity to tell the world that he was my godson. As a result of this, when my book finally came out, all that the few critics who bothered to review it could come up with was that, given the astoundingly implausible aspects of my story, I should have asked my godson to turn it into a comic book, which would at least have given the reader something interesting to look at. Obviously, I was virtually ignored by both the television and radio media, and my book was pulled altogether because of sluggish sales.

To say that, given the circumstances, my editor behaved in a completely odious manner would be an incredible understatement. When I voiced my displeasure at the way he was handling my novel, he replied that word of mouth was the best form of advertizing there was, but the word of mouth on my novel was pretty poor, and that the only way it could be marketed at all would be to highlight, in bold letters, the fact that the book was written "BY ED GARPO'S GODFATHER." I slammed the door as I stormed out of his office. When I walked down the hallway, a colleague greeted me derisively, as did the interns, the receptionists, the administrative assistants, and even the doorman: They all looked at me in a contemptuous manner.

Don't think that I wasn't listening! I could hear you perfectly as you whispered "Paranoia" into each other's ears. I suppose you're going to suggest that I was paranoid. Why "paranoid"? Of course, I was always a little hypersensitive, but who would be so cruel as to bring attention to it with such exaggeration? "Paranoid"? You had better reflect on your choice of words and notice the lucidity—or rather, the cold-bloodedness—with which I am telling you this story.

My extreme sensitivity allowed me to perceive all the different forms of derision of which I was the target—even the most dissimulating and treacherous kinds. And when I say that I could no longer attend a cocktail party or a dinner without seeing the derision that was behind the most innocent of glances and between the most inoffensive of words it's because DERISION WAS IN THE AIR! Don't make me yell it out.

And who was responsible for all this derision? The most derisive one of them all continued to dwell right under my roof and to come to dinner at my apartment with great regularity. Every week, I had to see his slug-lips embrace and disentangle themselves from each other as they sucked on his fork, as they oozed a viscous blend of admiration and gratitude while seemingly (and derisively) remaining oblivious to the humiliation I had to endure because of him.

I can't say for sure when exactly the idea came to me, but once it was conceived, it pursued me day and night. It had to be the lips. Every time I looked at them, disgust and panic grabbed me by the throat. And, slowly but surely, it dawned upon me that Ed Garpo had to be destroyed before he and his slug-lips could swallow me up, digest me, and relegate me to being "Ed Garpo's godfather" until the end of time.

And yet, there was still time: He had only published one comic book. Sure, it was a big hit, but a book has a short life span; in two weeks it would be completely forgotten. More than quality, what makes an author is quantity. There was still time to stop him before he could come out with a *Phantasma-Gore II*,

III, IV . . . which his editor would no doubt ask him to crank out with great urgency.

If you have any doubts about my mental state, behold the brilliance, the art of exploiting circumstances to their fullest, the skill with which I proceeded.

In order to crush a man, one must always make use of his passions. Besides Edgar Allan Poe, Ed Garpo's other passion was *U.L.M.* single-engine flying.[4] Thanks to the apparently generous advance he received on his next comic book, he was able to obtain a U.L.M. pilot's licence, purchase, with four other U.L.M. fanatics, a U.L.M. plane, and leave all the horrors of civilization behind by taking off, as he did regularly, at the Persan-Beaumont flying club. The airfield was easy to get to from my house. He could easily have found larger accommodations with more amenities than my little studette, with a bathroom that would have eliminated his need to use mine. But because of Persan-Beaumont, he wanted to stay in my neighborhood, which complicated his apartment search by limiting his options—but which, in fact, suited me perfectly. For the extraordinary ingenuity of my plan demanded that he continue to use my bathroom for a certain amount of time.

The beauty of it all lay in the fact that he himself had inspired the plan when, one evening, as an answer to one of my wife's questions, he had said that what he found particularly thrilling about U.L.M. flying was that it was fraught with danger. I can still hear him now: "By definition, the planes are ultralight, and therefore ultrasensitive to the slightest wind, and because they lack any power reserves, they must maintain the same speed in flight as during takeoff. At two hundred, four hundred meters in

---

4. *U.L.M.*, for "*ultra leger motorisé*," an ultralight single-engine plane which can also resemble a hang glider with a propeller on it

altitude, even in ideal weather, that kind of flying necessitates an intense level of concentration. The slightest moment of inattention, the slightest loose bolt, and you crash. . . ."

My wife's eyes opened wide as she oohed and aahed. I just nodded my head as I finished my soup. If you had seen me, you would never have imagined the kind of explosion that "crash" made in my head.

A fiery image of slug-lips spit out into the sky.

My sabotaging the plane by unscrewing some bolts was out of the question, of course, because of certain insurmountable obstacles that cropped up, not the least of which was the fact that I have absolutely no mechanical knowledge.

But I knew a lot about eye drops.

Not too long before, I had asked my wife a few questions after a strange type of eye drop had popped up in the medicine cabinet. She informed me that they belonged to Edgar, which didn't surprise me in the least: Ever since he'd started taking his baths in my bathroom, he'd had a tendency to consider my medicine cabinet as an extension of his own. Without my having to prompt her at all, my wife explained to me that he used the eye drops right before he flew in order to insure optimal visibility.

I suddenly recalled this bit of information when Edgar brought up the dangers of flying, and my scheme was hatched shortly thereafter: Thanks to his drops, I would insure that he would fly with *minimal* visibility, with all the predictable consequences that such a detail would entail.

I just wanted to make sure that "right before he flew" was to be taken literally and did not mean approximately: "right before *going off* to fly"—which would have killed my idea right there and then.

I was relieved to find out that, despite her gender, my wife had expressed herself with precision: The flask disappeared from the medicine cabinet when Edgar left for Persan-Beaumont (twice a week, on average), and reappeared upon his return. Edgar therefore brought it with him and made good use of the drops *right before he took off.*

You will never understand how this idea came to me, nor how I could have concretized it with such precision and talent if you are unaware that, like all sensitive creatures, I was always in some sort of pain. A creative writer who is continuously sitting at his desk or in front of his typewriter in the silence of his office is surely concentrated on what he is creating, but also has an eye on his gut. At the mercy of my daily woes, I thought that I was afflicted with all sorts of grave illnesses, from intestinal obstructions to interstitial nephritis, in addition to the more familiar types of cancers. These slightly hypochondriacal tendencies pushed me to consult a plethora of medical works and instilled in me a strong passion for medicine and medications in general. That's why, even though I might have been incapable of sabotaging a little plane, I was most competent when it came to dealing with eye drops.

As such, I knew that atropine causes intense dizziness through the dilation of the pupil and a suspension of ocular adjustment. It was imperative that this sort of dilation, which could eventually trigger a certain amount of suspicion, be compensated with eserine which, in turn, causes an opposite contraction within the pupil.

I also had to add a pinch of coniine (which causes blurred vision) as well as—the cherry on the cake—a dash of stramonium (which can cause dizziness and hallucinations). Some of these substances can be found in over-the-counter products, others in homeopathic herbs. With Edgar spending all of his time drawing in his studette and my wife spread thin across the four corners of the neighborhood in search of an apartment for him, I was free to extract, mix, and dose in perfect peace. The dosage was of crucial importance because the product could not be activated until Edgar was up in the air. That's why my project would have been impossible to carry out if he had put the drops in before leaving the apartment, as I would never have been able to concoct a deferred version of the drug that could have taken effect as soon as he arrived at Persan-Beaumont. At best, he would have gotten into a car accident, but the last thing I would have wanted was to have another motorist get killed—or worse, to have someone actually save *his* life.

There was little likelihood of anyone saving his life after a plane crash. The real risk was in the ensuing investigation, which could potentially reveal the visual difficulties he would endure and lead to an analysis of the drops. In my eyes—I dare say—that presented only a moderate risk, and therefore a risk worth taking.

Obtaining the exact dose became exceedingly difficult, and all the more annoying in the sense that I had to use myself as a guinea pig, which caused all sorts of dilations and contractions to my very own pupils, in addition to some partial blindness and dizziness.

And one hallucination.

Once, during a lugubrious afternoon of work, I heard a gentle knocking at the door of my office, and with a silky swish of material, a man dressed in elegant nineteenth-century attire entered the room. He made no effort to say hello and, without the slightest hesitation, walked right up to me and sat down on a corner of my desk. He sat down, looked at me, and that was it. He had a high and bulging forehead under black, curly hair; thin and sardonic lips beneath a short moustache; and deep-set black eyes, eyes that were filled with horror, with pity—and irony. "Who are you?" I cried out as I sat up straight. "Get out! And

WHO'S AFRAID OF ED GARPO?

don't come back!" He remained motionless. He said: "Nevermore!"—and disappeared.

My vision and my reason were so perturbed that I almost "crashed" right down on the floor. My concoction was apparently right on the money.

All that was left for me to do was to substitute my own mixture for the drops that were in the flask—which I did on the eve of Edgar's flight date.

It was a long night, and I couldn't sleep a wink. That morning, as I was lying in a catatonic state next to my wife, who was snoring peacefully, I heard Edgar enter our apartment, then go into the bathroom to run his bath. I would have preferred staying in bed, but I usually got up when I heard Edgar and had breakfast with him. I had to do what I usually did.

So, courageously, I forced myself to get up, went to make some coffee, and, greeting Edgar cordially, asked him how he had slept. Apparently, he had slept better than I had, even though—he admitted—he always felt a little apprehensive before a flight. But his apprehension actually excited him. I asked him if, at his age, he couldn't find any other sources of excitement. He shook his head, grinning ear to ear: No, he couldn't, because he had no woman to share his life with. Until further notice, therefore, he would be devoting his life exclusively to Ed Garpo.

Fine. If that's what he wanted. I gazed at him with curiosity as he downed his last cup of coffee: Could he not feel that it was his very last one? As I watched his slug-lips, I thought about how I would no longer have to see them flap up and down again.

As soon as he left the apartment, I raced toward the bathroom. The drops were gone: All I had to do was wait.

Everyone knows that there is nothing more torturous than waiting. It was even harder to take in my case because I had to put on a good face in front of my wife. In order to avoid her, I could have locked myself up in my office and pretended to work, but I still had to have lunch with her, and she obviously noticed that I was hardly touching my food at all. She looked me over with concerned tenderness:

"You're not hungry? You're not feeling well? You're so pale! You wouldn't be hiding some sort of flu from me, would you?"

In a rather lively fashion, I told her that I was indeed fighting something, but I was fighting it all alone, and was old enough to take care of myself like a grownup. In the wake of her pained expression, however, I apologized and told her that I was tormenting myself over the ending of the novel I was working on—which was not a complete lie.

In fact, my anxiety was oppressive and was giving me cramps to the point where I was having difficulty breathing.

After lunch, I went to stretch out on my bed with the help of a tranquilizer. But I could find no rest: When and how would I learn of the news?

I began to imagine how I was going to come up with the most appropriate response: shock and grief, but within reason. Above all, I couldn't overdo it. It was at that point that I heard the front door open. And men's voices. And among those voices . . . I leapt to my feet: There were three men wearing aero-club jackets. My wife had already gone up to the door to greet them. Edgar was among them. Bandages wrapped his stomach and held up his arms; his head was also wrapped in bandages. His slug-lips managed a grin and pronounced with a flap, "Hey there! Don't panic! But I just had a close call!"

Apparently, I no longer needed to think about how to react: A red-hot branding iron sizzled across my stomach, another one seared my back. I could hear myself scream out in agony, and felt myself falling into the depths of darkness.

• • •

I didn't regain consciousness until I was in a hospital bed, in intensive care, in too much pain to ask anyone what had happened to me, and too weak for anyone to tell me.

Then, little by little, my condition started to improve, and I found myself right here, in this room. With you, Professor, who looked at me with such pride and benevolence, with you, Doctor and Nurse, smiling as you watched me, and you, my wife, who stared at me with great affection.

But no Edgar.

Professor, you informed me that I have been suffering from a congenital heart deformity (the only deadly illness that escaped my mind) which came to light only as a result of the intense shock that I experienced upon seeing Edgar when he came home after his accident. I survived only because of an astonishing string of circumstances which led to a successful but serious and delicate operation. I was now out of harm's way and back in the affectionate hands of my loved ones.

"And what about Edgar?" I asked. "How is he doing?"

You looked at each other, and my wife was the one who answered first, with a wistful smile on her face:

"You're strong enough now, so I don't have to beat around the bush with this: He's dead."

"Dead?" I cried out as I sat upright in attention. "But when did this happen?"

"Almost right after your attack. Miraculously, he had walked away from his accident practically unscathed; all he had was a broken wrist and some cracked ribs. Or so we thought, at least. We had overlooked a slight nick on his head . . ."

"Which occurs quite frequently with this kind of wound," (as you continued, Professor). "Your godson was able to come home, in full command of his faculties. But in fact, he had sustained a skull fracture, which led to a fatal hemorrhage. . . ."

It was highly imprudent, but I absolutely had to know:

"And the accident," I enquired, "was caused by . . . ?"

"Some sort of mechanical glitch, no doubt. It's hard to know for sure given all the debris from the aircraft. Your godson, though, had complained about some visual difficulties, as well as some dizziness and hallucinations, but . . ."

"But?"

"But he must have been suffering already from the effects of the brain trauma he had just undergone."

"That must have been it," I said. "Poor boy!"

I shook my head in sadness, while inwardly being overwhelmed with an intoxicating sense of triumph.

"A heroic end to a heroic life," I added profoundly. "He was a very talented artist. His death is a great loss to the B.D. profession."

I was feeling confident enough to allow myself this brazen bit of sarcasm. You were all too clueless to have even detected it. As a matter of fact, I don't think you were listening to me at all. There was a pregnant silence. My wife looked at you, then turned toward me and gently whispered in my ear, as she squeezed my hand, "His death saved your life."

Now it was my turn to remain speechless as I stared at you all, not daring to understand what had happened. You took it upon yourself to dot all the *i*s for me:

"Your condition required an emergency heart transplant—and therefore a compatible donor. That donor was brought to you by the Heavens in the form of your godson. And since he left no document behind opposing such an operation . . ."

I was still staring at you all, petrified, as my heart began to beat through my ears.

"I know that he would have endorsed it," my wife insisted. "He really liked you, you know!"

The poor woman ascribed my incredulous stupor to some

sort of sorrow, when, in fact, I was feeling quite elated! Yes! Not only did I succeed in knocking off Ed Garpo, but I had also . . .

A cold chill suddenly swept through my bones. My head began to throb, and it seemed to me that the pounding was getting louder and louder in my ears. I would have liked to have been all alone, but you had pretty much settled into my room.

"Me too," I said in a halting manner, "me too. I'm positive he would have agreed to this. I'm positive that the author of *Phantasma-Gore* would have appreciated it. Wouldn't he? It's worthy of his great talent, don't you think?"

I talked and I talked, to get rid of that noise in my ears—until I realized that the noise was *not* within my ears.

As much as I tried to heighten my voice, the noise increased, becoming louder and louder . . . a low, dull, quick sound . . .

I sat up in my bed in a cold sweat. Couldn't you hear it? And yet the noise became louder, louder, and louder! You were all looking at me in such a benign fashion with your smiles stuck to your faces like cotton candy! You *pretended* not to hear anything! *You suspected me from the beginning!* And you did it on purpose, didn't you, Professor, putting *THIS* in my chest! And, at the moment, you're enjoying my disgust! I understood it all! And it took this for me to finally understand why I'd always had a visceral disgust for Edgar Allan Poe!

The incessant, infernal noise filled the room. I couldn't bear it any longer and I was at the end of my rope when I shrieked:

"That's it, you bastards, I confess! I was the one who killed him! Take a good look at those eye drops! BUT STOP THAT BEATING FROM HIS HIDEOUS HEART!"

Beatrix Kramlovsky

Silk Road

Translated from the German by Mary Tannert

Austrian Beatrix Kramlovsky was a respected visual artist with works exhibited in galleries in Germany and elsewhere before she turned to the literary arts and began to write plays, crime novels, and short stories. She has thus far contributed two stories to EQMM's Passport to Crime series. The German-language original of the story anthologized here was a nominee for Germany's Friedrich Glauser prize for best short crime fiction of 2004. The author often assists in the translation of her own work into English, bringing to the prose a poetic quality not always found in crime fiction.

Toward seven in the evening, Armin Pewlacek headed quietly up to his bedroom, double-checked the pens and papers he had spread out on the desk, looking for telltale signs that would reveal an unannounced motherly visit to his room, breathed a sigh of relief as he pulled off his clothes, and enjoyed a leisurely shower. A short time later, the telephone rang downstairs. He heard her light step, the creaking of the pearwood floor as she stood before the telephone, shifting her weight restlessly, waiting, as she always did, for the ring tone to finish before she picked up the receiver. Wasn't it comforting, this predictability in all she did?

"Pewlacek." Her voice was high when she spoke, rising on the last syllable like a question, as if she were unsure, after all these years, that this really was her name.

He stood motionless, and waited.

"Papa won't be home till later; we're supposed to go ahead and eat."

Armin grunted his agreement, even though he knew she couldn't hear him, and pulled on a sweat suit. One more look in the mirror. He hadn't missed anything. Everything was under control. Whistling cheerily, he pounded down the stairs into the kitchen, where his mother stood working at the stove, her skin shiny from the steam.

The table had already been set for three. Armin hesitated only a moment before he cleared away the extra place setting and got out the candles and matches and the round glass candleholder he had given her for her last birthday. She turned around when she smelled the smoke, first startled, then smiling. To Armin, her pleasure felt like the softest flannel, warm from sleep. For a moment he closed his eyes and was, once again, a small boy lying in bed in the evening.

Why can't I fly, Mama?

Because you have no wings.

If you were a bird, I would sit on you like Nils Holgerson on his goose, and we could fly out into the big wide world. Far, far away.

Oh, but that would make Papa sad.

Well, I hope so, he had thought, but he hadn't said it.

She set down the steaming pot and lowered the ladle into the thick broth. He loved her economical movements. She didn't fumble unnecessarily like some other mothers, artificially spreading their manicured fingers. She rarely wore anything but her wedding ring. Only once had he seen on her arm the ruby bracelet that his father had given her on their fifteenth wedding anniversary. In her simple way, Mama had a touching beauty, and it annoyed Armin every time his father felt it necessary to enhance it. But now she reached for her spoon, and smiled at him before she began to eat.

"Isn't it cozy here, just the two of us?"

Her lips opened wider and the spoon, full of soup, vanished between them. It hurt so much to watch her, and at the same time it made him so inexplicably happy.

"Papa will be late again tonight. Work. Much too much work."

Armin said nothing.

"I hope nothing will hold him up on Saturday."

"Saturday?"

"Oh, Armin, now don't tell me you've forgotten his birthday!" She laughed. He listened as she planned the dinner, named the guests. In a voice that was light and suddenly young.

"What are you giving him?"

"I'm not telling!" She laughed again, and he knew everything even before the sweat broke out on his hands as it always did. In his mind he saw his father untying the ribbon, folding back the tissue paper, carefully and with a very special expression on his face that Armin otherwise only saw when his parents believed themselves to be alone. His eyes would drink in the lace, the flowered straps, before he folded the tissue paper shut again and said, "I'll save this for later." And none of his friends was allowed to peek. Every year it was the same.

Mama was much more casual. Her gifts lay around to be looked at, pored over. It didn't bother her at all when Aunt Margot ran her hands longingly across the silk ribbons, when Uncle Herbert plunged a greedy fist inside a still virginally-wrapped satin camisole. Papa didn't like that. Armin knew this, and understood that these instances were among the rare occasions when the two of them agreed on anything.

"Papa has so much to do," she complained, and he asked himself yet again why she had married him, why she waited patiently, for nearly two decades now, for him to come home, bringing his horrible work and all the thoughts that belonged to it into their small house.

"Why do you have such a hard time showing him how much you care for him?"

Her eyes focused on him, brooding, moss green with yellow flecks. In the sunlight they reminded him of light amber. He pushed back his empty soup plate. Her timing for "serious" talks had always been catastrophic, in his opinion. He made a noncommittal noise and stood up to clear away the dishes. He knew she was studying him intently. A view of his back, clad in gray. Presumably her forehead was wrinkled in consternation.

Did she look like that when she talked to his father about him? In their bedroom. Wearing the burgundy-red neglige, birthday 1997. Or the emerald-green boy-cut pants, Christmas 1999. Had she already noticed that the bodysuit was missing? The apricot one with five pale flower appliqués on the front, with vermilion-red pistils and lime-green stems embroidered in the finest, thinnest thread? Their wedding anniversary in 1996. He had torn it unintentionally along the side seam. His shoulders were too wide; he'd really grown over the last year. That cool feeling on his skin, the faint scent of White Linen, her favorite perfume these last few months, had pricked his senses so much that the hair had stood up on his arms and legs.

"I mean, you show me how much you care."

Her voice had a pleading tone now. But loving your mother doesn't mean telling her everything. Even with Mama there was a limit as to how much she understood intuitively, and it was dangerous to expect too much from her. Armin turned around, the dirty plate still in his hand.

"Oh, Mama, don't worry so much. Everything's fine. We're a happy family. I'm giving him something really special this year. It's a surprise. So I'm not telling you, either."

He was still smiling when he reached the top of the stairs and the door to his room. No, Father would never forget this birthday. The question was merely whether he would solve the puzzle in time, because he hadn't shown any sign of that yet. The silk flowers, hadn't they provoked any spark of recognition? But Father almost never talked about his work, at least never when Armin was there. Did he mention his investigations in the bedroom, as he gently pushed the satin camisole up over Mama's shoulders? Did he say: You know, I saw one just like this today, on a corpse, the apricot-flower murderer.

No, Father wouldn't talk like that. Work is work and schnaps is schnaps. I don't bring the dead home with me. That's the way he always interrupted colleagues at social events who began carelessly to talk about a case. Armin would have liked to know whether the investigations were conducted the way they showed them on television. If they were, his father would arrive upon the scene of the crime, follow the police officers to the body, look around him, observe all the tiny details, make notes, declare open season on the killer in the quietest of voices. He must have recognized the bodysuit. So carefully chosen; all the dark blue and black silk undies and bras had been considered and discarded. Armin had taken a lot of time for the decision. Did Father ask Mama about her underwear? Did she wear what he suggested or did she select it herself? Had she already begun to search for the pieces that were missing? The plum-colored ensemble had only been gone for two days, the high-cut panties and the underwire bra. The finest embroidery in eggplant and reddish-purple thread on stretch tulle. But just a little, just enough that you could run your finger over it. The fabric was so soft, you just couldn't help holding it to your own skin. The woman this afternoon had understood that.

He got ready for bed, humming, and turned the light out. Subdued noise rose up from the first floor; Mama had turned on the radio. Armin liked the dark. The blackness didn't frighten him. The woman, on the other hand, had gasped underneath the pillow, even though he spoke soothingly to her and told her it would be over soon. Yes, he'd really grown this past year, become a strong young man, broad-shouldered and imposing, according to Aunt Margot. And good-looking. In his own kind of way.

"You wait and see, now he'll go out with the other boys and come home drunk for the first time and discover girls!" Aunt Margot had found this idea very amusing.

Mama, on the other hand, knew that remarks like this made him nervous, that he didn't like them. Mama was sensitive and respected his silence. The woman this afternoon had talked so much. Talked and talked about nothing at all. Useless conversation. It never ceased to amaze him how easily he gained entry to strangers' homes, how he was positively urged inside.

November. Soon Christmas decorations would appear in town, strung across the street to swing spectrally in the fog above the cars. As a small child, he had sung Christmas songs with Mama, for what now seemed to him like weeks and weeks. He had baked cookies with her, dipped lumpy candles. He loved the short days, the long twilight, the smell of damp wool. The first snow, the flakes drifting down hesitantly. He and Mama in a circle of light inside the warm house. Father's arrival home in the evening came as a loud disruption of that idyll. His hand on the child's shoulder was just the hint of a hug, but Armin always pulled quickly away.

My little man, Father often called him.

November. There had been pumpkins in the apartment of that other woman, the one three weeks ago, and colored corn cobs in a wooden bowl; a leafless branch of wild rose hips, glowing red, stood in a floor vase. Mama would have liked the sparely-furnished room. Only the plants added any color. And the apricot-colored bodysuit suited the scene perfectly.

Father hadn't said anything. Only Mama had occasionally mentioned the new case since then. She probably didn't know enough; the lingerie hadn't been mentioned in the newspaper. Sometimes, when Armin brushed her hair for a quarter-hour, hard, the way she loved, she speculated on Father's work and how it must be to be so close to crime.

The house had now grown very quiet. He heard the kitchen door squeak, and then her steps, moving into the living room. She would wait. For half her life she had waited. Had let time dribble away. Had oriented everything toward that moment when her husband came home. Toward creating a meaningful life for him. Thus the child: something for the lonely hours. Armin, there to fill the gaps in her days. Without Father it would be different. Better, he thought. For her, too. Finally her own life, with new goals. Would she still wear silk underthings then?

He stretched and looked at the glowing hands on his old alarm clock. The woman this afternoon had told him that she was expecting visitors this evening. They must have found her by now. And by now it would surely be dawning on the investigators that the murder three weeks ago wasn't just an isolated case, it was the beginning of a series. Father was the specialist in cases like these.

Father would stand in the door and stare at the bared body, noting the synthetic blanket that had been drawn carefully over her head, over the pillow on her face. The hands laid across her naked belly, the fingers folded in a last prayer. The legs straight and close together, alabaster with fine blue veins. Like a statue that had fallen over. Father would recognize the dignity with which the body had been handled. A still life of death. Father would observe the silk panties and risk a brief moment of near-recognition. He would lift the blanket from the torso and suddenly see the purplish lace at the décolletage as if it were covering other breasts, against familiar skin. And how would he react then?

Armin turned over in bed. He'd have loved to be there, to watch it all, while Mama sat unsuspecting in the living room, reading and looking occasionally at the clock and the hands that moved much too slowly.

Father would have to think of the bodysuit. He wouldn't be able to help himself. The uncertainty would tear at his mind. He'd run home, rummage through the drawer. Note the absence. One apricot and two plum-colored. Oh, how that would pain him. Armin groaned with pleasure.

What a dilemma! Father would have to cover up for him. He'd be the only one who knew. There were no other clues, no traces. Armin had been careful, had considered everything. And then the birthday this weekend! The package with Mama's gift. Delicate underwear. Or maybe, this time, satin pajamas for him, wrapped around a book. Father loved coffee-table books on historic gardens and famous roads. *Europe's Amber Roads. The Via Appia. Route 66. The Silk Road.* Armin giggled. No more silk for Papa! And just how would he explain that to Mama? Or would he be able to bring himself to go on buying lingerie, pandering to this secret vice in their relationship, all the time knowing everything? Imagining the dainty things on strange, cold, dead skin, and simultaneously on her, rosy and alive?

What a choice! What a life! Father in the vise grip of all the variations on deceit and silence. Mama would never forgive him either the one or the other. Father would be terrified that she might leave, terrified that the truth might come out. Career over. Marriage over. It was too wonderful!

A car drove by, and stopped in front of the neighbors' house. Then a second. Armin's brow creased. Usually nothing happened on their street in the evening. The house door opened. Father was home! At that instant, the apartment doorbell rang. But Father never rang the bell. Armin jumped out of bed. Downstairs, he heard his mother's voice, astonished. A step creaked. Someone threw open his bedroom door, turned on the overhead light.

Blinded, Armin shut his eyes.

"You filthy . . ." whispered his father hoarsely. "You disgusting beast." The voice broke.

Then Armin heard his father turn and go into his bedroom, and he opened his eyes. Two police officers stood there, shocked into breathlessness.

"Get dressed."

They focused past him at the sky-blue window curtains with their pattern of white clouds. His mother appeared, her hair disordered, her hands covering her mouth. She gazed at him in horror, stared as if he weren't merely a stranger, but also incomprehensible, unfathomable to her.

"Mama!"

He began to cry, and then suddenly to tremble all over. His body was seized with shudders. He shook so hard that he fell to his knees, and yet he went on screaming for her, wailing her name in desperation even between the spasms of nausea that made him vomit his dinner all over the floor.

"Now he's throwing up the last remnants of his soul," he heard one of the police officers say in disgust. His mother turned on her heel and disappeared. As if through a fog he registered that someone was handing him something to wear, insisting again that he get dressed. There was no answer to his cries. He heard nothing from the next room, nothing, just a silence that swallowed and utterly buried his hopes.

Minutes later, as they pulled him from the house, he was still shouting her name through his sobs, outraged that his father had chosen this response, aghast that his mother had made a choice that called into question everything he was, everything he believed. All his plans, all his prospects had turned out to be false, without substance. How could that have happened?

Hands pushed him into a car. He huddled there, a foul-smelling bundle of misery. Not a single neighbor would have given him credit for the evil of his thoughts, the ruthlessness, the cool planning. He tilted his runny-nosed, tear-streaked face up toward the brightly lit window of his parents' bedroom. Naturally the curtains were already closed against the dark, but he could see the silhouettes of two heads, like black paper forms against the light.

He had no idea what they were saying, how they were looking at one another. He couldn't imagine what lay dumped unceremoniously on the bed between them. A crumpled pile of stretch lace and Swiss guipure embroidery, flowers flocked on fabric, baroque richness in charmeuse, satin, and silk. And of course, he couldn't possibly imagine his mother's feelings, his father's feelings, the purgatory he had made of their future.

And as he lay in his cell, his thoughts circling obstinately around the question of why his father had turned him in, his mother left the house, a sack in her hand. She ran down the street, turned the corner, ran again, until finally, at a safe distance, she came to a stop next to a garbage container. She raised her arm slowly and turned the sack over, allowing the contents to spill. The streetlight illuminated a glowing waterfall of lingerie slipping languidly down into the container, steel blue, the purple of figs, white, burgundy-red. Peach-colored chiffon wafted down to join the odors of decay and mildew.

Then she turned and staggered, crying, back to her home.

Boris Akunin

Table Talk, 1882

Translated from the Russian by Anthony Olcott

The more than eight million copies of his novels that have sold in Russia since they first started appearing in the mid 1990s make Boris Akunin (a pseudonym of critic Grigory Chkhartishvili) far the brightest star on the Russian crime scene. Translations of his books were already a hit in Continental Europe and Britain (one of them claiming a prestigious Dagger Award nomination in the UK) before they began to be available to American readers in 2004, in Random House trade paperback. Most of the Akunin novels feature late-nineteenth-century Sherlock Holmes-like special agent Erast Fandorin, and combine humor, espionage, detection, adventure, and multiple plot twists in such an original way that Akunin is sometimes said to have invented an entirely new Russian literary genre. The first four Fandorin books—The Winter Queen, Murder on the Leviathan, The Turkish Gambit, and Death of Achilles—are in U.S. bookstores now. Upcoming in 2007 is Special Assignments, also starring Fandorin. Grigory Chkhartishvili recently began a second mystery series under the Akunin pseudonym. Its first two novels in English translation are Pelagia and the White Bulldog and Pelagia and the Black Monk.

After the coffee and liqueurs, the conversation turned to mystery.

Deliberately not looking at her new guest—a collegiate

assessor[1] and the season's most fashionable man—Lidia Niko-laevna Odintsova, hostess of the salon, remarked, "All Moscow is saying Bismarck must have poisoned poor Skobelev. Can it really be that society is to remain ignorant of the truth behind this horrible tragedy?"

The guest to whom Lidia Nikolaevna was treating her regulars today was Erast Petrovich Fandorin. He was maddeningly handsome, cloaked in an aura of mystery, and a bachelor besides. In order to inveigle Erast Petrovich into her salon, the hostess had had to bring off an extremely complex intrigue consisting of many parts—an undertaking at which she was an unsurpassed mistress.

Her sally was addressed to Arkhip Giatsintovich Mustafin, an old friend of the house. A man of fine mind, Mustafin caught Lidia Nikolaevna's intention at the first hint and, casting a sideways glance at the young collegiate assessor from beneath his ruddy and lashless eyelids, intoned, "Ah, but I've been told our White General[2] may have been destroyed by a fatal passion."

The others at the table held their breath, as it was rumored that Erast Petrovich, who until quite recently had served in the office of Moscow's Governor-General as an officer for special missions, had had a most direct relation to the investigation into events surrounding the death of the great commander. However, disappointment awaited the guests, for the handsome Fandorin listened politely to Arkhip Giatsintovich with an air suggesting that the words had nothing whatever to do with him.

1. "Collegiate Assessor" was a civil title—one of fourteen that Peter the Great established when he reformed Russia's bureaucracy—indicating a high rank, the threshold at which someone attained life nobility. The equivalent rank in the army was major.
2. Skobelev: general whose militant pan-Slavic views and predictions of inevitable conflict with Germany got him in trouble with the government in St. Petersburg and resulted in his recall to the capital, where, in 1882, he died of heart failure.

This brought about the one situation that an experienced hostess could not permit—an awkward silence. Lidia Nikolaevna knew immediately what to do. Lowering her eyelids, she came to Mustafin's assistance. "This is so very like the mysterious disappearance of poor Polinka Karakina! Surely you recall that dreadful story, my friend?"

"How could I not?" Arkhip drawled, indicating his gratitude with a quick lift of an eyebrow.

Some of the party nodded as if also remembering, but most of the guests clearly knew nothing about Polinka Karakina. In addition, Mustafin had a reputation as a most exquisite raconteur, such that it would be no penance to hear even a familiar tale from his lips. So here Molly Sapegina, a charming young woman whose husband—such a tragedy—had been killed in Turkestan a year ago, asked with curiosity, "A mysterious disappearance? How interesting!"

Lidia Nikolaevna made as if to accommodate herself to her chair more comfortably, so also letting Mustafin know that she was passing nourishment of the table talk into his capable hands.

"Many of us, of course, still recall old Prince Lev Lvovich Karakin,"—so Arkhip Giatsintovich began his tale. "He was a man of the old sort, a hero of the Hungarian campaign. He had no taste for the liberal vagaries of our late Tsar, and so retired to his lands outside Moscow, where he lived like a nabob of Hindi. He was fabulously wealthy, of an estate no longer found among the aristocracy of today.

"The prince had two daughters, Polinka and Anyuta. I beg you to note, no Frenchified *Pauline* or English *Annie*. The general held the very strictest of patriotic views. The girls were twins. Face, figure, voice, all were identical. They were not to be confused, however, for right here, on her right cheek, Anyuta had a birthmark. Lev Lvovich's wife had died in childbirth, and

35

the prince did not marry again. He always said that it was a lot of fuss and he had no need—after all, there was no shortage of serving girls. And indeed, he had no shortage of serving girls, even after the emancipation. For, as I said, Lev Lvovich lived the life of a true nabob."

"For shame, Archie! Without vulgarity, if you please," Lidia Nikolaevna remonstrated with a stern smile, although she knew perfectly well that a good story is never hurt by "adding a little pepper," as the English say.

Mustafin pressed his palm to his breast in apology, then continued his tale. "Polinka and Anyuta were far from being horrors, but it would also be difficult to call them great beauties. However, as we all know, a dowry of millions is the best of cosmetics, so that in the season when they debuted, they produced something like a fever epidemic among the eligible bachelors of Moscow. But then the old prince took some sort of offense at our honored Governor-General and withdrew to his piney Sosnovka, never to leave the place again.

"Lev Lvovich was a heavyset fellow, short-winded and red-faced, a man prone to apoplexy, as they say, so there was reason to hope that the princesses' imprisonment would not last long. However, the years went on, Prince Karakin grew ever fatter, flying into ever more thunderous rages, and evinced no intention whatsoever of dying. The suitors waited and waited and in the end quite forgot about the poor prisoners.

"Although it was said to be in the Moscow region, Sosnovka was in fact in the deep forests of Zaraisky district, not only nowhere near the railroad, but a good twenty versts even from the nearest well-traveled road. The wilderness, in a word. To be sure, it was a heavenly place, and excellently established. I have a little village nearby, so that I often called on the prince as a neighbor. The black grouse shooting there is exquisite, but that spring especially the birds seemed to fly right into one's sights—I've never seen the like in all my days. So, in the end, I became a habitué of the house, which is why the entire tale unfolded right before my eyes.

"The old prince had been trying for some time to construct a belvedere in his park, in the Viennese style. He had first hired a famous architect from Moscow, who had drawn up the plans and even started the construction, but then didn't finish it—he could not endure the prince's bullheaded whims and so had departed. To finish the work they summoned an architect of somewhat lower flight, a Frenchman named Renar. Young, and rather handsome. True, he was noticeably lame, but since Lord Byron our young ladies have never counted this as a defect.

"What happened next you can imagine for yourselves. The two maidens had been sitting in the country for a decade now, never once getting out. They both were twenty-eight years old, with absolutely no society of any sort, save for the arrival of the odd fuddy-duddy such as myself, come to hunt. And suddenly— a handsome young man of lively mind, and from Paris at that.

"I have to say that, for all their outward similarity, the two princesses were of totally different temperament and spiritual cast. Anyuta was like Pushkin's Tatyana, prone to lassitude, a touch melancholic, a little pedantic, and, to be blunt, a bit tedious. As for Polinka, she was frolicsome, mischievous, 'simple as a poet's life, sweet as a lover's kiss,' as the poet has it. And she was far less settled into old-maidish ways.

"Renar lived there a bit, had a look around, and, naturally enough, set his cap at Polinka. I watched all this from the sidelines, rejoicing greatly, and of course not once suspecting the incredible way in which this pastoral idyll would end. Polinka besotted by love, the Frenchie giddy with the whiff of millions, and Anyuta smoldering with jealousy, forced to assume the role of vessel of common sense. I confess that I enjoyed watching this comedy at least as much as I did the mating dance of the black grouse. The noble father, of course, continued to be oblivious of all this, because he was arrogant and unable to imagine that a Princess Karakina might feel attracted to some lowly sort of architect.

"It all ended in scandal, of course. One evening Anyuta chanced . . . or perhaps there was nothing chance about it . . . Anyuta glanced into a little house in the garden, found her sister and Renar there in flagrante delicto, and immediately informed their father. Wrathful Lev Lvovich, who escaped apoplexy only by a miracle, wanted to drive the offender from his estate immediately. The Frenchman was able only with the greatest difficulty to plead to be allowed to remain at the estate until the morning, for the forests around Sosnovka were such that a solitary night traveler could well be eaten by wolves. Had I not intervened, the malefactor would have been turned out of the gates dressed in nothing but his frock coat.

"The sobbing Polinka was sent to her bedroom under the eye of her prudent sister, the architect was sent to his room in one of the wings to pack his suitcase, the servants scattered, and the full brunt of the prince's wrath came to be borne precisely by your humble servant. Lev Lvovich raged almost until dawn, wearing me out entirely, so that I scarcely slept that night. Nevertheless, in the morning I saw from the window how the Frenchman was hauled off to the station in a plain flat farm cart. Poor fellow, he kept looking up to the windows, but clearly there was no one waving him farewell, or so his terribly droopy look seemed to say.

"Then marvels began to occur. The princesses did not appear for breakfast. Their bedroom door was locked, and there was no response to knocks. The prince began to boil again, showing signs of an inevitable apoplexy. He gave orders to splinter the door, and devil take the hindmost. Which was done, everyone rushed in, and . . . Good heavens! Anyuta lay in her bed, as if in deepest sleep, while there was no sign of Polinka whatsoever. She had vanished. She wasn't in the house, she wasn't in the park . . . it was as if she had slipped down through the very earth.

"No matter how hard they tried to wake Anyuta, it was to no avail. The family doctor, who had lived there on the estate, had died not long before, and no new one had yet been hired. Thus they had to send to the district hospital. The government doctor came, one of those long-haired fellows. He poked her, he squeezed her, and then he said she was suffering from a most serious nervous disorder. Leave her lie, and she would awake.

"The carter who had hauled off the Frenchman returned. He was a faithful man, his whole life spent at the estate. He swore to heaven that he had carted Renar right to the station and put him on the train. The young gentle-lady had not been with him. And anyway, how could she have gotten past the gate? The park at Sosnovka was surrounded by a high stone wall, and there was a guard at the gate.

"Anyuta did wake the following day, but there was no getting anything from her. She had lost the ability to speak. All she could do was weep, tremble, and rattle her teeth. After a week she began to speak a little, but she remembered nothing of that night. If she were pressed with questions, she would immediately begin to shudder and convulse. The doctor forbade such questions in the very strictest terms, saying that it endangered her life.

"So Polinka had vanished. The prince lost his mind utterly. He wrote repeatedly to the governor and even to the Tsar himself. He roused the police. He had Renar followed in Moscow— but it was all for naught. The Frenchman labored away, trying to find clients, but to no avail—nobody wanted a quarrel with Karakin. So the poor fellow left for his native Paris. Even so, Lev Lvovich continued to rage. He got it into his head that the villain had killed his beloved Polinka and buried her somewhere.

He had the whole park dug up, and the pond drained, killing all his priceless carp. Nothing. A month passed, and the apoplexy finally came. The prince sat down to dinner, gave out a sudden wheeze, and *plop!* Facedown in his soup bowl. And no wonder, really, after suffering so much.

"After that night it wasn't so much that Anyuta was touched in the head as that her character was markedly changed. Even before, she hadn't been noted for any particular gaiety, but now she would scarcely even open her mouth. The slightest sound would set her atremble. I confess, sinner that I am, that I am no great lover of tragedy. I fled from Sosnovka while the prince was still alive. When I came for the funeral, saints above, the estate was changed beyond recognition. The place had become dreadful, as if some raven had folded its black wing over it. I looked about and I remember thinking, *This place is going to be abandoned.* And so it came to be.

"Anyuta, the sole heir, had no desire to live there and so she went away. Not to Moscow, either, or someplace in Europe, but to the very ends of the earth. The estate manager sends her money to Brazil, in Rio de Janeiro. I checked on a globe to find that Rio is absolutely on the other side of the world from Sosnovka. Just think—Brazil! Not a Russian face to be seen anywhere!" Arkhip Giatsintovich ended his strange tale with a sigh.

"Why do you say that? I have an acquaintance in Brazil, a former c-colleague of mine in the Japanese embassy, Karl Ivanovich Veber," Erast Petrovich Fandorin murmured thoughtfully, having listened to the story with interest. The officer for special missions had a soft and pleasant manner of speaking, in no way spoiled by his slight stammer. "Veber is an envoy to the Brazilian emperor D-Don Pedro now. So it's hardly the end of the earth."

"Is that so?" Arkhip Giatsintovich turned animatedly. "So

perhaps this mystery might yet be solved? Ah, my dear Erast Petrovich, people say that you have a brilliant analytic mind, that you can crack mysteries of all sorts, like so many walnuts. Now here's a problem for you that doesn't seem to have a logical solution. On the one hand, Polinka Karakina vanished from the estate—that's a fact. On the other hand, there's no way she could have gotten out of the garden, and that's also a fact."

"Yes, yes," several of the ladies started at once, "Mr. Fandorin, Erast Petrovich, we so terribly want to know what really happened there!"

"I'm prepared to make a wager that Erast Petrovich will be able to resolve this paradox quite easily," the hostess Odintsova announced with confidence.

"A wager?" Mustafin inquired immediately. "And what are you willing to wager?"

It must be explained that both Lidia Nikolaevna and Arkhip Giatsintovich were avid gamblers whose passion for making wagers sometimes approached lunacy. The more insightful of the guests glanced at one another, suspicious that this entire interlude, with a tale supposedly recalled solely by chance, had been staged by prior agreement, and that the young official had fallen victim to a clever intrigue.

"I quite like that little Bouchet of yours," Arkhip Giatsintovich said with a slight bow.

"And I your large Caravaggio," the hostess answered him in the same tone of voice.

Mustafin simply rocked his head a bit, as if admiring Odintsova's voracious appetite, but said nothing. Apparently he had no qualms about victory. Or, perhaps, the stakes had already been decided between them in advance.

A bit startled at such swiftness, Erast Petrovich spread his hands. "But I have not visited the site of the event, and I have never seen the p-participants. As I recall, even having all the necessary information, the police were not able to do anything. So what am I to do now? And it's probably been quite some time as well, I imagine."

"Six years this October," came the answer.

"W-well then, you see . . ."

"Dear, wonderful Erast Petrovich," the hostess implored, "don't ruin me utterly. I've already agreed to this extortionist's terms. He'll simply take my Bouchet and be gone! That gentleman has not the slightest drop of chivalry in him!"

"My ancestors were Tartar *murza*, warlords!" Arkhip Giatsintovich confirmed gaily. "We in the Horde keep our chat with the ladies short."

However, chivalry was far from an empty word for Fandorin, apparently. The young man rubbed the bridge of his nose with a finger and muttered, "Well, so that's how it is. . . . Well, Mr. Mustafin, you . . . you didn't chance to notice, did you, what kind of bag the Frenchman had? You did see him leave, you said. So probably there was some large kind of trunk?"

Arkhip Giatsintovich made as if to applaud. "Bravo! He hid the girl in the trunk and carted her off ? And Polinka gave the meddlesome sister something nasty to drink, which is why Anyuta collapsed into nervous disorder? Clever. But alas . . . There was no trunk. The Frenchman flew off as light as an eagle. I remember some small suitcases of some sort, some bundles, a couple of hatboxes. No, my good sir, your explanation simply won't wash."

Fandorin thought a bit, then asked, "You are quite sure that the princess could not have won the guards to her side, or perhaps just bribed them?"

"Absolutely. That was the first thing the police checked."

Strangely, at these words the collegiate assessor suddenly

became very gloomy and sighed, then said, "Then your tale is much nastier than I had thought." Then, after a long pause, he said, "Tell me, did the prince's house have plumbing?"

"Plumbing? In the countryside?" Molly Sapegina asked in astonishment, then giggled uncertainly, having decided that the handsome official was joking. However, Arkhip Giatsintovich screwed his gold-rimmed monocle into one eye and looked at Fandorin extremely attentively, as if he had only just properly noticed him. "How did you guess that? As it happens, there *was* plumbing at the estate. A year before the events that I have described, the prince had ordered the construction of a pumping station and a boiler room. Lev Lvovich, the princesses, and the guest rooms all had quite proper bathrooms. But what does that have to do with the business at hand?"

"I think that your p-paradox is resolved." Fandorin rocked his head. "The resolution, though, is awfully unpleasant."

"But how? Resolved by what? What happened?" Questions came from all sides.

"I'll tell you in a moment. But first, Lidia Nikolaevna, I would like to give your lackey a certain assignment."

With all present completely entranced, the collegiate assessor then wrote a little note of some sort, handed it to the lackey, and whispered something quietly into the man's ear. The clock on the mantel chimed midnight, but no one had the slightest thought of leaving. All held their breath and waited, but Erast Petrovich was in no hurry to begin this demonstration of his analytic gifts. Bursting with pride at her faultless intuition, which once again had served her well in her choice of a main guest, Lidia Niko-laevna looked at the young man with almost maternal tender-ness. This officer of special missions had every chance of becoming a true star of her salon. Which would make Katie Polotskaya and Lily Yepanchina green with envy, to be sure!

"The story you shared with us is not so much mysterious as disgusting," the collegiate assessor finally said with a grimace. "One of the most monstrous crimes of passion about which I have ever had occasion to hear. This is no disappearance. It is a murder, of the very worst, Cain-like sort."

"Are you meaning to say that the gay sister was killed by the melancholy sister?" inquired Sergey Ilyich von Taube, chairman of the Excise Chamber.

"No, I wish to say something quite the opposite—gay Polinka killed melancholy Anyuta. And that is not the most nightmarish aspect."

"I do beg your pardon! How can that be?" Sergey Ilyich asked in astonishment, while Lidia Nikolaevna thought it necessary to note, "And what might be more nightmarish than the murder of one's own sister?"

Fandorin rose and began to pace about the sitting room. "I will try to reconstruct the sequence of events, as I understand them. So, we have two p-princesses, withering with boredom. Life dribbling through their fingertips—indeed, all but dribbled away. Their feminine life, I mean. Idleness. Moldering spiritual powers. Unrealized hopes. Tormenting relations with their high-handed father. And, not least, physiological frustration. They were, after all, young, healthy women. Oops, please forgive me...."

Conscious that he had said something untoward, the collegiate assessor was embarrassed for a moment, but Lidia Nikolaevna let it pass without a reprimand—he looked so appealing with that blush that suddenly had blossomed on his white cheeks.

"I would not even dare to imagine how much there is intertwined in the soul of a young w-woman who might be in such a situation," Fandorin said after a short silence. "And here is something particular besides—right there, always, is your living mirror image, your twin sister. No doubt it would be impossible for there not to be a most intricate mix of love and hatred between them. And suddenly a young handsome man appears. He demonstrates obvious interest in the young princesses. No doubt with ulterior motive, but which of those girls would have thought of that? Of course, an inevitable rivalry springs up between the girls, but the ch-choice is quickly made. Until that moment everything between Anyuta and Polinka was identical, but now they were in quite different worlds. One of them is happy, returned to the land of the living and, at least to all appearances, loved. While the other feels herself rejected, lonely, and thus doubly unhappy. Happy love is egoistical. For Polinka, no doubt, there was nothing other than the passions that had built up through the long years of being locked away. This was the full and real life that she had dreamed about for so many years, the life she had even stopped hoping for. And then it was all shredded in an instant—indeed, precisely at the moment when love had reached its very highest peak."

The ladies all listened spellbound to the empathetic speech of this picture-perfect young man of beauty, all save for Molly Sapegina, who pressed her slender fingers to her décolletage before freezing in that pose.

"Most dreadful of all was that the agent of this tragedy was one's very own sister. We may agree, of course, to understand her as well. To endure such happiness right alongside one's own unhappiness would require a particular cast of the spirit which Anyuta obviously did not possess. So Polinka, who had only just been lounging in the bowers of Paradise, was cast utterly down. There is no beast in this world more dangerous than a woman deprived of her beloved!" Erast Petrovich exclaimed, a tad carried away, and then immediately grew a bit muddled, since this sentiment might offend the fairer half among those present. However, there came no protests—all were greedily waiting for the story to continue, so Fandorin went on more briskly, "So then, under the influence of despair, Polinka has a mad plan, a terrible, monstrous plan, but one that is testament to the enormous power of feeling. Although, I don't know, the plan might have come from Renar. It was the girl who had to put the plan into action, however. . . . That night, while you, Arkhip Giatsintovich, were nodding drowsily and listening to your host pour out his rage, a hellish act was taking place in the bedroom of the princesses. Polinka murdered her sister. I do not know how. Perhaps she smothered her with a pillow, perhaps she poisoned her, but in any event, it occurred without blood, for otherwise there would have remained some trace in the bedroom."

"The investigation considered the possibility of a murder." Mustafin shrugged, having listened to Erast Petrovich with unconcealed scepticism. "However, there arose a rather sensible question—what happened to the body?"

The officer of special missions answered without a moment's hesitation, "That's the nightmarish part. After killing her sister, Polinka dragged her into the bathroom, where she cut her into bits and washed the blood away down the drain. The Frenchman could not have been the one to dismember her—there is no way he could have left his own wing for such a long time without being noticed."

Waiting out a true storm of alarmed exclamations, in which "Impossible!" was the word most often heard, Fandorin said sadly, "Unfortunately, there is no other possibility. There is no other solution to the p-problem as p-posed. It is better not even to attempt to imagine what went on that night in that bathroom. Polinka would not have had the slightest knowledge of anatomy, nor could she have had any instrument more to the purpose than a pilfered kitchen knife."

"But there's no way she could have put the body parts and bones down the drain, it would have plugged!" Mustafin exclaimed with a heat quite unlike him.

"No, she could not. The dismembered flesh left the estate in the Frenchman's various suitcases and hatboxes. Tell me, please, were the bedroom windows high off the ground?"

Arkhip Giatsintovich squinted as he tried to recall. "Not especially. The height of a man, perhaps. And the windows looked out on the park, in the direction of the lawn."

"So, the remains were passed through the w-window, then. Judging by the fact that there were no traces left on the window sill, Renar passed some kind of vessel into the room, Anyuta took it into the bathroom, put the body parts in there, and handed these to her accomplice. When this evil ferrying was done, all Polinka had to do was scour out the bathtub and clean the blood from herself. . . ."

Lidia Nikolaevna desperately wanted to win her bet, but in the interests of fairness she could not remain silent. "Erast Petrovich, this all fits together very well, with the exception of one circumstance. If Polinka indeed committed so monstrous an operation, she certainly would have stained her clothing, and blood is not so simple to wash away, especially if one is not a washerwoman."

This note of practicality did not so much puzzle Fandorin as embarrass him. Coughing slightly and looking away, he said quietly, "I im-imagine that before she began dismembering the b-body, the princess removed her clothing. All of it. . . ."

Some of the ladies gasped, while Molly Sapegina, growing pale, murmured, "Oh, *mon Dieu* . . ."

Erast Petrovich, it seemed, was frightened that someone might faint, so he hastened to finish, now in a dry tone of scientific detachment. "It is entirely probable that the extended oblivion of the supposed Anyuta was no simulation, but rather was a natural psychological reaction to a terrible tr-trauma."

Everyone suddenly began speaking at once. "But it wasn't Anyuta that disappeared, it was Polinka!" Sergey Ilyich recalled.

"Well, obviously that was just Polinka drawing a mole on her cheek," the more imaginative Lidia Nikolaevna explained impatiently. "That's why everyone thought she was Anyuta!"

Retired court doctor Stupitsyn did not agree. "Impossible! People close to them are able to distinguish twins quite well. The way they act, the nuances of the voice, the expressions of their eyes, after all!"

"And anyway, why was such a switch necessary?" General Liprandi interrupted the court doctor. "Why would Polinka have to pretend that she was Anyuta?"

Erast Petrovich waited until the flood of questions and objections ebbed, and then answered them one by one. "Had Anyuta disappeared, Your Excellency, then suspicion would inevitably have fallen on Polinka, that she had taken her revenge upon her sister, and so the search for traces of the murder would have been more painstaking. That's one thing. Had the besotted girl vanished at the same time as the Frenchman, this would have brought to the forefront the theory that this was a flight, not a crime. That's two. And then, of course, in the guise of Anyuta, at some time in the future she might marry Renar without giving herself away. Apparently that is precisely what happened in faraway Rio de Janeiro. I am certain that Polinka traveled so far from her native land in order to join the object of her affections in peace." The collegiate assessor turned to the court doctor. "Your argument that intimates are able to distinguish twins is entirely reasonable. Note, however, that the Karakins' family doctor, whom it would have been impossible to deceive, had died not long before. And besides, the supposed Anyuta changed most decidedly after that fateful night, precisely as if she had become someone else. In view of the particular circumstances, everyone took that as natural. In fact, this transformation occurred with Polinka, but is it to be wondered at that she lost her former animation and gaiety?"

"And the death of the old prince?" Sergey Ilyich asked. "Wasn't that awfully convenient for the criminal?"

"A most suspicious death," agreed Fandorin. "It is entirely possible that poison may have been involved. There was no autopsy, of course—his sudden demise was attributed to paternal grief and a disposition to apoplexy, but at the same time it is entirely possible that after a night such as that, a trifle like poisoning one's own father would not much bother Polinka. By the way, it would not be too late to conduct an exhumation even now. Poison is preserved a long while in the bone tissue."

"I'll bet that the prince was poisoned," Lidia Nikolaevna said quickly, turning to Arkhip Giatsintovich, who pretended that he had not heard.

"An inventive theory. And clever, too," Mustafin said at length. "However, one must have an exceedingly active imagination to picture Princess Karakina carving up the body of her own sister with a bread knife while dressed in the garb of Eve."

Everyone again began speaking at once, defending both points of view with equal ardor, although the ladies inclined to Fandorin's version of events, while the gentlemen rejected it as improbable. The cause of the argument took no part in the discussion himself, although he listened to the points of both sides with interest.

"Oh, but why are you remaining silent?!" Lidia Nikolaevna called to him, as she pointed at Mustafin. "Clearly, he is arguing against something perfectly obvious simply in order not to give up his stake. Tell him, say something else that will force him into silence!"

"I am waiting for your Matvey to return," Erast Petrovich replied tersely.

"But where did you send him?"

"To the Governor-General's staff headquarters. The telegraph office there is open around the clock."

"But that's on Tverskoy Boulevard, five minutes' walk from here, and he's been gone more than an hour!" someone wondered.

"Matvey was ordered to wait for the reply," the officer of special missions explained, then again fell silent while Arkhip Giatsintovich held everyone's attention with an expansive explanation of the ways in which Fandorin's theory was completely impossible from the viewpoint of female psychology.

Just at the most effective moment, as Mustafin was holding forth most convincingly about the innate properties of the feminine nature, which is ashamed of nudity and cannot endure the sight of blood, the door quietly opened and the long-awaited Matvey entered. Treading silently, he approached the collegiate assessor and, with a bow, proffered a sheet of paper.

Erast Petrovich turned, read the note, then nodded. The hostess, who had been watching the young man's face attentively, could not endure to wait any longer, and so moved her chair closer to her guest. "Well, what's there?" she whispered.

"I was right," Fandorin answered, also in a whisper.

That instant Odintsova interrupted the lecture. "Enough nonsense, Arkhip Giatsintovich! What do you know of the feminine nature, you who have never even been married! Erast Petrovich has incontrovertible proof!" She took the telegram from the collegiate assessor's hand and passed it around the circle.

Flabbergasted, the guests read the telegram, which consisted of three words:

"Yes. Yes. No."

"And that's it? What is this? Where is it from?" Such were the general questions.

"The telegram was sent from the Russian mission in Br-Brazil," Fandorin explained. "You see the diplomatic stamp there? It is deep night here in Moscow, but in Rio de Janeiro right now the mission is in attendance. I was counting on that when I ordered Matvey to wait for a reply. As for the telegram, I recognize the laconic style of Karl Ivanovich Veber. This is how my message read. Matvey, give me the paper, will you? The one I gave you." Erast Petrovich took the paper from the lackey and read aloud, " 'Karl, old boy, inform me the following soonest: Is Russian subject born Princess Anyuta Karakina now resident in Brazil married? If yes, is her husband lame? And does the princess have a mole on her right cheek? I need all this for a bet. Fandorin.' From the answer to the message it is clear that the pr-princess is married to a lame man, and has no mole on her cheek. Why would she need the mole now? In far-off Brazil there is no need to run to such clever tricks. As you see, ladies and gentlemen, Polinka is alive and well, married to her Renar. The terrible tale has an idyllic ending. By the by, the lack of a mole shows once again that Renar was a witting participant in the murder and knows perfectly well that he is married precisely to Polinka, and not to Anyuta."

"So, I shall give orders to fetch the Caravaggio," Odintsova said to Arkhip Giatsintovich with a victorious smile.

Ingrid Noll

Fisherman's Friend

Translated from the German by Mary Tannert

Often called Germany's Queen of Crime, Ingrid Noll was born in 1935 in Shanghai, where she began to write stories at a very young age. She and her family returned to Germany in 1949; later she studied philology and history in Bonn, and married and raised three children. It was only after her children left home that she returned to fiction writing. Her first novel, Hell Hath No Fury, *appeared in 1991, to rave reviews. Its huge success in print was followed by its adaptation for television. In the years since that stunning debut her popularity has only increased: Her work has so far been translated into twenty-three languages.*

A s fate would have it, I met both men at those stupid anglers' parties. Even when I was just a girl, once a year mother and I had to attend a summer party with father's sporting friends and their families. As if fish were in short supply the rest of the year. . . . The women made potato salad, coffee cake, and other culinary tours de force, and the men saw to it that there were kegs of beer and grilled fish. The children sprayed each other with their water pistols and howled because the wasps stung them. People gorged themselves, swilled beer, sang loudly and badly, and hopped about the dance floor, but the event always retained a semblance of discipline and order. The whole thing was held in a clubhouse by the lake, or, in good weather, on the meadow next to the dock. It was under the festive lanterns that I met Eugene and later Ulli.

I was seventeen at the time, and as dumb as they come. I didn't understand that Eugene only had designs on me because he had heard the clock ticking and had begun to panic: He was nearly forty and hadn't managed yet to find a woman who would take the bait. I thought his age was a sign of distinction. A man who was nearly as old and conservative as my father, and who wanted me, of all people. What a stroke of luck! Eugene was short and scrawny and neither funny nor interesting, but at least he had some money. He had an old and established specialty store that sold umbrellas, gloves, and hats. Up until that day I had always worn the mittens that Grandma knitted for me, but from then on I became the owner of a collection of the finest leather gloves.

My parents weren't much smarter than I was, because they too regarded Eugene's courtship of me as the purest good fortune. *Don't dillydally, just take him!* they urged. I wasn't merely naive, you see; my career as a postal carrier wasn't turning out to be too promising, either.

And so I was married at eighteen, and a mother at nineteen. At the beginning I was supposed to help in the shop, but I lost interest quickly after my first attempts. I didn't know the first thing about the business, and the salesladies couldn't take me seriously as their superior. It offended me that they whispered about me behind my back, and not kindly, either. I probably annoyed Eugene so much with my miserable whining that he never wanted to see me in the shop again. So I stayed at home. There was enough to do with my child and my home, and at the beginning I was almost content.

It took awhile before I got to know Eugene better. His hobbies were fishing and cars. He had a Land Rover for sporting activities and a big Mercedes for the city. Since he was so short, he always wore a plaid hat from his shop so that at least a smidgen of him was visible behind the wheel. He was the first in the store in the morning and the last to leave at night. When he got home, he wanted to eat, watch television, read the ADAC[1] motor report or an anglers' magazine, and be comfortable in his bathrobe and slippers. He spent the weekends, if it wasn't raining buckets, at the lake in purely male company. After he had produced an heir to his realm so swiftly, he appeared to have lost all interest in providing the world with a second.

However, Eugene knew that a young woman has certain expectations in general, and this gave him a permanently bad conscience. This he dealt with by being very generous financially. I had a sizable allowance and could buy clothes, cosmetics, shoes, and bags to my heart's content without his ever complaining. He was even proud that the little brown sparrow at his side had molted and gradually acquired the luxurious plumage of a golden pheasant. Sometimes we went out for dinner, and he enjoyed the way I attracted attention from men as well as from women. When our son was born, he gave me a string of pearls, and for our fifth anniversary a fur coat. Not particularly original, but well-meant.

My changed appearance—in addition to the chic clothes I had simply become prettier—also resulted in an enhanced self-image and a desire to get out and do things. Every afternoon I took my little one to the castle park, let him play for a while on the playground, and then visited the cafe there. Jonas got a big dish of ice cream, and I ordered a double espresso. Unfortunately,

1. ADAC, for *Allgemeiner Deutscher Automobil-Club*; similar to the United States' AAA.

at this time of day it was mostly elderly ladies or mothers and children who were out and about, so that I had no opportunity to flirt with any men.

But that changed at the next summer's anglers' party. I had known Ulli since we were both children, but then my family had moved away. Ulli had finished school and become a textiles engineer. He had recently gotten his first job in the weaving mill here in town. He was the exact opposite of Eugene—young, good-looking, tall and strong, fun and not a bit boring. Naturally all the girls were after him, and I figured I didn't have much of a chance, but sometimes fortune helps a girl along. Ulli was looking for a used car, and Eugene wanted to sell his Land Rover. They agreed to meet on Sunday at our house.

I had put on coffee and made myself pretty even though they would almost certainly not take me along on their test drive. But luck was with me again: Just before Ulli arrived, the police called. Eugene's store had been broken into during the night. My husband drove over right away to assess the damage, and I was supposed to take care of our guest in the meantime, lead him to the garage and show him the car. Our son always spent the weekend with my parents—"So that you can sleep late," they always said, an offer doubtless directly related to their hope for a granddaughter.

Ulli wanted to do more than just look at the car; he wanted to test it off-road. We got in, drove into the woods, stopped, and kissed. Then we drove home without a word. When poor beset Eugene got home, he didn't even notice how wound up I was. I had fallen in love, probably for the first time in my life.

From that point on, there was no stopping me. Twice a week in the afternoon, I dropped Jonas off with my parents, met Ulli in his apartment around five o'clock, and was back home by the time Eugene arrived at seven. My illicit excursions were, naturally, risky—in a mid-sized city such as ours, the identity of Ulli's visitor would scarcely escape his neighbors for long. It was just a matter of time until someone would drop hateful hints to Eugene in the store or at his regular pub night. But now that I loved Ulli, I simply couldn't stand my husband anymore. At first I imagined the divorce; later I pictured Eugene's death. The second scenario had the advantage that I would receive a good widow's pension and the proceeds of the life-insurance policy. I would then be financially independent, because I never again wanted to forgo a certain luxury.

Although I am not a particularly creative person, I began to form a plan to systematically arouse Ulli's ire against Eugene. In Phase I, I painted myself as a saint at the unprotected mercy of a sadist. This awakened both Ulli's chivalrousness and his sympathy; he wanted to rescue me from the clutches of the devil by spiriting me away. In Phase II, I got more concrete: I planted the idea in Ulli's mind that marriage would be the solution to all our troubles, and intimated that, in the event of a divorce, Eugene would try to cheat me out of all the money. After mature consideration, it was obviously preferable to my lover to acquire a wealthy wife. Phase III took aim directly at the threat to our lives: If Eugene were to learn of our relationship, he would probably kill us both. Ulli was, as I mentioned, a tall, strong, and handsome lad, but not an overly intelligent one. He believed me utterly, and saw that we had to get a jump on Eugene.

My husband was therefore surprised when, one evening, I asked him about his fishing grounds. "Since when are you interested in my hobbies?" he asked, and then told me how he had recently discovered a little lake in the Odenwald Forest where he could catch marvelous fish in complete solitude. But it was just like gathering wild mushrooms, he noted: He would never reveal his secret locations to a single soul. "But you could tell me, I'm no rival!" I protested. "Take us with you sometime," I begged. "It would be absolutely heavenly for our son. . . ." Up to now, Jonas had never had much fun fishing; he was too small to sit still for hours staring into the water. Eugene wasn't really very enthusiastic at the prospect, but he understood that he would have to accustom his son gradually to the manly joys of the wilderness.

That little lake really wasn't easy to find. We had to drive down dirt roads and through muddy meadows, but that was child's play for the new sport-utility vehicle. I sat in the back with Jonas, furtively making notes and drawing little maps. I almost began to regret never having accompanied Eugene on his Sunday jaunts. It was marvelous here. Even though it was still early in the year and quite chilly, the sun came out occasionally, lit up the still, glassy water, and warmed us. Wild ducks went about their business undisturbed, pussy willows bloomed, and Eugene and Jonas set up the folding chairs we had brought and cast their lines. I went for a little walk. When I got back a quarter of an hour later, Jonas had already gotten cold and bored and was sitting in the car reading comic books.

"If you can feel the peace out here," said Eugene, "then maybe it'll be clearer to you that my real life doesn't just take place in the store. Out here, I'm Robinson Crusoe; I feel alive."

Not for long, I thought. *I'll see to that!*

A few days later, I drove out there with Ulli and showed him the hidden lake.

"Now when you 'run into' Eugene out here on Sunday, you have to behave as if you've just discovered this paradise. It shouldn't be any problem to throw him into the water accidentally and hold his head under just a little while you're 'rescuing' him. Don't forget to put on your waders!" Ulli nodded. We wandered around the lake, holding hands and standing still occasionally to kiss or look at a water bird. I broke off several cattails before it occurred to me that I couldn't take them home. Suddenly a forest ranger turned up. What were we doing here? This was a wildlife sanctuary! Couldn't we read the signs? Obviously, Eugene had found a roundabout way into the sanctuary, a route that lay far from any posted notices. We were given a friendly warning and sent home; people are considerate of lovers.

Unfortunately, I couldn't tell Eugene that he was fishing in forbidden waters. On the other hand, it was entirely possible that he knew it already, that he had special permission from the forest ranger. Eugene had helpful pals and sports buddies everywhere. For his part, he was always ready with a generous discount off the purchase of fishing hats, olive-green scarves, and fingerless hunting gloves.

Ulli wanted to try his luck next Sunday, anyway. Because it was still early spring, it wasn't likely that anyone else would be around to run into. And if the forest ranger turned up again, he'd just have to change his plans at short notice.

On the Sunday in question, Jonas was with my parents, as always, and I waited for Ulli's phone call. I would never have thought that I could become so agitated: I hadn't slept a wink at all the night before. I couldn't eat a thing, but I drank cognac to soothe my nerves. The house was completely quiet: Nothing stirred. I dialed Ulli's number in vain. Gradually it grew dark and I had to go pick up Jonas, and of course I had to behave as if nothing was out of the ordinary.

Jonas and I had been home for ages and we were sitting in front of the television—although I remember nothing of the program we watched—when I heard Eugene's car. I ran to the door. Ulli and Eugene climbed out, the best of friends. They seemed unimpressed by my face, white as a sheet. Instead, they turned their attention to a large plastic bag that they took from the trunk. "It's almost too good to freeze," said Eugene. "I've never caught such a large pikeperch myself—that was definitely beginner's luck!"

Ulli had apparently forgotten all our plans: Eyes shining, he presented me with his fat fish. "I'd never have managed that without your husband," he assured me gratefully.

The two men pottered around the kitchen while I put Jonas to bed. They had decided on the spot to cook the pikeperch for dinner. Ulli peeled potatoes while Eugene cleaned the fish and removed the scales. However, that was the extent of my husband's kitchen prowess, and it wasn't long before the two fishing buddies sat in the living room drinking beer while I, tears in my eyes, fried the fish in one pan and the potatoes in another. They had left me a nice pile of fish innards and potato peels in addition to spilled schnapps and splattered kitchen tiles. It all stank to high heaven.

The two of them ate with obvious gusto. Eugene told tall tales about his previous successes and Ulli bragged about today's catch. I sat there and couldn't eat a bite or say a word. The two men made plans for next weekend—they had obviously become the best of friends in an astonishingly short time. Naturally, more than half of that magnificent fish was left over even though both men had eaten like farmhands. "We'll eat the rest tomorrow," suggested Eugene. I shook my head. Neither Jonas nor I liked a constant diet of fish leftovers, and I had promised the boy schnitzel with french fries tomorrow. "I'd rather freeze it all," I said.

I resisted the impulse to consign the remainder of the hacked-up fish to the garbage. Carefully I removed the fishbones, pulled off the skin, and put the flesh in the blender. Then I mixed in some softened bread crumbs, salt, curry powder, capers, finely minced onion, and crème fraîche and put together a tasty batch of fish croquettes. Just as I was about to fry them and then put them in the freezer, I had a brilliant idea. Carefully I removed some larger and smaller fish bones from the garbage and inserted them lovingly and unobtrusively in the croquettes I had just formed. Only then did I fry and freeze them so that my sportsmen could take a surprise picnic along on their next fishing trip. Buttered black bread and a green salad would be the perfect accompaniments.

Next Sunday, they were touched by the bountiful picnic basket I had prepared. As a loving wife and secret mistress, I had included, along with the croquettes garnished with lettuce and tomatoes, red-checked napkins, a salt shaker, and even little bottles of schnapps, even though a genuine angler always has his own hip flask along.

My initial fury at Ulli had, meanwhile, given way to an unbridled thirst for revenge. He had actually dared to play the injured party after I called him to complain. "Your husband is really very nice," he insisted. "I really don't understand what you have against him! Thank God everything turned out different than you planned. Or did you really think that I could commit murder?"

That day, too, I had to wait an eternity for a sign of life from the anglers. I painted mental pictures of the various fish bone catastrophes that could occur, from panicky coughing to suffocation attacks. Maybe they had scented the danger and my evil intentions at the very first bite, and any minute now they'd be standing at the door, their hunting knives drawn. But Eugene came home alone and barely said hello. Only upon insistent questioning on my part did I discover that Ulli had already gone home. The following morning, Eugene continued to behave strangely. He left the house early without either eating breakfast or saying goodbye. I couldn't find the picnic basket, either in his car or in the garage. Even though pride nearly kept me from it, I called Ulli at his office. His secretary informed me that he wasn't available. And he didn't answer the phone at home long after he surely had to be there.

Two days later, I read in the newspaper that a dead forest ranger had been found in a wildlife sanctuary on a little lake in the Odenwald. The owner of a Land Rover was being sought as a witness, since tire tracks at the scene had to have come from such a vehicle. Whether death was due to murder or an accident could not be determined until an autopsy had been conducted, but signs pointed to death as the result of asphyxiation. Other puzzling finds included several small schnaps bottles and the remains of a picnic.

I confronted Eugene. It had to be the lake he had shown me, those were surely the tire tracks from his Rover, and the picnic must be the one from my kitchen. Had the forest ranger caught him fishing illegally? Eugene broke down. The forest ranger collected a regular "donation" for allowing illegal fishing; they were acquainted and understood each other. On that Sunday, they had exchanged meals. The trade netted Ulli and Eugene two kinds of sausage—Hungarian *Kabanossi* and *Landjager*—plus black bread with goose schmaltz. For his part, the forest ranger fell on the croquettes. When he suffocated after a horrifying attack of choking and coughing that could not be helped even when they pounded on his back, shook him, and stuck fingers down his throat, they had been overcome by panic and had run away. But they hadn't gone directly home, they had gone to a pub near our house. "We had to calm down first," Eugene explained, seeming at that moment even shorter to me than usual. Naturally, I couldn't tell a soul about his confession: My own role in this drama had to be kept in the dark. I just hoped that Ulli could hold his tongue.

All three of us probably suffered disturbing dreams for the next few days and weeks, and every ring of the phone, every stranger's step at the door seemed to threaten us. But nothing happened. Neither Ulli nor the police got in touch. Slowly I stopped thinking constantly about the dead man at the lake, began to wipe the treacherous Ulli from my memory, and returned my attention to everyday life. Jonas was about to start school—an important event for mother and child.

Several months had gone by when I received a phone call from a woman I did not know. "My name isn't important; just call me Adelheid," she said, and hinted that she knew things that were of great importance to me. In the event that I wasn't willing to meet her as she suggested, she wouldn't hesitate to bring to public attention a certain secret that we both knew.

What choice did I have? In my fear, I thought she could only be a blackmailer who would threaten to inform my husband of my relationship with Ulli—which had long since ended. I would probably have to pay.

Jonas was with my parents, Eugene was off fishing, and I sat in a cafe across from this unfamiliar woman, prudently in the nearest metropolis and not in our little city. This so-called Adelheid let the cat out of the bag right away. Over a double espresso and warm apple strudel with vanilla ice cream, I discovered that she was the widow of the dead forest ranger. On the basis of his notes she had discovered who was responsible for the monthly "donation." Her husband had even confided to her that he sometimes met a "pal" at the lake whose financial boosts were contributing to their planned vacation in the Caribbean.

"When the police came to tell me of my husband's death, they brought a picnic basket with them, which they set down in my kitchen. It didn't belong to me. I examined the basket and its contents while I was making them some coffee. I already suspected that someone had poisoned my husband, so I removed one of the two fish croquettes. I mean, you hear everywhere that they're so careless in the labs."

She didn't look like the grieving widow. She was well-dressed, nicely made-up, and well-preserved, I noted, and moreover, she knew how to tell her story with a certain liveliness and suspense. But what did she want from me?

"The police took the basket and its contents with them when they learned that none of it came from our house. Moreover, my suspicion of the labs was justified; the result of the chemical analysis merely confirmed that there was no poison in the fish. However, during the autopsy they had discovered immediately that my husband's death was ultimately due to a fish bone in his throat; that is, he had choked on his own vomit. So those clever fellows concluded that it must have been an accident, because, naturally, fish croquettes can contain a few bones."

"And what does this have to do with me?" I asked, unable to prevent a feverish blush spreading across my face.

She went on. "The fish mixture was prepared in a blender, I could see that right away. If a few fish bones had gotten in unbeknownst to you, they would also have been chopped to pieces. Every homemaker knows that. So it was clear that you had introduced the fish bones intentionally afterward, and not in the most loving frame of mind." I looked "Adelheid" full in the face. She returned my gaze without protest, even with a certain admiration. Finally, we both smiled.

"You have done me a great service," she said, "because I've wanted to get rid of that simpleton of a wilderness man for a long time, but he couldn't be bothered to do me the favor of taking out any life insurance. He said that it wasn't necessary, since as the widow of a civil servant I would be well-off."

That was indeed unfortunate, I had to admit. "And how would you be situated in such a case?" she asked sympathetically. Proudly I related that Eugene was not so petty. In the event of his death I was very well provided for.

We met several times until all the details of the plan were mature. It was summer by the time she called and, in a mysterious voice, lured a fearful Eugene to the lake. She claimed to have found something there that belonged to him. Strangely enough, Eugene confided in me. The forest ranger's wife had insisted that he come to the lake. She probably wanted to blackmail him on the basis of his earlier payments to the forest ranger, he surmised. If he wasn't back by seven on the dot, I should call Ulli and hurry to his aid. Unfortunately, he couldn't take anyone with him: The woman had explicitly insisted that he come alone.

In the still part of the lake, we had propped one of Eugene's hats over a willow branch. We lay in wait in the reeds, crouched in a shallow rowboat, clad in heavy men's shoes to leave a false trail, and drinking from the dead forest ranger's hip flask.

Eugene arrived punctually, waited in nervous agitation, looked constantly at his watch, and finally noticed the hat on the willow branch. He was obviously puzzled, and hesitated at least ten minutes before he finally pulled on his hip waders and waded into the water. We were on the spot quickly, felled him with the oars, held his head for a suitable length of time underwater, and left him to his beloved fish.

My vacation with Adelheid is shaping up nicely. We've outfitted ourselves with some chic new clothes, and it won't take long before the good-looking, wealthy men in the Caribbean flock to our sides. Sportsmen who go in for deep-sea fishing generally have the good sense to choose rich parents.

Mitsuhara Yuri

Eighteenth Summer

Translated from the Japanese by Beth Cary

Mitsuhara Yuri is a writer of poetry, children's stories, and fantasy and mystery fiction. Her story "Eighteenth Summer," selected for EQMM's *Passport to Crime series and reprinted here, was the co-winner (along with Norizuki Rintarō's "An Urban Legend Puzzle," which also appears in this volume) of the 2002 Mystery Writers of Japan Award for best short story. Her first mystery novel,* Let's Forget Our Watches and Go to the Forest, *was published in Japan in 1998, but is not yet available in English translation. Please note that the author's name and names in this story are rendered in Japanese order: surname first.*

1.

A sky colored pale, as if smoothed by a brush dipped in water. Faint sunlight falling on the river's surface. A row of cherry trees halfway to full bloom lining the far bank of the river. On this side, a woman seated near the river sketching. He could still see it all. If it were a painting, he would have called it "Spring."

Alas, the scene no longer existed. The sky was deeper now; the sunlight unbearably hot and harsh. The cherry trees were fully green and silent. And near the riverbank, a gaping hole that could never be filled.

• • •

On that spring evening, Miura Shinya stopped to stare back across the bridge just before he left it. This pause had become a habitual part of his evening jog. A few days earlier, just as the cherry blossoms began to open, Shinya's own pale fragile hopes had fallen. He would have to spend another entire year studying to retake the university entrance exams.

He always felt somewhat unsettled during spring vacation. But this year he felt more completely adrift than ever before: vaguely lonely, at loose ends, and yet oddly relieved. He was afraid that he would become slack, especially physically, so he started jogging, even though he realized that jogging would look like slacking to others. He told his family that he would spend the rest of March recovering from the long, drawn-out cramming for exams. This was hardly an adequate explanation, but it was the best he could offer. Then, unexpectedly, something happened to rekindle his interest in life.

The bridge Shinya jogged across overlooked the grassy riverbank. In the distance, just about twenty meters away, she was sitting on the grass, tracing with colored pencils on paper clipped to her drawing board. *I hope it looks like I'm just taking in the scene,* Shinya thought. He stood there staring, content to feel the breeze come and go.

Suddenly, she put the drawing board down, stood up, turned around, and bent over to look at the far side of the river through her legs. She put her hands wide apart on the grass and gracefully stretched up into a handstand. Her white cap fell off and her ponytail hung down. From the handstand, she rolled gently forward onto the ground. It wasn't the first time he'd observed her, and once in a while he'd seen her move like this, with graceful ease. She reminded him of fairies he'd seen in animated videos.

She lay there looking up at the sky for a while, her arms and legs outstretched. Then she stood up, picked up her cap, and reached for her drawing board. The sun was sinking, and the river breeze was turning chilly. A gust of wind blew across the river, catching her drawing. It fluttered away from her, a bird flying from her hands. It turned, twisting in the wind, moving toward him. He could see pale colors on one side.

When the breeze carried it over his head, without thinking, Shinya ran after it. Eventually, the breeze weakened and the paper drifted down to dance along the grass, but just as it seemed sure to stop, another gust took it farther. Shinya felt that the sketch was mocking him, daring him to "Come over here." His impatience got the best of him and he dove for the irritating piece of paper, finally stopping its flight.

The sketch centered on the row of cherry trees on the opposite bank of the river. The delicate lines of colored pencil captured the faintly tinted trees, which seemed to rejoice in their springtime rebirth. A gray roof peeked through the trees. He couldn't tell about technique, but he thought it was a good drawing. If only there wasn't a crease down the middle. When he had collided with the paper, he had crushed it.

When she finally caught up, the first thing she said to Shinya, who was trying to get up off the grass, was, "Hey, you, what are you doing?"

She was wearing a pink T-shirt, a tight apple-green jacket, and slim white jeans. The spring colors on her slender body made her seem almost as young as a student, but he couldn't really tell a woman's age. She was definitely over twenty-five, and maybe almost thirty.

"Oh, I'm sorry. I messed it up."

She stamped her foot as if annoyed at his apology.

"That's not what I meant. You shouldn't chase so wildly after something I'll throw away anyway. If you got hurt, that would be idiotic."

"Throw away?"

"Sure. I don't have any interest in keeping my own trash."

"Trash? . . . But you went to such effort to draw it."

"Yes, I did. But only because I enjoy sketching. Once I've finished, I don't even want to look at it."

Feeling as if he had suddenly been tied in knots, Shinya looked at the beautiful "trash" and then back at her. If her eyes had been half a millimeter larger, they would have made her face overbearing; her nose was pointed like a small bird's beak. Her blunt manner of speaking with those naturally light pink lips was at odds with her delicate beauty, but this only called forth more images from his childhood and increased his nostalgia. Wasn't she called Tinkerbell in *Peter Pan*, that whimsical, sassy, cold-hearted fairy with the miraculous dust that enabled children to fly?

"Come on, get up already. . . . Oh!"

Her husky alto voice went up a notch when she stretched out one hand toward Shinya and saw a cut on the palm of his hand. He had scraped it when he dove for her drawing.

With the efficient manner of one accustomed to getting things done, she quickly decided what to do. "That needs to be looked after. I live right over there."

She took the drawing out of Shinya's hand and tucked it onto her drawing board.

Shinya mumbled that he was all right, but he decided to follow her lead, even though licking the scratch would have healed it.

"Won't it disturb your family?"

"No, I live alone."

"Oh, then . . . won't it annoy your boyfriend?"

He was feeling his way around, but she just laughed scornfully and said, "This is it."

Shinya looked up, surprised at the building where she stopped, just below the levee where she had been drawing her picture. He knew about this building. It was not far from his house just across the river. It had been built a few decades before, and there were numerous cracks in the gray outer wall. It was sure to collapse in the next strong earthquake. Only the lights in several of the windows at night kept it from being mistaken for an abandoned building: It was that sort of apartment house. Its name, Shōˉ raisoˉ , was old fashioned as well. With his average grade in Japanese, Shinya wasn't able to pronounce the old-fashioned characters. He had heard the rumor that there was a dispute between the owner and his son and daughter-in-law. The owner didn't want to evict any tenants, while the son wanted to convert the property into a fashionable, upscale apartment building while interest rates were still low. Because all the tenants were elderly, it was only a matter of time until the son and his wife won the battle. The rumors were tinged with black humor, and some said that all those old people were unnaturally tenacious and might outlive the younger couple. In any case, Shinya did not think it was the sort of place where a young female artist would live.

Her room was on the second floor, up a flight of stairs that creaked each step of the way. The door was dented in toward the bottom, no doubt a souvenir from a previous tenant. Pasted on it was a small piece of paper with the surname Suō hurriedly written on it. She must not have wanted it known that she was a woman living alone.

The inside of her apartment matched the outside of the building. The kitchen space offered merely a plain sink and cooktop. Then came the main room with a closet. It appeared that there was a door to a toilet, but he was willing to bet that there was nothing as fancy as a bath. Shinya had never been to a Zen temple, but he thought he would have to go to one to find living quarters more Spartan than these. Also, she had hardly any furniture, so that even this cramped living space felt bare. There was a small refrigerator in the kitchen, and in the living room, a little dresser and a low table. By the window stood an old desk and wastebasket. This was all the furniture he saw. How was it possible for a woman to live like this? It was so different from his older sister's room, cluttered with all her belongings. Faded, weathered-brown tatami mats edged around the heated carpet in the center of the room.

"Go on in," she said, impatient behind him. "I've just moved in."

Without realizing it, he had stared through the door for so long that it had seemed rude. Shinya felt flustered as he took off his shoes. He had thought the "Rooms for Rent" sign posted at the entry to the building was a joke. Now he had the strange impression that it was effective. Even so, you would think that a person who had recently moved in would have had a bit more furniture.

It crossed his mind that perhaps he should leave the door open, since he was alone with a woman. But she closed it without any sign of concern.

After she put her drawing board on the desk, she took a bottle of Mercurochrome and a packet of tissues from the drawer. What a makeshift life, if you kept your first-aid kit in your desk.

Without the least shyness, she grabbed Shinya's hand and applied the disinfectant. She said, "You must think it strange that I don't have anything here."

"Yes." His candid reply made her laugh out loud.

She let go of Shinya's hand. For a while he could still feel the touch of her slender fingers.

"I use my home in I—— as my office." She mentioned a station on a private line twenty minutes away. "But it's too small now—I've had a lot of work recently, and there's no room left even to sleep. I was thinking of moving when I found an empty room here. I try to work at home during the day and sleep over here."

"And sometimes you sketch in the early evenings."

She looked wide-eyed at Shinya, momentarily at a loss as to how to respond. Then she said, "I suppose so."

She stood up. His chance remark had let her know that he had been watching her. Actually, he wasn't entirely sure it was a slip of the tongue. Maybe he'd intentionally let it slip out.

She'd gone to the refrigerator to get something.

Shinya made another attempt at conversation. "You mentioned your office. What type of work do you do, um . . . Ms. Suō?"

She turned to face him, surprised by his blunt question.

Shinya hurriedly added, "That's right, isn't it? That is how your name is pronounced? It was on the front door."

"Ahh," she said. "I'm surprised you could read it. It's written in very old characters for dark, purplish red. My name is Suō Kumiko. Kumi is written with the characters for crimson and beautiful. My whole name is steeped in red tones. I feel that it sounds unpleasantly hot."

"No. It's very pretty."

She laughed disdainfully at his trite response and set a can of iced coffee down in front of him.

She told him that this was all she had to offer, then she answered his question. "I'm a freelance designer."

"Really? So that's why you like to draw."

"I've liked drawing ever since I was a child, but my work doesn't require that I draw."

"Even though you're a designer?"

Kumiko seemed used to this kind of question, and her reply was matter-of-fact. "That's right. A designer's work . . ." She stopped, stuck for a good example. "Well, that's why sometimes I simply want to draw for the pure pleasure of it. . . . What about you?"

Shinya drank his coffee while he thought over her question. It was not so difficult, she probably just wanted to know his name.

"My name is Miura Shinya. I live nearby."

"Are you a high-school student?"

"Starting in April, I'll be an exam prep-school student."

She told him to study hard, giving the standard response without much enthusiasm. She put the medicine and tissues back in the desk drawer. Then she took her picture from the drawing board and tore it in half and then in half again. She threw the shreds into the wastebasket. What she had said earlier was true. She looked at Shinya, raised her well-shaped eyebrows, and said, "What?"

"Well, if you were just going to throw it away, I would have liked to have it."

"No."

He had kept his tone light and teasing and was surprised that her response was so severe. There was nothing more to say about it. He drifted back to their previous topic.

"This apartment, um . . . isn't it inconvenient?"

"Well, it hasn't bothered me because I just come here to sleep, but I might feel that way once I get used to it."

Shinya gulped down the coffee, which was too cold for this season, and tried to shake off the thrill he felt when he heard her say, "come here to sleep."

"I don't mean to insult your landlord, but why did you pick this place?" He felt he sounded pushy, but Kumiko didn't seem suspicious.

"It was partly by chance. I happened to see the sign when I passed by. And then . . . I was taken with the view from the window."

Kumiko reached across the desk and opened the window. Shinya stood and walked over to it. Kumiko took his place sitting near the low table. With her long legs, it suited her just right to sit cross-legged on the floor.

Outside the window was a balcony, too small to call a veranda, but just right for drying laundry. There were four pots on the balcony. This seemed out of keeping with the rest of the apartment, which lacked even basic furniture. The pots were plastic, small enough to be encircled by two hands. It might be dangerous to place heavy terra cotta pots on such a tiny drying-balcony. Something might have been planted in the pots, but nothing poked through the surface of the black dirt.

The evening light was turning lavender. The riverbank, the river, and the row of cherry trees were all about to melt quietly into the evening dusk. It was such an ordinary scene. Yet, in the magic of the spring sunset, it was strangely nostalgic and comforting—the kind of scene many Japanese would identify as one of their original childhood memories. Shinya did not tell her then that the gray roof peeking through the trees was his house.

"Besides, the rent on this apartment is incredibly low."

Kumiko, who looked like a fairy or woodland sprite, suddenly came out with this pragmatic explanation. Shinya was amused by the incongruity, and it gave him an idea.

"Are there any empty rooms left?" he asked.

"I think so. Why?"

"If it's that cheap, I might as well rent a room here to use as a study. My older sister is living at home now; she's going to have a baby. It's already very chaotic at home, and it'll only get worse after the baby is born. I was wanting to have some quiet space for myself."

Shinya kept his gaze on the landscape outside, so he couldn't see Kumiko's expression.

"Really?" she said. "Then it would be just right for you."

She sounded a little surprised, but she didn't seem to object. Maybe her mind was on something else.

2.

When he went to talk to the landlord, who lived next-door, he was able to reach an agreement right away. Perhaps the landlord was reassured because Shinya was the son of a family who lived in the neighborhood. Or perhaps he didn't want to take his eyes off the rerun of the samurai drama he was watching. Anyway, he told Shinya, "You can move into any empty room anytime you like."

It fact, the room rent was astonishingly low. The rumor may have been true that the old man refused to give up managing the apartment building only to spite his son and daughter-in-law. However, he wasn't joking when he glared at Shinya from beneath his long white eyebrows and said, "There's no fire insurance. So it's up to you to be careful."

When Shinya told his parents he'd rented a room to study in, they didn't have any serious objections. Shinya felt reassured on many levels. At first, his mother thought it would be too expensive, but when she heard how low the rent was, she must have been relieved, and she seemed unconcerned about her son living alone. After all, she was fully occupied with the family's major event—the birth of her first grandchild. She really had no time to think about her son.

Shinya privately thought his mother was much improved. She was now forty-eight years old and had become worried about her health. The doctor told her that there was nothing wrong with her, so it must have just been menopause. Shinya thought the various minor complaints she had were tedious, and he'd largely ignored her. But about a month ago, it seemed to affect her mentally. She seemed very depressed, and several times he saw her lost in thought, sitting in the dark, too listless to bother turning on the lights. Both Shinya and his father began to think there must be something seriously the matter with her. Even though they began to feel worried, at such times men are utterly useless. They were lucky, because just at that time, Shinya's sister returned home to await the birth of her baby.

Shinya's sister had nerves of steel, and because she was a woman, she was able to be more sympathetic to their mother. Shinya and his father never inquired about the details, but his mother was able to pour her heart out to her daughter. And, as the due date drew closer, his mother became so involved in all the preparations for this solemn event that she had no time to complain of general malaise.

He was glad that she was in better spirits, but the trade-off was that she had become obsessed with preparing for the arrival of her grandchild. Now, if Shinya's behavior or his father's bothered her, she would scold them or shout at them. And Shinya knew that once the baby came, he wouldn't be able to stand the stress of studying for his exams in such a crazy household. He needed an escape. If he could move into that apartment, he could kill several birds with one stone.

Once Shinya left home, he knew his father would bear the brunt of his mother's irritable temper, and he felt sorry for him. But she was his wife, after all. He had only himself to blame. As for his sister, she seemed to think that everything should revolve around the baby she was carrying, so her mother's hysterics wouldn't affect her very much.

His mother's only concern about his living alone was his eating habits. So he agreed to eat at home, as she wished. The apartment was only a three-minute walk away, so it wasn't such a big deal. He also decided to continue to sleep at home, because he didn't want the hassle of buying a whole new set of futon and bedding. And, with this sort of "semi-independent" living, he didn't have to care about the lack of fire insurance.

In the end, all he bought was a small low table. He took an extra electric kettle and some coffee cups that his parents had received as gifts. These few things furnished his modest retreat. He carried his study materials back and forth. If he should find that he needed something else, he would get it at that point. He took Kumiko as a model: She was already set up in her simplified life.

Kumiko's room was just above his. She was a quiet resident, out at work for most of the day. He pretended to go to his prep school, but came straight to the apartment instead. He hung around and thought he could sense her presence. Even on her days off or at night her apartment was quiet, with no sound of a television or voices from possible visitors. Still, he could tell she was there. He couldn't figure out what she was doing, but he listened to her movements. And he realized that she was not a sprite from a fairy tale—she had the heft of a real person. He would stop turning the pages of his book, lost in listening. He had to force himself to focus and continue reading. By the middle of April, just a little over two weeks after he had moved in, he had finished reading two of Shiba Ryōtarō's historical novels: *Ryōma Goes Forth* and *Burning Sword*. He wished his life were as exciting as that time past, when the whole course of Japan's history shifted because it had to open to the West and to modernity. He wanted to feel vital and determined, no matter how hard the struggle might be.

His reference books and review texts stayed in the shoulder bag he carried back and forth between apartment and home.

One day, Shinya knocked on Kumiko's dented front door. She peeked out, and when she saw him, she looked surprised.

"What about your school?"

"My sister went into labor this morning."

"Oh?"

"It was sheer chaos, with my mother beside herself."

"So?"

"That's all."

"That's not an excuse to miss school."

"What about you?"

"It's the prerogative of a freelancer. I don't feel like working today, so I'm taking the day off."

"In that case, here's something for you."

Shinya showed her the package of strawberries that he'd lifted from the refrigerator at home.

Kumiko was taken aback. "Come on in," she said.

The heated carpet had been taken up. Other than that, the room looked the same as it had three weeks earlier. She was wearing a bulky beige sweater and blue jeans. She seemed to have been drawing. Her drawing board and colored pencils were out on the low table. Clearly there was nothing else for her to do in this barren room. In soft colors, she had drawn the scene outside her window. The plastic pots on the veranda were there. Small seedlings pushed up through the dirt, just as he remembered they had when he was in elementary school.

Kumiko cleared the table, putting away the drawing board and colored pencils. She rinsed the strawberries and returned them to their package. Again, he realized how stark her room was.

"How old is your sister?"

"Um . . . twenty-five."

"So, she's seven years older than you, kid."

She sat cross-legged as she had done before. He wasn't pleased that she called him "kid," but it sounded so natural that he didn't feel like objecting.

"I guess so. And what about you, Ms. Suō?" he asked.

"Let me see, I'm much, much older," she said, stressing the difference.

She took her third strawberry. He felt she had avoided answering his question.

"Are you drawing morning glories?" he asked, glancing at the sketch lying on the tatami mat.

"Yeah, sort of, since they've finally sprouted."

Kumiko pointed to the balcony with a shiny red strawberry. Then she slowly put it in her mouth.

"You must really love morning glories to have planted four pots of them."

"I don't know. I just wanted to plant the same flower to see which one would bloom first."

"Are you making them compete?"

"Yes, I've even named them. From the right: Father, Mother, Boy, Girl."

"What's that about?" he asked, barely able to keep from laughing.

Kumiko didn't notice. She stared into the distance, focused on the sky beyond the balcony.

"Your sister will probably say to her baby, 'Grow up quickly.'"

"I suppose so. Most parents do, don't they?"

She ignored Shinya, who was confused by her comment, and continued, "It's strange. All living things must die. Growing up means getting closer to death. The earlier a flower blooms, the sooner it will wither and die."

Kumiko smiled faintly, a very beautiful smile. But at the same time, it was a heavy smile, so heavy that a fairy's delicate wings wouldn't be able to carry it.

Once again, Shinya appeared at her door when he should have been at school. Again, Kumiko seemed surprised. She was wearing an old oversized T-shirt, and her face was flushed.

"What on earth are you up to?" she asked.

"This should tell you." He pulled a can of peaches out of a paper bag.

"What am I supposed to see?"

"Isn't this a typical get-well gift?"

"That's not what I meant. What about school . . . ?" She only got that far before she surrendered to a fit of coughing.

"Just go back to bed. Our landlord told me you were in bed with a terrible cold."

Muttering a string of epithets such as "you disobedient no-good son" under her breath, Kumiko turned and went back. She sat down on her futon and folded her legs beside her. Then she pulled the covers over her knees. Each movement was labored.

"Did you go to the doctor?"

"No, it takes too much effort."

"Do you have a fever?"

"I don't have a thermometer."

"Are you eating?"

"I'm not hungry. I think I ate yesterday."

"You'll die sooner or later."

"That would be a blessing."

"That doesn't sound like you. I think the fever has gone to your head."

Shinya innocently reached out to put the back of his hand against her forehead. Kumiko roughly caught his hand—and time stood still.

Presently, she whispered, "Don't be so forward."

She pushed his hand away and then gave in to another coughing fit.

"Well, I brought you some home-cooked rice with vegetables. Please eat this." Shinya cleared his throat and took a Tupperware container out of the paper bag.

Kumiko looked at him warily, like a cat.

"Rice cooked with vegetables? Did your mother cook it?"

"Yes. It's one of my sister's favorite dishes, and she cooked so much we had leftovers."

"I don't want it."

"Don't be so polite. It's pretty good."

"I said I don't want it."

"Why not?"

"Because I said so."

Kumiko waved him away, knocking the container he held out to her onto the tatami. She took refuge under the blanket, and he could barely hear her say, "I'm sorry."

Shinya sighed. "Actually, I cooked it, hoping you would eat some. Won't you taste it, since I made it specially for you?"

"Liar," Kumiko said, half poking her head out from under the blanket.

"No, I swear, it's true."

"Then tell me how you made it."

"Let me see. Here's the recipe. You soak the rice in the water used to soak shiitake mushrooms or kelp. You chop the vegetables into identically-sized pieces so they will be flavored evenly. Then you put them in with the rice, add the right amount of water and seasonings, and switch on the rice cooker."

He answered smoothly and without pause for thought. Actually, he didn't mind cooking. It would be too much trouble to cook every day, so he left that to his mother. But occasionally he enjoyed making a simple dish.

Kumiko sat up. "I guess I believe you."

"Look, I even brought chopsticks."

"Come on, even I have chopsticks here."

"What about a fork?"

"Well, what about it? . . ."

Shinya congratulated himself on remembering to bring a can opener. He used it to open the can of peaches. Kumiko opened the disposable chopsticks he had brought and was eating small, birdlike mouthfuls of the rice dish. Shinya glanced at her, and then went to the kitchen to get something to put the peaches in. He took a dish from the dish drainer—a large dish, the kind you'd eat curry from. It was too large, but it would have to do, because he didn't see any other dishes. He emptied the can of peaches into it.

"How's it taste?"

"You'll make a good husband."

"Would you like anything else?"

"A beer."

"Don't be silly. I'll go buy you a sports drink and some vegetable juice later."

"Make it the kind with fruit juice, okay?"

"Sure, of course."

"And could you water the plants?"

Shinya handed the dish of peaches to his demanding patient and went to open the window. He noticed that the room was stuffy. It would be good to let in some fresh air.

All of the four improbably-named pots—Father, Mother, Boy, and Girl—had sprouted seedlings with tiny leaf buds shaped like butterflies.

He didn't expect her to have a watering can, so he filled a cup from the dish drainer with water and watered the plants, taking care not to spill a drop.

"Which one has grown the most?" Kumiko asked.

"I can't tell. There doesn't seem to be much difference."

"Do any have permanent leaves?"

"Um . . . maybe one has the bud of a permanent leaf. It's on the 'Girl' plant."

"Hmm. . . . How's your sister?" she asked, suddenly changing direction.

"She's back from the hospital, with my niece."

"So she had a girl. What's her name?"

"They're still thinking about it. They can't decide between Asami for morning glory and Aoi for hollyhock, so they're playing 'Eenie, meenie, minie, moe.' But whenever they settle on one, then the other starts sounding better."

Kumiko barely chuckled. Maybe it was because of the fever. "Oh, you mean like 'Whatever the gods in heaven say'?"

"Yes, but my sister's husband is from Nara, so there they call it 'Whatever Buddha says.'"

This made quite a hit. "That's so local." She laughed through another coughing fit.

"But don't you find it strange? The 'gods in heaven' chant is exactly twenty-two syllables, so whenever you're deciding between only two choices, you know that you can't possibly end up with the one you start with."

"I've never thought it through like that."

"Even if you didn't count ahead, after chanting it a couple of times, you ought to realize how it was going to work out. Maybe people use this chant because they have already decided unconsciously on the second choice. So they start the chant with the one they don't want to pick. This way, they can have divine will validate their choice."

". . . Have you ever been told you're obnoxious?" Kumiko frowned as she ate a slice of peach.

"Why?"

"You're just too logical. I bet girls don't like you."

"Don't go there," Shinya cautioned. "Besides, I'm planning to major in psychology."

"Okay, but even using that chant, your sister is still unable to make up her mind."

"Well, you've got me there."

"People's choices aren't logical," Kumiko said with a sigh, and added nothing further.

As he went to leave her, Kumiko sat up in the formal position, with her legs tucked under her. Like a well-behaved child, she raised one hand to her chest in a prayerful pose.

"Thank you very much."

"It was no trouble. But, remember, it's customary to repay kindnesses twice-fold, you know."

" . . . You devil."

"Yes, yes. Go to sleep and get well soon so you can repay me."

Shinya laughed as he closed the door. Kumiko was easier to deal with when she was sick.

3.

"Ms. Suō."

When he called out to her, Kumiko glanced back and stared at him, wide-eyed. She turned around to face him and stood as tall as she could. She was simply dressed, as usual, in stretch jeans and a light blue shirt. She wore no accessories and used almost no makeup. He spoke before she could say anything.

"I went to school today. I'm telling the truth. I'm on my way home."

Of course, he had been waiting secretly for two hours at the McDonald's across the street, hoping that she would come out of the building where she had her office.

"Oh yes. You did say that your school was nearby."

Her response was flat, perhaps because he hadn't let her speak first. It was two weeks since she'd gotten over her cold. She must have had a lot of work to catch up on because she was hardly ever at Shōraisō.

"I still haven't repaid you, have I?" Kumiko said.

"I'm still waiting."

"You're a tactless kid, aren't you? All right. I'll treat you to whatever you want to eat."

"Are you finished with work?"

"Yes, finished for today."

"Let's go to one more place."

Shinya was starting to feel that she was punishing him with kindness. She treated him to supper. Then, she also took him to his first bar, but since he was a minor, she insisted that he drink only colas and iced tea while she downed one drink after another. As he guided Kumiko, in a happily drunken state, through streets crowded with weekend revelers, he had his feet trampled so many times he was already tired of partying.

"It's about time to go home."

"No, let's drink some more."

"I haven't been drinking at all, you know."

"Ha, if you haven't been drinking, then you should still be ready to party."

There was no way to keep this conversation going.

"Oh no," she remembered, "I haven't watered the morning glories today." Her words were slurred and almost incoherent.

"You haven't?"

"Will they die if I miss one day of watering?"

He knew nothing about growing morning glories, but he said, "Yes, yes. They'll wilt. They absolutely will. So we need to go home."

She answered, "Do you think so? Then that's great. I won't go home."

She didn't make sense to him.

Kumiko swayed. Flustered, Shinya grabbed her elbow to steady her. Then she put her other hand on his.

"I don't want to go home. . . . It's all right, isn't it?" she said with a sweet-sounding sigh.

His entire body felt heavy, like a sea sponge. No, he thought, that's not right. It should be like a sponge soaked with water. He was sleep-deprived and only nonsense drifted through his head.

He had thought staying out all night would be sexier than this. When she had suggested it, Kumiko had looked up at him, a melting expression in her big brown eyes. She had never looked at him like that before. And he'd felt excited in spite of himself. He didn't want her to know how he felt, so he nodded in agreement. He had no idea that he was agreeing to go on an all-night binge of karaoke singing. What's more, when they got to the club, she announced that she wanted to sing theme songs from old cartoon programs that Shinya had never heard of. Finally, to fight back, he sang a slew of schmaltzy Japanese-style popular songs. It was a pointless battle. How irritating to feel so pushed around.

Although he felt like snapping at her, he saw Kumiko safely back to her room, still drunk after this all-nighter. Shinya decided to drag himself back to his house.

He was just about to cross the bridge when someone behind him called his name. He turned and picked some leaves of grass as he looked behind him. He pretended to make a grass whistle in an effort to hide his agitation and his swollen eyes.

Fortunately, the man behind him was also exhausted. Drooping eyelids half hid his father's intense, sarcastic eyes. His hair was a mess, his face unshaven, and his classical good looks had deserted him.

Whenever Shinya's female classmates called him at home, they always wanted to know who the man with the sexy, low voice was.

Now the voice said, "You look sleepy."

"So do you."

"I've been editing proofs all night."

"Your hours are irregular, as always."

"It's mostly responding to man-made disasters," he said, yawning. "Some author claimed he'd mistaken his deadline by two weeks."

"Should you be deriding your source of income?"

"When an author always mistakes the due date, I end up feeling very annoyed. If it's a genuine mistake, why don't they ever think the deadline is two weeks earlier? That would make the production process go much more smoothly for everybody involved."

"Didn't you tell your author that?"

"As one with dependents to support, I can't say that to my source of income. I'm just hoping you become financially independent soon."

"If you hurt the feelings of this sensitive student suffering from exam-rejection, I might become a derelict."

"Keep saying that. I've never known anyone who announced that he was turning into a derelict who actually became one. . . . And you, have you been out studying all night?"

"Something like that."

Shinya couldn't possibly admit that he'd been out all night singing karaoke with some woman.

When he'd first rented the room, he'd always gone home to sleep. But now that it was warm enough to sleep with just a light blanket, he often slept over in the apartment when he stayed up late. Returning this late (or this early) didn't raise any suspicion.

"It's better not to stay up all night. You feel self-satisfied because you feel tired, but in fact it's not very effective."

"You should talk. You stayed up all night, didn't you?"

"The printer's deadline was nine o'clock this morning. There was no time to worry about efficacy. You're not under that much pressure yet, are you?"

"That's true."

"I won't object if you want to take another year to study for your exams—that is, if you really like to study."

"Why, you're so kind."

"No need to thank me. Anything I spend on you after you reach twenty, I'll consider a loan."

Shinya's father, an editor at a publishing company, was always sharp-tongued. He said that he was more circumspect at work. But Shinya wondered whether he didn't disparage his authors, and whether he would one day anger them into assaulting him in a dark alley. If he were stabbed, it wouldn't be a laughing matter, but if he were only beaten up a little, Shinya would be able to appreciate it.

"Are you satisfied with your granddaughter's name?" Shinya thought to ask as they reached the gate to the house.

"Yes . . . especially since Buson's haiku about morning glories is so dazzling." He said this seriously, without a trace of sarcasm.

It confused Shinya to think his dad was both disagreeable and an unrepentant romantic.

"And what about you?" He stopped when he asked Shinya this question. "When your sister goes home, are you going to give up your apartment?"

"I don't know. I've gotten used to studying this way."

"If it really helps you concentrate on studying, I don't mind."

"I wonder. Won't it bother you, absorbing the brunt of Mom's bad temper once Sis leaves?"

"Don't be silly."

Gazing into the face of this man, a man of whom people said "he looks best when he's angry," Shinya wondered if he, too, looked that way to others. He still hadn't figured out what parts of him were like his father.

"Well, I'll think it over," Shinya said with intentional arrogance. Then, grinning, he stepped to the side to let his father precede him through the gate.

As he passed in front of him, Shinya's father took a parting shot. "Don't say too much to your mom this morning. She'll wonder why you have such a hoarse voice if you've only been up all night studying."

Damn this man, Shinya thought.

His father opened the front door and stood stock-still. Wondering why, Shinya peered around him to see a man seated on the riser leading into the house. The visitor looked to be in his early thirties and was wearing a polo shirt. His manner was so stiff and earnest that Shinya thought if he tapped him, he would give off a metallic echo. Shinya didn't think he knew him, but he felt he had seen him somewhere. His eyes were bleary with fatigue. Clearly he hadn't had any sleep. This morning their neighborhood seemed to be filled with people who had stayed up all night. It was much too early in the morning for a courtesy call, but since his mother was kneeling in the entryway, offering him tea, he must be a guest.

When he saw Shinya's father, the man stood up so abruptly that Shinya pulled his father back to protect him from being stabbed by this potentially irate author.

Then the man bowed deeply and said, "Mr. Miura, sir! I'm so sorry. Please forgive me!"

The man did not straighten up.

Shinya's mother reported, with a troubled look, "I asked him to come inside and wait for you, but he insisted on waiting here."

"Please, Mr. Mineo, don't. It is I who should be congratulating you, sir."

It was extremely rare for his father to sound so deferential.

"Please don't treat me so formally. If you hadn't been there for us, I don't know what would have happened to my wife or me. . . . And yet I acted so abominably."

This visitor named Mineo seemed to be very excitable, and he was all choked up. As he went on talking and thanking and apologizing, despite his father's reassurances, Shinya was able to piece together the situation.

Mineo was the son of an alumnus of Shinya's father's university. When Shinya's father had been at university, Mineo's father had befriended him in some way. For some reason, this situation had inspired Mineo, a budding novelist, to take his manuscript to Shinya's father's firm.

(" . . . You read my manuscript so carefully, just because I was the son of someone who had been ahead of you in college. . . .")

"No, no. I'm not that soft. I read it over because instinct told me there was something there."

" . . . But you worked with me and instructed me, like a partner in a three-legged race. . . .")

Evidently, Shinya's father had polished Mineo's manuscript, which was raw and immature in places. Then, just when Mineo's prospects brightened and his novel looked as if it would be published, his wife, who'd been supporting him, fell ill. Without her income, and with the added expense of medical treatment, their financial situation soon became desperate. Mineo's parents were no longer living, and as Mineo's marriage had practically been an elopement, the young couple could not turn to her parents.

Mineo's long apologia continued.

"At that point, sir, you gave us a substantial amount of money. As a struggling writer, I should never have presumed on your kindness, but we were desperate."

"Not at all. . . . When I ran out of money, your late father would always treat me to dinner. And your book was scheduled to be published soon."

The publication of the book was suddenly put off indefinitely, however, due to problems at the company. This was not unusual at a small publisher like the one Shinya's father worked for, but for Mineo, it was a life-or-death matter.

"That's what I can't excuse. Even though I knew the delay wasn't your fault, I let my emotions overtake me. I said some terrible things to you, the man to whom I owe so much."

"Don't think about it that way. I was embarrassed by my company's decision, and I didn't think that you were out of line, given what you were going through."

Mineo engineered this unpleasant parting. Then, all the while ruing his misfortune, Mineo was forced to look for a job. Just before he started looking, he submitted his novel to a famous literary competition. He felt almost the way a destitute person feels when he buys a lottery ticket. And he also wanted to show the publisher Shinya's father worked for that the company had made a mistake. Mineo was unable to find a decent job, and at just about the time that he could no longer make ends meet doing odd jobs here and there, he heard the surprising news that he had won the prize.

"When I heard the news I realized for the first time how ungrateful I'd been. I shouldn't have submitted the manuscript to another publisher on my own."

"Don't be silly. The company made a mistake in delaying publication indefinitely. It was your manuscript to do with as you wished."

"Not at all! It was only because of your help that the manuscript was finished and presentable. You spared no pain in reworking my manuscript to improve it. It was hard to go through, but I really enjoyed the time we spent together working on it. . . ."

In the end, the author started sobbing violently.

And Shinya had finally recalled why he looked familiar. This was Mineo Hidenori, the writer who had received the prestigious Newcomer's Prize for his first novel two months ago. He had seen an article with the author's photograph. The interview conveyed the impression that the young author was unsophisticated, but the photograph hadn't revealed how emotional he was.

Shinya's father, who disliked such emotional displays, seemed uncomfortable. He stood watching the sobbing author. Shinya could tell from his posture that his father felt uneasy.

When was it that his father had told him that there was nothing better than seeing a manuscript he'd worked on turn out to be a good book? It had been a long time since Shinya had begun avoiding this type of conversation with his father.

"I didn't feel that I could return the money I owed you because I felt it wouldn't make up for my sins. Here . . ." Still sobbing— it was rare to see someone who was not a child so consumed with crying—Mineo took an envelope and a floppy disk from his shoulder bag. "Here is the money I owe you. And if you can forgive me, I should like to have the novel on this diskette published by Ryokuinsha." This was the name of Shinya's father's company. "It is topical now, so it should sell quite well."

His father, in a voice filled with regret, said, "That's not a good idea. Your first novel written after the award should be published by Taiyōsha, the company that sponsors the award."

"No! . . . I mean, yes, I'm aware of that. But I wanted my next novel to come from your publisher as soon as possible. That's the least I can do to make amends. During the past two months I've written two novels. I'll take the other one to Taiyōsha. I'm confident that both are equally good."

"Well, I'm impressed. I didn't realize that you were such a fast writer."

Shinya saw that his father could choose his words carefully when he was dealing with work-related matters. But Shinya understood that his father really meant, "Yet, you write so slowly."

Mineo smiled through his tear-stained face. "Somehow, when you're under enough pressure, you can get it done."

So that was it. Shinya now understood the situation. Mineo had worked late into last night finishing up the novel and had brought it to Shinya's father first thing in the morning.

His father politely received both the envelope and disk.

"I'll read it right away. And we'll be happy to publish it as soon as possible."

"But knowing you, Mr. Miura, you won't give it the go-ahead sign until you're satisfied with it."

"Of course not. Please prepare yourself for several revisions."

The author laughed and then started crying again. Shinya was surprised to see that his mother, sitting still on the floor, was also weeping. To top it all off, deeper inside the house the baby started crying.

What commotion, Shinya thought, feeling very lighthearted.

4.

The *noren*[1] curtain hung down to his knees. It was becoming unbearably hot and humid in Kumiko's second-floor apartment, with no cross breeze and no air conditioning. The humorous phrase "pushing against a noren," which means to waste your effort, was printed across the navy blue curtain.

Shinya knocked on the door, which was wide open.

"What do you want?" came the surly reply.

"Am I not to come by unless I have some business?"

---

1. *noren,* split doorway curtain that provides privacy while allowing air to circulate

"If you don't have any business, then you wouldn't come by, would you?"

"It's not okay if I come by just because I want to see you?" he asked recklessly.

After a while she answered, "If you have so much time to kid around, shouldn't you be studying?"

"I'll make you some tea."

"Well, in that case, all right."

Given permission to enter, he slipped off his sandals.

Kumiko had on an orange tank top and beige shorts that exposed three-quarters of her body. She was drawing a picture, as usual. Her sketchbook was propped up, making it impossible to see what the drawing was.

Shinya stood in the kitchen and asked, "What would you like?"

"Black tea."

"Shall I make it iced?"

"Hot."

"In this heat?"

"On a hot day, it is more effective to drink something hot and perspire to lower your body temperature."

"Really?"

He was afraid that he might have to go out and buy some tea, but fortunately he found some tea bags on a shelf. He used the only mug in the drying rack for Kumiko and selected a handle-less teacup for himself.

Kumiko said she didn't take sugar, so he carried the tea-filled cups over to her. He placed her mug on the low table in front of her. Then he moved away and sat on the window sill.

"What's been happening?"

"Nothing."

He felt like keeping distance between them. Kumiko's slim shoulders and legs looked very white and smooth.

"Have you lost weight?" he asked.

"I haven't had enough sleep."

"You're pushing yourself too hard."

"On what?" She looked up to glare at him.

"I don't know."

Their conversation seemed to be going nowhere. Shinya shifted position and turned the other way.

"I seem to have insomnia. I've gotten some medicine for it."

"Does it work?"

"I don't want to rely on something that's not natural."

"That sounds inconsistent." He laughed and then turned his head. The pots of plants with the strange names had stakes stuck in them. The vines were vigorously growing up the poles.

"They've gotten so big," he noted.

"Do you think that they'll bloom soon?"

"Let me see. There are a few small buds."

"Which pot will be first?"

"I can't tell."

She traced a light blue pencil sideways back and forth across her paper and spoke harshly again. "You were saying before that even if it seems that one is undecided, unconsciously one may already have decided."

"Yes, I suppose so."

"That's irresponsible of you." Kumiko frowned, and lines formed between her eyebrows.

"We were talking about playing 'Eenie, meenie, minie, moe' to decide on a name, weren't we?"

"So, you do remember. That's what made me think of it. I may think that I'm interested in which plant will bloom first, but I may be hoping unconsciously that this one or that one will bloom first. And if so, I may be treating that plant slightly differently from the others. That would make the competition unfair."

"That could be true psychologically, I suppose. Are you that compulsive about which plant blooms first?" he replied in amazement, thinking to himself that she didn't seem intent on caring for them.

Kumiko frowned again. "I have my reasons." She then took a dark blue pencil and said, "The flowers should be blue because those are the seeds I bought," as she began to rub the pencil across the sketch paper.

"Do you like blue?"

" 'Morning glory / a single circle the color / of a deep pool.' Don't you know it? It's a famous haiku poem by Buson about the morning glory."

" . . . 'The morning glory / has taken my well-bucket / I go to borrow water' is actually better known," Shinya retorted, feeling angry.

"But I don't like that haiku. I can't see how you could not notice that a well-bucket you use every day had been overtaken by a morning glory vine. It's disingenuous. It's so obvious in saying, 'Aren't I kind?'"

"Perhaps the poet Chiyojo had been away from home for a while."

Kumiko stopped drawing, and she sat deep in thought.

"Well, if you can confirm that she continued to borrow water from her neighbor until the morning glory finished blooming and withered, I'll take back what I said."

"I don't think it's possible to confirm that."

He didn't feel as interested as he usually did when they bantered back and forth. Then, he let slip what had happened.

"That reminds me, they chose Asami for my niece's name after all. In the end, her grandpa got his wish."

"Oh," Kumiko said, without interest. She said nothing more.

There was a long pause. Shinya couldn't keep his mind from racing.

"There was a man here yesterday, wasn't there?"

Kumiko looked up so quickly he almost heard a snap.

"Weren't you at school?"

"Is that what you thought? Actually I was in my room."

Strictly speaking, this was a lie. He had returned from school early and had only seen the man from the back as he had left. Yet it was such a disagreeable sight that it had extinguished all the lightheartedness he'd been feeling. Shinya continued the lie, as if to share the negative feelings that had overtaken him.

"Do you know that I can tell what is going on up here when I'm down below?"

Suddenly Kumiko became wary. "What are you trying to say?" She tucked her legs under herself in an uncomfortable formal sitting position. Shinya noticed that all at once he was facing her across the low table.

"He seemed like a middle-aged guy. Are men who have a wife and children that good?"

"What kind of ugly suggestion are you making? Anyway, you wouldn't know; you're just a kid."

Kumiko looked at him with an expression of anger mixed with threat. Shinya placed his hands on the table and pushed himself to his knees.

"Even if I'm just a kid, you and I are closer in age than you and he are. Isn't that true?"

He couldn't recall the order in which things happened next. He flung the table aside and grabbed her shoulders. She let out a small, sharp scream.

When he came to himself again, he had pushed her down onto the tatami. One of the straps on her tank top had slipped, partly exposing the edge of her breast. His heart was beating wildly, as if it might burst out of his rib cage.

What was he to do now?

Kumiko turned her face to the side and closed her eyes tightly. Her lips were moving, and he was afraid that she might scream. But her voice was faint.

"Don't make me feel contempt for you."

He felt himself grow hot. "I'm the one who has contempt for you," he replied, his voice hoarse as well.

Kumiko kept her eyes closed and said nothing more. When Shinya put his sweaty hand on the hem of her tank top, he heard the rustle of paper. Kumiko had grabbed her sketchbook, which had also fallen onto the floor. Shinya glanced at it and saw the drawing on the page—the figure of a youth in a light blue shirt and jeans—a figure that had been Shinya just a few minutes before.

The figure in the drawing was so relaxed that Shinya felt like crying. He let go of Kumiko's fragile shoulders and stood up unsteadily. He turned and looked back as he fled from the room, and he saw that Kumiko was still lying where he'd left her. He thought he saw tears in her eyes.

He didn't want anyone else to see her like this, so he selfishly closed the door on his way out. The door felt heavy. He wondered if he had the strength to open it again. He put his hand on the doorknob, but didn't have the courage to turn it.

5.

The stairs to the second floor looked steep and insurmountable. Yet he felt he must climb them. Several days had passed since the incident. If Shinya didn't go to apologize, he was sure Kumiko would remember him as an animal for the rest of her life. She wouldn't just detest him, she would be disgusted by him, as if he were something repulsive. It was frightening to imagine her beautiful face contorted with disgust every time she thought of him.

Shinya stood in front of the sea-blue noren feeling like a

grade-school kid waiting to be scolded. He knocked timidly on her door.

"I've been waiting for you."

When he heard this, he wondered if she had mistaken him for someone else. Feeling painfully insecure, he poked only his head through the noren, so that she could see clearly who it was.

Kumiko was sitting on the window sill with the potted plants behind her. One of the plants was on the low table. A withered blossom still hung from the plant.

"I've been wondering how many days it would take before you felt like apologizing."

Kumiko kept her hands clasped behind her head and gestured toward the corner of the room, indicating that he should sit far away from her. The day was hot, yet Kumiko wore jeans and a long-sleeved shirt buttoned to the top. Her face was the only skin exposed.

Shinya wished he could shrink. He moved to sit in the corner. He put his hands on his knees and lowered his head.

"I'm sorry for the other day. But I really have feelings for you—"

She whipped out her response. "Don't joke with me."

Shinya bit his lip. She was not the kind of woman who would permit him to tell her how he felt after what he had said and done.

Kumiko stood up gracefully and walked weightlessly to the kitchen. She seemed to ignore his presence. He heard the sounds of water running, filling the kettle, and of the stove being turned on.

"Um . . . don't bother about me."

"Shut up." Another curt response to counter his hesitant effort.

Kumiko returned. Shinya, his head still bowed, saw a tea cup placed on the tatami directly in front of him. The sweet fragrance of milk tea drifted up from the pale liquid in the cup. As she walked away, he could see that blue socks completely covered her feet. Shinya felt like crying.

"You said you had contempt for me, didn't you?" she said.

"Oh, that . . . I didn't mean it."

"Are you the type who says things that you don't mean?"

He was powerless to counter her ridicule.

"It's not like you to be involved in a shabby affair with a married man."

"Not like me? What do you know about what is and isn't like me? Don't say such irresponsible things. You don't know me well enough to know what I'm like."

"I know that much about you because I love you."

He could tell that Kumiko was at a loss for words. Shinya felt some satisfaction at being able to shock her after all that had happened.

"You've misunderstood everything," she said, calm again. "I'm not having an affair with him. I just happened to fall for a man with a wife and children. Then I came to hate him of my own accord. . . . Hey, drink up."

He looked up and saw that Kumiko was sipping from her mug. She must be drinking the same thing. Shinya gingerly sipped his milk tea. It wasn't very hot because she had added a lot of milk to the tea. She must have put in a lot of sugar, too. He found it too sweet for his taste.

"You said such a shabby thing wasn't like me, didn't you? Well, I'll tell you something. The reason I moved here was because I wanted to kill someone in his family and destroy his household."

Was this the way a bomb was dropped, so nonchalantly? Shinya's hand quivered ever so slightly.

"Are you afraid?"

He answered, "No," and drank the milk tea all at once. "I'm not afraid. I couldn't forgive a man who caused you to think such thoughts."

Shinya blushed and looked back at the floor. He had no right to blame anyone. Kumiko continued talking in a strange, flat voice.

"I thought I couldn't control my longing for him or loathing for him unless I killed someone. But I couldn't figure out who it should be. Should I kill him, the one person I hated over anyone else; or should I kill his wife, who had him all to herself; or should I kill his son, who was the center of the happy family he left me for. The morning glories were going to help me decide whom to kill. Like playing 'Eenie, meenie, minie, moe.' I planned to kill the one whose flower bloomed first, like a game of Russian roulette."

Shinya remembered that Kumiko had said, "Growing up quickly means getting closer to death quickly." He remembered how she smiled when she said it and he began to feel afraid.

"But . . . but you couldn't have been thinking of killing someone in earnest."

"I was in earnest."

"You couldn't have been. 'Cause that night—when we stayed out together—when I said the plants would wither if you didn't go home to water them, you said, then you wouldn't go home. In your heart you must have been thinking that it would be good if the plants died. Then the game would be over."

"You're still so arrogant, deciding that you know all about another person's feelings." Kumiko sighed as if completely exhausted. "Of course I said that. No matter how much I meant it, murder isn't something you can plan and then have no second thoughts. It's been three months since I found this place near his house and started observing his family. I vacillated between thinking it was all so senseless and all so necessary. I wanted to stop the whole thing. I even went to see a psychologist. I wanted someone to stop me."

"Do you know what substitute behavior is?" he asked, using her tactic of introducing a completely unrelated topic.

"Yes, I know that much jargon, Mr. Psychologist."

"If you can't have the real thing, then can't you put up with a substitute? Wouldn't I do?"

"Do you have any pride, kid? Begging to be his substitute."

"If it's for you. And if that will make you forget him."

"I don't like men who have no pride."

She's like ice, Shinya thought, as he rubbed his eyes. He suddenly felt extremely sleepy.

"Besides, the flower has already bloomed—the one on the table there." Her voice was as cold as ice.

"Which plant is it? 'Father' is the man, 'Mother' is his wife, 'Boy' is his son, and 'Girl' must be his daughter."

"No, that's not it." She laughed. "The daughter has left home. She's not involved. *So this isn't about your sister.*"

Shinya looked up and raised his heavy eyelids. He looked Kumiko full in the face for the first time that day.

Kumiko stared back at him; she realized that he understood. They spent a long moment staring into each other's eyes. Then sleepiness overtook him and Shinya closed his eyes again.

"The 'Girl' is myself," Kumiko said. "Because I knew the easiest solution would be for me to die. I thought it would be unfair if I didn't include myself in the game."

Shinya struggled to fight his way back to consciousness. Kumiko—this cold, selfish, violent, yet beautiful being—might die. Incomprehensibly, this was more of a shock to him than the possibility that his father or mother might die.

"Which plant bloomed? You mustn't die. You mustn't . . ."

How much did she hear of what he was barely able to say? He

could tell that she had stepped across the tatami and moved closer to him.

"I'm sorry I didn't say anything. I knew you were his son from the very beginning. I could tell as soon as I saw you on the bridge. I knew I shouldn't get close to you, but I couldn't help it. . . . You know, you look so much like him."

He felt her small hand stroke his cheek with unexpected gentleness.

Sleeping pills. She had gotten them for her insomnia. From a psychologist's clinic. That's why she made milk tea. To disguise the taste. Fragmented thoughts floated around in his head.

—So it was my plant. But that's all right, if that's the way it is. My dying means she'll live. But I wanted to say one thing. I knew about you and my father from the very beginning. I knew, but still . . . Then Shinya lost all consciousness. . . .

Shinya sat facing his sister. They were at a family restaurant near the house. It must have been early spring.

"The old man's having an affair?" he said.

Shinya nearly spit out his coffee. His sister had insisted he meet her here to discuss something she couldn't talk about at home. So this was it.

"I can't believe it. How could anyone be attracted to such a middle-aged bore?"

"That's just your opinion. He's the type young women find attractive."

His sister, who was drinking milk in deference to her pregnant belly, sounded like a middle-aged woman.

"I still don't believe it."

"It's Mom's intuition. She says sometimes he smells like a soap that we don't use at home. Woman's intuition is very powerful about this sort of thing."

"From the smell of soap? Really? Couldn't she be delusional?"

He'd noticed that his mother had started to behave strangely as she entered menopause. It had improved considerably since his sister had moved back and become his mother's confidante. He was grateful to her, but he thought she shouldn't believe everything their mother said. But his sister was insistent.

"That's not all. You remember the elaborately designed New Year's cards that Father's received over the last few years, from before I got married until now? He said they were from a designer he often worked with."

"Yeah, I guess so."

His mother always wanted to see the cards that came to Shinya and his father, saying she wanted to use them as examples for the next year's cards that she would have printed up to send out—though by the next year she was too busy to do anything about it. Shinya did not want to hear his mother's comments on the cards girls sent him, so he had refused to let her see them. But his father didn't have that kind of freedom. His cards had to be available to the whole family. And it was true. There had always been an exceptionally beautiful card in purple and red.

He remembered his father talking in his usual gruff way when this card came up for discussion. "It's from one of the designers who work for us. It would be easy for her to make this."

Shinya had asked, "Designers design clothes, don't they? Why would you know her?"

"Ah, there are all kinds of designers," he answered. "Some designers do work like putting clothes on books. So it's really close to editing. They decide where the photographs and illustrations go, what kind of paper to use for the cover, what kind of font to use for the title . . ."

Even though his style was gruff, his father always sounded

cheerful when he talked about work. Shinya felt sad when he remembered when he was young and still called his father "Dad."

"Her name was difficult to read, wasn't it?"

"Mom showed me the card. Her name is Suō Kumiko."

His sister picked up a customer survey card on the table and wrote out the characters.

"Really? You read these characters Suō?"

"It's the name of a color, a purplish red. I can't understand how your Japanese can be so weak when you read so many books."

"Reading is not as shallow as studying vocabulary for entrance exams."

"Who said that?"

"I just made it up."

" . . . Don't scatter the cherry blossoms by failing again next year, okay?"

"No need to worry. I want to go into psychology, which is in the sciences."

This was an empty boast. When he was pressed about his lack of knowledge in mathematics, Shinya had taken to saying, "Psychology is in the humanities." Shinya's image of psychology was that it was hard to categorize, like a bat hanging upside down.

"In any case, apparently this year there was no New Year's card from her. By this time Mother had been looking forward to the card, so she asked, 'I wonder if there was a misfortune in her family?' She said Father's response seemed very nervous. He said something like, 'I haven't had much to do with her recently. I wasn't ever that close to her.'"

"Couldn't Mom be overreacting? Wouldn't you normally think that if New Year's cards stopped coming, the relationship was no longer a close one?"

"Silly," his sister responded condescendingly. "When a woman becomes involved with a married man, she no longer feels like sending him a New Year's card. She would make herself crazy imagining his family looking at the card as they sit around the table, warming their feet in the *kotatsu*[2] heater. And the worst possible thing would be to receive a response with all the names of his family members on it."

Shinya vacillated, thinking that she might be right. He wondered if his sister had experienced something similar.

"But I wonder. You really don't have any solid evidence."

"Yes, I do have solid evidence." His sister grew even more serious. "You know Father opened savings accounts for us, right? He closed mine out when I got married. But he still should have the one for you."

"So?"

His father had secretly been saving a few thousand yen at a time. He planned to use these accounts for his children's future. Several years ago, his mother had found the passbooks in his father's desk drawer and had been deeply moved. But once she found out, she said she felt she had to raise her husband's allowance, and that she felt she was the one who was losing out.

"Mom said since Dad had started the savings accounts, she had left them up to him and refused to get involved at all. But when she started feeling suspicious, she checked the passbook."

"Why on earth . . . ?"

"You need money to conduct an affair, don't you?"

"Ah . . . I get it. So?"

"The account was practically empty when there should have been a total of several hundred thousand yen."

". . . Did she say anything to Dad?"

---

2. *kotatsu*, an under-the-table foot warmer, usually sunk into the floor; its heat is contained by a quilt draped over the laps of those seated at the table.

"If she'd felt she could ask him about it, she wouldn't be suffering this much now."

Shinya crossed his arms. It sounded suspicious. Yet it all sounded so vague. When he said that, his sister responded calmly.

"That's why I'm telling you. You should be the one to confirm whether or not it's true."

"What?"

How was it that she had to drag him into this?

"I don't expect you to be as good as a private detective. We can get her office address from the old New Year's cards. I just want you to go there and see what she's like."

"I'm studying for my exams, you know."

"That's no excuse. This is a family crisis."

"Why can't you do it yourself?"

"You can't demand that much from a pregnant woman."

No matter what he said, he couldn't get through to his sister, who thought the world revolved around her.

—*It was all too real for it to be a dream,* he thought, *I must be ruminating about my memories,* as he drifted in and out of sleep. . . . *If I argue too much, she will just scold me again*—

Shinya felt an indescribable sense of loss as his thoughts wafted back and forth.

When he awoke, he was lying with his face pressed against the tatami. His head felt heavy because of the sleeping pills. *I'm still alive,* he thought, as if he were thinking of someone else. He tried to sit up.

He looked around and saw that the stem of the morning glory vine on the table had been cruelly broken off. Its leaves were wilted. Next to the plant was a sheet of paper torn from the sketchbook.

"The plant was 'Girl.'" This was how the letter started,

written in identically sized characters like printed lettering. "To use your words, perhaps I was subconsciously hoping that I would be the one to die. But, it doesn't matter anymore. What did you call it, substitute behavior? Since you were so insistent that I not die, I'll let breaking the morning glory substitute for killing myself. Though it's a shame for the morning glory. By the way, the reason your father came the other day was because he noticed that you and I had made contact and he was concerned. He saw the woman who had been in love with him coming home in the morning with his son, so I don't blame him for being worried. We just talked politely, and nothing like what you imagined took place. When I served him some tea, I almost put in some sleeping powder. But it was just a thought, and I couldn't go through with it. I told myself that the flowers hadn't bloomed yet. I wonder now how serious I was about all of this. I don't even know myself.

"I don't think it's unlike me to fall for a man with a wife and children. I don't regret that I loved your father. But trying to kill someone to get closure on my feelings was certainly unlike me. I feel humiliated that I had to be argued out of it by a kid like you. I'll never do anything so foolish again.

"Can I ask you for a favor? Tell the landlord goodbye. I won't be returning, so he can do as he wants with the stuff in my room. And, if you feel like it, it would please me if you would take the rest of the morning glories. They'll only last until the end of summer.

"Thanks for everything. The rice with vegetables, particularly. It tasted good.

"Please turn into a terrific adult, all right?"

What a stubborn way to end it. All along treating me as if I were just a kid.

When Shinya turned the paper over, he saw the sketch she'd made of him the other day.

He sat there for a while, tears running down his face.

6.

Shinya stood on the bridge thinking about the three months he'd been able to be close to Kumiko.

When he'd followed his sister's orders, he'd ended up reluctantly spying on this unadorned young woman. She didn't seem to be the type that his father would be supporting. As he watched her from the McDonald's across the street, she looked straight ahead and walked quickly into and out of her office. He began to feel disgusted by what he was doing. He told his sister, "Your suspicions are groundless. I'm taking myself off this case."

Then, when he was jogging and noticed the sassy, spritelike beauty drawing on the riverbank near his house, he was more than surprised. He was curious: He wanted to know why she was there. He couldn't help wondering if maybe she really was having an affair with his father.

He didn't tell his sister about it, but from then on it became part of his daily routine to watch over her from the bridge. He wasn't sure if he watched to get to the truth about the situation and her intentions or if he was content just to be able to stare at her.

Then one day, because of a chance meeting, they became acquainted, grew close, and then parted. No doubt their fate was determined from the moment the drawing blew across his path, fanned by the wind. And now, Shinya held her last picture, in a different form, in his hands.

As Kumiko had vowed, she never again showed up at Shōraisō. But he was surprised that she also cleared out of her office near Shinya's school and moved away. She was thoroughly consistent, as he would have expected her to be. With this realization, Shinya moved beyond his own sadness to being impressed with her strength. If she was still doing work for his father's company, he could find out where she was. But he didn't want to know, because Kumiko would not have wanted him to look for her.

Of course, Shinya's father had not used his savings to set Kumiko up as his mistress. He'd used the money to support that writer. If his father had told anyone he wanted to lend the money to a stranger, he would have had to explain the whole thing and he hadn't wanted to go through that tiresome process. He thought his wife wouldn't notice right away because she didn't involve herself in that savings account. So he had advanced the money without saying anything.

After the sobbing writer had finally left, his father had explained everything. Neither Shinya's mother nor his sister ever told him of their suspicions. Men are no match for women when it comes to feigning ignorance. In the end, his father never knew that he had avoided a family crisis. Since then, his mother had dropped all of her suspicions about his father. She was returning to her usual cheerful, easygoing self, and her menopausal symptoms seemed to be lessening. His sister had returned to her husband's house, and seemed to have forgotten all about the troubling task she'd forced on him. She often came back to visit, bringing Asami, and taking home food for supper.

When his sister left, Shinya moved out of Shōraisō and back to his house with the three morning glory plants. They were now on the balcony outside his window, blue flowers in bloom. His father, who must have seen these plants in Kumiko's room, started several times to say something to Shinya, but he never managed it. His father looked depressed, bereft of his usual self-importance. Shinya found it galling that he undoubtedly looked exactly the same. This was a secret that the two men shared; they never told the two women in the family.

One thing Shinya didn't know—when Kumiko had said her love for his father was one-sided, had that been the truth? His uncertainty grew stronger when he saw his father look at the morning glories. At the very least, they must have had a deep connection if it allowed them to share their impressions of Buson's haiku—'a single circle the color of a deep pool.' And maybe it hadn't stopped at that. Perhaps she had told Shinya that there had been no intimate relationship to protect his feelings. Maybe she didn't want him to lose his trust in his father? Or maybe it was something else?

It was probably better not to know. Kumiko had discharged her ambivalence and anger toward his father and then had left. She had chosen a particularly thrilling way to do this, in keeping, no doubt, with her deepest nature. He hoped she would always stay true to that nature. He hoped no man would appear in her life to get in the way of that. He didn't know if he, as one person who had hurt her, had the right to pray for this, but he would always be praying thus every time he thought of her. Most likely his father was doing the same thing.

His view of the riverside was dull now, with her slim figure no longer there. The thing that brought perfect beauty into his world was lost forever.

But he was being overly sentimental. If Kumiko could hear his thoughts, she would ridicule him. *And whenever she ridiculed me, I felt angry.* Shinya cheered himself up this way, and he opened the handkerchief he had used to wrap the ashes of her sketch. The Kumiko who wished that he would turn into a terrific adult would have wanted him to do this. Two months after she had vanished, he'd finally made this decision. He stood on the bridge and threw them into the air. They rode on the wind, and spread out like a flock of black butterflies. Then they slowly drifted down onto the shining surface of the river.

His eighteenth summer was soon to end.

Theo Capel

The Red Mercedes

Translated from the Dutch by Josh Pachter

Born in Amsterdam in 1944, Theo Capel is a child psychologist who began reviewing crime fiction in the mid 1970s, and wrote his first novel in 1981. The book became a series whose tenth entry appeared in Holland in 2002. "The Red Mercedes" is the author's first work in English translation. Another of his short stories was recently dramatized for Dutch radio.

From where I stood, I had a clear view of the red Mercedes E240. It was bathed in afternoon sun, which made it seem even redder. If you gashed your hand and watched it bleed, you'd see the exact same shade.

So the car *did* exist, after all, which meant we had a chance to get it back. Klop's uneasiness had been misplaced.

Klop runs the Personal Loans department of the Geldkrediet Bank. His job is, on the one hand, to lend out as much money as possible, then, on the other hand, to get it all back with interest. It doesn't always work out the way it's supposed to, and that's where I come in. My one-man firm is called Stammer's Collections, but Klop and I know each other from way back and are on a friendly basis.

That morning he'd sounded more nervous than usual, and

the fact that he was waiting for me when I presented myself at the reception desk was a clear sign that something out of the ordinary was up.

"Seen the paper, Hank?" he said as we walked down the Geldkrediet Bank's cool corridors towards his office. "The accident in the Keizersgracht?"

I shook my head. Klop and I read different newspapers.

"Guy's lived his whole life in Amsterdam, run over on his doorstep by a French tourist. Must have had too much wine at dinner, the Frenchman. And then, while the guy's lying there in the gutter waiting for the ambulance, he's robbed by a German drug addict. What a world, Hank. What's it all coming to?"

In my newspaper, they're called "junkies," not "drug addicts." Maybe that sounds more interesting. I didn't answer Klop's question—his paper'd already done that for him. The world was going to hell, you could read all about it every day.

We walked on in silence, with me still wondering what was up. The answer came at Klop's office door.

"You hear about Schepers, Hank?"

"Schepers? No, what's the old man done now?"

"He's dead. Heart attack."

This *was* news. I'd known Schepers during my own time at the Geldkrediet Bank. He was an old-school manager, totally authoritarian. His fight against women in pants had made him notorious.

"But, Mr. Schepers, pants cover up more of my figure than a skirt," one courageous secretary had dared to argue.

"Madam, pants accentuate, a skirt conceals," was his honeyed response. Since that day, those words had been used around the bank to put an end to uncomfortable conversations.

"It was a disaster," Klop said. "You see, it happened in a— in a club."

"A club?"

He gave me a pained look. "You know what I mean," he said.

The penny dropped. "A sex club? Schepers? Really?"

He winced. "You don't have to say it out loud, Hank. The walls have ears. Let's just call it a 'club,' okay?"

That was fine with me, but I knew there had to be more to the story. Klop might be a latter-day Puritan, but he didn't really care what other people did with their private lives, as long as they didn't scare the horses. Work, that's all he was really interested in.

He ushered me into his office and sent his secretary off for coffee.

I sat there quietly, waiting for the rest of it. It took Klop several moments to work his tight mouth around the words.

"He left a hell of a mess behind, Hank. He broke more rules than I can count, and it looks like he knew exactly what he was doing. I'm afraid the bank stands to lose a bundle."

His face reddened. Klop was convinced that his customers were always trying to rip the bank off. But he couldn't bring himself to believe that his colleagues were capable of the same bad behavior.

"So far, we've been able to keep it quiet. Only Internal Affairs knows anything about it. We're talking about a hundred thousand, here. Euros, Hank. A hundred thousand euros."

Klop hadn't really adjusted to the euro yet. He still thought in guilders. Personal loans were generally in the 5,000–10,000 euro range. It would be the end of Klop's world if twenty such loans suddenly went up in smoke.

"Is the money gone, Klop? What did he do with it?"

Given the scene of Schepers' death, there was an obvious answer to my question, but even for that sort of situation, it was an awful lot of money.

"You knew Schepers was in charge of Auto Loans?"

I hadn't known.

"Well, for starters, he seems to have approved two car loans which ought to have been denied. He took care of all the paperwork himself, didn't go through the ordinary channels. Then he made it look like the payments were coming in on time—but actually it turns out that the man who got the vehicles never paid a cent on the loans."

"How did he manage that? If no payments were being made, it would've shown up in Accounting, wouldn't it?"

Klop shook his head sadly. "He made the payments himself. Well, not really. He made it *look* like the payments were coming in, juggled the books, sort of a robbing-Peter-to-pay-Paul situation. And because he's been here so long, and knows our systems, he was able to cover it up."

"Until he died."

"Well, yes. When he stopped faking the payments, the loans were red-flagged and investigated, and that's when the truth came to light. Now we need to repossess the cars. You think you can handle that?"

"We'll see," I said. "But why did he do it? What did he get out of it? And why *two* cars?"

Klop scowled. "That's where the story turns really nasty. Schepers was speculating on the dollar market—apparently with embezzled funds. He bought an option for three months, the dollar fell against the euro, and he lost it all. Naturally, he was hoping to make a big enough profit to pay everything back."

For a man in Schepers' position, it would have been easy to place a large dollar order with a fairly small up-front investment.

"If he could have held on for another two weeks," Klop said, "everything would have worked out the way he'd intended. The dollar turned around, and it's still going up against the euro. Schepers saw it coming—but he got the timing wrong and lost it all."

Klop looked as if he'd made the doomed investment himself. He was far too cautious for such speculation, though.

"Upstairs has put me temporarily in charge of Auto Loans. They're positive there's more bad news to come."

"Upstairs" meant the bank's directors.

"Will you take a look at this for me, Hank, see if you can at least find out what happened to those two cars?"

Before I'd finished my coffee, though, Klop's telephone provided another shock. Auto Loans also handled insurance, and now it turned out that one of the two Mercedes had been reported stolen several months earlier. Quite quickly—suspiciously quickly—Auto Loans had paid off on the claim.

"It could be worse, Klop. At least it was the cheaper of the pair, just a C320," I said, only half joking. "The buyer must still be driving the other one, and that one's a lot pricier. Second time around, he had a better idea of what he really wanted."

Klop was not amused. "Do you realize how much even the C-series costs, Hank? You can't find one for under forty thousand."

Disgust, despair—Klop's tone spoke volumes.

From my vantage point, I watched the blood-red Mercedes E240 stand there glittering in the sun. You could almost smell the wealth and privilege, especially in that neighborhood. The cars parked around it were mostly midrange, none of them new. They were all on at least their second owners.

The little square in Amsterdam-South where I stood was intersected by a wide cross street. The Mercedes was registered to Marco de Bruin, salesman. That didn't really fit the neighborhood, either. You'd expect to find a salesman on the other side of the irrigation canal, where the houses were bigger and there was even the occasional villa to be seen. Of course, salesmen come in all shapes and sizes. Maybe de Bruin was just a minor hustler, but then what was he doing with a Mercedes? Maybe trying to look like a major hustler . . .

In this part of Amsterdam, many of the blocks were housing projects, originally thrown up for laborers and office personnel. The buildings, most of them, were due for their first major renovation. Trucks full of construction materials offered excellent cover for the itinerant investigator.

There was a playground on the other side of the square. There was a jungle gym and a sliding board, a knot of kids clambering up the one and whooshing down the other. The word "Fuckaduck" had been spray-painted on the side of the slide. The children looked Turkish to me. It surprised me to think that they knew English, on top of Dutch and their own language.

I stepped out from behind the truck and crossed the street, heading for the Mercedes. Klop had warned me that the E240 might also have been stolen by now, same as the C320—"stolen" in quotation marks, he'd said. I took a good look at the license plate, though, and it was the right car. All four doors were locked.

"Hey, you! Get away from the car!" someone shouted.

I turned, and thought I saw a figure behind the curtains in one of the downstairs apartments. I couldn't make him out clearly, but that didn't bother me. What bothered me was the pistol pointing straight at me.

The downstairs apartments had tiny front gardens, with access via sliding-glass living-room doors. On each side of these doors was a small curtained window. There was a broken pane in one window, and the pistol's barrel was sticking through the hole in the glass. A man held the curtain a little to one side so he could aim in my direction.

"That's right, you see it. You want to *feel* it, too? Get the hell away from my car!"

"Mr. de Bruin? Marco de Bruin?" I called in an official voice.

It was quiet for a moment.

"What if I am?"

"My name is Stammer. I'm representing the Geldkrediet Bank."

The pistol disappeared, and a few moments later the dark green front door opened. I saw a thin young man. As I walked toward him, I saw that he'd been threatening me with an air pistol. It had seemed far more dangerous when I hadn't known for sure what it was.

"They're always messing with my car," he said.

He made a sweeping gesture with his arm, encompassing the children crowding the playground, but also, apparently, everyone else in the neighborhood. Even the grown-ups. Even me.

"Every once in a while, you have to scare them a little. And don't get me wrong, this thing can *sting*." He raised the pistol. "I shot a pigeon right out of a tree last week. Thought I was out there washing the car just to give it a clean place to take a dump."

"I'd be careful, if I were you," I said. "Especially around the kids. All you need is a bunch of pissed-off parents banging on your door."

He shook his head stubbornly. "Not a problem. They find out one of their brats touched my car, they'll beat the crap out of him themselves. Those foreigners know exactly how much a Mercedes costs. One of them came by the other day, wanted to know what I'd take for it."

"As long as the bank still holds the paper, though, you wouldn't try to sell it, would you?"

He stared at me in silence. I noticed that he'd cut himself shaving. He didn't look like he could afford a new razor, let alone a car. He definitely fit the minor-hustler mold. His trousers were wrinkled, and his striped shirt was a Goodwill special. On his feet were cheap, off-brand sneakers.

"I'm here for the keys," I said. "No payments, no car."

For a second, I thought he was about to spit on my out-stretched palm.

Then, "What's your problem?" he said. "That's not the deal I made with your dude. I'm waiting for the cash. You guys know that. It won't be much longer—you'll get your money."

"We want it now, Marco. A deal's a deal. You haven't kept up the payments, so we take the car back. That's the way it works. You signed the papers yourself."

"Papers? What papers?" he said, stroking his chin. He glanced down at the air gun and stuck it clumsily in his pants pocket. "Mr. Schepers was supposed to take care of all that for me."

"Mr. Schepers isn't with us anymore."

"Naturally," he muttered. "I knew this would turn to shit. Look, I can explain everything."

"Including the stolen C320?"

He was dumbstruck. "What are you talking about?" he demanded. "Somebody stole it. Stuff happens. But the insurance covered it, it was all taken care of."

"I see," I said. "So then why did you need to finance *this* car, too? Why didn't you just pay for it with the insurance from the first one?"

He stared at me. "What do you care about the insurance? The insurance company doesn't care. They've got zillions."

"The insurance company is owned by the bank."

There was a momentary pause, and then he grinned. He was missing a tooth, I noticed.

"So you took quite a hit, then," he said.

He was starting to annoy me. "The keys," I said.

I took a step toward him, which put me practically inside his apartment. He was getting nervous: He took a step back and looked shiftily from side to side.

"You don't mean that," he said. "It's all gonna be fine, the money. I need the car for work. I can explain everything." He thought a moment. "You know what? We'll go see the dealer. They know the whole story."

"I'd be happy to believe you," I said, "if you'd let me see some cash. I'm not leaving without three thousand euros or the car. You pick."

"Three grand!" His voice was suddenly shrill. "You know I haven't got that kind of money. You have to give me a little time!"

He started in again about business, without explaining exactly *what* business he was in. I kept quiet. I knew the routine.

Finally, I agreed to ride along with him to the Mercedes dealer—who was sure to advance him a few thousand, he insisted. After all, he was a good customer.

What changed my mind was the realization that he was inviting me to sit inside the car, with the keys within hand's reach. And I was going to have to check out the dealer anyway.

De Bruin went inside to get a jacket. I watched him poke around for a piece of cardboard to prop inside the broken windowpane. He came out in an old leather bomber jacket with a wide collar and epaulets. The keys were in his hand.

Crossing the street, we had to jump out of the way when a heavy black Honda motorcycle carrying a rider and passenger roared past.

"Hey!" de Bruin called after it. "Watch it, you jerk!"

The biker slowed down, and his passenger turned back to face us. You couldn't see their faces through the tinted visors of their helmets. Both of them wore full leathers with the Honda logo on the back.

"Bikers are such jackoffs," said de Bruin, opening the Mercedes' passenger door for me as the motorcycle picked up speed and disappeared around a corner. "They think they own the road."

During the drive, de Bruin bragged nonstop about the beauty of the E240, and I had to admit that he was right. You barely heard a whisper from under the hood. It accelerated smoothly and ran like a dream. When I didn't argue with him, his self-confidence accelerated as smoothly as the car. He assured me four separate times that the Mercedes dealer would lend him the three thousand euros I was demanding. He even chewed me out when I made a minor readjustment to the side-view mirror on my side.

The dealership was in Buitenveldert, in a big showroom on the ground floor of a huge apartment block. There was a parking area in front, and no kids around to smudge the car's brilliant paint job with their greasy fingers.

We were the only customers at that hour. A fellow about my age came out to meet us. He wore a spiffy blue-gray suit, a white shirt, and a striped silk tie. He was perfectly clean-shaven. His gaze seemed slightly clouded, and he forced a smile when he saw de Bruin.

"Ah, Mr. de Bruin. What can we do for you? No problems, I hope. I saw you pull in, and everything looks just right—but I told you, it's a heck of a car." He turned to me. "Or is your friend interested in a Mercedes?" He said it dubiously, unsure whether I *was* de Bruin's friend or something else.

"I'm with the Geldkrediet Bank," I said as we strolled towards the showroom. "Mr. de Bruin has been having some trouble making his payments, and the bank has decided to repossess the car."

"It's not gonna come to that," de Bruin snapped. "I told you, they'll take care of it. Just give me five minutes to work it out!"

The car salesman had edged away from him, and I also stepped back, leaving him standing all by himself, like a ship-wrecked sailor on a desert island.

"Well," the salesman said hesitantly. "This can't be very pleasant for you, Mr. de Bruin."

"Pleasant?" de Bruin snarled. "You want to talk about pleasant? I'll tell you what won't be pleasant. If you don't hand me three thousand euros, I'm going straight to your wife, and I'm gonna let her know what you've been smoking back there in your office between customers. You knew damn well I didn't have the money when I bought the car, but you were happy to sell it to me and you haven't said no to those bags of herb I tip you with. Now you're going to help me out of a jam—three thousand euros doesn't mean a thing to you."

He grabbed the salesman by the lapels. He didn't really seem dangerous to me; his bluster looked more like begging than a threat. But the salesman took him seriously. He kneed de Bruin hard in the groin, and de Bruin staggered back, his face drained of color. For a moment it looked as if he might throw up on the showroom floor. He collapsed, and covered his crotch with shaking hands. If I hadn't been there, the salesman would have kicked him in the head with a perfectly polished wingtip.

"I should have done that when you first came in here, you dirty little loser," the salesman hissed. "You think I let a nobody like you threaten me in my own place? You watch yourself, little man. You ever set foot in here again—you go anywhere *near* my wife—I'll have a couple of my mechanics teach you some manners."

His face was red with anger.

"Okay, now," I said, just to be doing something.

"It's *not* okay," the salesman cried. "You've got your own problems with him—otherwise you wouldn't be here."

"Well, you're the one who sold him the car," I said. "Wait a minute, what am I saying? You're the one who sold him *two* cars. You figured you could make some money off him. Or am I missing something?"

De Bruin had risen to his knees and was sucking in deep breaths. His hands were still clutching his privates.

"Sure, I sold him two cars," the salesman argued, "but only because Mr. Schepers vouched for him. You don't think *I* sent *him* to Auto Loans? They came in together, and Mr. Schepers guaranteed me the financing wouldn't be a problem. What was I supposed to do? I mean, I sell cars, that's what I *do*. And you can't always judge by appearance. I had a rock singer in here, he looked to me like he was stoned to the gills, but he had a pocket full of five-hundred-euro notes. Fifty thousand euros, cash, and he wasn't leaving without a Mercedes, he said. I had to go to the bank with him to make sure the bills were real. Not that I was worried. I've seen him on TV, his records sell like crazy. My own kids buy them, so do all their friends. The guy's rich, but you wouldn't know it to look at him."

"This one says he's a salesman," I said, pointing down at de Bruin.

Who reached out a hand to me.

I helped him up.

"Jesus," he groaned. "Jesus, that hurts." His face spasmed. "I gotta ralph."

Before I could make a move, the salesman took him by the arm and had him halfway back to the big glass showroom door. I tagged along, and a minute later de Bruin was tossing his cookies on the asphalt of the parking area. He didn't have all that many cookies to toss, but it took him quite awhile to toss them. When he was finished, he stood there bent forward at the waist, gasping.

"Sit in the car," I said. "Try to pull yourself together."

He nodded and handed over the keys. I opened the door on the passenger side and helped him in. He leaned back against the leather, but he didn't seem to appreciate the comfort he'd been bragging about twenty minutes earlier. I got in behind the wheel.

After a while, de Bruin seemed to be tracking again.

"Bastard," he said, looking over at the showroom.

The salesman was nowhere to be seen. He'd apparently gone back to his office.

"He's a freaking liar. He's the one who put me and Schepers together. I'll tell your boss the whole story, if you want; he'll be very interested. I could write a book about all the dirty little games he and Schepers were playing." He was getting his nerve back. "You saw it yourself, he attacked me. I'll get even."

I thought about it. I had the keys. I had to deliver the car to the bank, anyway. Why not take de Bruin along and let him talk to Klop?

De Bruin insisted we stop off at his office to pick up what he called his "evidence."

"Where *is* your office?" I asked.

He glared at me as if I'd insulted him, but then told me to head for the Central Station.

"And be careful with my car," he added when a light turned red and I didn't come to a stop quickly enough to suit him.

By the time we hit downtown, I was feeling more comfortable behind the wheel. All I had to do was stop thinking about my own car, an old VW. Every once in a while, de Bruin did some backseat driving, but for the most part his attention was still focused between his legs.

"Stop here," he said at last. "I'll be right back."

I watched him go into an old warehouse in Spui Street, not

far from a line of pricey tourist hotels. An illuminated yellow sign over the warehouse door said "Club Kitty" in English. "Open all day and all night."

"That's some car, mister," a voice said.

A slim young woman, maybe twenty-three or twenty-four, had appeared beside the Mercedes, running the tips of her long white acrylic fingernails slowly along the edge of the half-open driver's window. Her hair was dyed the same dead white as her fake nails, and she wore a faded black micro-skirt over fishnet stockings and a V-necked T-shirt with the sleeves slit off. It too had been white, once upon a time, but too many wash cycles—or too few—had left it a dingy gray. Her face was probably the same color beneath too much clumsily applied makeup.

"Can you spare a cigarette? Or maybe we could take a ride?"

The way she said it suggested she wasn't really interested in smoking or riding. Her Dutch was clumsy, her accent Slavic.

"Buzz off, Vera," said de Bruin, swinging open the passenger door. He eased himself carefully into the seat.

"This is your office?" I said. "So you run the sex club where Schepers died, is that it?"

"Like you didn't already know," he said. "Yeah, this is my place. At least, I'm one of the partners. Why do you think I needed that insurance money? And I use the car to pick up customers and bring them home after. It makes a nice impression. I was supposed to take Schepers home that night, and then all of a sudden he was dead in one of the rooms. We had to straighten him up a little—didn't want it to look like the girls had killed him." He gazed over at his sex club. "I thought the publicity would be bad for business, but go figure: Soon as the story leaked out, the thrill-seekers started showing up, wanting to see where it happened. A couple more days like this, I'll be able to pay off all my debts. You'll get your share, don't worry."

He groaned, but that was still because of the pain. "And that bastard at the dealership, he'll get what's coming to *him*, too."

I started the car and pulled carefully out into traffic. I gave a little gas, then stomped on the brake when the car in front of us unexpectedly came to a halt.

"Hey, watch out!" cried de Bruin. He hadn't fastened his seat belt. "What are you doing?"

Two men jumped out of the car.

"Police!" they shouted. "Step out of the Mercedes. Step out!"

"Dammit," de Bruin muttered, reaching inside his leather jacket.

I jumped when he pulled out the pistol. My seat belt unclasped easily, but de Bruin still beat me out of the car. He aimed his weapon at the detectives, who dodged behind their vehicle. I heard a motorcycle behind me, and then a man in black leathers and a helmet with a tinted visor grabbed me by the neck. A second man, similarly outfitted, was dismounting from the bike and setting it on its kickstand. I recognized them by the Honda logos on their leathers.

"Police!" the second biker screamed from under his helmet. "Don't move! Drop the gun!"

"Don't shoot," I cried. "Don't shoot! It's just an air pistol!"

"Right, I'm an idiot," said de Bruin. "You think I'd go up against that ripoff artist at the dealership with a stupid air gun? This one's the real thing. You bastards want my car? Come and get it!"

To my astonishment, he shot a giant star in the rear window of the car the officers had been driving. I saw one of them waving a badge folder from behind the front bumper. I don't know why he bothered. Nobody was doubting they were cops.

Out of the corner of my eye, I saw that the biker had unzipped his leathers and pulled out a gun. His colleague pushed me into the asphalt and pressed his knee against my spine. On the other side of the Mercedes, de Bruin fired again. Two more shots sounded from much closer to my ear.

I lay with my cheek pressed against the road and could see de Bruin's legs and feet on the other side of the Mercedes. I watched him slump to the asphalt.

"He's hit," the man holding me down called out. "His buddy's unarmed."

He let me go. I got slowly to my feet and assumed the position. De Bruin wasn't moving. One of the cops pulled his jacket open. The brown leather was drenched with blood, which had also spattered onto the hood of the Mercedes.

"There's nothing on him," the man yelled. "Where's the damn weed? I don't see anything in the car."

My policeman slapped the side of my head.

"Where is it?" he demanded.

He patted me down, but I had nothing for him to find.

"This one hasn't got it, either," he called to his colleagues. "You check the club, maybe it's still in there. I'll check the trunk." He pulled me away from the car. "Open it."

I wasn't really paying attention. I was looking at de Bruin's blood on the hood of the Mercedes. They weren't quite the same shade of red, after all.

Kjersti Scheen

Moonglow

Translated from the Norwegian by Tiina Nunnally

It was Kjersti Scheen's art, not her writing, that first saw print in book form. Born in Oslo, Norway, she began illustrating books in 1964 and by 1976 she'd written and illustrated her own first picture book, Fie and the Darkness. *A wide range of books for children and adults followed. Her debut as a crime writer came in 1994, when P.I. Margaret Moss was introduced in the novel* Final Curtain *(now available in English from Arcadia). Critics loved the book and since then Kjersti Scheen's star on Norway's mystery scene has continued to rise. She has more than half a dozen crime novels in print in Norway.*

It's late May, and the city is having a heat wave. The asphalt is soft and sticky, a stale odor of salt water is rising up along the streets from the harbor. Summer has done what it usually does—caught Oslo napping, switching from icy roads and a north wind to tropical nights without any polite transitions. Fish is on the menu at the Theater Cafe; the aroma of steamed turbot is seeping out the big doors with the brass trim. It's not yet time for the dinner rush. There are still empty tables in the cafe's rotunda and in the section on the right which the regulars call Bunne Fjord.

Margaret Moss is sitting with a glass of expensive white wine, pretending to read the newspaper. She regrets taking this job; it's not the first time in her life. She's not one who appears in the papers under reports of fashionable murder cases. She usually has to settle for unfaithful husbands and missing wives. But this time she really should have said no. What is she doing here in the Theater Cafe on a stifling hot day about to eavesdrop on four respected elderly gentlemen having their annual spring dinner together?

It was all because of Herman.

The city between the mountains was panting. It had been doing the same thing four days ago. That's when Moss was lazily drinking a beer as she sat under the apple trees in her aunt's yard in Smestad, where she rented the third floor.

"Look how comfortable you are, sitting there in the shade!" her aunt called from the porch. Over the years, Maisen Moss Pedersen had developed a great deal of trouble with her legs, and she seldom attempted the steps down from her porch without assistance.

"Well, I don't know if I'd call it shade," replied Moss gloomily. "There's mildew on the trees again. And there aren't a lot of leaves to speak of."

"Good gracious, what are you telling me?" shouted her aunt in a worried-sounding soprano. "We'll have to get the trees sprayed!"

Moss didn't reply. She pulled her sweaty T-shirt away from her body and blew down at her chest. Her aunt was saying something again up on the porch. "Actually, somebody's on the phone for you, dear."

Moss sprang to her feet. "A job? I hope so. I'm totally broke!"

"Er, no. It's just Herman."

"Just Herman" was Herman Hoff Siversen, retired tax attorney and old friend of the family.

"I wonder what he wants with me," muttered Margaret Moss as she walked down the gravel path in her bare feet and headed for the telephone.

"Hello, little Margaret, it's Herman. How are you, sweetie? You must be taking full advantage of the spring, I imagine. Ah yes, that's life. What would you say to dinner at the Theater Cafe? It's actually sort of a job, at your standard rate and extra for expenses. Plus a glass or two of chilled Chablis in this heat."

That's how the whole thing started.

With the obsessive idea of an elderly gentleman who had too much time on his hands.

"It's about my record collection, you know," he told her.

His unique collection of swing jazz tunes on old-fashioned shellac records, 78s, those heavy platters, the collection he had put together with such care and which had inexplicably vanished in the late 'sixties. Margaret's father, who was Herman's law-school buddy in the bad old days, had been most definite about it: Herman is a splendid fellow, but for goodness' sake don't let him get started talking about his record collection!

Now he was not only talking about it, he claimed to have definitive information about what had happened to the records. But to prove it, he needed an unbiased witness, an outsider who wasn't weighed down by old prejudices. Apparently all the others were: Herman's closest friends who had stuck with each other through thick and thin for almost sixty years. Once upon a time there had been seven of them. Now there were four, and over all these years they had held on to one tradition: They met at the Theater Cafe for dinner four times a year. To rehash old memories: the girls of Havna Island in 1949, the unforgettable grouse hunt in 1956, and jazz—which was no longer what it used to be.

This isn't either, thought Moss, taking another gulp of her wine as she sat in the Theater Cafe, waiting for the old guys to show up. She took out her notebook and pen. Herman had pictured a cassette tape recorder, slyly positioned, but Moss had explained that it would pick up so much background noise that their voices would be hard to distinguish. The secret police were probably the only ones who possessed the kind of recorders that wouldn't have that problem—and were also invisible.

"We always sit in the same place," Herman had explained. "A table for four next to the wall in Bunne Fjord. So I'll reserve a little table for you next to us. You know how close the tables are. The guys won't recognize you, will they? You don't have a fake moustache you could wear, do you?"

She didn't laugh, just paused for a moment to consider whether they would know who she was, but decided they wouldn't. None of them had seen her since she was a skinny kid climbing trees in the yard in Fredrikstad, back when her mother and father still had frequent guests in their home.

She'd be able to take notes in peace.

People often took a few notes at the Theater Cafe.

Then they arrived.

First Herman, who cast a piercing glance at Moss before, with great waves of his hands and much hearty bluster, he showed the others to their seats: Nicolai Nielsen, Nic, a former tennis ace, now retired attorney, and Thorvald Torgersen, a businessman who once had offices on Drammensveien. Then Birger Bøe arrived and sat down behind the table that the waiter attentively pulled out. Bøe had been a G.P. on the west side up until a year ago. Birger Bøe, with a sprinkling of angelic tufts of hair around his ears, a rosy face with deep dimples, discreet glimpses of gold in his teeth. He would have been a great doctor, as Moss's father used to say, if it weren't for a certain soft-heartedness that was almost too much of a good thing. Her father thought this was because he had never married and so he never stopped romanticizing women. Apparently there was Someone Who Had Turned Him Down.

Then there was Thorvald Torgersen. Tall, awkward, with a big nose, a great mane of bristly, iron-gray hair that revealed big, suntanned ears. An outdoorsman, through and through. After he turned over his businesses to his sons, he had devoted himself to his main hobbies: botany and deer hunting. His wife Erna was from the Ålesund region, where they had owned a little house on the lake for many years. And that's where Thorvald spent long stretches of time, whenever he wasn't rummaging around in used bookstores searching for botanical treasures.

Nic Nielsen was sitting closest to Moss. He had just raised his glass to give a welcome toast, but his hand was shaking so badly that he had to support it with the other one.

"I swear, you're going to make your drink foam the way you're shaking it," said Thorvald Torgersen so loudly that Moss realized he was hard of hearing. It seemed as if the others were, too, and she noted with pleasure that it was going to be easy to follow their conversation even though the other tables were slowly filling up and the clatter of glasses and silverware had increased.

If only they wouldn't start playing music! For the time being the balcony up near the ceiling was deserted. She could only hope for the best. Herman was clearly in his element as he issued instructions to the waiters and handed out the menus. His trimmed black moustache and his hair with the perfect part had been dyed. That wasn't something he would ever admit, but Aunt Maisen claimed he'd been doing it for a good twenty years. Moss abruptly looked down at her newspaper as the headlines swam before her eyes. She felt suddenly touched, darn it all. Here sat these old guys, fumbling with their reading glasses and holding the menus at arm's length in their big, brown-spotted hands, with ruddy cheeks and bushy eyebrows and hair sticking out of their ears. Herman and Thorvald were wearing blue blazers with Royal Norwegian Yacht Club emblems on the pocket; Birger and Nic wore impeccable gray summer suits.

Study their faces, Margaret! That's what you should do. And listen to what they say! Your cue is when I mention the name Rowland Greenberg; that's when I'll start talking about the serious issues, that's when I'm going to talk about my record collection! But that won't happen until we're well into the main course. Is everything clear?

Oh yes, it was all quite clear.

The night before, Herman had insisted on personally presenting the main points of the matter, as he said, although the main points got more and more detailed as they sat there drinking Aunt Maisen's cloying port wine. He started digging up all sorts of stories about Nic and Birger and Thorvald, while Maisen nodded off in the corner of the sofa and Margaret got a cramp in her jaw from trying not to yawn. But he kept coming back to the famous *weekend at the cabin,* that long weekend the four friends had spent together one summer long ago when they were all younger, livelier, and more fun, in every sense of the word. That was the weekend the record collection disappeared.

It was right after midsummer in 1967. And it was just Herman, Birger, Thorvald, and Nic. Alf was dead by then, Sigurd was in Japan representing a Norwegian company, Einar was abroad working for the Foreign Office. The four of them all drove together in Herman's big station wagon out to Nøtterøy near Vrengen, to Nic's cabin. They were boisterous and exuberant, in the best of spirits. Before they had even left Oslo, they were all talking at once: *Hey, remember that time, boys . . .* by God, that's the Mills Brothers . . . No, it's the Ink Spots, man . . . that was the year that . . . "The Hankø Waltz," do you remember "The

Hankø Waltz"? . . . Geez, boys, what was it that Alf used to . . . it wasn't Teddy Wilson who . . . but what about Einar Rose?

That's how it started.

Herman felt like the luckiest man in the world that night. (Yes, I know, Margaret, I see you looking at me! But friendship like that, well, women have no idea what it's like!) Everything was perfect, the sun set in the northwest and night fell, utterly still. At dawn the next morning they went out to pull up the net they had set out, just Birger and Herman this time, and Herman never forgot it: the gentle, silky smooth swells out on the sea, the oars creaking in the oarlocks. They didn't get many fish, but the *mood!* And Birger, who was always the merriest of the lot; but out there he was quiet, pensive, even *humble!* He confided something to his oldest friend. Said that he had found the love of his life, but she was married to someone else. It was a tragedy, it had *been* a tragedy, but now he could start to breathe again. She had promised to leave her husband.

Herman was touched by his friend's story. He rowed to land and started cleaning the net, and they didn't say anything more about it, but those kinds of moods you didn't forget.

Up at the cabin the guys were in the midst of frying bacon, and it was still only Saturday morning, and the sun would soon be high overhead. Thorvald had a hangover, it's true. He was taciturn and distant and hid himself in a book. And yet, Margaret! said Herman. And yet!

"Uh-huh," said Margaret, wondering when he was thinking of getting to the point. "So did you play any records? Did you take out your records?"

Of course! That was one of the reasons for the trip! They were going to listen to the old records without interruption from women or children! And so they played records all Saturday night. And talked. And drank.

A lot.

But what great discussions they had! A regular debate about jazz, Margaret, a bit influenced by alcohol toward the end, of course, and yet. Thorvald had gradually gotten quite loud and opinionated. Thorvald had actually been rather difficult the whole weekend, now that Herman thought about it. Argumentative and irritable one moment, silent and standoffish the next. At three in the morning, when Birger, with bloodshot eyes and his hair in disarray, stood swaying in the middle of the room and wanted to play "Moonglow" for the third time in a row, Thorvald flew completely off the handle. "But it's so beautiful," said Birger with a hiccup. "They're playing our song. Not yours, Thorvald."

" 'Moonglow'?" said Moss.

"Benny Goodman's recording from nineteen thirty-six," said Herman. "Goodman on the clarinet, you know, and Teddy Wilson on piano, Lionel Hampton on vibes and vocals, and Gene Krupa on drums. A famous recording."

"I see," said Moss with a sigh. "But then the record disappeared?"

"Not just that one," said Herman. "The whole collection, with the case and all."

"When did you last see them?" asked Moss, feeling like a cross between a mother and a police officer.

"That's the thing," said Herman, "I never saw them again after that weekend."

They were all in a big rush that Sunday. Thorvald was restless and eager to get home, and when rain and wind swept in, their departure was pushed forward. The cabin had to be cleaned up, the fireplace emptied, the boat pulled up on shore. When everything was stowed in the car, Herman asked about his case of records and was assured that it had been carefully stashed

with the knapsacks and bags in back. It so happened that he
didn't personally unpack the car. When he had dropped off the
others and finally pulled up in front of his own place, he found
his wife Lillen standing on the steps wringing her hands.
Herman's old mother had suddenly fallen ill, so he jumped into
a cab and let Lillen unload the car and put it away in the garage.
Not until weeks later did he discover that the record case was
not in its usual place. Lillen couldn't remember if she had taken
it out of the car—so many things had happened that evening,
what with all the phone calls as the condition of Herman's
mother grew worse.

"So you don't know whether the case even made it back from
the cabin at Nøtterøy?"

"No," said Herman, "but Nic insists that it wasn't there when
he and his family went out to the cabin a few weeks later."

"And now you think it was one of your friends who took it?"

Yes, that's what Herman thought. That's what he had always
thought, deep in his heart. And he thought it was now time to
get this confirmed. Birger had called Herman recently, osten-
sibly to remind him that their spring dinner was coming up, as
if Herman couldn't remember that himself! But then he, Birger,
had hinted that there might be occasion to clear up some old
mysteries.

"I see," said Moss.

"I think I'm going to get a confession," said Herman tri-
umphantly. "But he may recant later on. Pretend that it was all
a joke. Birger has always been a slippery devil!"

And so here she was. Keeping an eye on four elderly gentlemen
who were trying to decide what to eat. "Okay, I'm ready," said
Birger with a loud whinny of a laugh. "I always have the shellfish casserole."

"Yes, we know that," said Nic. "But the question is, what am *I* going to have! Hmm, let's see . . . trout, that's what I'll have!"

"That's what you always have," said Thorvald, who was already scanning the wine list. "For my part, I've decided on steamed turbot."

Herman also ordered the turbot, and then that was that.

Moss read her newspaper. With half an ear she kept tabs on the proceedings to her left. It's true that the tables stood close together. Once, Nic, who sat the closest, absent-mindedly tapped the ash from his cigar into the ashtray on her table. Then he gave her a distracted but apologetic glance, although there was no recognition in his eyes.

Moss had finished with her newspaper long ago. She was also done with her salad and had nearly finished her wine. She left half a glass so that it wouldn't look like she was completely done with her meal. She scribbled in her notebook, mostly to indicate to the waiter that she wasn't about to leave anytime soon.

Then Herman's sonorous baritone suddenly cut through the buzz in the cafe: "Greenberg, Rowland Greenberg!"

Moss flinched and quickly turned her head.

"But they often spelled the name of the club wrong, remember that? Sometimes it was called The *Pinguin* Club; once I even saw it called The *Pingvin*," said Nic Nielsen.

Now Thorvald jumped in: "What you might have expected was The *Penguin* Club," he said, carefully enunciating each syllable. "It would have been—"

"Of course," interrupted Herman. "But that's not what I'm talking about. I'm talking about Rowland Greenberg!"

He practically bellowed the name. *Okay, okay!* thought Moss, annoyed. She'd heard what he said!

"Who was he playing with at that time?" said Nic. "Wasn't it the Pastor on piano and . . ."

"Uh-uh, it was Carsten Kloumann," mumbled Birger, his mouth full of shellfish.

"There were lots of people who played with Rowland Greenberg!" said Herman.

He gave Moss an imperious look, and she flashed him a look in return as if to say: *Yes, I'm listening!* And then it came. Herman cleared his throat and said: "But in that great record collection that I once owned, there was a recording with Rowland Greenberg in which there wasn't any piano! Instead, Eilif Horn played the vibraphone!"

There it was: the record collection.

"That's right, your record collection," said Thorvald as he leaned back and straightened the napkin on his knees. "That was strange, wasn't it? It just disappeared. It must have been your wife, Herman. Lillen probably just gave it away to the flea market or something. You know how women are. A worn-out case full of old records . . . Women don't have any sense for things like that."

Herman interrupted him. "Thorvald! I'm trying to have a conversation here! And it couldn't have been Lillen. She knew, more than anyone, how much those records meant to me."

He looked at Birger and put down his knife and fork with a slight clatter. "Isn't it your turn now, Birger? Aren't you the one who had something informative to tell us about what actually happened to my records back then? So come on now, let's put all our cards on the table!"

Margaret Moss clutched her pen tightly, her neck aching from staring without looking as if she were staring.

Birger sat motionless, his back erect, without speaking or looking at any of the others.

"Really," said Nic Nielsen, leaning toward Herman. "Do you have to be so bombastic? I mean, it's all so long ago. Water under the bridge, don't you think? Surely there's no point in dredging up these old matters."

All at once it was very quiet at the neighboring table, so quiet that the steady restaurant hum seemed suddenly very loud. Up on the balcony a violinist was tuning his instrument.

"Birger?" said Herman urgently. "Birger!"

Everyone looked at Birger. Suddenly the quartet started in on the Radetzsky March, making the chandeliers ring. Birger Bøe shoved aside the table and stood up. "Excuse me," he said with compressed lips. "I need some air."

Then he headed off for the cloakroom, walking unsteadily.

Moss waited a fraction of a second, then she too stood up, slipped between the tables, and hurried after him.

In the Theater Cafe, a steep little stairway leads down to the men's room. That was no doubt where Birger Bøe was headed, but before he got that far he collapsed and fell to the floor between the cloakroom counter and the stairs.

Moss and the stout doorman in the wine-red jacket looked at each other.

"Ambulance," said Moss. "It must be his heart."

She squatted down and loosened Birger's bow tie and the top buttons of his shirt. He opened his eyes and tried to focus. Then he murmured: "It . . . prickles on my lips. Muss . . . the mussels. Paral . . . ysis of the airway . . ."

"He's a doctor," Moss said, looking at the doorman. "He must know what he's talking about. Hurry!"

The doorman dialed the emergency number.

An observant waiter showed up shortly and closed the glass door to the restaurant.

Moss tried to move the gasping Birger into a more stable position. His lips had now taken on a terrifying bluish tint.

Inquisitive faces were peering through the front door from Stortingsgata.

"Wait just a minute, please. A guest has taken ill," the doorman told the spectators. "The ambulance is on its way," he added in Moss's direction.

She heard footsteps behind her. It was Herman, who had finally started to worry.

Birger Bøe curled up on the floor and then vomited.

The ambulance arrived.

Apparently very few guests had noticed what was happening. Up on the balcony they were playing something from *The Merry Widow*, which had always seemed so appropriate to the Viennese interior of the cafe, thought Moss. She had not introduced herself to the group of four gentlemen, and she chose not to do so now. They paid for their dinner and had a long, discreet conversation with the frowning female maître d'. She was undoubtedly even less happy about what had happened than the three gentlemen.

Outside the restaurant, they said brief goodbyes.

Thorvald disappeared into a cab going to Bestum. Nic just managed to catch the tram for Briskeby. Herman looked at Moss. "Maybe you'd like to come to my place?" he said. "So we could have a little talk about all this?"

His black moustache looked even more artificial than usual against the pallor of his face.

Herman lived on a side street in the Frogner district.

He hung up his jacket and went to the kitchen to busy himself with glasses and ice cubes. He reappeared with a bottle of whiskey. "Maybe you'd rather have sherry?" he said to Moss, but she shook her head.

"What you have there is fine," she said.

He sat down and they were both silent.

"It was my fault," he said at last.

"I don't think so," said Moss. "And if it was the shellfish, then it really wasn't your fault."

Herman stood up. "I think I'll call and find out how he's doing," he said. "They were taking him to Ullevål Hospital."

He disappeared into his office.

Moss took small sips of the whiskey and water, trying to relax her shoulders. The bright sky of the summer evening was visible through the balcony door. Somewhere a lawnmower was droning, and the tram screeched as it took the curve at Frogner Square.

Finally she heard Herman's footsteps crossing the parquet floor in the hallway. She put down her glass.

"Birger's dead," he said, sounding indignant, as if someone had just told a highly inappropriate joke. "Poison, they said. They don't know exactly what kind yet. But it wasn't a heart attack. When I indicated to the nurse or whoever it was that I was talking to that it must have been bad shellfish, she told me quite sternly that they couldn't be sure what it was yet. Have you ever heard the like! What else could it be?"

He went over to lean against the balcony door.

Neither of them spoke. The lawnmower had stopped. Some kid on a skateboard skidded past down on the sidewalk.

"I don't understand it," said Herman at last, turning to face Moss. "I can't for the life of me . . . this couldn't end up being a criminal investigation, could it?"

Moss sighed. The thought hadn't left her mind for even a moment. "Yes, it could," she said. "I wish I didn't have to give evidence, but I'm sure I will."

She thought gloomily about the looks that were bound to greet her down at police headquarters.

Oh no, that's not private investigator Moss again, is it? So what is it this time? A missing cat?

"Maybe we should get a little headstart," she said, pursing her lips thoughtfully.

"What do you mean?" asked Herman, looking at her. "It's the Theater Cafe's case."

"But it's odd that nobody else got sick," said Moss. "The maître d' told me that they'd served that shellfish casserole to a couple dozen people since lunch. But no one else collapsed on the floor because of it. Of course, the poison might have been added *after* the shellfish was brought from the kitchen." Moss gave Herman a sidelong glance.

"That's sheer nonsense!" he said.

"I know," replied Moss. "But I'd still like to know how shellfish poisoning works. I thought it would just make you vomit. You don't happen to have Internet access now, do you?"

"Yes, actually, I do," said Herman, and for a moment he almost looked cheered up. "In my old age, I've gotten interested in researching my ancestry, and so . . ."

He led the way into his rather dusty office, pulled out a chair for her, and switched on his computer. Then he went out to the kitchen to make some coffee.

Moss sat down and drummed her fingers on the desk. What was it called? Poison information? She tried that. And there it was: Poison Information Agency, with a phone number that was available twenty-four hours. Well, it was too late to get help for Birger. She skimmed through the general information, then clicked her way to shellfish poisoning. The usual symptom was diarrhea of varying severity. The less common kind was PSP, or paralytic shellfish poisoning, which caused paralysis: numbness, prickling on the lips and fingers, dizziness, difficulty in breathing, and muscular impairment which could end up paralyzing the heart. That's what she read on the flickering screen.

It definitely sounded like what Birger had experienced.

It often took only thirty minutes for PSP to set in, but it could also take longer. The poison was "not significantly affected by cooking or freezing." Moss started drumming her fingers on the desk again.

"It's rare," she told Herman when he brought two cups into the office. "The type that causes paralysis, I mean. And where would someone get poisoned shellfish, anyway?"

"I hope you're joking," said Herman as he put down the cups. "You can't seriously think that . . . Who would have done it? Me?"

"No, I don't know," replied Moss absent-mindedly. "I need to use your phone."

She called the number listed on the homepage of the Poison Information Agency. She told them it wasn't an emergency, she just needed some information for a poor . . . Then she hesitated before she boldly said into the phone: "I'm a writer. I'm working on a murder-by-poison plot, ha, ha!"

And someone there was actually willing to answer her questions, provided it didn't take too much time.

Herman was now sitting in an old armchair. He had a hand over his eyes, and he looked terribly tired and worn out.

"But are there any other kinds of poison?" Moss said at last into the receiver, after having exhausted the subject of shellfish poisoning. "I mean, that would produce similar paralysis of the airway and heart . . . and that anybody could easily obtain?"

The person on the other end of the line cleared his throat. The Poison Information Agency was apparently starting to think this was going a little too far. "There could be lots of things, but if you're thinking of plant poisons, then we have, for instance, friar's cap or aconite. *Aconitum napellus*, as it's called in Latin. All parts of the plant are poisonous and produce symptoms that are similar to PSP."

"Friar's cap? Is that in the same family as monkshood?" she asked quickly. "Monkshood, isn't that the plant with the tall, elegant, helmetlike blossoms that grows deep in the woods?"

"Yes," said the person on the phone. "It's actually a venerable old plant poison that has been used since ancient times. It's said that Emperor Trajan prohibited the cultivation of aconite in Roman gardens because it became so popular to use it whenever anyone wanted to get rid of troublesome opponents."

"Thanks so much," said Moss. And she put down the phone.

"Where's your encyclopedia?" she said, glancing around the room.

"It's an old one," said Herman. "From before the war."

"That doesn't matter," said Moss. "What I'm looking for is even older."

And in the row of worn brown-leather spines she found not only the appropriate volume, but also the entry for aconite. A blurry picture of a tall bellflower, with the description: "Garden plant. As far as is known, grows wild in Norway, in the areas of Borgund, Møre, and Romsdal."

"Aconite," she clarified, looking at Herman, who took his hand away from his face. "Extremely poisonous."

"What you're implying is completely monstrous," he said, suddenly angry. He straightened up.

"Plus we don't have a motive," said Moss, unperturbed. "Maybe you could call Nic. Apparently he knew what Birger was thinking of revealing today."

"Hmm," said Herman. "Well, all right. I have to call him anyway to tell him that Birger is dead."

With great effort he got to his feet, creaking in all his joints.

Moss considerately stepped into the living room as he made the call.

Aconite. It could be detected, of course. Somebody would have to be crazy to kill a man with plant poison in this day and age. She sighed. The scent of birdcherry had suddenly gusted in through the balcony door, and she thought to herself that she should have been somewhere else entirely. It was that old sense of yearning that she could never get rid of, a yearning for something she couldn't define. She yawned and thought that either she would have to do something with her life, or she'd have to accept the way it was in a more respectful fashion. Then she heard Herman come into the room.

"Dort, wo du nicht bist, isn't that how that Schubert song goes, Herman—you who graduated with my father and majored in German?"

But he wasn't listening. He raised the whiskey bottle and poured a healthy shot into his glass. Then he downed it in one gulp. "Well," he said at last. "Nic says that he didn't know what Birger was planning to tell us, but he's positive it was some kind of revelation. He thought it had something to do with Thorvald. And he came to the conclusion that Thorvald had made off with my record collection back then; and that Birger knew about it and thought it was about time to say something. Although Nic did *not* agree."

He stood up, went over to the balcony door, and closed it. "It's getting chilly," he said, and remained standing there, looking out. "Nic took it hard, the news about Birger. He had just been talking to Erna. She called to hear where Thorvald was. He hasn't come home yet."

"Is that right?" said Moss. "Do you usually go home this early after one of your dinners?"

"Yes. We started early, after all. I think I'll call Erna."

"Do you feel up to it?"

"Sure, why not?"

"The bearer of bad news," said Moss. "Keep in mind that she was once in love with Birger Bøe."

"What did you say?" said Herman in dismay. "Where did you hear that?"

"Come on, Herman," said Moss. "It's obvious from everything you've told me. It was Erna that Birger was talking about in the boat on that early morning when the two of you were together. And that's why Thorvald was so gloomy; he must have suspected. And then he found out for sure when Birger got so drunk that he forgot himself and wanted to play 'Moonglow' and talked about it being 'their' song—his and his lover's. You can bet that Erna must have also played it plenty of times at home back then!"

"Margaret, this is romantic hogwash!" said Herman.

At that instant the phone rang in his office. Moss followed on Herman's heels when he went to answer it.

"Erna! My dear! Who called you and . . ."

He put his hand over the receiver and whispered: "Nic called her!"

There was a great deal of agitated talking on the other end of the line. Herman alternated between nodding and shaking his head, uttering alarmed little noises. He looked at his watch. "Yes, I'll do that, my dear," he said, obviously trying to sound both resolute and reassuring. "Of course I will. Take something, Erna . . . maybe you should have a drink. I'll call you later!"

He put down the phone and looked at Moss. "She discovered that the keys to their summer house are missing. It seems strange that Thorvald would go out there. Without any luggage or anything."

"Tell me again where that house is," said Moss.

"It's just a small place. On the outskirts of Ålesund, not far from Borgund Church."

Moss gave a long whistle, and Herman looked at her. "Margaret!"

But she was already on her way into his office. She leaned over the computer and started clicking. Waited, clicked again. "Look at this," she said. "A flight took off for Ålesund at seven-twenty P.M. He could have made that easily. He must have arrived there by now. With a fire in the fireplace and everything." She suddenly laughed out loud. The whole thing was so crazy.

"There's nothing to laugh about," said Herman gloomily. "You were right. It was Erna that Birger meant that time when he said he had found the love of his life. But she says that Thorvald threatened Birger and made him give her up. She's completely shattered by the news of his death. I really don't know what I should do, I'll have to . . ."

Moss interrupted him. "Have you been to their summer house in Borgund?"

"Sure, lots of times. Why?"

"Write down the directions for me. I can just make the last flight to Ålesund if I take a cab to the airport!"

It was still light when the Braathen plane landed at Vigra. Beyond the steep contours of Godøya island the sky was a bright yellow. A sharp wind blew through the grass near the runway, and Moss shivered. The cab driver—a short old man with a big visored cap—looked at the directions she handed him and nodded. A man of few words, he didn't say a single thing during the whole ride through two tunnels, across a bridge, and along miles of gravel and asphalt. The radio was playing accordion music. Moss leaned her head back against the seat and tried to relax. She was exhausted and wound up at the same time, and the whiskey that she'd had at Herman's place was searing beneath her ribcage. They had passed Borgund Church when the driver slowed down, pulled over to the curb, and stopped.

"This is it," he said.

She paid the fare, pulled her big shoulder bag out of the cab, and closed the door as silently as possible. The night was so quiet, with every noise exaggerated.

The cab made a U-turn and vanished while Moss cautiously walked down the narrow gravel road. She caught a glimpse of the lake through the trees; somewhere a gull squawked.

She could smell the tidewaters, and a fire burning.

The house was almost hidden among the gnarled fruit trees. It was a small building with a pointed gable and a high cellar wall. There were lights in two of the windows on the first floor. She walked through the grass toward a high porch, took the stairs without making a sound, and peeked through the glass pane in the door.

Thorvald Torgersen was sitting in a chair with his hands in his lap, staring straight ahead.

She raised her hand and knocked on the glass pane. Then opened the door and went in.

The smells of a summer cottage, of soot and ancient timbers. Somewhere a clicking sound from what she at first thought was a clock, but then she realized it was a record player on which the needle had long ago reached the paper label in the center of the record.

He gave her a rigid blue-eyed stare from beneath bushy brows. Then he apparently recognized her, and what looked almost like a smile spread across his bony face. "So you found me. That was faster than I thought."

He got stiffly to his feet and went over to turn off the record player. Then he cast a glance outside at the blue darkness before he returned to his seat.

She glanced around the room. Everything looked very neat and proper. A dried bouquet of heather from the previous autumn in a copper container on the dining room table, woven rugs placed at right angles on the hardwood floor. There was even a fire in the fireplace, smoldering and smoking around crumpled paper stuck under a few birch branches. Was he burning old letters?

He followed her glance. "Yes, I took her letters. She probably didn't realize that I knew they had resumed contact again, so she didn't hide them. That's fine. You're from the police, aren't you? I knew it as soon as I saw you after Birger . . . after he fell ill. You were sitting at the next table, weren't you?"

She nodded. "My name is Moss," she said. "Margaret Moss. Wilhelm's daughter."

He looked surprised. Then he said, "I see."

A crackling came from the fireplace, and partially burned scraps of paper rose up the chimney.

"Was Herman the one who blabbed?" he said at last.

"That doesn't really matter," said Moss. "What did you have on your wife that she would give up so easily back then, in 'sixty-seven?"

"Erna? I didn't have anything on Erna," he said, staring at her. "It was Birger—he didn't have his physician's papers in order. Everybody knew that he was educated in Austria, but no one knew that he dropped out. He established his practice based on false documents. The popular and clever Dr. Birger Bøe. So, what do you say to that?"

He had grown agitated. He got up and started pacing back and forth. "But I knew about it. I happened to have contact with an Austrian who was the head of a big pharmaceutical company that wanted to sell its products in Norway. It turned out that he had studied medicine with Birger, and that's how the cat got out of the bag. It was a piece of information that came in handy, let me tell you! Just a few days later, while I was still in doubt as to what I should do with the information, the bomb fell. Birger Bøe—that cheat and—well, enough said . . . he was the one my wife was going to leave me for!"

"And that's what you found out during the famous weekend at the cabin?"

He looked at her and then nodded. "Yes. Or at least I had my suspicions confirmed. And I told him about it, the day we left the cabin. I told him that I knew he was sailing under a false flag and that I would tell Erna about it unless he kept away from her. I said that if he didn't, I was going to make public the whole scandal, and it would ruin her life. He believed me. He was stunned and utterly ashamed and he had every reason to be. He did as I said. From then on, he kept away from her!"

"Was that when the record collection disappeared?" asked Moss.

He gave her a wry look. "The record collection! That idiot Herman has been babbling about that lousy collection all these years. Yes, I was the one who took it when I got out of the car at home. Nobody saw me. I was the first one to be dropped off, and they were all sitting inside the car, chattering away like a bunch of old ladies, which is what a couple of them are! I really only wanted the one stupid record with Goodman. I got rid of the rest a few years later; I don't really remember where. The case probably ended up with the records at some flea market."

"And Erna never found out why Birger Bøe disappeared from her life?" said Moss.

"No," he said. "Birger did as I said."

She looked over her shoulder, out into the dusk, and then glanced at her watch. He followed her gaze. Then he said: "Up until recently, that is. They saw each other only on those rare occasions when we included our wives in our . . . gatherings. But I was always on the alert. Then Erna and Birger happened to run into each other in town this past winter. She probably didn't think I would find out; she hid the letters afterward. But I knew it was only a matter of time. When our annual dinner was approaching, Birger started talking about having something to tell us. Then I realized I had to do something fast. Unlike our good friend Herman, I didn't think it had anything to do with his confounded record collection!"

"How could you think that the aconite poison wouldn't leave any trace?" she said, studying him carefully. He seemed to be growing more nervous.

He stepped out in the hall for a moment and looked into what she assumed must be the kitchen. Then he came back. "Do you know what hubris is, Margaret Moss? Arrogance! I knew so much about botany, especially the historical aspects. I planned this very carefully and was actually very proud of myself !"

Moss glanced at the front door again. "But you didn't know anything about traces of poison in a dead body."

"No," said Thorvald Torgersen. "Obviously not. Well, I suppose they're waiting outside," he said. "It was considerate of you to come in alone. You can tell them that I'm at their disposal. I just have to get my bag."

He went toward the door but something seemed to occur to him, and he took a detour over to the record player and set the needle back on the record. It crackled and popped a bit, and Moss watched as he went back out to the hall as the record began playing.

Piano, and then a soft clarinet. "Moonglow."

She opened her bag and pulled out her cell phone. She took a few soundless steps toward the door, punched in the number of the Ålesund police, which she had entered in advance. Just as someone answered the phone, there was a bang, and she realized that she knew this would happen, and now it was too late.

When the medics came driving down the gravel road fifteen minutes later, she was waiting for them on the porch. The man who was lying on the kitchen floor wasn't much to look at anymore.

The rest is quickly told. Thorvald had shot himself with his hunting rifle. Twenty-four hours later, the presence of aconite poison was proved, to the great relief of the Theater Cafe, which under no circumstances wanted anyone to think their shellfish was poisonous. Thorvald had bought his plane ticket to Ålesund four weeks earlier. The techs from the crime lab found residue from the plant poison on the compost heap behind the small summer house, along with some withered scraps of the plant. Thorvald Torgersen had aconite growing in his garden.

He left a letter behind, not addressed to Erna but to his friend Nic. According to the letter, Thorvald had been certain that Birger's death would be attributed to shellfish poisoning. Then he was going to go to his summer house in Borgund and commit suicide—and it was supposed to look like an accident. He had taken out old rags and some oil and the other things needed for a thorough cleaning of a gun, done by a man who loved his hunting rifle and often cleaned it to calm his nerves. This was meant to make life easier for the surviving Erna. He didn't want her to be left feeling any sort of shame.

He had taken his revenge, and that was enough.

Herman never mentioned his record collection again.

And "Moonglow" was never the same again, either for him or for Margaret Moss.

Marco Denevi

Victor Scarpazo, or The End of the Pursuit

Translated from the Spanish by Donald A. Yates

Marco Denevi (1922–1998) was one of the most important Argentine writers of the twentieth century and author of the enormously popular crime novel Rosaura a las diez *(1955), still in print and published in English as* Rosa at Ten O'Clock *(Holt, Rinehart, 1964). The following story is one of seven short accounts of fanciful disappearances that formed part of a 1982 volume, in Spanish, of the author's work.*

The clue was provided by a paragraph in Terisio Pignatti's book *Carpaccio:* "We are unaware of the existence of any portrait [of the artist], in spite of the fact that in his time he was also renowned as a portrait painter. We imagine that he took pleasure in painting his own portrait onto some of his models and that some day, closely examining the countless subjects of his canvases, we will experience the surprise and delight of suddenly encountering his face."

This was all it took: He himself would undertake that adventure of finding the revered maestro's face among the many that populated his paintings.

Something instinctive, a hunch, or perhaps something in his blood, led him to believe that what he was looking for was hidden somewhere in "The Legend of Saint Ursula," a series of eight large paintings that Carpaccio executed for the chapel of the Scuola di Sant'Orsola in Venice, and that were now displayed in the *Academia* of that paludal city.

The Italian government generously welcomed his petition to study those paintings. (He did not reveal the true reason for his request.) In possession of substantial financial support and carrying a bundle of letters of introduction and recommendation, Victor moved from his solitary room in a pension near the Retiro train station in Buenos Aires into a room in a third-class hotel near the *parroquia de San Canciano* in Venice and daily visited the Academia, where they ended up treating him like one of the staff.

The eight enormous paintings, all nearly three meters in height and some six or seven meters in width, filled with crowds that spread out before a background of imaginary geographies that are neither Brittany nor Rome nor Colonia but a Venice of fables and dreams, inspired in him a frenzy that bordered on erotic passion and perhaps even insanity.

From his letters I know that he began his search of the eight canvases with "The Arrival of the Ambassadors" and ended it with "Martyrdom and Funeral of the Saint," following the chronology of the legend as recorded by Jacobo de Vorágine and the order in which, a cornu Epistulae of the altar, they once graced the long-since demolished ancient chapel.

I also know that he dedicated an entire year to his enterprise and that the search for the maestro's face across the expanse of the enormous paintings was repeated again and again.

In short, I know that he lent to his investigation the obsessive obstinacy and meticulous patience of a fanatical police officer who pursues a criminal, the unrelenting cruelty of Javert on the trail of Jean Valjean. But it was love that guided him.

In a letter to me he writes: "I have no information on the features of Vittore,"—he invariably referred to him thus, by his first name—"nothing except what Geralamo delle Colombe says about him: He was blond and handsome. But nonetheless I am sure that when I see him an irrepressible throbbing of my heart will tell me 'This is he.'"

He adds: "In any case, it will not be easy for me to find him. There are hundreds of faces that have to be examined one by one. At the Academy they have lent me a ladder and a magnifying glass. They light the great crystal Murano chandeliers for me. I have lied to them, saying that I am studying Vittore's portraiture techniques."

Another letter might well have alerted me: "I paused next to a page accompanying the English ambassadors because I sensed that it was he in disguise. I circled him two or three times, I looked at him from the front and in profile, but my heart remained still." I interpreted these otherwise senseless sentences as metaphorical, and attributed their oddity to overenthusiasm.

A letter dated some time later opened my eyes: "It has occurred to me that Vittore may be one of the persons who, in 'The Departure of the Newlyweds,' are looking down from the balconies of the palace to the right. The distance, even when shortened by the magnifying glass, prevents me from distinguishing his features. I will try to go into the palace and look at them all, face by face."

I should have warned him then about third-dimension hallucinations. I failed to do so and he wrote: "Yesterday, in 'The Arrival at Colonia,' I penetrated too far into its complex perspectives and nearly got lost. I can't tell you how hard it was to find my way back. Fortunately, no one noticed my momentary absence."

I was on the verge of writing him a stern reprimand when I received these laconic and premonitory lines: "I think I have discovered where he is hiding. Even though in order to get there I will have to cross that small bridge that is blocked by the throng of onlookers, I am confident that tomorrow I will reach him." Evidently, he was referring to a detail in "The Return of the Ambassadors."

Just as I feared, his correspondence, which up until then had been steady, was interrupted, never to be resumed.

I wrote to the proprietors of his hotel: They replied, testily, that *quello mascalzone* had taken off without paying his bill (and without his luggage, they failed to note).

I wrote to the authorities of the Academy. I could have foreseen their reply: The distinguished and most pleasant Signore Scarpazo had not returned for several months. The last time he was seen, contrary to his custom, he had left without saying goodbye to anyone, and abandoning his ladder and magnifying glass.

I planned to let them know of my suspicions, or rather my certainty, that "The Return of the Ambassadors" had suffered a slight alteration. I intended to have them investigate the other side of the bridge. I also planned, as a final proof, to say that I could guess that the ladder and the magnifying glass had been left at the foot of that painting.

Later on, I thought better of it and instead requested that they take a photograph of "The Return of the Ambassadors" and send it to me. The request fell on deaf ears, and other concerns drew away my attention, time passed, and there's no longer any point in insisting.

No matter. Someday I will go to Venice. Someday I will go to the Academy and will contemplate "The Return of the Ambassadors." I expect to see, among all the faces that Carpaccio painted, a face that Carpaccio did not paint. And even if I don't find it, because the intruder is hiding behind the motionless multitude, I will not doubt that he is there.

But I will feel no regret over his end. I truly believe that, trapped forever by the object of his pursuit, Victor Scarpazo is the happiest of pursuers. Perhaps the secret and powerful force of a bloodline was at work, for Victor's surname, like Carpaccio's, derives from the Latin "Carpathius."

Carmen Iarrera

The Wind

Translated from the Italian by the author

Italy's Carmen Iarrera is the author of two spy novels, three mystery novels, and numerous short stories, as well as many cartoons, radio plays, and telecasts. Her short stories have been translated into several different languages, with the English translations appearing in anthologies by Cumberland House and in Ellery Queen's Mystery Magazine. *She has twice won the Gran Giallo Cattolica Award and has been the president of the Italian branch of the International Association of Crime Writers.*

They say that it can reach up to a hundred and twenty kilometers per hour."

"What can?"

"The bora. You know, the wind around Trieste, the strongest in Italy. It can become really dangerous. I wonder what it's like to get caught in it."

He didn't answer. His eyes were fixed on the road; he was concentrating, and his jaw was quivering—his face had contracted. She sighed, mortified. It had been like this for months. He was always tired, increasingly on edge and irritable. He no longer smiled at her. Gone were the days when he'd come home with a bunch of flowers hidden behind his back. Restaurants were a thing of the past and, what baffled her more than anything, he no longer laughed at their usual jokes. He'd get home late, eat without caring what it was, and start to read the papers, oblivious to any of her attempts at small talk. She was far from happy about this but tried to find excuses for him.

It's because of his job, she told herself, that new assignment has him under too much pressure.

She tried, in every way possible, to make allowances for his bad behavior. If he tried to apologize for an outburst of temper, she'd immediately soften and try to comfort him.

"You work too hard," she'd say. "If only you could travel less, spend more time at home, relax a little."

But if he did stay home, it only made things worse, because then he'd turn all his anger back on her. "Not enough for you to organize my life, is it? You want to poke your nose into my job now as well, don't you?" He'd stare at her coldly and grab the paper. And she'd go silent, pained.

Every day was like that, and it was getting worse, so when he suggested spending a weekend in Trieste, where they'd gone on their honeymoon, she had to stifle her cry of joy, knowing that even a show of pleasure could set him off. It seemed that anything these days could cast him into a bad mood.

But now, though he was sullen, at least they were travelling. And the idea had been his. She wanted to make him smile on this trip. What could she do that would make him smile? What about one of those childish games that used to make him laugh so lovingly?

She glanced at the speedometer. 140 kilometers. Too fast. She waited for him to finish overtaking. 130, here we go, 120 . . . perfect. She rolled down the window and shoved her head out. The wind, strong and rumbling, jerked her head backwards. It felt like a slap on the face, making her close her eyes and whipping back her hair. It took her breath away.

He was mouthing something, shouting something.

"What the hell are you doing?"

"I wanted to see what a hundred-and-twenty-kilometer-per-hour wind felt like," she murmured, disheartened.

She could feel his contempt in the glance he directed at her. She tried to put it aside. She'd made a mistake, but sooner or later she'd find some little thing to make him laugh. She had to, or the weekend would be spoiled.

Huge, thick, unmoving clouds seemed to crown the city like dirty gray cotton wool. The pavement was clammy, the air sharp. The sea, lead-colored, like the sky, rippled with long, powerful waves that strode to the horizon. She stifled a sigh. Not even the weather was on her side.

"Shall we go and get something to eat?" She smiled as if she didn't have a care in the world. They'd just unpacked.

"If you want."

"Maybe that little bistro where we went on our honeymoon is still there . . . you loved it there, remember? They made that piping hot pork broth with mustard."

"Makes no difference to me," he interrupted her with a grimace, which he then tried to counteract by stroking her shoulder.

He hadn't touched her for weeks, not even accidentally, not even when passing the salt.

They ordered the broth and, naturally, some of the strong red wine from the area. He knocked back three glasses as if it were water—as if he needed it.

People were talking about only one thing in that suffocating, hot restaurant: the wind. It was rising quickly. Even the TV said it would be violent.

Outside, the wind whipped. It messed up their hair, got into their jackets, caused their trouser bottoms to slap against their ankles. She forced herself not to complain about it. She tried to think how wonderful it would be if he suggested going back to their room, curling up under the sheets, hugging one another, and making love.

"Fancy a little walk?" he said instead. A rhetorical question, as he'd already moved off towards the shore. He seemed oddly animated, as if something had energized him—maybe the wine.

She watched him move away, hunched up against the increasingly bitter wind. He pressed ahead . . . one, two, three, four steps. She looked lovingly at his lopsided shoulders, his long stride, and his slightly rigid walk.

Melancholy as she was, that short distance between them suddenly seemed intolerable. Everything about the last few months seemed intolerable. All the hopes she'd pinned on being kind, patient, and understanding, time and time again, had vanished into thin air. This was it, she couldn't go on. She had to confront him, speak to him and clarify things.

She ran to catch up.

"Wait for me."

He turned around sharply. His eyes were hard.

"What is it?"

"Something's wrong—" She was shouting now so he could hear over the whistling wind. "Terribly wrong. I can't go on. Will you tell me what is happening? Why are you behaving like this? Why are you treating me this way? What the devil has got into you? Can't you see what you've become? You're disagreeable, irritable, and edgy. I can't speak to you anymore, everything I say is wrong. You're never satisfied. What's wrong, will you tell me?"

He looked at her as if he were incapable of speaking.

"Yes," he said eventually, "I'll tell you. I need to tell you. Let's go and sit down."

So there was something! But what?

She couldn't get the question out of her mind as she followed him, facing into the wind now, toward the jetty. It was ridiculous to go there: The wind gusts were so strong now they even made the lamppost lights flicker, and the waves, foamier and larger than ever, crashed against the huge dark mass of solid earth that projected out into the sea.

He sat on one of the bollards and she sat alongside him, half turned toward him, a precarious enough position even without all that wind and spray. She waited.

"There's someone else," he eventually said, staring at the horizon.

She didn't understand, or at least she pretended not to.

"What?"

"There's someone else," he repeated, louder now, without looking at her. "I don't know how it happened, but it did. That's it. There's nothing I can do about it."

Her heart skipped a beat and she felt a cold dizziness sweep over her. She stood up, as did he.

"What do you mean, 'That's it'?" she shouted. "That's it? Look at me!" He looked at her with the cold indifference of a stranger.

"I love someone else. I'm leaving you. I'm sorry."

Sorry? . . . He was leaving her for someone else?

He'd been deceiving her for months, she'd been beside herself, letting herself be humiliated. Because that's what she'd done by coddling him, always trying to get a smile out of him. He was sorry?! Years of love, dedication, tenderness—nothing. There was nothing left for him. He was sorry.

She was trembling. Shaking because of the icy cold inside her, the freezing wind, and the violent sprays of water that struck her like needles of ice. She thought she would faint. She moved backward slowly until she could clutch onto a lamppost.

So, that was it. She'd been blind. Blind and stupid, so very stupid. She felt sorry for herself, terribly, terribly sorry. It was such an unbearable feeling that it soon changed into rancor and then, in turn, into a spasm of anger.

She looked at him, this thin figure struck by the howling wind, near the edge of an increasingly violent sea. And suddenly she felt that all the great, eternal love that she'd felt for him had turned into a clot of hatred.

A push. A simple push was all it needed for him to lose his balance and the wind and the sea would whisk him away. He would disappear, vanish into the deep, he and his vile selfishness and his feelings for another woman. He, with his horrible desire to abandon her, would go away.

She pulled away from the lamppost and swayed in the wind like a drunkard, her arms tense, hands held out in front of her, her eyes crazily unfocused.

And then it happened. A dull sound, like a roar, and a huge wave, higher than all the others, came right up to the dock. It took him, threw him up in the air, twirled him around, hurled him onto the pavement, and sucked him into the sea.

She remained where she was, staring into a void, with her hands still outstretched. And in the same way that love had transformed itself into hatred, the hatred turned back into love. A desperate, desolate, useless love.

Useless, just like her. Her arms fell to her sides and she looked around. It was all gray and rough and jolted by an ever-raging wind. She took a couple of steps forward to the place where he had just disappeared.

It would be easy. Very easy. She needn't do anything, just wait for another high wave, another powerful gust of wind.

Luis Adrián Betancourt

Guilty

Translated from the Spanish by Donald A. Yates

For forty years, Cuban Luis Adrián Betancourt has been one of the most important contributors to and supporters of the crime-fiction genre in his native land. He is the author of many mystery novels and short stories, all published in—and available in—either Cuba or Spain. The following story is his first to appear in English translation.

H e did not like traveling by train because train trips were slow and boring. They brought back sad memories of farewells, absences, and inevitable emotional distress. In his teeming recall, the train evoked a tangled blend of distances and sleeplessness. All in all, an unpleasant experience.

But this time it would be different. He was coming back. Ignoring the hours, the miles, the stops, he was returning home, to the place where waiting for him would be Rosario, anguished over the lost years spent alone and deserted, Chela, well along toward becoming a young woman, unsuited now to a child's dress, with her hair pulled back into a bun, and Ivan, with more curiosity than feeling for the father he didn't remember and who, after so many years, was returning to his home.

They all were wondering what their lives would be like from now on living together. Antonio himself did not have a clear idea of his immediate future. He needed to sit down with them and humbly, without omitting any details, tell them the true story of that nightmare and ask them if, in spite of everything, he deserved another chance.

Soon after passing under the overhead crossings on the out-skirts of Havana, it began to drizzle. Just as it did on that afternoon when a rainfall coincided with the funeral of Pancho Vasallo. The gravediggers had drunk a whole bottle of Bacardi and stumbled through the mud, cursing the weather and their task.

The sky was an unbroken gray. It had been raining gently and without letup for hours, like tears falling from above. Only the deceased man's family and the two rural policemen on duty remained to the very end, unaffected by the rain that soaked them. Amalia had wept for some time, tormented by the thought that she was responsible for that tragedy and incon-solable over the loss of her beloved father.

Vicente, the agronomist, gave the eulogy, taking only five minutes to say that the man whom they now covered with damp soil had been, above all else, generous and a good friend.

By then, the killer had confessed. It was a simple matter for the authorities—a complete and spontaneous statement, leaving no doubts. Antonio meekly admitted his guilt. At moments it seemed that he had no interest in defending himself.

There was no need to waste time with interviews or ques-tioning. The weapon had not been found, and no one suggested looking for it. Antonio was the only one to mention it, when he gave his statement, saying he had thrown it into the river. No one ever attempted to determine if Vasallo had been killed by a bullet fired from an old Parabelum. The confession eliminated any need to be concerned about proof.

The motive emerged from the testimony of witnesses present, all of whom repeated the same series of tedious facts.

Their statements were so similar that a single one of them would have sufficed to satisfy the needs of the investigation.

The trial was carried out promptly, and since the crime was so recent and the victim so widely respected, a sentence of twenty years seemed fitting to everyone except Rosario and her children.

Standing as his sentence was read, Antonio learned with little surprise that he would spend the next twenty years behind bars, far from his family and his town. His gaze cast down, biting his lip, he came to the understanding that there would be many blank pages ahead in his life and that he would experience that death in life that is called solitude. He also did some figuring. By the time that he ceased to be State Inmate 33455, on his release, he would be fifty-three years old, his hair turned gray, and his body weakened. But in this he was mistaken.

After hearing his sentence, he was given a few minutes to say goodbye at the door of his house, while the dogs howled mournfully, as if they understood the role of those accompanying strangers. When he was leaving, Antonio said only one final thing:

"Wait for me."

"We'll wait for you," his wife replied. And she embraced him. She could offer him no encouragement, for she could feel none for herself. The children remained asleep even at the last kiss. They had no way of knowing what that farewell meant.

Standing on the train platform, Antonio took a long, anguished look at the town, as if he wanted to preserve the image of that place in a corner of his memory.

That day the train was on time. The villagers whispered to each other as the prisoner shuffled by. His head was bowed, his hands bound. One of the soldiers helped him onto the train. The other one offered him a cigarette. His face looked out from the coach window until he was lost from sight.

Now, so many years later, the countryside had changed. That

may have been the reason the trip back seemed to take so long. The soldiers with him were relaxed, giving little attention to keeping an eye on him.

They were almost there now. Antonio closed his eyes and remembered the morning many years earlier when he had first arrived in that town. It was July and the hives were full of decanting honey and the *tomeguines* were in full bloom in the fields and on the floor of the pine forests.

He found her strolling amidst the hovering bees and the flowers. He watched her come and go, fascinated by her fleeting smile. He attempted a flattering remark that made the girl smile again, and Antonio knew then that he would remain to live in that town for many years, perhaps for the rest of his life. They were married. There were happy times and others not so happy.

"I would have liked to start all over again," he wrote to her from his prison cell, "and then I would not have wasted a single moment at your side. No one understands what he has until he loses it."

It was something he had discovered when he least expected to. When it was too late to act on that understanding and he was being taken away on a train with only a one-way ticket.

Rosario could not bear to go to the station, but she knew the time when the train would leave and the sound of the departure whistle confirmed it. That night she received an unexpected visitor. Lorenzo Puente indicated that he was there to offer her assistance. She reacted with distrust, suspecting that he was intent on taking advantage of the situation. He did not rate favorably in her estimation.

Lorenzo had not been a particularly good friend of Antonio. He had never wanted to give him a job on the Vasallo ranch. It was easy to see that the nature of their relationship was based on casual circumstances and shared interests, but in no way was it a true friendship. It was rather that life had led them down similar paths of parties, drinking, and casual women. In truth, they had been more like accomplices than friends. The last thing she found out about that superficial connection had ultimately turned into a public scandal.

Rosario was embarrassed by what people were saying. Antonio wanted to save the marriage, begged her forgiveness, and in the end she once again forgave him. She said her reason was the children, who were innocent of any blame. They decided to work to keep the family intact at whatever cost. But for now there was nothing he could do. The matter of Pancho Vasallo's daughter did not emerge in Antonio's confessions and he persistently denied any suggestion that it was relevant. But the death of the old man indicated otherwise.

In view of all this she cautiously let Lorenzo speak his piece.

"I don't want people saying that just because of a drunken argument I could desert my close friend in his hour of need. Let me help you."

Rosario asked for some time to consider his offer and wrote a letter to her husband filled with doubts and anxieties. The reply took two long months to arrive, during which time she refused to accept any help. Finally, Antonio's answer came, urging her to agree without questions or hesitation to what Lorenzo was proposing. He said that she should accept the offer of help as something she rightfully deserved, but that in all other respects she should keep her distance from Lorenzo.

"I owe you an explanation," Antonio added, and that would not be the last time he would leave her perplexed over an explanation that was not forthcoming.

"You owe me two," she replied, alluding to Amalia.

Lorenzo took charge of the family's debts, day-to-day expenses, and other matters such as the children's schooling and medical care, the upkeep of the house, and other emergencies that unexpectedly arose.

At no time did Lorenzo try to take advantage of his role as a benefactor, and never did he attempt to play on the woman's helplessness for his own purposes, even when circumstances seemed propitious. Nonetheless, throughout the neighborhood there circulated dark rumors, gossip, wagers, surveillance behind shutters, all nurtured by the desire to discover what mysterious reason was behind the rancher's generosity.

Even the most distracted of townspeople wondered why that proud and lustful neighbor was making such a cult out of friendship. No one had ever seen that sentimental side of Lorenzo.

The gossip increased. Rosario learned about all of the suspicions and assumptions and patiently put up with the constant spying. She tried to protect the children from the rumors, but at times people came to call on her and report the latest lie. On other occasions, it was the children themselves who came home with questions that were hard to answer.

On several occasions, Rosario received terrible anonymous letters, whose offensive content was aimed at both her and Antonio. In a large scrawled script, the first of the messages assured her that her husband had killed because of another woman, and she would be well advised to pay him back with similar currency. The second letter was a warning from someone who was waiting for Antonio's return so that he could administer his own justice, since that meted out by the court was too lenient and did not demand an eye for an eye. Despite the seriousness of the matter, the pages were burned in Rosario's fireplace without her having reported them to the authorities. The important thing was for her to alert her husband in one of her letters. But he replied that it was nothing more than the provocations they had to endure, possibly organized by old Vasallo's relatives.

Rosario dedicated more than one sleepless night to trying to find a way out of her situation. She was prepared to make any sacrifice for her children, but she saw no other path of action than the one she was following, which was causing so much cruel speculation. She ended up going along with the arrangement, trusting to her own integrity and the approval that her husband had given her.

From his cell Antonio managed to keep informed of virtually everything that was going on. In time, he set up a rapid and dependable means of communication that involved a series of individuals: a lobster fisherman from Batabanó, a truck driver, and the firemen on a train. He wrote lengthy letters that tried to capture features of the unattainable reality of home, that tried to control it and make decisions from his remote position, all in an effort to overcome the consequences of his separation. Even though he shared in Rosario's suffering and wondered about the strength of her resistance, he urged her to wait for him, to trust in him, and to continue accepting what Lorenzo offered. He explained that his generosity was not motivated by charity or the desire to do a favor, but rather by something associated more with a duty, the carrying out of a sworn promise. Just what that promise was he could not reveal until the day when, free to speak, he could tell her in detail what was involved. Antonio also wrote a lot about his intimate feelings and made repeated promises of loyalty and eternal love. This made her cry.

Lorenzo religiously kept the vow that he had made to the prisoner. He never failed to carry out what he promised, nor did he deny any of Rosario's requests. This continued each day, each month, each year up until the morning when he awoke with the realization that he did not have long to live.

It was an old condition that at times he was able to forget, but that suddenly would reappear and affect him severely. It was winter, and that season helped to speed up death's work. The moment arrived when he understood that there would be no reprieve, no doctor, no medicine, no miracle cure or accident that could save him.

After a long night of feverish reflection, he had his wife call a clergyman, an old family friend who had married them and baptized their children, a Franciscan priest who came immediately to tend to his soul, since there was no hope for his body.

"Father," he said, "I feel that I am dying and I don't want to go without confessing my sins."

The priest listened to him patiently. At first there were everyday issues, minor sins, the Devil's little tricks, but then he went on to capital sins, mentioning pride, anger, and lust. Then he said:

"I have a great debt before God, and before man. I committed a grave mistake and I scarcely have time left to do anything about it."

The proximity of death terrified him, but worse was facing it burdened with guilt. He scarcely had the strength to make that accusation of himself. The dying man's wife placed a white cloth on the table and the priest laid out on it the objects of the extreme unction: the cross, the candles, the saucer with the bread and the cotton, the holy water. The priest's words were not enough. He needed someone other than God to hear him.

"My son, you have good reason, but it is not in my power to help you. Not even your wife could be a party to what you have told me."

The priest explained to him the necessary secrecy of his confession. It was intimate and inviolable even if it involved a crime in the eyes of the law. Death came before the dying man had ceased to protest. Thus it was that Lorenzo's carefully guarded secret remained forever with the Franciscan. If human justice had been as benevolent as that of God, he would have confessed much earlier and to a court of law.

Vicente the agronomer gave the eulogy. Since he didn't know the deceased very well, he had to make inquiries concerning his person and he was careful about the words he used. Based on what he was told, he offered this observation:

"If death is seen as a punishment of God, only Lorenzo will

know which of his sins provoked that blind rage. I merely want to give this farewell by acknowledging at least one of his virtues: silence."

Rosario felt abandoned now for a second time. She wrote to Antonio telling him about the unfortunate death of Lorenzo and asking him what he would suggest that she do about this new crisis.

For the first time, Antonio reread his wife's letter several times. The news of Lorenzo's death was unbelievable, but there it was, clearly described, with details from the funeral that left no room for doubt. He did not sleep that night, and the next morning he requested an interview with the prison counselor. The counselor, Lieutenant Ramos, was familiar with his case. As a consequence of several previous discussions between Ramos and Antonio and the examination of his file, there was a pending application for a reduction of sentence for inmate 33455. It was supported by the prisoner's exemplary behavior over the period of more than ten years. Contrasting with that, however, was the fact that Ramos had never been able to understand that inmate's refusal to speak openly. When he committed the crime, he had no previous record and a reputation as a peaceful man, which matched his behavior in prison. When the regime of Fulgencio Batista collapsed in 1958, the word reached Antonio through a group of prisoners who came to him announcing their liberation. One of them was carrying the keys to all of the cells and the locks were soon opened. The few guards who remained on duty were paralyzed with fear. It was now just a matter of walking out of prison, into the street, and finding liberty. There was no longer a Batista, no longer a government.

All of the other inmates made their escape, but Antonio felt compelled to honor something above and beyond those events. He remained behind, stretched out on his bed, together with an old man who refused to leave because his sentence was nearly over and he didn't want to endanger his release with new infractions.

When his new custodians arrived, they found him there, meekly waiting, just as he had been the day when he held out his hands to be handcuffed after confessing to the murder. At that time, Ramos was an army private who met Antonio when he worked for him in the prison kitchen. Even then, Ramos found it hard to believe that Antonio had taken a man's life.

His behavior had always been impeccable, the only exception being when he was involved in a violent incident when he was trying to prevent a killing behind bars.

Lieutenant Ramos had had frequent conversations with inmate 33455, whom he called by his first name. The reason for the murder was a constant topic, since Ramos had trouble squaring Antonio's character with the facts in his case. He had always been skeptical about prisoners' claims of innocence. They rarely accepted any guilt, and in most cases claimed to be victims themselves. They were in prison because of a miscarriage of justice, or some unfortunate coincidence or error. At other times they refused to talk about what sent them to prison just to show that they were tough and thick-skinned. But when Antonio assured him that he had no reason to feel repentant, he believed him.

At the time he began to attend the therapy sessions for men convicted of homicide, Ramos realized immediately that Antonio was an exception. The group was very diverse, and the personalities varied widely. There were morally depraved persons, others given to uncontrolled aggression, and those who were the victims of circumstances, like the man who came home drunk and found his wife with a lover, or a man driven to despair by a blackmailer, or one who had been humiliated in front of his woman, or a peasant who could not stand by when authorities came to evict his parents from their home and burn it to the ground.

Antonio clearly did not fit into the therapy group, although he adapted to it and the others ended up calling him "the secretary" because his handwriting was good and he agreed to write letters and petitions for them. Antonio's conviction was based on a common situation, a dispute over a woman, yet he continued to be devoted to his wife and children.

So when on that morning Ramos heard Antonio insist that he was innocent, it was like the confirmation of an old suspicion. But there was no easy way to deal with it. Or was it possible that Antonio was simply echoing the protests of his fellow inmates, who all swore that they were unjustly convicted?

Antonio scarcely offered any support for his claim of innocence. All he did was tell Ramos that if he examined the case against him carefully he would soon see where the truth lay.

The officer asked to hear Antonio's version. In response, Antonio alluded vaguely to how he had gone to the Vasallos' celebration and how, after a stupid argument, he had decided to get his horse and leave. It was when he had already started for home that he heard the gunshot.

The account seemed too simple to be believed. Moreover, there was no explanation for his ten-year-long silence. Antonio said that he became confused when he was arrested and saw no way of defending himself, that he was very young and the authorities refused to listen to him, that everything happened so quickly and so he resigned himself to his fate. But now, he said, with so much time gone by and his children now of an age to begin asking questions, he wanted to take steps toward allowing the truth to be known.

Nonetheless, Ramos sensed that the man was lying, or that at least he was offering an incomplete account. He promised Antonio that he would see that the investigation was reopened according to regulations. They took him to the prison's administrative office; there also he had to answer questions. He kept to his story without adding or eliminating details, as if it all was a memorized statement. He made a formal declaration. The decision was that in two weeks he would be returned to "the scene of the events." An official investigator was named who began making the first new inquiries. Time elapsed and the faulty memory of witnesses complicated the process.

The death of Pancho Vasallo was now recalled in a series of personal anecdotes, some of them obviously contradictory. It was very hard to find dependable witnesses, and equally difficult to locate family members, since they had in many cases moved away, and in any event were not interested in digging up the past. The only unassailable fact was that no one would be able to bring Pancho Vasallo back.

The victim's immediate family members were no longer in the area. Amalia Vasallo had married and lived abroad and Celso Vasallo could not be found. The death of his father had left him shaken. All of his plans had been destroyed with that one shot and he had thereafter wandered about aimlessly with no permanent home.

The judge from the old trial was now retired and spent his time raising fighting cocks outside town. He remembered the case very well. With one sentence he gave his final judgment: "Let the hearing go ahead, but I don't know what's going to change."

The letter of the law had been observed.

Now, as the train approached, Antonio was thinking ahead to the moment of his arrival. He imagined different ways in which it might occur. The idea of being able to spend a few hours in his town filled him with happiness.

Ramos had promised him that before the new hearing he would take him first to his home and find something else to do while he spent a few hours with his family.

Lulled by the movement of the train, Antonio's thoughts turned back to the fatal evening. The party had gotten into full swing and the dancers were swaying to the rhythm of the music when he arrived dressed in his Sunday best, a fancy cigar lit up and his spirit lifted by a few strong drinks under his belt. The musicians were warmed up and playing at their best, performing a sultry melody:

"Mama, I want to know the place
From where the singers come . . ."

Antonio glanced into the dance hall and saw her immediately. She was off in a corner, talking with Lorenzo, a foreman from the Vasallo ranch, El Paraíso. He knew that that rancher had his eye on Amalia, but he didn't particularly care, or at least that was what he told himself. He was going to turn away and ignore the couple, but then it appeared to him that the girl was being harassed and that called for some action. So he made his way across the dance floor, now feeling quarrelsome from the effects of the alcohol.

The rancher was trying to get Amalia to agree to something and she was attempting to turn away when Antonio reached them, now openly aggressive like a prize gamecock. But the girl ignored him also.

Belén, who was a kind of watchdog for the Vasallo family, saw what was happening and went to look for the old man. He gave him the message, adding his own interpretation and saying that it was a family issue that needed to be addressed. He asked Vasallo for permission to intervene, but the old man said that it was his matter to attend to personally.

Rumor had it that the two men had both enjoyed Amalia's favor, but that she had ended things with both of them. The discussion had become heated when Pancho Vasallo arrived. He dealt with the situation in his own way: He slapped Amalia across the face and ordered the two men to leave the party. Lorenzo withdrew immediately. Antonio cursed the old man and said that his treatment of him left an account to be settled.

Pancho Vasallo responded to the threat with an oath: "From now on, as long as I live, you will never set foot on my property."

"I don't have to come here to be with Amalia."

"Then I'll have to go to your home and let Rosario know the kind of husband she has."

"Amalia is your daughter, not your mistress."

"She won't be yours, either, you son of a—"

Suddenly they were struggling. The dancers managed to separate them. Since no blows had been struck, they glared at each other, hurling curses.

"I'm going to settle this with you. And soon!" was the last thing Antonio said before going for his horse. At least, that was what the witnesses recalled.

Belén clapped his hands together over his head and announced that the party was not over, that the night was still young. He called to the musicians to play a lively *guaracha*. The people returned to the dance floor. It was soon after that the gunshot was heard. The men came running out of the dance hall, looking in all directions. They saw Antonio riding off at a trot. They recognized his Stetson hat. They called out to Pancho Vasallo, but he did not answer. They found him sprawled on the paving stones, gravely wounded. Lorenzo ran for his jeep, brought it around, and many arms helped lift the dying man. Lorenzo drove recklessly down a long and winding muddy road. It took almost an hour before he reached the doctor, who, after one glance, said:

"This man is dead."

The bullet had struck him in the chest and had not exited. Lorenzo, in time, took charge of everything, assumed all the expenses, saying that he did not hold a grudge and that Vasallo's death had put an end to any resentment. Back at the El Paraíso, one of the ranch hands said to Belén:

"It was Antonio."

Someone claimed to have seen him escaping at a gallop. Everyone set out to look for him. The first to arrive, in his jeep, was Lorenzo.

Antonio was prepared to continue their fight, but Lorenzo cut him short.

"They're coming for you. They think you killed Vasallo. But I know you're innocent."

Antonio's first urge was to flee, to go into hiding until the incident could be cleared up. Lorenzo pointed out to him how slow and ineffective justice was, that he couldn't desert his family. What would they live on?

"Unless you could leave them enough money."

"Where would I get money?"

Lorenzo said he could provide it, that he would pay generously for what Antonio gave him, if he was willing to make a sacrifice for his family.

Antonio protested that he was innocent, that it would be just a matter of time before the truth would come out. Lorenzo pointed out that it was a time when justice was hard to come by. Antonio would be dealing with the police and with judges, which was difficult without having money and the type of connections that he himself happened to have.

"I want to make you a proposition."

"Well, I suppose I can listen." Antonio began to adjust his horse's saddle. "But you'd better talk fast."

"It's simple. I'll take on all of your family's problems and you'll confess to the murder."

In case he hadn't understood, Lorenzo added: "I'm paying you a lot for the only thing you have, your freedom."

Antonio thought about his sick mother, his children, the debts and the deprivations of his family.

"And what if you don't do what you promise?"

"Then all you would have to do is tell what you know."

The deal was sealed.

Lorenzo returned home and described to his wife the enormous tragedy.

Antonio resigned himself to being arrested, and understood that it would be a long time before things would be as they had been.

Now the arrangement had ended. Death had put an end to his wait. The train began to slow down. After it rounded a curve, Antonio could see the train platform. There was only a small group gathered there, but they were among them. Rosario and Chela were weeping. Ivan stood quietly, his arms crossed.

The train came to a stop. Antonio moved with deliberate slowness. Now every second held profound meaning. He let two old people laden with packages get off, and a couple with two noisy children. Then he helped several nuns with their baggage.

Finally, his feet were on the ground. He breathed a deep sigh and began walking toward his family. They, too, were moving forward to the encounter. Two steps away from their embrace, someone stepped out from behind a pile of boxes and fired. Celso Vasallo had come from far away to fulfill an unjust promise on his father's soul when there was no way to avenge his death, and now his bullet found its mark.

Since it was raining the gravediggers had had a lot to drink and were having problems with their footing and the job at hand. Rosario, Ivan, and Chela, their weeping behind them, stood huddled at the graveside. Few people had come to the funeral service.

Vicente, the agronomer, gave the eulogy. He took only one or two minutes to state that the man whom they were covering with earth had been, in spite of everything, a family man.

Baantjer

DeKok and the Hammer Blow

Translated from the Dutch by H. G. Smittenaar

Albert Cornelis Baantjer, who signs his fiction "Baantjer," is the most widely read author in the Netherlands. In a country with less than fifteen million inhabitants, he has sold almost five million books. Baantjer's most popular fictional protagonist is the hero of the following story, Detective Inspector DeKok. Like DeKok, Baantjer was himself an inspector for the Amsterdam Police for thirty-eight years. He bases his stories and novels on actual cases, and there are, to date, more than fifty titles in his DeKok series. Some two dozen of them are available in English, including February 2007's DeKok and Murder by Installment *(Speck Press).*

've come to turn myself in."

The woman who sank down in the chair next to DeKok's desk still panted slightly after her exertions on the stairs to the detective room. The old police station at Warmoes Street, in the oldest part of the old quarter of Amsterdam, boasts no elevators.

"I've come to turn myself in," she repeated. "I've murdered my husband."

She took several deep breaths, pressed her spine into the back of the chair, and folded her hands in her lap. There was an expression of resigned expectation on her reddish face.

"I've come to turn myself in," she said once more.

DeKok barely hid a sarcastic grin. Almost thirty years as a cop had taught him to react in a laconic manner to that type of confession.

"How?" he asked.

She did not answer.

"How did you do it?" urged DeKok.

She raised her chin, almost defiantly.

"With a hammer."

DeKok looked at her more closely. She was a stout woman. DeKok estimated her to be about fifty years old. A motherly type with a generous bosom and streaks of gray in the black hair. He studied her eyes, but could not detect the slightest hint of derangement.

"Where is he now?" tried DeKok carefully.

"Who?"

"Your husband."

"In hell . . . I hope."

There was so much hate and disgust in the tone of voice that DeKok felt a shiver run down his spine.

"I meant, where did it happen?"

She gestured toward the back of the room.

"At home, in the bedroom." She searched in the pockets of her overcoat and produced a bunch of keys. She slapped them on the desk. "Here, go have a look."

DeKok left the woman in the care of the desk sergeant and, accompanied by Vledder, went to the woman's house. It turned out to be an apartment on the second floor of a somber old house in a narrow street between two canals.

They opened the front door and climbed the worn wooden stairs in the dark. On the landing, DeKok searched for the right key while Vledder played his flashlight over the surroundings. He noticed that the wooden front door to the apartment was ripped open in several places and the frame was damaged. Apparently the door had been busted down several times and makeshift repairs had been made.

Inside, the inspectors found appalling destruction. In the living room, the kitchen, everywhere there was broken glass and earthenware. The furniture was mostly ruined. Springs protruded from the upholstery and poked through slashed material. A once-fine sideboard had smashed mirrors and the hinges of the doors were distorted and in one case, ripped out of the wood. The china it had once contained was in pieces all over the floor. One of the drawers had been removed and was in splinters on the floor.

On the bed in the bedroom, lit by the weak light of a bedside lamp, they found a heavily built man. He was dressed in a stained blue suit. He was on his stomach with his face pressed into a pillow. There was a ring of clotted blood on the back of his balding head.

DeKok leaned closer. A disgusting smell of stale, cheap booze came from the corpse. The man was dead, there was no doubt about that. The woman must have hit him while he was sleeping off the effects of his intemperance.

DeKok especially noticed a chair next to the bed. A kitchen chair. The only chair in the home that was still intact. The chair was standing there as if somebody had kept watch over the corpse for hours.

On the night table, within easy reach of anyone sitting on the chair, was a hammer. A heavy claw hammer, the type used by carpenters. There was blood on its head. Apparently it was the murder weapon.

After the photographer had left and the coroner had officially pronounced the victim dead, the corpse was taken to the morgue.

DeKok carefully locked the apartment, Vledder sealed the door, and the two inspectors went back to the station house.

It was a simple case. The woman had killed her husband and the motive was easily determined. The destruction of the premises made it obvious. DeKok had run across similar cases often enough . . . a brute of a husband who had driven his wife to murder as a last resort, to end intolerable living conditions.

DeKok took the woman to one of the interrogation rooms. She was calmer now. Less tense than a few hours ago. "How about a cup of coffee?"

The woman nodded gratefully.

DeKok went over to the coffeepot and poured her a cup. Meanwhile he gathered his thoughts, wondering how to start.

Where does marital trouble originate? In the courthouse . . . with the first child . . . the third? How could one pinpoint the first act of lovelessness. The cup was uneven on the saucer, but he managed to put it on the table without spilling. For a while he remained silent and watched her drink the coffee.

"I . . . eh, I went to your home," he began hesitantly.

"I understand."

"It was a mess. Just about everything was broken, or torn apart. The doors hung crooked in the buffet."

She smiled sadly.

"It's been like that for months."

DeKok frowned.

"Months, you say? I thought it happened more recently."

She shook her head.

"In the beginning I used to clean up . . . tried to bring everything back in order. But in the end it became futile." She stared for a moment into the distance. There was a despondent look in her eyes. "After twenty or thirty times," she continued, "I just gave up. I just left things as they were. That's what he wanted, a pigsty."

She moved in her chair and tapped herself on the chest.

"He knew that, despite everything, I wanted to keep things neat, clean, and tidy. I was always trying to keep up. That buffet, sir, that you mentioned, that sideboard was my pride and joy. It's from shortly after the war. I had a newspaper route then. From the money I earned, I saved for years. I was so proud and happy when I had enough to buy it. It's real oak. It must have absorbed pounds of wax . . . rubbed in with my own hands. And every time he was angry, my buffet had to suffer. He kicked the doors, took an ashtray to make dents in the wood. You see, that's how he was. As soon as he knew I was attached to something, he had to ruin it."

DeKok sighed deeply. Baffled, he rubbed the back of his neck.

"But surely that's no reason to brain somebody."

She grinned grimly.

"No, in that case I would have killed him ten years ago."

DeKok gestured in her direction.

"But you waited this long. Why?"

She leaned closer to DeKok, fire in her eyes, suddenly vehement.

"What choice did I have?" she screamed. "Should I have waited for my boy to do it?"

DeKok was taken aback.

"Your boy . . . your son?"

She sank back in the chair.

"Henk, my oldest. I have four children, two boys and two girls. None of them lives at home anymore. One by one he's driven them away. They don't visit me anymore, either. 'As long as you're with that guy,' they said, 'you won't see us.'"

She swallowed a few times.

"The only one who remained loyal was Wimpie, my grandson. He's such a sweet boy . . . nothing bothers him. Even when my son, Henk, told him he could no longer visit his grandmother, he came anyway . . . on the sly."

She started to cry. Her body shook. Big tears dribbled down her cheeks. DeKok offered a clean handkerchief. She dried her eyes.

"Last week he hit the child, just like that, for no reason."

"Your husband?"

"Yes."

"He hit Wimpie?"

Again she started to cry.

"Yes," she said after she calmed down somewhat. "You should have seen it. The poor lamb. His face was all red from the slaps.

"I fled outside with him . . . gave him ice cream, chocolate, money for the movies. Don't tell your father, I said, please don't tell your father."

She rubbed her tear-stained eyes.

"Mister, I know my Henk . . . he's my own son. If he found out that my husband had hit Wimpie, he would have killed him. That's why . . . that's why I was so afraid. I hoped and prayed that Wimpie wouldn't say anything."

"And?"

She looked sadly at DeKok.

"The child could hardly keep quiet about it. The first thing they asked, when he came home, was about the bruises."

She fell silent.

"Go on," prodded DeKok after a while.

"Henk has been around twice. Pale as a sheet. Luckily, my husband wasn't home. Henk swore that he would kill him. And he wasn't bragging . . . not my Henk. He would be back, he said."

Again she fell silent, apparently calm and completely under control.

DeKok let her be. He could find nothing to say. Her last words reverberated in his head. The old sleuth stood up and poured another cup of coffee for her and one for himself.

After he had sat down again, he took a few sips. Then he looked up.

"When did it happen?" he asked gently.

"Last night."

"Last night?"

She nodded, sipped her coffee.

"About two in the morning, I think," she said after a long pause.

"But," protested DeKok, "that's almost twenty hours ago. What did you do in the meantime?"

She looked him straight in the eyes.

"I sat with him."

"With your husband?"

She nodded slowly.

"In a chair next to the bed, the hammer in my hand."

DeKok looked a question.

"But why?"

She closed her eyes, as if to shut out a painful memory.

"To wait and see . . . to see if he would come to."

DeKok licked his tongue along dry lips.

"But he didn't come around?"

She shook her head.

DeKok hid his face in his hands. There was no need to ask what she would have done if her husband had come around. He already knew that answer.

Bertil Falk

There Are No Pockets in Our Graveclothes

Translated from the Swedish by the author

Bertil Falk is a retired Swedish newspaper and TV journalist who spent ten years on assignments in Britain, India, and the United States. His fluency in English has allowed him not only to do many translations of English novels and stories into Swedish but to flip the coin and translate his own stories into English. He is the author of fourteen novels in the mystery and science fiction genres, all published in Sweden, and the producer of numerous TV documentaries, some of which have been shown in the United States.

It was an incredibly hot summer in Sweden. The meteorological institute reported that for a couple of days the night temperature in Stockholm had been tropical. It had not fallen below sixty-eight degrees, which is very rare.

I spent my summer on a small island in the archipelago. I sat in the shade sipping at my lukewarm coffee, for I had learned during my years in Kenya that in hot weather cold drinks make things worse. My neighbour, whom I thought of as a "young lady," spent her days painting landscapes. Every weekend her husband, who worked in the capital, came to join her, on board the regular skerry cruiser. They rented a typical small "Falu red" cottage with white-painted trim. So did I, as well as many other summer visitors. In their garden and against the heavenly backdrop of blue skies and

189

the yellow sun, the yellow cross on blue ground fluttered in the wind from a white flagpole with a golden boss at the top.

She was about twenty-five years old and during the week she used to seek the company of the retired missionary who was her neighbor—me, that is. One evening, after she had complained about the difficulty of painting in the heat, she told me that she had just read a strange true story about a case that had taken place about seventy years ago in Gothenburg. A jealous young man had killed his girlfriend in a barn. A simple case of murder? Yes, but the odd thing about it was the aftermath. Some days after the funeral, the police found a dead woman's body in the home of a mentally deranged man. To his astonishment, the pathologist recognized it as the body of the murdered girl he had performed an autopsy on the week before. It turned out that the deranged man had stolen the corpse on the evening of the day it had been buried. He simply lifted it from the grave, which had been left open till the next day.

"Is that really possible?" she asked me.

She looked so young and so fresh. She reminded me of a girl I had been in love with half a century ago, similar blue eyes, fair hair, an attractive smile.

"I remember that story," I said. "What would be impossible about it?"

"Do they keep graves open overnight after an interment?"

"Why not?"

"In the night, people could fall into an open grave."

"Most people don't run about in graveyards in the night. And it has happened that drunken people have fallen into graves in broad daylight. But yes, sometimes the gravedigger waits till the next day before he covers a grave. Once it happened to me."

She looked at me, somewhat surprised. "You've been a gravedigger?"

"Certainly not." And I told her the story.

• • •

It happened about ten years ago. Evert Svensson was an old friend of mine. For many years he worked as a mining engineer in a South African diamond mine before finally returning to Sweden. His wife Laura was the daughter of a Social-Democratic municipal commissioner, a very good-looking woman. She successfully devoted her time to inducing young women to use cosmetics and to turning her own children into good consumers of the unneeded things that a greedy industry portions out in a never-ceasing stream. She was a very warm and pleasant person, and she had a bizarre sense of humor. The Svenssons had a son and a daughter. The son, Lars, was a computer scientist, married to Ulrika, who was a surgeon. They lived—or as they would say, "resided"—near Evert and Laura. The daughter, Lena, was a housewife and married to a plumber by the name of Sven. They lived a long way off.

Evert and I used to meet quite often for a couple of whisky tumblers at his place. Or rather: Evert took his Bowmore and soda, while I, as the teetotaller I always have been, had my Ramlösa water. He would talk about his time as a mining engineer. Once he even showed me an uncut diamond about the size of a walnut. In my opinion it was not much to look at, but he said that it was worth a fortune.

When Evert died and Laura became an aging widow, she now and then invited me for a dinner in their mansion with its view of the sea. Her relationship with her children was not the best. She used to complain that they wished to see her dead so they could lay their hands on the fortune she had at her disposal, for as long as she lived, she retained undivided possession of the estate.

Her health eventually gave way, and one day she asked me to come over and see her. I had no idea then that she was dying. On the porch, she sat in a deck chair in a semi-recumbent position. It was a sunny afternoon in August. I saw that she had fallen away since the last time I had seen her. But her eyes had their usual acuity.

"I've not long left," she said. "Soon the brats will have their way. Unfortunately, there are no pockets in the cerements, so I can't bring anything with me to the other side. Or do you think I could? As a staunch Christian, you should know."

I was puzzled. I did not get what she was driving at, and she was not kidding. She was calm, her voice weak but firm.

"What are you talking about?"

"This," she said. "Look here."

She handed me a small case.

"Open it!"

There on a bed of dark blue velvet was that uncut diamond that Evert had shown me many years ago.

"Do you know what this is?" Laura asked.

"A piece of uncut coal that is worth a fortune," I answered with the words Evert had once used, and I returned the case to her.

"I don't want the brats to get it," she said. "They don't deserve it. I want to give it to you. Evert always enjoyed those afternoons and evenings together with you. And he once told me that he would like to give it to you. So I've made up my mind."

I shook my head. "I don't want it. I don't need it. Give it to your children."

"Don't worry about them. They'll get more than they deserve," Laura tried to persuade me.

"I'm not fond of these kinds of things," I said.

"You can give it to charity," she said.

"No. These things have a tendency to bring ill fortune. You give it to charity."

"It's too late. I'm dying."

"Oh, come on, Laura."

We were interrupted by her home help. She came to serve us coffee. With some water Laura swallowed some pills that her doctor had prescribed. Understanding that this was our last conversation and feeling the atmosphere turn solemn, I bid her goodbye, bent forward, and kissed her forehead. It was feverish and cold at the same time. When I left her, she sat there with the case in her hands. There was a bewildering smile on her lips. I had never before seen her smiling that way.

Three days later, Laura died. She still lay dead in the living room when I came over to express my sympathy. Sorrow and distress were not exactly palpable. Instead a quarrel over property was in full swing.

The brother and sister and his wife and her husband could not agree on who would have the bisected antique mirror or the Gustavian rococo furniture. And above all, they were excited about the uncut diamond:

"On Sunday morning she was there in her bed stuffing herself with those damned pills her doctor prescribed. She did not trust me to attend, of course. It had to be some other doctor. Her daughter-in-law was not good enough. She bluntly told us that she had disposed of the diamond, and then she died. Just like that. We've looked everywhere and can't find it."

It was Ulrika, her tongue as sharp and her voice as piercing as the tools she used in her profession.

"It was in a case," I said.

"It's empty now," Lars explained.

The small case was indeed empty. A small depression in the velvet indicated where the diamond had been all those years.

"I wonder where she hid it," Ulrika said.

At the funeral a week later, the diamond was still missing. I understood from the line of reasoning they followed, which was as far removed from mourning as imaginable, that the house had been meticulously searched. The home help had been the target of insinuations. She was red with weeping.

"Perhaps you have some notion of where the diamond could be?" Lars said to me.

I had no idea, and even if I had had one, I did not feel like assisting them in finding a fortune that I knew the deceased had grudged her heirs.

"Laura said that she disposed of it," I said to Ulrika. "So why do you suspect the home help?"

Ulrika looked intently at me with her big brown surgeon-eyes, as if she reflected on performing a kind of live autopsy on me.

"For the simple reason that the home help could have helped Laura to hide the diamond," she said. "Haven't you any idea where it can be?"

"Well, if I had been Laura, I would have thrown it into the sea," I said, suppressing my anger.

"We've thought of that," Lars countered. "But it's a hundred and fifty yards to the sea and she could not possibly have been near the shore the last weeks of her life, certainly not in her last days. We were here most of the time, and she told us she had only just got rid of it. We were by her side as she swallowed her pills with her glass of water, but she refused to eat anything. And for your information, I don't think she had any opportunity to give the diamond to the home help as Ulrika thinks."

He looked reproachfully at his wife.

The funeral service was sparsely attended. The usual psalms were sung. "Earth to earth," the minister said. The home help wept a little. "Ashes to ashes," the minister continued. Lars puckered his brows. "Dust to dust." The coffin was carried out and lowered into the prepared grave. The next day it would be covered by the gravedigger. My eyes moved from one face to another as we stood gathered there around the pit in the ground. At the request of the deceased, there were no flowers and no wreaths. Laura hated cut flowers. Her opinion about this was crystal clear: "It's enough that I fade away. No flower shall fade on my coffin lid."

The home help's face was red and swollen. Lars looked in a pondering way at his mother's coffin, which now touched the bottom of the grave. Ulrika, who had looked serious, suddenly seemed to have thought better of it. Her face lit up, and for a moment a smile of—was it triumph?—was on her lips. It lasted for a second and then she looked serious again. Lena, the daughter, bit with her upper row of teeth at her bloodless lower lip. Sven, her husband, nervously fingered his left lapel with his right hand.

"Well, let's go back and continue the search," Lars said.

"Is there any sense in searching?" Sven wondered.

"Hardly," Ulrika said. "Lars and I will go home."

"I don't know," Lars said, but stopped speaking as Ulrika caught him with her sharp eyes.

Lena shook her head. "We decided not to have any funeral feast," she said, her voice tired and flat, "so that Sven and I could go on searching."

She turned to me. "How about you?" she asked.

"None of my business."

But I was not sincere when I said that.

The glimpse I had had of the momentary expression on Ulrika's face bothered me.

"I think that you should come with me and Lars," Ulrika said to Lena and Sven. I saw them driving away in their cars, Lars and Ulrika in a flashy Volvo, Lena and Sven in an even flashier Chevrolet of a vintage kind. I myself sat in my cheap Skoda Felicia and pondered.

Later that evening, I tried to read but I could not concentrate on the speeches of Cicero. I still pondered as the wall clock in my library struck eleven o'clock. It was then that the pieces fell into their proper places. I shook my head in despair and called my friend Roland Franzen, the police superintendent. I told him about my conversation with Laura a few days before she died. And I told him my theory.

"I think she took the opportunity to swallow the diamond when she took her pills," I said. "She could have done it under the very noses of her heirs. Maybe she got the idea when she told me that there are no pockets in the graveclothes. I suspect that her daughter-in-law guessed the truth. And she is a surgeon. And the grave is open till tomorrow."

Roland listened to me and I fairly saw him nodding on the other end of the line. I picked him up in my Skoda. The church clock hit the midnight mark as we arrived. The grave was open. I shone my torch. The lid was on the coffin, but it was unscrewed. Roland leaped down and took it off. The coffin was empty.

"They will either get rid of the corpse or they will return it to the grave," I said.

"We'll take no chances," Roland decided, and sent for reinforcement.

The perpetrators' cars were parked outside the house of Lars and Ulrika. The door was unlocked. We did not ring the bell but walked straight in. We stopped in silence in the doorway of the dining room. There, on the oblong dining table, was the naked body of Laura. Her daughter-in-law Ulrika leaned over the corpse. We saw how she brought up something from the insides of her mother-in-law, while Lars, Lena, and Sven stood gathered stock-still around the body. In her hand Ulrika held a small capsule. She opened it and unfolded a paper.

"Damn it," the surgeon said. "She has cheated us."

Ulrika gave the paper to Lena. She read aloud: "That's what you get, body-snatchers and desecrators of corpses!"

At that moment Roland intervened.

"Enough is enough," he said.

The four of them turned their surprised and horrified faces toward the door where Roland and I stood.

My neighbor had hung upon my words as I told her the story. Now she thoughtfully looked out over the narrow strait that separated our island from another small rocky islet.

"I guess they had to pay a price for their outrage?" she said.

"Not very much," I told her. "Ulrika was sentenced to three months' imprisonment for desecration of a grave and disturbing the funeral peace. The others got off with no more than a fright and a fine. According to the statute book, they could all have been given six months. The court obviously considered Laura to have provoked the crime, and they may therefore have found the circumstances somewhat extenuating. I don't know. I wasn't there."

"And that's the end of the story?"

"Not at all. You see, the week after this ghastly occurrence took place, I, as usual, went for my evening stroll. I put on the jacket I wore the last time I visited Laura and I walked down to the shore. I sat down on a mole, contemplating. It was windy with scudding clouds. The sea ran high and the waves dashed in and flooded the shore over and over again. There were drops of rain and I regretted that I had not put on my rain suit and sou'wester. I was on the verge of returning home when I put my hand in the pocket of my jacket and felt something."

"Of course! Laura had slipped the diamond into your pocket when you kissed her feverish forehead," my neighbor whispered.

"That's right."

"Don't tell me that you have the diamond here and will show it to me."

I smiled at her. "You see, I stood there and I looked at the sea-gulls. They felt, as I did, the storm brewing. I walked out on the pier, and summoning all my strength I threw that calamitous thing worth a fortune as far away as I could into the sea."

"Calamitous?"

"Yes, jewels such as Kohinoor and the Hope are not calami-tous in themselves. But our greed makes them so.

"Anyhow, Laura had a strange sense of humour and she proved it with the last thing she did. She was right in what she said, too: There are no pockets in our graveclothes."

Rubem Fonseca

Winning the Game

Translated from the Brazilian Portuguese by Clifford E. Landers

*Since the 1960s Rubem Fonseca's often violent, totally unsentimental short stories, marked by unstinting realism and sometimes discomfiting emotional honesty, have been capturing the attention of Brazil's reading public. His novels have consistently made Brazil's bestseller lists. His fiction has been embraced by readers in many other parts of the world too: Translations of his works have appeared in French, German, Spanish, Dutch, and several Scandinavian languages. Three of his novels—*High Art, The Lost Manuscript, *and* Vast Emotions and Imperfect Thoughts—*are currently available in English.*

When I'm not reading some book I get from the public library I watch one of those TV programs that show the life of the rich—their mansions, the cars, the horses, the yachts, the jewels, the paintings, the rare furniture, the silverware, the wine cellar, the servants. It's impressive how well served the rich are. I don't miss a one of those programs, even though they're not of much use to me; none of those rich people live in my country. But I enjoyed hearing a millionaire interviewed during a dinner say that he acquired a yacht worth hundreds of millions because he wanted to have a yacht bigger than some other rich guy. "It was the only way to put an end to the envy I felt of him," he confessed, smiling, taking a swallow of the drink in his glass. The dinner companions around him laughed a lot when he said that. The rich can have everything, even envy of each other, and in them it's humorous; with them, everything is amusing. I'm poor, and envy in the poor is looked upon badly, because the poor repress their envy until, eventually, it turns to hatred of the rich; the poor don't know how to retaliate without a spirit of vengeance. But I don't feel rage against any rich person; my envy is like the guy's with the bigger yacht: like him, I just want to win the game.

I've discovered how to win the game between a poor guy, like me, and a rich one. Not by becoming rich myself; I'd never manage that. "Getting rich," one of them said on a program, "is a genetic proclivity that not everyone has." That millionaire had made his fortune starting out from zero. My father was poor, and I inherited nothing when he died, not even the gene that motivates you to make money.

The only possession I have is my life, and the only way of winning the game is by killing a rich man and coming away alive. It's something like buying the bigger yacht. I know this seems like odd reasoning, but one way to win the game is by making up at least part of the rules, something the rich do. The rich man I kill has to be an heir; an heir is a person like me, without the predisposition to get rich, but who was born rich and blithely enjoys the fortune that fell from the sky into his lap. Actually, to relish life to the fullest, it's preferable that just the father, and not the heir, be born with the gene.

I would prefer killing one of those foreign rich guys that I see on television. A man. Their wives, or their daughters, are even more ostentatiously rich, but a woman, however many jewels she has on her fingers and around her wrist and neck, isn't the bigger yacht. Nor would I be interested in one of those women who obtained their fortune by working—clones who appear on television in suits—though they are certainly carriers of the gene. No, it would have to be a man. But since the ideal rich men live in other countries, I have to be satisfied looking for one who lives right here, one who inherited the money and goods that he enjoys.

The difficulty in achieving this goal doesn't worry me in the least. I painstakingly draw up my plans and when I lie down I'm asleep within minutes and don't wake up during the night. Not only do I have peace of mind but a well-functioning prostate, unlike my father, who used to get up every three hours to urinate. I'm in no hurry; I must choose with great care, somebody at least at the level of the rich guy who bought the big yacht. The majority of the people who appear in the magazines published here in my country can be called rich and famous, but killing one of them would be easy and wouldn't make me win the game.

Every rich person likes to show off his wealth. The nouveaux riches flaunt it more, but I don't want to kill one of them, I want a rich man who inherited his fortune. These, belonging to the later generations, are more discreet, normally displaying their wealth through travel. They love shopping in Paris, London, New York. They also like to go to distant and exotic places that have good hotels with genteel help, and the more sports-minded can't pass up an annual ski trip, which is understandable because after all they do live in a tropical country. They display their wealth among themselves (there's nothing to be gained from playing with the poor), at millionaires' dinners where the winner can confess it was because of envy that he bought what he bought, and the others merrily drink to his health.

A guy like me, white, poor, skinny, and starving, has neither brothers nor allies. It wasn't easy to get a job with the most expensive and exclusive catering service in town. It took deliberate planning and maneuvering; I spent two years at it. Perseverance is the only virtue I possess. The rich had the habit of hiring that catering service when they gave a dinner. The owner, the descendant of an illustrious family—I'm not going to mention her name, just as I'm not going to mention anyone's name, not even mine—was a domineering woman who kept her notes and time charts in a small computer that she carried in a bag over her shoulder. She imposed rigid standards on those who worked for her—cooks, decorators, buyers, waiters, and all the rest. She was so competent that the employees, besides obeying without batting an eye, even admired her. If some employee acted in a way not in keeping with the established model, he was fired. That was rare, because all, before being hired, were subjected to a rigorous selection and training process. We did as we were told, and I was one of the most obedient. And the service charged a small fortune to cook for and feed those rich people. The owner of the catering service had the gene.

Before the evaluation and training to which I submitted to become a waiter at the catering service, I did an apprenticeship of my own. First, I did something about my appearance. I found a good, cheap dentist, which is very rare, and bought some decent clothes. Then, which was more important, I learned, as part of my solitary training, to be a happy servant, as good waiters are. But faking those feelings is very difficult. That subservience and happiness can't be obvious, they must be very subtle, perceived subconsciously by the recipient. The best way of playing that impalpable dissimulation was to create a state of mind that could make me truly happy to be a waiter to the rich, even temporarily. The owner of the catering service pointed me out as an example of the employee who did his job by taking pride in what he did, which is why I was so efficient.

The rich, like the poor, aren't all the same. There are those who like to ramble on with a cigar between their fingers or a glass of precious liquid in their hand, there are those who play the gallant, those who are reserved, the solemn, those who sport their erudition, those who flaunt richness with their designer attire, there are even the circumspect ones, but deep down they're all show-offs; it's part of the pantomime. Which ends up being a true sign language, for it makes it possible to see what each of them really is. I know that the poor also do their pantomime, but the poor don't interest me, it's not in my plans to play with any of them; my game is that of the bigger yacht.

I waited patiently for the ideal rich man to come along. I was ready for him. It wasn't easy to get the poison, tasteless and odorless, that I transferred from one pocket to the other in my pilgrimage. But I'm not going to relate the risks I took and the vile things I did to obtain it.

Finally, a rich man of the type I was looking for appeared at the reserved-seating dinner at one of the five tables in the mansion's dining room. I knew his story, but I'd never seen him, not even his photo. It was the owner of the catering service who told me, and for the first time I saw her excited, because "he" had just arrived and I was designated to serve him personally. Rich people like to be well attended. I would remain at a certain distance, without looking at him, but at any gesture of command of his I was to approach and say simply, "Sir?" I knew how to do that very well; I was a happy waiter.

He had arrived, like the other guests, in a bulletproof car, surrounded by bodyguards. He was a short, dark guy, balding, with discreet gestures. His wife, his fourth, was a tall, slim blonde who appeared even taller thanks to the high heels she was wearing.

There were eight guests at each table, four men and four women. Even though the service wasn't French style, each table was attended to by a pair of waiters; my colleague was a tall black man with perfect teeth. There were drinks for every taste, even beer, but I don't remember anyone at my table asking for that vulgar and fattening beverage. As per the owner's instructions, the other waiter was my subordinate. Discreetly, I decided that my colleague would handle the requests of the other diners, who were so engrossed in their conversations that they didn't notice the special treatment I afforded one of them.

I waited on him with perfection. He ate little, drank in moderation. He didn't use, with me, the word "please" or "thanks." His orders were laconic, unaffected. The dinner was nearing its end.

"Sir?" I approached when he turned his head an inch to the side, without looking at anyone, but I knew it was for me.

"Half a cup of coffee."

It was the chance I'd been waiting for.

I went to the kitchen and made the coffee in the state-of-the-art Italian machine supplied by the caterer. I added the poison.

"Here you are, sir."

He sipped the coffee, chatting with the lady beside him. Unhurriedly, I picked up the empty cup, went back to the kitchen, and washed it carefully.

It took some time for them to discover that he was dead, as he had rested his head on his arms on the table and appeared to be sleeping. But since millionaires don't do those things, taking a nap at a banquet table, those around him found it odd and realized that something serious had occurred. A heart attack, probably.

There was a commotion, confronted with appropriate elegance by the majority of those present, especially his svelte wife. The bodyguards, however, were much more nervous. The dinner was brought to a close shortly after a private ambulance took the corpse away.

I think I'm going to continue serving the rich for a time. It'll have to be another catering service; the one I worked for suffered a reverse of fortune. At first the newspapers said only that the cause of the rich man's death was a sudden illness. But one of the weekly magazines published a long cover story talking about poisoning, with pictures of the guests at the banquet, especially those, men and women alike, about whom malicious insinuations could be made. The life of the dead millionaire, his businesses, his marriages and divorces, especially the scandalous circumstances of one of the latter, were given extensive coverage.

The police are investigating. I enjoyed going to the precinct to make a statement. I wasn't there long; the police thought I couldn't have much to say about poisoning. After all, I was a stupid and happy waiter, above any suspicion. When I was dismissed by the interrogator in charge of the case I said casually, "My yacht's bigger than his."

Someone had to know.

"I told you, we're through here, you can go."

As I was leaving, I heard him tell the recording clerk, "One more shitty statement."

I won the game. I'm uncertain whether I should play again. With envy but without resentment, just to win, like the rich. It's good to be like the rich.

Paul Halter

The Call of the Lorelei

Translated from the French by Peter Schulman

Paul Halter is from Alsace-Lorraine, but it isn't easy to find stories by him set anywhere in France, for he most often writes about an English detective in an English setting. The following tale, one of several Halter stories published in EQMM's Passport to Crime series, does take place in the author's homeland. It's an impossible-crime story, in the vein of John Dickson Carr, whom Halter greatly admires. One of France's most esteemed mystery writers in the classic tradition, Halter has authored more than twenty novels, including La Quatrième Porte (The Fourth Door), *which won the* Cognac Festival Award in 1987, and Le Brouillard Rouge (The Red Fog), *which won the French Adventure Novel Prize in 1988. Surprisingly, only one Halter book is currently available in English, a collection of short stories entitled* The Night of the Wolf *(Wildside).*

Beneath a gloomy sky, the white boat full of tourists ploughed through the murky waters of the Rhine. Seated at a table near the railings, Dr. Alan Twist, a tall and thin sexagenarian, staidly dressed in tweed, watched as the old feudal villages passed by one after the other. Still and defiant, their haughty silhouettes were perched along the peaks of hills like sentinels, complementing the twilight beauty of this romantic landscape. Were those old stones hiding the ghostly Walkyries? Were they the keepers of the Rhinegold? The old British detective asked himself these questions as he succumbed to the strange charms of the legendary river.

Suddenly, a murmur rose from the tourists on the bow. Twist followed their gazes and saw a dark and threatening elevated craggy mass emerging like a ghost ship from the mist. The word "Lorelei" buzzed through everyone's lips.

So that was the famous rock. . . . That was where the famous siren would use her enchanting melodies to lure the unsuspecting boatmen towards their rocky deaths.

"Striking, isn't it?" he remarked mechanically to the person sitting next to him. "I don't know why, but I've always been fascinated by these old legends. . . ."

The man ventured an answer only after some time had elapsed and the German tourists had finished singing *"Die Lorelei."*

"Old legend?" he said. "That's how you put it? I can tell you that I knew someone who bloody well saw the siren. . . ."

Dr. Twist turned to look at his interlocutor, a bearded man in his fifties with a somewhat embittered look about him. There was nothing in his demeanor which would suggest that he was joking in any way.

"His name was Hans Georg," he began again, as his eyes looked up towards the deadly rock. "Unfortunately for him, he was unable to resist the call of the Lorelei. . . ."

The detective eventually befriended his companion, one Jean-Marie Vix, who promised to recount the strange tale of Hans Georg one day if Dr. Twist would honor him with a visit to his house in Munchausen, a small village in northern Alsace. Twist, who, coincidentally, was planning to see some friends in nearby Haguenau, took his new friend up on his offer by paying him a visit.

Munchausen hugs the right bank of the Sauer, which, in

turn, flows into the Rhine. It is a rather wild region which, despite being subject to flooding by the devastating river, is also home to a picturesque scenery made up of ponds and oxbows over which willows cast their latticelike foliage.

Just north of the village, Jean-Marie Vix's home seemed to erupt from a dreary plain in the midst of a thicket of beeches that surrounded the last few houses. It was an imposing half-timbered two-story house which did not seem to suffer from its isolated location. An ornamental (but slightly askew) border of tiles ran above the first-floor windows. The front door opened onto a large hallway which ran all the way through the rest of the house to the back door; its lime-bleached walls enhanced the reddish patina of the ground-floor windows, as well as the studwork and the polished wood of the doorways. The old house radiated a pleasant warmth that made Dr. Twist feel immediately at home, as did the ebullient welcome from the master of the house, who relieved him of his tweed coat by placing it on the coatrack by the entrance. Without attaching any particular significance to them, Twist noticed, to his left, a few long and beautiful peacock feathers, which had been placed in a terra-cotta vase resting on a low table.

His host apologized for his wife's absence. She was busy with a parishioners' meeting that night but hoped to be forgiven for her absence by having prepared an amazing *choucroute*[1] especially for their guest. Dr. Twist was delighted and rejoiced in the *mirabelle*[2] which was served to him after the meal. It was at that moment that Jean-Marie Vix finally began the strange tale of Hans Georg.

"It all happened in the mid-nineteen twenties. Hans Georg, a

1. A typical Alsatian dish made up of sauerkraut, meat, and vegetables.
2. A regional type of plum brandy, often homemade and very strong.

young, blond, athletic German traveling salesman, had an uncomplicated approach to life. He had great confidence in himself, and in humanity in general, as though there were no such thing as evil on this planet. When his work brought him to Munchausen, he wasted no time courting my sister Clementine, even though we had just barely been freed from the German boot. Although about ten years had already elapsed since the armistice had been signed, the Alsace region was still licking her wounds. Alsace had been affected more deeply than any other region in France; she had to pay a heavy price for the conflict. Some of her sons, who had been forcibly conscripted into the Prussian army, had to confront their brothers on the battlefield. . . . Our family, therefore, was hardly overjoyed when Clementine told us that she was planning on getting engaged to Hans Georg, the German. . . . It was thanks only to the wisdom he had acquired with time . . . as well as to a few glasses of mirabelle that my father, Panaleon Vix, was able to contain his wrath. My mother simply asked her daughter if she knew what she was doing. I was only thirteen or fourteen years old at the time, and as far as I was concerned, Hans Georg was quite nice, with his direct manner and his resounding laughter. Most importantly, he never forgot to bring me a present when he came over to visit. On the other hand, my brother Hubert, who was just a bit older than Clementine, could barely suppress his rancor. He cooled down eventually, at least sufficiently enough to suffer through the German's company, but he never failed to mock our neighbors on the other side of the Rhine, and that is exactly what he did on the day when Hans Georg, who was always filled with a boundless initiative, took us all on a cruise along the Rhine.

"As we approached the Lorelei's rock, Hans Georg brought up the old romantic legend. Hubert then proceeded to declare drily that the story had been fabricated to explain why so many fatal crashes had occurred at that particularly dangerous spot. Hans simply shrugged his shoulders and laughed, admitting that, after all, such a thing was quite possible. Yet, a few minutes later, when the rock became more perceptible, he became quite tense and his face appeared visibly confused. Only on the way back did he admit to having seen a young blonde woman at the top of the promontory. We all dismissed it as a mere coincidence. A few weeks later, however, he thought he had seen the young woman again several times in a row. In town, in the crowds, at a detour on a country road . . . he had seen her signaling to him discreetly. He turned right around each time he saw her, despite his hesitations. He felt an intense attraction to the young blonde's charms, but his instincts urged him to be cautious.

"Clementine, however, was convinced that these sightings were proof that a rival existed, a rival who hoped to snatch her fiancé away from her by some sort of cryptic trickery. Hans Georg was not spared a few jealous scenes. She eventually began to agree with her mother, who was very superstitious, and saw the uncanny female apparitions as a bad omen. As for my brother and father, they seemed rather skeptical at that point. Then winter came. . . .

"It was around mid December, when we were celebrating Clementine and Hans's engagement right here in this house. It was bitterly cold at that time. Munchausen and its surrounding towns shivered beneath heavy layers of snow. But our home was blessed with a deliciously warm ambiance. There were about twenty of us in attendance: our family, some friends, my bachelor uncle Joseph who had limped ever since he had been wounded in the trenches by a shell explosion. He was a jolly chap who was unmatched when it came time to enliven an evening with his accordion. For Hans, the vision of the young woman had become but a distant memory: He no longer made the slightest mention of it. But the moment Uncle Joseph launched into a rendition of the 'Lorelei,' an icy frost seemed to envelop the dining room. . . . My parents and the affianced couple suddenly became pale. There was something incongruous about their frozen countenances and the accordionist's lilting melody. Without probing or attempting to understand what was going on, Uncle Joseph quickly switched to a more engaging tune. It was a minor incident that the others had hardly noticed, but Hans began to show signs of great concern. He continued to act as jovially as possible, but was caught occasionally shooting quick and furtive glances at the windows.

"By midnight, all the guests had gone home with the exception of Hans. It was still snowing, but not a single snowflake was falling an hour later when the fiancé finally took his leave. He had kept my father company in the kitchen for one last drink, while my mother, my brother, my sister, and myself had gone to bed. When the clock struck one, he finally left the house. It must have taken him two attempts, however, as the first time he tried he had to come back for his umbrella, which he had forgotten to take with him. According to my father, he was a little tipsy but not drunk. He usually spoke quite loudly, and we all heard his thunderous: *'Ach! Donnerwetter! Ich habe mein parapli vergessen!'* A few minutes later, the door slammed a second time. He had opened his umbrella even though it was no longer snowing. My mother was the one who followed his strange behavior from the first-floor bedroom. The heavy snow clouds lifted, and the veiled moon seemed to bathe the landscape in a cadaverous hue. Hans had barely advanced a few meters in the direction of the village. He turned around and appeared to extend his ear. He then went back on his steps, tentatively. . . . Each time he returned, he wanted to go back out toward the village but he seemed to be attracted by something mysterious coming from the north. . . .

Had he stumbled upon the famous siren's song? My mother asserted that she did not hear anything in particular at that moment, neither a song nor a cry, but she was half asleep, and couldn't say for sure. She had been awakened from her slumber by the German's door-slamming, and his shouting. Thus, she had seen Hans circle the house from the left side and waited in vain for him to reappear, but then went back to bed because sleep had overtaken her. Hans was found the next morning drowned in the frozen little pond, about a hundred meters north of the house, and not far from the Rhine. . . . The malevolent siren had succeeded in drawing him into her lethal trap!

"The police officer from the *gendarmerie*, who was dispatched to the scene that very afternoon, undertook an extremely detailed investigation. As it had not snowed since the previous evening, he was able to retrace the victim's path with ease. Hans Georg had indeed followed the contours of the house, working his way along the entire left side of it before making his way to the back door. His steps were not entirely clear because he had been so visibly hesitant, advancing and then retreating. Moreover, the layer of snow was not thick, as the roof had sheltered the edges of the house. Curiously, when Hans veered decisively northward, the steps became quite distinctive. Even though the steps seemed uncertain after an evening of heavy drinking, the footprints here evidenced a rather heavy gait. Hans had headed straight toward the pond, the frozen surface of which had disappeared beneath a pristine layer of snow. He did, however, know it was there. He knew that it was a dangerous place to tread, and yet, this had not been enough to stop him from making his way to the center of the pond, where the ice collapsed beneath his feet. It reconstituted itself during the night above the unfortunate fellow's corpse, which cast a vague shadow from the depths of the icy water. As for his umbrella, it remained on the ice's surface, right next to the fatal jaws of the opening he had fallen through. Because the water temperature had been particularly cold that night, he must have died rather quickly.

"But what would have propelled Hans Georg toward such a dangerous spot? What had he heard right after leaving the house? The officer from the gendarmerie was asking himself that very question, especially after learning of the existence of the enigmatic blonde, who, it turns out, had only been seen by the victim himself. Did she actually exist? He firmly rejected the 'diabolical siren' theory which my mother and sister seemed to completely believe. And yet, Hans's death was shrouded in mystery. The suicide hypothesis did not hold up, given the victim's personality. Hans Georg had apparently no reason to put an end to his days, especially on the eve of his engagement. An accident? That, too, was unlikely, so bizarre had been his behavior that night. The investigator never brought up the possibility of some criminal mischief, but it surely must have crossed his mind at some point or another. Nonetheless, it was established that no one could have approached the victim on the path he took after leaving the house, either to push him from behind or otherwise make him fall through the ice. The distinctive and isolated footprints Hans left behind proved at least that much. Nor could anyone have walked in his footsteps, tracing them back to the shore, or performing any other perilous act of that nature. Furthermore, the space around the house and the pond were perfectly untrammeled as well. The trees which bordered the north bank of the river were too far from the spot where the ice had cracked to imagine the possible involvement of a tightrope walker or any other kind of acrobatic trick. The theory that the victim's death had been caused by his own momentary alcoholic frenzy was the one that was ultimately accepted, but I can assure you, Mr. Twist, that from my family's and my point of view, there is another explanation for Hans Georg's tragic death."

"What you're saying, then, if I understand you correctly," Dr.

Twist playfully suggested, "is that you believe the siren may have played a role in all of this?"

His interlocutor seemed embarrassed. He stroked his reddish beard before sighing. "Yes, since there is no other conclusion that I find satisfactory. . . ."

With these words, he took the bottle of mirabelle, filled the glasses, then added: "But something seems to tell me you are not entirely convinced of this, Mr. Twist. . . ."

"Well, let's say that my experiences with criminal affairs have taught me to be somewhat skeptical. . . . But before giving you my opinion, I would like to ask you a few questions. . . . Do you remember any kind of detail that might stick out, any kind of innocuous event that might have occurred then?"

"No, not really," Vix answered, making a concerted effort to think long and hard about it. "Nothing except for the peacock feather, which intrigued the officer, but I don't think that it could be of any importance. . . ."

"A peacock feather?" asked the astonished visitor. "Similar to the ones I noticed in the hallway, near the front door?"

"Yes. The day after the dramatic event, we found one on the floor, at the far end of the hallway. My mother had the silly idea of alerting the officer to this fact, as neither she nor anyone else could explain its presence there."

"How peculiar. . . . Besides that, was there anything else?"

"No, not that I can remember. . . ."

"Did Hans Georg speak German with you?"

"Yes, of course," Jean-Marie Vix answered, feebly attempting a smile. "He knew a bit of French, but began with the premise that we were all expected to be completely versed in his native language. . . ."

"And what about the Alsatian dialect?"

"No, not even that. . . . Nothing but German. . . ."

"That's just what I thought," Twist answered, nodding. "But then there is something strange about your narrative.... Are you quite sure of the words he used that night when he came back to get his umbrella? *'Ach! Donnerwetter! Ich habe mein parapli vergessen!'*"

"Yes, absolutely, since everybody heard it.... (The master of the house's face lit up at that point.) Ah! I see. It's the *'parapli'* that bothers you! Believe me, that would not be the case if you knew how to speak the dialect. Alsatians use the French word for umbrella. That's what threw you off in your reasoning...."

"I'm rather afraid that the opposite has occurred, in the sense that none of you noticed this anomaly because you were all used to the dialect. Think about it for a moment: Hans Georg should have used *Regenschirm*, the German term, in fact ... and yet he did no such thing!"

The master of the house seemed surprised.

"Yes, you're right ... but there could be a million reasons why he didn't.... (He scratched the back of his head.) Let's see ... First of all, because he had a drop too much to drink that night ... but is this really important?"

"I fear that it is indeed.... It could mean, for example, that someone else uttered those words...."

"But that's absurd! And who on earth could that have been if that were the case?"

"To that we can add the detail of the peacock feather," Twist continued as though he hadn't heard that last remark. "No, really, none of this leads me to believe for a minute that ... Unfortunately, I have too much experience in criminal matters to believe that this Lorelei had anything to do with it...."

The Alsatian frowned: "What? Are you implying that Hans Georg was ... *murdered?*"

"That is a term that cannot be disregarded, alas!"

"But then, we would have to look for his killer . . . here, amongst ourselves!"

Twist downed his glass of mirabelle in one shot before asking: "By the way, whatever happened to your family?"

"Sadly, there are not a lot of us still around! Time took its toll and then the Second World War came rumbling through. . . . My brother was shot by the Germans as a spy shortly after the liberation. My parents died soon afterward, as well as Uncle Joseph. Clementine, who had taken refuge in the Perigord[3] region during the upheaval, simply stayed there. She recently married a childhood friend who moved to her village. Unfortunately, we rarely see each other. . . . No, really, I find it difficult to believe that one of them could have committed such an act. . . ."

"Are you quite certain of that, monsieur? It has become quite apparent from your narrative that few of you approved of your sister's choice. Moreover, as it turns out, I am rather familiar with the historical context of the period. World War One and France's defeat at the hands of the Prussians left a large number of Alsatians with intensely hostile feelings toward the invaders. Hans's nationality made him an intruder, a vile stain on your family's honor. It was only because of his irreproachable behavior that everyone was able to calm down. But it did not take much to reawaken this ancestral hatred. As a matter of fact, you are all suspects! With the exception of your sister, because she was in love with him. . . ."

Jean-Marie Vix emptied his glass with a gulp and asserted: "Hans Georg could not have been murdered, Mr. Twist, the investigation officially proved it."

"Wouldn't a crafty soul have been able to skillfully lure him to the pond?"

"By imitating the siren's voice?" Vix shot back with an acerbic

3. A region in the southwest of France.

grin. "I admit to having thought of that possibility myself at that time . . . but there are two elements which weaken that particular argument. Nobody in the house heard any such call, and allow me to remind you that there were no other footprints besides Hans's throughout the entire circumference of the lake. . . . So I don't see how anyone, by virtue of their magical cries, could have convinced this victim to march towards the lake by his own volition as though he were some sort of zombie mesmerized by the sheer artifice of a song. . . ."

A tinge of malice flashed through the detective's eyes: "You are forgetting his hesitations after his departure. Your mother did indeed see him return several times before going around the house. . . ."

"Precisely, there can be no explanation for that! Which proves without a doubt that we are dealing with a supernatural creature. . . ."

Twist shook his head gravely: "No, there *can* be a perfectly rational explanation . . . an explanation that solves the entire mystery, the mystery of the '*parapli*' as well as the peacock feather."

Silence once again fell on the room while Vix hung onto the detective's every word.

"Obviously, my idea is just a hypothesis, but it has the merit of dissipating all the incoherent aspects of your story. First of all, I think Hans Georg was poking fun at you from the start with all that Lorelei business. During your cruise along the Rhine, his ego was probably wounded by your brother's remark, as though the entire German nation had been targeted directly. He therefore came to the defense of the legend and, in order to convince you that the siren really existed (for fun as much as out of spite), he claimed to have seen her at the top of the rock. The worried looks from your mother and your sister encouraged him to continue his little game. It was a hoax that your father eventually uncovered, with the assistance of Hans Georg himself, no doubt, who had in all likelihood confessed to it that night, or perhaps even had bragged about it while they were having one last drink together. . . . Your father, whose temper had undoubtedly also been fueled by alcohol, would have wanted to get even . . . and by the same token, he must have told himself that his family's honor and his daughter's well-being were now in his hands. . . . *So Hans Georg claimed to have seen the Lorelei? Well then, it would make sense for him to join her!* he must have told himself.

"At around one in the morning, when the young man had left the house, he got into a coat resembling the one the German was wearing, took an umbrella similar to the one he was carrying, then, in German, cried out the sentence in question in order to attract attention and to lead everyone to believe that Hans had returned, but he had also made the mistake I have alerted you to. He then proceeded to go out and perform the pantomime that your mother followed from her bedroom window. The opened umbrella made it quite difficult to recognize him. He went around the house but for him there was no problem using the back door upon his return. His hesitant footsteps and his comings and goings were doubly judicious as they scrambled the footsteps to the point where they could not be determined to be someone's other than Hans's, which were very distinctive, and which in fact began from the back of the house. . . ."

"I don't understand. . . . What was the point of that particular maneuver?"

"To lead people to believe that Hans had just heard the siren's call and that he hadn't exited through the rear of the house directly, because that would have seemed too odd. . . ."

"But how was he able to lure Hans Georg towards the lake?" Jean-Marie Vix interjected, his eyes round as saucers.

"This is when the peacock feather comes into play. Earlier, when I walked through the hallway, I noticed that what made it remarkable was its extreme uniformity—the red checkered floor, the equal number of wooden doors at each side, as well as one on each end leading outdoors. A person who was not aware of this, or who was simply disoriented when exiting through the rear door (which opened up to a vast blanket of snow with a clump of trees at the end of it), could well imagine that he was going toward the village, as the scenery is pretty much the same in either direction—especially at night or when one's thinking is clouded by alcohol. The 'last drink' your father served now becomes crucially important. It allowed him to be more efficient in his abuse of this person he wanted to drive away from his family. In order to accomplish this, he took advantage of a strategy which, despite its incredible simplicity, was quite ingenious and should not have taken him more than one or two minutes to execute. After making some vague excuse, he went out into the hallway and simply moved the coatrack and the low table with its conspicuous peacock feathers and placed them both by the back door. . . . The feather fell without his noticing it when, a little later, he put everything back in its place. You can guess the rest of the story: The unfortunate Hans Georg marched towards his fate with great confidence . . . and joined the rest of the Lorelei's victims all the way down to the bottom of their watery graves."

Translator's Note: *It is not unusual for furnishings such as those that play a part in this mystery to remain the same for generations in a French home that is passed down within a family.*

Daliso Chaponda

Heroic Proportions

Translation wasn't necessary for the following story by Malawian Daliso Chaponda. The author's native tongue is Chichewa, which he spoke as a small child, but years of British education gradually made English the language in which he was most fluent, and in which he writes all of his fiction. This story was the author's first to see print in any language, though previously he had been a finalist in an L. Ron Hubbard Writers of the Future contest. He makes his living as a stand-up comic, a career that began in Canada with such one-man shows as Black History YEAR: A Month Isn't Enough. *He is currently living and working in Manchester, England.*

"**D**ICTATOR DIES WHILE SITTING ON TOILET." That was the headline. Beneath it, a full-page photo showed General Ebeso, self-proclaimed "Lion of the Savannah" and "Leader for Life," sitting on a ceramic throne with trousers pooled around his ankles. As always, he was in full military regalia. The bullet wound in his chest was a crater in his bloated mass.

Detective Kachani leant his head back in an uninhibited laugh.

Govinda Patel's eyes flickered dangerously behind oversized, pink-rimmed glasses. "This is funny to you? The police not take me serious?"

He pointed at the *Malawi News* on her counter. "I wasn't

laughing at you." He reached for the newspaper. The photo was a grainy black-and-white. If ever there was a time when a color photograph would have been appreciated, this was it. Still, the image was sufficiently comical. Kachani mentally picked out a spot on his fridge on which to tape it. Better yet, he'd buy a frame.

The paper was abruptly whipped from his grip. "You can buy your own," Mrs. Patel snapped. "Do your job."

This was the last straw. All morning Kachani had been badgered by an increasingly infuriating sequence of proprietors who acted as if their stores were the center of the universe. "Listen," he said. "I doubt anyone is planning to start a carpet-smuggling ring with four carpets. They were probably stolen by rioters too drunk to know what they were taking. You can take some satisfaction in imagining the moment they wake up and realize that while others took televisions, stoves, and bags of flour, all they stole were some useless rugs."

Mrs. Patel tensed as though preparing to pounce. "I sell highest quality Persian carpets, imported . . . first rate . . ."

Kachani darted out of Carpet Nirvana before her rage peaked.

Bunda Avenue was crowded. People milled among the debris of the previous night: glass shards, knocked-over billboards, garbage from upturned bins, and the carcasses of battered cars. Beneath, the deeper scars eleven years of Ebeso had left on the city lingered: streets with potholes and ruptured gutters, neglected buildings with collapsing roofs, people so thin their arms looked like twigs. And now, what? Everything would miraculously become better because Ebeso was gone? Kachani could not make himself feel the jubilation he saw in the faces of people he passed. He made his way back to the station slowly. His eyelids sagged and his muscles ached. He was forty-three, but he walked like a much older man. His face, too, had been worn down. His eyes and thick lips were framed by dark lines, and he was balding. A few grey curls flecked his beard.

He had parked a kilometer north of the ravaged city center. He stopped at a newsstand and bought a copy of the *Malawi News,* and laughed again at the front page. Definitely worth buying a frame.

The police station was almost empty. Kachani found a slip of paper that said "Come and see me" stuck to his desk. No name was needed; Station Commander Patrick Chundira's messy scrawl was unique. He found him in the middle of what seemed to be a very taxing phone conversation. His tight-boned face was gleaming with sweat. A series of exchanges climaxed in Patrick shouting, "I don't care if you have to arrest them all, just do it!" He slammed the receiver into its cradle.

"What was that about?" Kachani asked after the commander hung up.

"A crisis at the hospital." Chundira dabbed his face with the corner of his sleeve. He took off his glasses and wiped them as he spoke. "There are not enough doctors for all the wounded. After hours of waiting, some of them have become violent. I don't have enough people to send."

"You want me to go?"

"I need you for something more important. I need you to figure out who killed Ebeso."

"What?! Did you somehow sleep through last night? We don't need to waste time trying to find the killer. Everybody's overjoyed."

"That is actually the problem. The killer has become a national hero."

"So?"

"He ran away after shooting Ebeso. I wish he hadn't. So far, three people have come forward claiming the credit."

Kachani grinned.

His boss met this response with a sigh. "I also thought it was funny at first, but I have been talking to the chief of police and this could escalate into disaster. Elections need to happen quickly or the chaos will get worse. Whoever killed Ebeso has an almost guaranteed win. But two of the people who have come forward are just political opportunists. And once their claims spread across the city their supporters will start fighting. Mark Lungu's have guns and I don't know about the others."

Kachani nodded. Mark Lungu was the leader of the Tembelelo rebels. They had been fighting Ebeso for the past three years and were loved by the masses, though Kachani personally felt their acts of dissent hurt civilians as often as they hurt the government. They set fires, hijacked deliveries, and engaged Ebeso's forces with no thought for people caught in the crossfire. "Who are the other two?" he said.

"Archbishop Mpocha and 'Lightning' Kalyati."

Kachani whistled. The archbishop's supporters were probably the largest group, but Zikomo "Lightning" Kalyati, Malawi's most famous ex-footballer, was rumored to have ties to the military. It wasn't an exaggeration to imagine the situation could lead to a civil war.

Chundira shook his head. "If we could have predicted this, we would have closed the murder scene to the press . . ."

"So the impostors had access to the crime-scene details."

"Exactly why I need your help."

"Why me?"

"Because you're brilliant. I can count on you for results."

Patrick was obviously more used to receiving compliments than giving them, because he hadn't mastered the art of pretending to be sincere.

"The truth," Kachani insisted. He had always done things his own way no matter what the circumstances, and he knew that this had often complicated his superior's life.

The left side of Chundira's mouth rose in his characteristic half-smirk. "All right. It's because you are notoriously apolitical. You have never backed one group or other. You don't care."

Kachani feigned resentment. "Not entirely correct. I simply mistrust all politicians equally."

"Either way, you're the only person I can trust."

Satisfied, Kachani rose. "I'll head to the palace immediately."

"Give me ten minutes," Chundira said, picking up the phone.

"You're coming with me?"

"Of course." He began dialing a number. "This is a sensitive situation. You have no tact or respect for people in positions of power."

Or rather, Kachani realized, there was no way Patrick was going to miss this opportunity. He didn't want to stay director of a small precinct forever, and one of the three supposed killers was probably going to be the next president. . . .

A little later, they were in Chundira's Toyota Corolla. The *Malawi News* article was spread between Kachani's thighs, shaking with the car's jerky progress. "Good," he muttered.

"What?"

"The woman who wrote the article hated Ebeso."

"Who didn't?"

"The impostors got all their information from this article. Anything I see at the palace that she didn't report accurately will show them to be liars."

"Clever." Chundira made a sharp turn off the main road. "Who do you think did it?"

"Haven't got an opinion yet."

"You must have a hunch. Why don't we bet?"

"No, thanks."

Patrick cast Kachani a disapproving look. "I think it's either Zikomo or Mark Lungu. It can't be the archbishop."

"Why not?"

"He's a man of God, not the violent sort. Also, you've seen him. He's short and weak."

Kachani almost remarked that his boss was only five foot six. Instead, he said, "You don't have to be a giant to pull a trigger."

"You have to be brave, though. A man like that would panic."

"Have you ever spoken to Archbishop Mpocha?"

"No."

Kachani let his silence speak.

Patrick let out a frustrated grunt. "You think he did it?"

Kachani closed the newspaper. "I didn't say that."

"Zikomo Kalyati, now there's a man with courage. Did you ever watch him play?"

"I'm not a soccer fan."

"Something is wrong with you. You're like a woman. He ran like a cheetah. I promise you, if it hadn't been for that car accident Malawi would have won the Africa cup. It was a tragedy, a great tragedy." The policeman's face collapsed into an expression of earnest grief.

Although he didn't follow soccer, Kachani would have had to be living in seclusion not to have heard about the Blantyre team's star player's car accident. His leg had been mauled by twisted steel. Unable to play anymore, he had chosen to exploit his popularity by running for parliament. Under Ebeso, parliament wasn't influential, but MPs still got to pose for photographs, attend official functions, and be introduced as "Your Excellency."

Chundira rambled on. "Mark Lungu is the obvious one, though."

"Why would Mark Lungu take the risk instead of sending one of his rebels?"

"He's not that sort of man. He's a man of action."

Again, Kachani was sure his boss's speculations were based on nothing but hearsay. He reached out and his fingers sandwiched the knob of the car radio.

There was a large crowd outside the palace. They had probably been there since the night before. Once-jubilant faces were now showing signs of exhaustion. Their voices, still screaming and chanting, were now raw and hoarse. Still, they remained gathered—almost as though they feared it was a dream and if they went back to their houses, they would wake to find Ebeso alive. Patrick mentioned that it had been hard to stop the crowds from rushing the palace the day before. Now, policemen stood lazily in front of the residence's gates watching the mollified masses. There was still some life in the weary multitude. It was localized around one man who stood on a makeshift podium of upside-down crates. He gesticulated ferociously as he shouted.

"Who's that, some community leader?"

Chundira didn't know, either.

They entered the palace. It was huge—excessively so. Eleven years earlier, when Ebeso had come into power, he had felt that the old presidential residence in Lilongwe was an inadequate representation of his heroism. He had demanded that a palace "of heroic proportions" be built for him. He inspected the plans drawn up by several architects and ordered them executed for insulting his magnificence. Eventually, one architect satisfied him and the Blantyre palace was built. It had cost more than Malawi's annual domestic budget. It stretched out over twenty-one acres and had twelve floors and elevators on opposite sides. The ceilings were high, and elaborate crystal chandeliers hung from them. The corridors were long and paved with ornate carpets that reminded Kachani of the wares of Mrs. Patel's Carpet Nirvana. Every few meters there was a tribute to Ebeso's magnificence: paintings and photographs of the dictator, wooden carvings of lions, and a large mirror (in front of which he would undoubtedly pose).

"Didn't the man ever get tired of looking at himself?" Patrick mused.

Kachani stopped to look at a nine-foot-tall portrait. Ebeso was always taller, thinner, and more handsome in his portraits. This one barely looked like him. He was identifiable only because of the array of medals for valor pinned to his chest. Ebeso had awarded them to himself. Military might had been essential in Ebeso's vision of Malawi, even though it had never been at war with another African country. It had no raw materials to be coveted, and its land mass was sparse. Hardly worth the effort of invasion. But then again, Kachani considered, how many African countries have ever been at war with another country? Still, all of them spend money and resources on the military. The armies, of course, never go to waste. They are inevitably used on the domestic population.

The bathroom was at the far end of the corridor, a bald policeman standing outside it chewing gum noisily. Like everything else in the residence, the bathroom was huge. It had four stalls and the tiles on the floor were a mosaic of a lion. The image was barely visible now because the floor was covered in a layer of grime. "Did you let every policeman in Blantyre in here to contaminate the evidence?"

"No," Chundira defended himself. "Ebeso had one of his big parties two nights ago."

Everybody who had attended that party, every guard who used to patrol the palace, and everyone else remotely linked to Ebeso had probably fled the country by now. The few followers of Ebeso who had been found by the mobs the night before had been beaten to death. Kachani walked about the bathroom taking meticulous note of everything he saw: three sinks, three urinals, a mop in a bucket, a large fan in the roof, a portrait of Ebeso on the wall . . . By the time he had made a complete survey, he was disheartened. Even with her bias, the *Malawi News* reporter had been very accurate. "I need to speak to the man who found the body," he told Patrick. "Did he leave his address?"

"He's right outside, sir," said the bald policeman.

"Great. Can you get him?"

A nod and a brisk march down the corridor followed.

"He's actually military," said Chundira, pointing at his back. "We didn't have enough police to keep control yesterday so we gave some soldiers police uniforms. Couldn't have them in military uniforms because of the stigma."

Kachani barely heard him. He was looking intently down the corridor himself.

"What is it?"

"Maybe nothing," replied Kachani.

The man who had found Ebeso's body was brought back in a few minutes. It was the man they had seen giving a speech outside. His suit was immeasurably old, with split seams about the shoulders and numerous stains. It was draped over his skinny body like a tarpaulin. He had a veritable glow about him; his smile was huge and his head was held aloft. "I am Arthur Ntaso."

"You found him?"

"Yes," was the proud reply. "I was mopping upstairs when I heard a loud bang. It was like thunder. It made my body shake. I know now that it was the sound of God's vengeance. I ran downstairs, and when I got here I found him gasping for his life. He was holding his wound and coughing blood. As he was dying he held out his hand and said, 'Forgive me, Malawi.' I told him, 'It is too late for you.'"

Kachani stifled a smile. Mr. Ntaso was obviously embellishing to make himself out to be a hero. Who could blame him? Here was a man who had probably been a servant all his life. Serendipity had suddenly placed him at the center of attention and he loved it. The untruths in his story were obvious. Even from looking at the photograph in the newspaper Kachani knew that Ebeso's hands had not been bloody. And the notion of Ebeso begging Malawi for forgiveness was laughable. Kachani kept these thoughts to himself. He could get the information he needed without tearing away Mr. Ntaso's moment of glory.

"Could you show me where you were when you heard the gunshot?"

Ntaso took Kachani and Patrick up a short flight of stairs. "Here. Just outside his study."

"And you ran?"

"As fast as I could."

"You didn't see the killer?"

"No, the instrument of God's fury was already gone by the time I got there."

Kachani had a few more questions and then he made for the car.

"That was a waste of time," grumbled Patrick.

"Why do you say that?"

"He was obviously lying."

"I know, but he still helped. Now, to the two suspects."

"You mean three?"

"Two," he insisted. "As much as Mr. Ntaso was adding to the story, you can be sure that if he had seen the killer he would have told us about it. He may have added a few things like a halo glowing around the killer's head, but he would have mentioned it. You saw how long the corridor was? The killer ran all the way down it in the time that Mr. Ntaso took to run down the stairs. With Zikomo's limp, he couldn't have run that fast."

Chundira opened his mouth, then shut it. "You're right."

Kachani smiled with satisfaction, then added, "St. Paul's Church is ten minutes away."

When Kachani was younger, he had been deeply religious. A crucifix had dangled from his neck and a Gideon's Bible in his back pocket had frequently been consulted. His religious and political disillusionment had occurred simultaneously. After Malawi's first dictator, Kamuzu Banda, had been removed from power, Kachani had been one of the most hopeful. He had praised God and thrown himself into trying to serve his people as a policeman. But in the face of poverty, AIDS, and harsh droughts, none of the presidents who followed Kamuzu helped Malawi. Neither had God.

When Kachani stepped into St. Paul's Church, he felt none of the awe he would have twenty years earlier. A lone figure knelt in front of the crucifix at the far end of the church. Kachani and Chundira approached Archbishop Mpocha. His skin was an inky black that seemed to blend into the suit he wore. His priestly collar was a thin white island in an opaque sea. He did not respond to their approach. His head remained bowed, his expression solemn. His mouth moved soundlessly.

It was a long prayer. Eventually the archbishop's eyes opened and he rose. His wrinkled face, graying beard, and penetrating stare made him look impossibly old. "I was praying for forgiveness."

Chundira jumped at the bait. "A great man like you doesn't need forgiveness."

"I took a life," Archbishop Mpocha announced. "Even a man as vicious as Ebeso was a child of God."

"You did Malawi a glorious service. It was a—"

"Why were you at the palace?" Kachani cut in.

"I had a meeting with Ebeso about the demonstrators he imprisoned last week."

"So after years of standing silent while he imprisoned and executed thousands, what was it about the latest incarcerations that moved the Church to action?"

"I'm sorry," Patrick said desperately. "Please excuse him, he—"

"Do you think this is the first time I have heard insults like that?" The archbishop was unruffled. The only part of him that moved were the fingers of his left hand. They played absently with the hem of his suit. "Blaming the Church is an easy thing for frustrated people to do. We did not stay silent."

"You're right," Kachani replied. "The Church was very vocal in supporting Ebeso. Whenever he ordered a judge removed or one of his rivals disappeared, the Church would denounce that person and every congregation in Malawi would hear how that man had been a sinful Judas."

Archbishop Mpocha's gaze still had a calm, superior veneer. He smiled as one would to a silly child. "So you are so much more righteous? While Ebeso was in power, how many murder investigations did you end prematurely when the evidence led to Ebeso's cabinet? And what did the police ever do when the people committing violence were Ebeso's followers?"

Kachani opened his mouth to reply but the archbishop held up his hand. "On some level, everybody collaborated with Ebeso. It is easy to say, 'You should have stood up to him, you shouldn't have been silent,' but we were all afraid. Of course we were. We did not want to be the next one eliminated. The most anyone could do was find ways to do some good within the restrictions. I was guilty every day because the Church had to support Ebeso and turn a blind eye to his deeds. Yesterday I had been pushed too far. When Ebeso went to the toilet, I knew he was vulnerable for once."

Kachani struggled to control his anger and think logically. "You were carrying a gun?"

"Yes."

"Why? If you didn't plan to kill him, why would an archbishop be carrying a gun?"

"Malawi is not as safe as it once was. I am ashamed to admit it, but I sometimes have to carry a gun."

"Weren't you searched when you arrived at the residence?"

"The guards who let me through were Catholic. My word was enough for them."

"Where is the gun now?"

"I panicked. I threw it away."

"Where?"

"I'm not sure. Somewhere on my drive back here."

Convenient, thought Kachani. "Where did you meet him?"

"In his study."

"And how did he react when you brought up the incarcerations?"

"He told me he did not care what I thought. That's why when he got up to go to the toilet—"

"You followed him down the corridor and shot him. In the toilet."

"Yes." The archbishop's restless fingers were now threading the rosary around his neck.

"Think about this. Are you saying that's what happened? You walked down the corridor after him, and shot him in the bathroom."

"Yes."

"We're done," Kachani said to Patrick and began to walk away. "He didn't kill Ebeso."

"What?" the archbishop objected. He finally sounded angry, and this pleased Kachani.

Chundira remained in the church for a few minutes more—probably apologizing and grovelling. He was enraged when he exited. "You can't talk to him that way."

"It's how he deserves to be talked to. Have you seen the house he lives in? He has a legion of servants, a pool, and a satellite dish. Many Malawians share a loaf of stale bread with their whole family for dinner, but still give money to the Church every week. This is what it's used for." Kachani pointed at a large red Volvo parked behind the church.

"You called him a liar with no basis."

"He said he followed Ebeso down the corridor and shot him in the bathroom, but he also claims to have met Ebeso in his study. You were there, Patrick; Ebeso's study was upstairs but the bathroom he was shot in was downstairs. The archbishop didn't mention the stairs."

Patrick thought about it. "That's hardly enough."

"I know, but every important thing about the murder is in the paper. Only the tiny details can reveal the liars."

"It's not much at all."

Kachani agreed. As they drove away from the church, he seethed with anger at himself. He had let his emotions get in the way. The smugness of the archbishop had reawakened old resentments. And when Mpocha had asked how many of his own investigations had been prematurely terminated, he had struck a nerve. Kachani could not deny it. There was a stack of "unsolved" cases. Some of them were horrendous—child rapes and murders of whole families. Yet he had done the cowardly thing. Many of the criminals would never be punished. They had probably left the country by now, no doubt with suitcases stuffed with money.

Kachani barely heard anything Chundira said to him as they drove.

They reached Kudya Inn in the late afternoon.

A scar, even a small one, has a way of commanding attention. People see the scar and they can't look away. Every time they look at the other features—eyes, nose, lips—it's a brief glance, and like twirling compass needles, inevitably their gazes return to the scar. Mark Lungu's scar began beneath his left ear and cut across his cheek in a keloid arc. The rest of his face was angled, immaculate, and refined. Without the scar, he would have had the air of a bothered university professor. With it, he seemed dangerous and unpredictable.

Inside Kudya Inn he was speaking to a group of men and women whose ragged garments were at odds with the inn's finery. " . . . Malawi has never been allowed to reach its potential," he was saying. "The British held us down. Kamuzu held us down. Ebeso was the most recent. Too much of the country's power has been in the hands of selfish bastards instead of with the people. I will return it to you." The speech continued for ten more minutes in this vein.

Afterward, Kachani and Chundira approached him in the foyer.

He greeted them with a jovial ease. "After years of running and hiding, I was so relieved at being able to return home that I forgot how much I hated making speeches."

"You did a fine job, anyway," observed Kachani. "You pointed fingers and made promises without explaining how you would do it, a by-the-books political speech."

The look of reproach Chundira gave him was exhausted. He was starting to accept that it was pointless to try and control what came out of Kachani's mouth.

Lungu replied in an even but strained tone, "I understand why you're wary. I'll have to earn your respect. What newspaper are you from?"

"We're not from a newspaper."

Lungu's irritation was palpable. "I don't have time for this."

"We just need to ask you a few questions and that'll be the end of it."

"All right." Lungu poured himself some water.

"Can you briefly explain the things leading up to your murder of Ebeso?"

The rebel's lips were beaded with tiny droplets of water when he spoke. "We were losing hope. Our activities were having little impact. Whenever we raided one of Ebeso's bases, he would take it out on the people. More and more rebels were being arrested and executed every week, but to kill Ebeso was a difficult goal because he was paranoid. He was always armed and surrounded by guards. At the big party he threw for his supporters two days ago, we knew he would be vulnerable. I slipped in with the guests."

"You weren't recognized? You?"

"There was a huge group. I just pretended to be one of them and waited. There was no opportunity, and when everyone started leaving I hid in the bathroom. You have no idea how long I waited in there, unsure of when I should come out. I didn't actually expect him to come in, so when I heard someone enter, I wasn't sure what to do. I didn't know it was him until I shot him. I was lucky."

Kachani asked him a few questions to clarify: what color the toilet stalls were, where he had been standing in relation to Ebeso, and other small details.

When they left, Patrick sighed with relief. "That solves it."

"I don't know."

"What do you mean?"

"He answered all the questions, but it didn't seem right. I feel I'm missing something."

"Why are you making it difficult? This is the best way it could have turned out. Mark Lungu is the best person to lead Malawi, he is a great hero."

"So was Ebeso," replied Kachani. "As much as I can't stand pathetic little cowards like Archbishop Mpocha, when they are in power at least things don't get radically worse. Occasionally they steal some money and promote a few of their friends, but that is the most they do. Men like Mark Lungu are more unpredictable. He said in his speech that the British kept Malawi down. Who knows if that will mean he suddenly decides to expel all Malawians of British blood? Leading rebels requires extreme thinking; leading a country is not the same. I don't know if Malawi can survive another hero."

"You're such a pessimist," Chundira accused, and Kachani did not disagree.

"I think we should go see Zikomo now."

"What? But you said . . ."

"I know, but . . ." Kachani hated to admit his mistakes, especially to Patrick, who would find ways to bring them back up at inopportune moments. " . . . I may have been hasty in discounting Zikomo. Zikomo could not have run away before Mr. Ntaso saw him, but maybe he could have hidden in an adjacent toilet stall and slipped away later."

"That's far-fetched."

"We need to check into every possibility."

Chundira grumbled something and Kachani did not ask for clarification. At the next intersection, however, Patrick turned left—toward Zikomo's house. After a few minutes of driving they came across a large group of people walking and running in the opposite direction.

"Now what?" Patrick sighed.

They slowed down and asked a bare-chested man who had a blue shirt wrapped around his head.

"We're going to the palace. At five o'clock Archbishop Mpocha is going to prove he killed Ebeso. It was on the radio."

Kachani turned to Chundira. "That's impossible."

"He wouldn't announce it on the radio unless he was confident."

"Why didn't he tell us?"

"After you insulted him?"

Kachani glanced at his wrist watch. "Hurry. We have to get there."

"I know," agreed Patrick, turning the car around.

They reached the palace at 5:26 P.M. Archbishop Mpocha's revelation was late. Kachani and his boss pushed their way through the amassed crowd. At one point they had to draw their guns and wave them in the air to clear a path. As they neared the front of the group, the archbishop caught sight of them. He gestured for them to approach. "I was hoping you would make it," he said to Kachani. His irritating smile had returned.

"What's your proof?" Kachani demanded.

"Have patience."

"What are you waiting for?"

"Them." The archbishop pointed.

A van from the Malawi Broadcasting Corporation had just arrived. A group of reporters got out, unloading equipment. They approached, clearly bubbling with excitement. After years of being nothing more than a propaganda machine for Ebeso, they were obviously eager to get some real reporting done.

The archbishop waved at the crowd and swaggered into the palace followed by the reporters, Kachani, Chundira, and a few others. He walked down Ebeso's majestic hallway and then to the bathroom. He waited for the reporters to give him a ready sign and then he began speaking. He enunciated crisply so that no word would be missed in the broadcast. "Malawi, here the Lion of the Savannah was slain. Here his reign of terror ended. I spent my life in the service of God. It meant more to me than anything else, but yesterday, when I saw an opportunity to kill Ebeso, I made a choice. It is not a choice I regret or would undo, but I am still sad because I must now announce that I am withdrawing from my position in the Church. This was a sacrifice I made willingly. It makes me angry that there are people who are telling terrible lies and claiming they killed Ebeso. Malawi cannot survive with the uncertainty, and I think God anticipated this. When I killed Ebeso I wanted to get the gun out of my hand immediately. I thought it was guilt, but now I think it was God who made me leave the gun here. The police searched this place, but God did not allow them to find the gun, though it has been here all along." The archbishop bent over the bucket in the corner of the room. He rummaged in the water and then rose with a flourish. He lifted a gold-plated gun in the air and held it aloft. Leisurely he walked out of the toilet and out of the palace. Chundira and the others darted after him.

Kachani stayed in the bathroom, transfixed to the spot. He cursed himself for being so stupid. He had allowed his dislike of the Church to cloud his judgment. For all his claims to Chundira of not making up his mind, he had been convinced the archbishop couldn't have done it. And the gun—there was no excuse for that oversight. In the bucket, of all places. He walked up to it and pushed it forward with his foot. It rolled. He looked down at the parallel wheel marks, cutting across the grimy floor like railway tracks. He stared at them intently. There was something that bothered him but he couldn't pinpoint what it was.

From outside he heard a wild cheer. As much as he disliked

the man, he had to recognize the archbishop's finesse. Resigning from the clergy so dramatically opened his way to running for president perfectly. Archbishop Mpocha was definitely a master of spectacle. He was probably holding the gun up to the crowd right now, like a holy relic. The image of the gun flashed in Kachani's mind and then he looked at the tracks left by the bucket again. "Of course," he muttered, and rushed out of the bathroom.

Thirty minutes later, he was knocking on the door of an apartment in Ndirande. A little boy of about five or six answered the door. He had a curly mat of black hair and large oval eyes.

"Is your father home?"

The boy welcomed Kachani into a small, single-roomed apartment. Arthur Ntaso was reclined on a sofa listening to the radio. He got up and flicked the radio off.

"Sorry to disturb you," Kachani said. "I forgot to ask a few things this morning."

Ntaso pointed at the radio. "It's over."

Kachani continued as though he hadn't heard. "You said you were mopping upstairs when you heard the gunshot and you ran downstairs immediately. Why, in your extreme hurry, did you carry the bucket and mop with you? There is no way you could roll the bucket down the stairs anyway. You must have used the elevator."

Ntaso opened his mouth, and then hesitated. He turned to his son. "Go play back there," he said, and the little boy ran out onto the balcony.

When the boy was gone, Kachani added, "The gun Ebeso was killed with was gold-plated. I didn't get to examine it, but I'd be willing to bet it had lions engraved on its barrel. You killed him."

"No, no, no," Ntaso replied, shaking his head vigorously. "I didn't kill him." He paused and considered whether or not to continue. Finally, he shrugged and sat back down on the sofa. "I found Ebeso in his study. I thought he was asleep, but when I came closer I realized he was dead. He had died naturally. Like that, so easily, after all the people he had killed." He pointed at a framed picture on the wall in which he was standing next to a woman. "Miriam died in prison for encouraging her students at the high school to commit treasonous acts. All she did was help some students write letters to Amnesty International, and for that she died alone after God only knows what had been done to her. And Ebeso died peacefully in his sleep. I was so angry. At least if he had been killed by a rival or suffered in some way it would have been bearable. Standing there, I got the idea of how to humiliate him. I could make sure I was the only one who ever knew how he had died. I loaded him onto the bucket and wheeled him to the elevator. I took him down to the toilet and—"

"Shot him in the chest with his own gun," Kachani finished. "Why didn't you just come forward and say you had killed him?"

"Who would believe that I, a cleaner, had killed him? They would ask too many questions and maybe find out how he had really died."

"But now the archbishop is taking the credit."

"I'm the one who told him where the gun was."

"What?!"

"When I found out he was claiming to have killed Ebeso I realized he would make it perfect. If people thought Ebeso had been killed by a man of God, the message would be clear."

Kachani could not find anything to say in response. He had totally misjudged Arthur Ntaso. "Don't you wish people could know what you did?"

"A bit," admitted the cleaner. "But this is the best way, and if I ever feel bad, I have these." He reached under his shirt and pulled out a selection of gold and silver stars. They were the medals for valor Ebeso had awarded himself. "I took them from his body. I'll give you one if you keep quiet about what I did."

"No need," replied Kachani. "You deserve them."

"Well then, maybe I can ask you to stay and eat with us. We are about to have dinner."

"Thank you," Kachani said.

Sometime later, Kachani was sitting at the dinner table with Arthur and his son Bidwe. Dinner was just cobs of maize and boiled cabbage. Not much of a meal, but Kachani looked at Bidwe. The boy had plump cheeks and a strong body. His clothes were faded to the point that Kachani couldn't make out the words printed on his shirt, but they were clean and ironed. Arthur clearly did what he could to be a good father. Kachani's eyes were drawn to the photograph Ntaso had pointed to earlier. How many other families were incomplete because of Ebeso? But then Kachani remembered the portraits of Ebeso in his palace. And of all the other portraits Ebeso had insisted grace the walls of every bank, school, and store in Malawi. In a few days they would all be torn down, defaced, and burnt. In a few years, none of those portraits would be remembered, but no one would ever forget the image of Ebeso's corpse on the toilet.

"Thank you," Kachani said to Arthur, taking a bite out of a cob. He could not remember maize tasting quite as good as it did at that moment.

Gunter Gerlach

Wedding in Voerde

Translated from the German by Mary Tannert

A native of Leipzig who currently lives in Hamburg, Germany, Gunter Gerlach has thirteen novels, more than three dozen short stories, and a number of radio plays, theater pieces, and poems to his credit. His most recent novel in the crime genre is Irgendwo in Hamburg (Somewhere in Hamburg), *published by Rotbuch Verlag. The following story won the 2005 Friedrich Glauser prize for short fiction, awarded by the German Crime Writers' Association. Nearly all of Gunter Gerlach's novels are widely available in German; none have yet been translated into English.*

1.

The noise of the motor is suddenly different.

I sit up, startled. "Where are we?"

Something's scratching and scraping under the hood. An animal, trying to get out.

"The coolant's overheated," says Ulrich. He's sweating behind the wheel. His plaid suit's gotten too small for him over the last four years. The pants are too short. His stomach rubs against the steering wheel. And the shirt buttons are about to pop. There's a red light blinking on the dashboard.

Ulrich turns on the warning flasher and begins to look for a parking lot.

"*Dinslaken*," he says. "We've almost made it."

He opens yet another button on his light-blue shirt. Then he guides the car into an empty parking space and turns off the motor. I unfold the street map.

"That's the road to Voerde," says Ulrich. "That's it, all right." He wipes the sweat off his forehead with the back of his hand.

"Why didn't you take the autobahn?" I ask.

"Because the coolant's overheating."

"How long?"

"Since Bochum."

I take a deep breath. Ulrich pats the air in a soothing gesture, palms toward me.

"Calm down. It's my car. And I want to get to that money just as fast as you do." He gets a rag from underneath the driver's seat. We get out. Ulrich takes off his jacket and rolls up the sleeves of his shirt, then opens the hood.

A thin hiss of steam rises from a hose. Ulrich grips the radiator cap with the rag and turns it. The cap jumps from his hand. Steam spurts out and envelops him. He emerges dancing and swearing, blowing on his arm.

I shake my head. "End of the line."

I go to the trunk and open it. "We're in luck; we've got everything here." I take out the heavy wire cutters. Bicycles are leaning against the fence around a building. I pick out two and cut through the locks. "It's not far," I say. "Is it?"

2.

The cool shade of the woods lines both sides of the road. It's too warm for Ulrich. He's riding in his shirtsleeves, his jacket rolled into a bundle on the bicycle's back rack. "Why do you have gears on your bike and I don't?" he shouts.

"Because you weigh more," I say. "That means more pressure on the pedals."

The district called Möllen is just along here, after the woods. It's part of the town of Voerde. There are houses on both sides of the street. But no people.

"We're too late," says Ulrich.

"We're also not invited."

My backside hurts. When you've spent four years in prison, you're not used to riding a bicycle. I stop, get off, and pull my pants out of my crotch. Ulrich leans his bicycle against a fence. He gasps for air, the corners of his mouth turned down, like a fish on land.

"All this just because of your car," I say. "Even though you had four years to get it fixed."

It's supposed to be a joke. Ulrich growls. "If Heinz doesn't have the money, I'll kill him." He shows me his arm. The scalded spot is swelling into a red egg. As he climbs on the bike again, his foot slips off the pedal and his toes ram the asphalt. He flings the bike away and hops around on the other leg, his teeth clenched.

"What's the matter?" I ask.

"Nothing," he hisses, and climbs onto the bike again. I ride ahead. After a while he catches up. "God help him if he doesn't have the money," he says, his eyes small and red.

3.

We find City Hall and push our bicycles into a bike stand.

"Have you ever noticed that everything's purple here?" asks Ulrich.

"Sure," I say, and point to the scalded spot on his arm.

"Nonsense," he says. "I mean the streetlights, the signs, the bike stand. That's purple, isn't it? Or is it dark violet?"

A woman comes out of the building. I ask where the registry office is. She laughs, tilts her head, and looks us up and down. "A friend of ours is getting married today," Ulrich tries to explain. I think she thinks we're gay.

The registry office, we learn, isn't in Voerde's City Hall, it's in "Haus Voerde," which is a castle with a moat. The woman tells us how to get there. Then she takes a little town map out of her bag and gives it to us. Meanwhile Ulrich is sitting on a bench and has taken off his right shoe and sock. The nail of his big toe is swimming in blood.

"Have you hurt yourself?" asks the woman.

"He's always bleeding from somewhere or other," I say.

Ulrich taps carefully on the nail and sucks in air through his teeth. "That hurts right down to the bone!"

The woman walks slowly away across the plaza and turns to look at us. "Do you have to tell everyone why we're here?" I smack my forehead with my hand. "It's a small town. By tomorrow everybody'll know. That's why everything's purple. It's a warning color. The gossip zone."

Ulrich dabs at his toe. Then he tries to put on his sock and shoe again. Everything's too small, too tight, his arms are too short. Sweat oozes from his hair. "I want my money," he whines. "And then we're out of here."

4.

"We've got to be careful," I say.

The castle glows whitely between the trees lining the road. We can hear voices and loud laughter. We push the bicycles into the shrubs on the side of the road and walk toward Haus Voerde. There are several wedding parties there. A large group is having a photo taken in front of the castle as a smaller party makes its way up the path.

"Out of here, move!" I push Ulrich back toward the street.

He limps and groans with every step. "The pain's making me crazy," he says.

We hide behind a tree. The bridal couple poses for a photo on a bridge over the moat. The bridegroom is Heinz. With his gray face and black suit, he looks just like a waiter from a basement nightclub who never sees the light of day. Next to him is his blonde bride in a yellow dress. She probably tends bar in the same nightclub.

Someone hands her a white bouquet of flowers. Just for the photo.

"Let's just walk in," says Ulrich.

"And if it gets serious? There are too many of them."

Down at the street, Heinz's wedding party gets into three cars.

"Let's go." I grab my bike. "We can't afford to lose them."

Ulrich turns to go and promptly runs into a tree.

5.

"Stupid bikes," I say. We're riding through a field, directly into the wind.

"I want my money," moans Ulrich. I turn to look at him. A drop of blood from the scrape on his forehead is running up into his hair, driven by the wind.

We find the cars in a parking lot in Götterswickerhamm, in the adjacent part of town. The wedding party is sitting in a restaurant with a view of the Rhine. We put the bikes in a rack. Heinz is just coming out of the restaurant with another man. They light cigarettes. When they inhale, their faces become bony, their eyes seem to recede in the sockets.

"Let's go get the money," says Ulrich, his face like a pufferfish. He limps toward the restaurant. Heinz recognizes him and his eyebrows shoot upward. He leaves the other man standing there and comes toward us.

"You're out?"

"We want the money," Ulrich sings out.

"Sure. You'll get it."

I shake Heinz's limp hand. "Congratulations."

"How do you know about the wedding?"

"*Some* people got a wedding announcement."

"I didn't know . . ." Heinz spreads his arms. "Well, I've got to get back."

He shows his yellow teeth.

"We're coming with you," says Ulrich.

Heinz curls his upper lip. You can see the narrow stumps of his teeth. They have cavities. "Nope," he says. "It's a wedding party. If I'd known you were out, I'd have sent you an invitation, honest."

6.

"If he doesn't have the money, I'm going to kill him!" Ulrich is behind me, sweating. We're pedaling through the fields again. I let him catch up with me. The noises he's making sound just like the bicycle seat squeaking and the chain scraping.

"You could have used those four years to lose a few pounds," I say.

"I want my money," he says, as if he's drunk with the exertion.

On the little town map, Heinz has marked the neighborhood where he lives. Friedrichsfeld am Markt. By the time we get there, Ulrich is completely exhausted. He drops heavily into a chair at the cafe and orders a cherry ice cream sundae. He eats it, choking and coughing. I order espresso.

"You get stomach cancer from that—and those deep lines from your nose to your chin," says Ulrich, pointing at the tiny espresso cup.

"I've had those lines all my life."

Ulrich eats another ice cream sundae, this time with straw-berries. I order cappuccino. Heinz doesn't turn up.

"Let's go, we're going to his place," says Ulrich. "I want my money. And then I'm going to kill him."

"It's his wedding day."

"So what?"

We get up and walk to the bikes. The front tire on Ulrich's bike is almost flat. I give him my pump. His hand slides off the valve and he catches his little finger in the spokes. I pump up the tire for him. Heinz emerges from one of the apartment build-ings. So that's where he lives. He waves us over to the middle of the plaza. He looks around him and talks softly.

"Listen, I can't get my hands on the money right away. It'll take awhile. Can't you come back in a few days?"

Ulrich shakes his head and sucks on his little finger.

I explain to Heinz about the car trouble. We follow him to an ATM. Five hundred, the machine won't give him any more than that.

7.

"Why didn't I just kill him?" Ulrich's little finger is swollen. He spreads his fingers on the handlebars as he rides.

"It's his wedding night," I say. "We'll get the money."

We're on our way through the fields again, pedaling back to Voerde. There's a hotel at the train station there. Heinz called and booked us a room. Ulrich rides slower and slower. He says he ate too much ice cream. He begins to weave and wobble and his face glows in the twilight as if it's sunburned. He says his stomach is pulling him from one side to the other. I let him ride ahead and set the pace, but just then his front wheel runs into a pothole and gets stuck. The bicycle tips over and Ulrich sails, arms outstretched, into a cornfield. I help him up, dust him off. His shirt has pulled out of his pants.

"Just look at that," he says, and pulls the shirt up higher. He has blood on his belly.

"I want my money," he says.

I wipe his belly clean with a Kleenex. A sliver of glass from a broken bottle is still sticking out of his skin. I pull it out.

"You should be glad you're so fat," I comfort him. "This was just stuck in a layer of blubber."

Ulrich sits by the side of the road, his hand pressed on the wound. I kneel down in front of him and look directly at him.

"I'm going to die," he says. He looks almost as if the beads of sweat are tears.

"Heinz is just bullshitting us," he says. "We should go back right now and demand the money."

"Tomorrow," I say, and point to the sky. "It's getting dark."

"No. Now," says Ulrich. "Tomorrow I'll be dead."

He braces himself and gets to his feet.

"You know what, we're going to kidnap him and extort the money from his wife. She knows where it is, I'll bet. That's why she married him. I mean, a guy like that, he looks like death. Why else would anyone marry him?"

8.

"We had an accident," I say into my mobile phone. "Ulrich's hurt. We're down here in front of the building."

"I'll come down," says Heinz.

There are four apartments in the building. Heinz's name isn't on any of the buzzers, just his wife's. We station ourselves on both sides of the door to the street. When Heinz comes out, Ulrich hits him on the forehead with a flat rock. I catch Heinz, and together we pull him back into the house, to the door to the cellar. I search through his pants pockets for the key. I can tell he's gotten thin. Just skin and bones. The pores in his face are much larger than they used to be. "You killed him," I say. Heinz's eyes are open, but he doesn't say anything or move.

I try all the keys in the cellar door until I find the right one. Ulrich tips Heinz over his shoulder. There's an old sofa in the cellar. We lay him down on it and tie him up with an extension cord.

"I'll go upstairs," says Ulrich.

"Let me do that," I say. "You'll just scare her." I point to his belly. It hasn't stopped bleeding. His whole shirt is bloody.

"Hurry up," he says. "I don't have much blood left."

9.

"Congratulations," I say. "I'm a friend of Heinz's."

"My husband will be right back." She laughs. "That sounds strange: 'my husband.'"

She asks me to come in. In the living room there's a bottle of champagne with two glasses. She laughs again. For no reason. Up close, she's older than I thought. Giggling, she introduces herself as Elisabeth and gets a third glass from the kitchen.

"I used to work with Heinz," I say.

"You mean when he was with the security service?" She laughs again. "I've never had a job," she laughs.

I tell her the story of the armored car. The whole story of the heist; of Ulrich, Heinz, and me. And then I say: "We've kidnapped Heinz. If you don't give us the money he owes us, then . . ." I draw my hand across my throat.

She smiles, bends forward, and asks, "Another glass?" And then she just pours. I think she must not have been listening, or maybe she's not right in the head and doesn't understand what I'm saying.

"Did you understand what I just said?"

"Yes. No." She laughs. "Heinz, that is, my husband, will be here in a minute."

"No, he won't." I stand up and bend over her, so close that I can feel her breath. "We've kidnapped Heinz," I shout. "We want our share. One hundred thousand euros. There's got to be that much left. And if you call the police, I'll tell them all over again about the armored car. Because we've done our time. Heinz hasn't."

She kisses me on the nose.

"You're sweet," she says. "But I don't know where he gets his money."

10.

"She doesn't know anything," I say.

In the dim light of the cellar, Ulrich and Heinz look Chinese.

"She doesn't know anything," says Heinz.

"I want my money," says Ulrich. He's holding his left hand.

"What happened?"

Heinz tries to sit up. "He mangled his fingers in that cabinet over there," he says. I go over to the cabinet and open it. There's wine in a rack inside.

"Open a bottle," says Heinz.

I use a screwdriver to push the cork down into the bottle, and drink a few mouthfuls. Then I give the bottle to Ulrich. He drinks and then holds the bottle up to Heinz's mouth.

"You're gonna knock out my teeth," Heinz complains.

"Where's the money?" I ask.

"Come on, tell us. You can see I'm dying," says Ulrich. "Shot in the gut. You can see. But first you talk." The wound in his belly looks like it's still bleeding.

"I changed the money into small notes, just a little at a time, and then I buried it. There's a transformer station behind the water tower. With three big fat generators." He laughs. "A hundred thousand volts for a hundred thousand euros. Easy to remember. It's lying a couple of feet underground. But you can't get to it. It's live, see. They only turn off the power once every three years to inspect the place. And you can only dig it up then. So you'll have to come back in three years."

"Nice story," I say. "Okay, then, we'll do that. Of course, you won't mind if we take your sweet little wife with us. We'll bring her back in three years, just a little the worse for wear."

"That's enough!" says Heinz. He closes his eyes and presses his lips together.

"You can kill him now," I say to Ulrich.

Heinz begins to tug against the extension cord. "Okay. I took all the money and bought a snack bar. Honest. Ask Elisabeth."

11.

Heinz has a lump on his forehead. It's getting bigger.

Elisabeth opens the garage door in the dark. Inside, a black station wagon gleams faintly.

"No money, you said? So where'd the car come from?" I ask.

"We got it for picking up supplies," says Elisabeth. "We'll buy the sausages directly from the factory."

Ulrich wants to drive, but as he walks around the car his pants get caught on something. The fabric tears.

"Not you," I say. "Get in the back with Heinz."

"I'll drive," says Elisabeth.

"Let me smell your breath," I say to her. She puts her arms on my shoulders and licks the tip of my nose. "Do you know today's my wedding night?" she asks. She tries to kiss me but I pull away from her.

"I'll drive," I say.

Ulrich pushes the still-tied-up Heinz onto the backseat and climbs in next to him. Elisabeth guides me onto a federal highway. After a short while we turn back toward Voerde.

"You're already past it," laughs Elisabeth. "You should have turned off back there."

I turn around and drive back. A dark road.

"Stop," says Elisabeth. Through the windows of the car we can see the snack bar on the other side of the road. Closed. Dark except for a neon tube twitching faintly over the counter.

"You have to see it by daylight," says Heinz. "It's a super place."

Paint is peeling everywhere. There's grass growing in front of the entrance. I look at Heinz, my mouth fallen open. "This dump?"

"It's lots bigger inside," he says.

"I'm going to kill him," says Ulrich.

12.

I don't want to get out. We all stay in the car, and Heinz tells us that he bought the snack bar a year ago from an old couple.

"They're only turning it over to me now. Next week," he says. "And there's a snack wagon, too. The old man used to take it to the farmers' markets. But then he went and died. And the old lady's sick and doesn't have anyone else. That's why it's been closed for two months now. I mean, what can you do? But we'll get the place into shape."

I look at Ulrich. He sits sunken into a heap on the backseat, his too-short arms and legs dangling from his body. Slowly he closes his eyes.

"You can make a first-class eatery out of it," says Heinz. "I'll hire a cook and the thing is practically the golden goose."

"It's a dump," I say.

"Bad location," says Ulrich. He shakes his head.

"They took you for a ride," I say.

"Shitty," says Ulrich.

"No, no, it just looks that way. I'll take the wagon to the markets and Elisabeth will run the snack bar here. In three years you'll have your money. With interest. It's really a good investment."

Elisabeth has gotten out of the car and is standing in front of the snack bar, arms outstretched, turning slowly in circles. We follow her and look through the windows. It's filthy.

"I want champagne," says Elisabeth. "How come they're not open?"

I untie Heinz. "I feel sorry for you."

Ulrich kicks the bicycle rack in front of the snack bar. He swears and hops around on the other leg. His face glows redly. Then he makes a fist and hits one of the glass panes in the door. It shatters.

"Let's get out of here," I say.

In the car, Ulrich winds the safety belt around his hand. He has a cut on the back of it.

"Idiot," I say. There's a packet of Kleenex lying on the dashboard. I toss them over the back of the seat to him.

13.

We take Heinz and Elisabeth home and drive the car back to the hotel at the train station in Voerde.

In our room, I unroll toilet paper and wind it around Ulrich's belly, fingers, hand, and big toe.

"At least we've got the car," he says.

"Won't get much for it if we sell it." I take off my clothes and get into bed. It's too warm for Ulrich under the covers. He lies on top of the bed like a lump of dough. "Tomorrow I'm going to kill him," he says.

I turn out the light.

"You know," I say after a while, "there oughta be a sign for the snack bar out on the highway."

"And a couple of flags out in front of the place," says Ulrich.

"Did you see, they didn't even have ice cream."

Ulrich tosses restlessly. "You can't get by these days just on sausages," he says. You've got to have Turkish *döner* sandwiches and hamburgers, that's what works. And soup—you've got to have soup, too."

"How do you know?"

"I used to work in a snack bar."

"Honest?"

"Yeah. That was a good time. You've got to have salads, too. I was good at those. They're easy. And I even introduced lunch plates. The place was really hopping then! But then I spilled the fryer grease all down my leg, and quit."

"You can do all that?"

"Sure. And crêpes, you need crêpes. Those are really good, lemme tell you."

I reach for the switch and turn the light on again.

"Listen, Ulrich," I say.

"I know," he says. "We'll take the snack bar."

Isaac Aisemberg

Ramón Acuña's Time

Translated from the Spanish by Donald A. Yates

A former director of the Argentine National Writers Guild, Isaac Aisemberg died in 1997. He was one of Argentina's most successful crime writers and enjoyed wide popularity. His celebrated story "Checkmate in Two Moves" was translated into nineteen languages, including English in the anthology Latin Blood *(1972), but none of his other work is currently in print in English.*

> *And on the seventh day God ended his work which he had made; and he rested on the seventh day from all his work which he had made.*
>
> —Genesis II: 2

I t so happens that the fiesta of the patron saint of Molinos, Our Lady of Candelaria, begins on the twenty-fourth of January and lasts until the celebrants surrender to utter exhaustion. Ramón Acuña, who was not from those parts, heard something about the celebration at the Molinos bank, but, being involved in his own concerns, he paid no attention to it.

Acuña had arrived from Buenos Aires not actually hounded by bad luck but rather, undone by his own underhandedness: a cheat at gambling and a perpetrator of shady business deals that rarely produced a gain. For Acuña had always been a petty crook, of no particular stature, one of those fourth-class felons that the police despised so much because they land in jail one day and then through the boredom or oversight of some judge end up out on the street the next. But in Buenos Aires he had run out his string, and even his fellow miscreants wanted nothing to do with him. He was an amateur from the word go.

So he began to look for new horizons. He saw the need to change the direction of his life and, if such were possible, his lifestyle.

Thus it was that after putting many miles behind him, he ended up in Molinos, situated in the distant northern province of Salta, and there encountered simple country folk, of the sort that extend credit even to strangers, welcoming them with unquestioned trust. He decided to make a new start, and set out to look for honest work. This, perhaps, because in some remote corner of his conscience there still remained traces of a sense of honor, the consequence of some single gene linked to the morality of his faintly remembered dead father, a law-abiding man who had cursed him on his deathbed.

"Can you handle accounting?" Señor Reyes asked him. He was the owner of the town's flour mill, a small-scale business that milled barely eighteen tons of wheat, which arrived from Orán, but that was sufficient to meet the needs of the district.

"I'm good with numbers, and I can manage accounting if it's not too complicated," Ramón replied forthrightly.

Señor Reyes smiled as broadly as his reserved small-town demeanor permitted, thus revealing teeth stained by tobacco and years of sipping on maté tea.

"We have an accountant," Reyes indicated. "You will be his assistant." And in keeping with the custom in Molinos, Ramón was not required to provide an identity card, nor was he asked for references.

They settled on a salary and Ramón took a room in a *pensión*, adapting to town life to the extent that his nature as a drifter permitted him to. For several months he carried out his duties with the seriousness typical of the mill's few employees. In his spare time, he would watch in wonder a spectacle that was completely new to him: the arrival of the wheat-laden trucks that filled the silos, the operation of the milling wheels, and the production of the flour, pure white and smelling of something clean and wholesome, that was finally placed in sacks destined to provide the bread for countless homes in the region.

He liked to stroll through the wide, shadowed streets of Molinos, eyeing the attractive village girls, whom he imagined to be receptive, although he never approached them because women never had any particular appeal for him, save for some fleeting relationship or an occasional physical urge.

He met all of the important men in town: the mayor, the justice of the peace, the police chief, and the pharmacist (there was no doctor). And he ended up sharing a table in the bar with the only Japanese in town, sipping the habitual vermouth while they chatted or discussed things that held little or no significance for him. In time, boredom set in, and along with the lackadaisical mood that descended on him, perhaps because of the oppressive heat, there came a faint twinge of nostalgia.

"Damned backwater town!" he grumbled after six months of life in Molinos, depressed by the solitude of his room, from whose window could be seen the single-story homes with red-tile roofs and beyond, far beyond, the mountains, which displayed the complete spectrum of colors of the landscape painter. But there was not even a railroad, only trucks. Nor was Molinos on the bus route. The only way to get out of town was to count on the friendship of one of the truckers or the driver of some passing antediluvian automobile. It turned out that Señor Reyes was the only person in town who owned a car.

Molinos had a small whitewashed church, a relic of the colonial days. Its priest was a corpulent, blond Italian, rotund and self-satisfied, who had come from God knows where. His name was Borello and he had preserved his Lombardic accent.

One day the priest spoke to Ramón:

"I never see you at Mass," he said.

"I've been planning to go," Acuña replied hesitantly.

"I'll be expecting you, then," the priest said, smiling, and continued on his way at a half-trot, as if trying to dodge the brutal rays of the sun that were beating down on the street, punishing the few passersby and a wandering, dazed dog.

I know how you feel, Ramón thought, regarding the poor animal, and headed on to the bank, where he regularly took care of deposits and check-cashing.

The bank teller confided to him.

"I'm from the city of Salta," he said, "and I was terribly bored here until I joined the Social Club."

Ramón had passed by the Social Club several times, but he had always preferred not to go in. Temptation lurked there. He had heard that people played for money, including the mayor, the justice of the peace, the priest (but only the Argentine card game *tute cabrero*), the pharmacist, several businessmen, and flour mill and bank employees.

It was Giménez, the accountant at the mill, who brought up the subject again.

"I'll put your name in and I'm sure that Señor Reyes will second your nomination. He's a member, but he never comes."

Christmas was approaching and the activity at the mill increased. They were not only receiving more grain from the normal sources, but were successful in marketing it all. It was gratifying to see the ancient machinery operating day after day around the clock at top efficiency. At that time, Señor Reyes was on the road from Monday to Saturday and always returned happy, having sold all the flour. An arrangement that used to be advisable only from time to time during the rest of the year now became routine. Reyes would leave blank checks that he had signed in advance. When a transaction was completed, the appropriate sum was written in and the accountant provided the second signature that the bank required. Everything was being done at a feverish pace that reminded Ramón of the hectic tempo of life back in Buenos Aires.

Before long, he began to feel that he was coming into his own.

He began showing up at the Social Club soon after his application had been quickly accepted. In the natural course of events, he won and lost, and then won and lost again. His fingers were now itching—as they did every day in Buenos Aires. Fingers that were eager to deal or to pick up cards and embark on a devious hand of poker that vividly brought back memories of his days in the capital.

During the first two weeks of January, Ramón alternated the demanding duties at the mill with visits to the poker tables that were often less than productive.

And when his fortunes hit bottom, Ramón Acuña did three things:

He practiced signing the accountant's name until he could produce a convincing facsimile and began to take forged checks to the bank, where they were cashed on the spot. He filled in the amounts of the checks with discreet sums and then falsified the sales receipts, a procedure that the accountant—a saint—never questioned, in part because the suppliers were so numerous at that time of year. He limited himself to presenting a single forged check at a time, so as not to arouse suspicion. And no one was the wiser. The activity at the bank was intense as well, because all the local businesses and their clientele were as busy as the mill.

The third step he carried out on the next Sunday. Inspired by the concept of public relations, he appeared at church and cordially acknowledged the presence of the faithful gathered there. Among those present was Señor Reyes, resplendent in his white Sunday outfit, alongside Señora Reyes, elegant, attractive, and subtly provocative. Reyes nodded his head with a certain air of solemn superiority, mixed with Christian fervor. And Ramón, following another direction of his plan, took confession—to the extent that in his position he could unburden his soul—bringing the wafer to his mouth and taking Holy Communion. After Mass, as he was leaving, the priest came up and spoke to him softly.

"We know that the paths that lead to God are infinite. It is all a question of choosing the right way."

His words were colored by his Lombardic accent. What he said was expressed in the tone of a holy saint who believes in and loves his fellow man and has complete faith in his ministry. Ramón considered that possibly he had overdone the dramatization of his religious fervor.

When he had finally made his way outside, the noon sun was beating down on the sidewalk and its brightness was nearly blinding. A glance at the brilliant blue sky told him that there was no hope for the slightest breeze to be stirred up. The air was oppressive and he felt like a hunk of meat in a stewing pot. He was assailed by a disturbing thought, but he dismissed it immediately. It was not right, the atheist and scoundrel said to himself, to bring God and the Devil together.

"Shall I take you somewhere?" asked Señor Reyes, pointing out his splendid late-model automobile. "I can take you to the bar or to the club."

"Thank you, sir," Ramón replied in a cultivated pious tone. "I attend Mass only rarely, but when I do, I like to sit alone in my room afterward and meditate."

He settled into the backseat of the car while Reyes took the wheel, seated next to Señora Reyes, who turned back toward Ramón, offering a friendly smile floating on a wave of perfume. The car started up, and Ramón could not repress a wave of envy toward Señor Reyes for his fine automobile and his lovely wife.

He tried to imagine what his old companions in Buenos Aires would think of him now. Arancibia, who knew what the north of the country was like, would probably say:

"Ramón has gone off his nut because of the sun, or maybe the lure of some lacy handkerchief doused in the perfume used by Señora Reyes."

Arancibia was an habitué of police stations and rarely emerged from the lower levels of the Hall of Justice.

Zaldívar, from the capital, who more than once occupied a cell in Villa Devoto Prison (in Buenos Aires) and was often a guest of the Olmos Prison (in La Plata), would doubtless observe:

"Ramón is getting on. He's doing a fine job. He has finally learned to take note of the things that are going on around him. Now he's a real professional."

On the morning of the twenty-third of January he cashed another of the special checks. The bank was crowded with people who were animatedly discussing something that was apparently of great importance. The teller blurted out a stream of words that mixed together things he didn't understand with the possibilities of romancing a few of the local females.

That night he went to the club. His fellow poker players were the chief of police, the pharmacist, and the justice of the peace. The card play was spirited. When dawn arrived, the only players left were those at Ramón Acuña's table. Ramón had started out with an incredible run of luck, and then began to lose consistently, until all that remained were a few coins in his pocket. A handful of small coins that weighed like lead.

He stumbled out of the club. The night was cool and the last of the stars shone brightly, seeming almost just within reach. Still, he thought in his humiliation, this was no time to be admiring the heavens. Moreover, he was sweating profusely, as if he were walking under the merciless sun that cracked open the earth and drove moisture out of the walls of the houses.

It was then that an idea that had been lurking in the back of his mind suddenly turned into a plan. So far, he had been taking single checks to the bank for fairly unimportant amounts. It was time now for a master move. The plan consisted in filling out several checks for large amounts, taking them to the bank and turning them into cash, and then getting a truck driver to take him to a neighboring town. And from there to another town that had a railroad station or that was on the bus route, and then disappear forever from Salta, from Molinos, from that suffocating town where, it was clear, there was no future for him.

He calmed down and slowly his confidence began to return. Deliberately, without altering his pace, he turned in the direction of the mill. Night was surrendering to dawn now, and dawn to the early-morning glimmer of the warming sun that was now appearing on the horizon. The mill was located on the outskirts of town and that gave him time to calculate the amounts he would place on the checks.

At that hour, there was no other soul about.

It was after seven in the morning of an inevitably torrid summer day. He could be sure that the townspeople would be snoring away in their gentle and blessed dreams.

There was no one around when he entered the mill office, whose door was never locked. The office was located in front of the silos and set aside from the main part of the operation.

He sat down at his desk. He didn't need to turn the light on. He took the pre-signed checks from the accountant's desk and began filling in the figures, then writing in the amounts, and once more imitating Giménez's signature.

He didn't hear the distant sound of an automobile that drove up and stopped. Nor did he hear the footsteps of someone approaching. Perhaps the sound of the car and the footsteps had been covered by the sound of the mill grinding on in full operation.

He looked up suddenly and encountered the angry gaze of Señor Reyes.

The expression on Ramón Acuña's face was not that of a model employee. On the contrary, it was that of a criminal, a thief, an embezzler caught with his hands in the till.

"What are you up to, Acuña?" Señor Reyes demanded.

"Sir . . . I . . ."

Señor Reyes snatched one of the checks from the desk, and then another.

Acuña was paralyzed, tears in his eyes, his face frozen.

"Swindling me, eh?"

"Señor Reyes . . ." Acuña managed to stammer. "I . . . I swear this is the first time." It was the whining of a trapped animal.

Señor Reyes took a deep breath, regarding him with scorn. And perhaps that scorn was the cause of what happened afterward. One can perhaps foresee certain things, but there are others that are not within the grasp of decent men like Señor Reyes, a simple miller from a town of humble people. There are the deceptions. Dark acts committed by the black sheep of the Lord's flock.

Señor Reyes's first intention was to gather up the checks, but he hesitated. Perhaps the poor devil who had gone astray would tear them up himself. Every sinner has his chance for redemption.

"Get out of here, Acuña. People like you make me sick. I don't want to lay eyes on you again. Not here and not in town."

Acuña didn't move. He was riveted to the chair, a miserable soul bathed in sweat. Señor Reyes turned and walked out of the room. Acuña finally drew air into his lungs. This was the moment to destroy the checks and run out. He had read that unexpected opportunity in Señor Reyes's eyes.

But there before him were the checks, urging him on. He stuffed them into his pocket and followed Reyes. The owner of the mill was striding decisively toward the silos. He was doubtless going to check on the latest deliveries. This was clearly more important to him than the squashed cockroach that he had left behind. Señor Reyes agilely climbed up the stairway that led to the top of one of the silos. Ramón was trailing him. He felt a sense of lightness that he had never known before.

He caught up with Reyes when he was looking down into the interior of the silo. Ramón's hand reached out for something and found a large set of iron tongs that someone had left there, and before Reyes could react he struck at him viciously until the man fell down, his head a battered and bloody mess. Ramón Acuña sucked into his lungs all the air in the world. He rejoiced.

If I throw him into the silo, he thought, *he won't be found for days.* An improvised crime, to be sure, but a perfect one.

He immediately set to work. But suddenly he had to stop. Two mill workers were approaching along the main walk below. By pure chance they didn't glance up toward where the attack had taken place.

Ramón moved the body away from the edge of the stairs to keep it from falling. He laid down the heavy tongs that carried the imprint of his bloody fingerprints.

He was now seized by a sudden sense of panic that had erupted from some corner of his conscience. He hastily went down the stairs, arranging his clothes and trying to produce a smile on his parched lips. But the workers had already disappeared into the shed where the empty flour sacks were stored.

Ramón Acuña went over to Señor Reyes's automobile. The key was in the ignition. A satisfied and calmer smile came over his face. It was still his time to be lucky. He noticed that the fuel-gauge needle rested almost at empty.

In a few minutes he had reached town and parked near the bank. It was three minutes to eight o'clock. He had to wait only 180 seconds. The seconds ticked by and the three minutes were up.

At that moment several loud explosions broke the silence. The homeless, flea-bitten dog he had seen in the streets before came running up to him. His ears were laid back and his tail was between his legs. The dog looked at him, terrified. He was asking for protection.

At that moment, in the distance, the sound of strident music could be heard, apparently produced by out-of-tune violins and wind instruments to the accompaniment of rocket bombs.

Ramón was the only person in the street, which was strangely empty for eight o'clock in the morning. Suddenly, in the distance, he saw a group of bedraggled children, none of whom could be older than seven. They were laughing and cavorting in a ragged procession. Behind them came the miserable band, playing a monotonous and tuneless march.

Then came another group of older children, dancing, leaping about, and circling the band like a swarm of bluebottle flies.

And after them, preceded by a group of barefoot men, husky and sweaty, came a rustic altar adorned with ribbons and rosettes of bright colors.

And after them a group of village girls in their best outfits, which accented wide hips, breasts as full as ripe peaches, shapely legs, and feet adorned in high heels, no doubt the alluring local girls that the bank teller had referred to. They kept their gaze lowered, and in their hands they held rosaries and missals.

Next came horsemen, the typical northern gauchos with their wide-brimmed hats, seated on high saddles, riding on elegantly trimmed horses.

And then the pharmacist and his wife, the police chief and his wife, the mayor and his wife, and the schoolteachers in their white smocks, each carrying an Argentine flag.

Another rocket went off and the sound momentarily blotted out the squeal of the music. The miserable, terrified dog quickly crawled under the automobile.

Ramón watched other townspeople parade by—Gutiérrez, the bank teller, other workers from the mill—as well as people from other nearby towns and the truckers that brought the wheat and others that carried off the flour. The band continued playing and then was joined by the church bells that began to peal.

He saw him as if he were by himself but still a part of the celebration: the Japanese from the bar, wearing a long jacket, a caricature of the Emperor. A few steps behind came the Turk, Salim, who owned the hardware store, decked out as if he were going to a wedding. And then there were women dressed in black with colorful kerchiefs on their heads, with their youngsters and babies, and high-spirited young girls, and excited dogs barking at everyone. It was the very picture of simple joy, a fiesta celebration.

They were all on their way to celebrate the day of the Virgin of Candelaria, whose image occupied the main altar of the church.

And Ramón, again transfixed, saw the priest Borello join the procession. The priest spied him and greeted him with the serene confidence of the blessed, exuding a sense of satisfaction over having brought his flock together.

And now Ramón Acuña understood that January

twenty-fourth had arrived. The festival would last for nine days, during which everything would be shut down, closed, locked up: the bank, the gas station, all businesses except the mill, which would continue operating at full capacity so that there could be bread on everyone's table. And during those nine days no trucks, save for those carrying flour, would leave the place. And now he could not return with the automobile to the mill and arrange to get a ride out of town seated next to some willing trucker.

Here was Señora Reyes, alone, waiting for her husband, who would surely arrive at any moment, and looking suspiciously at the car in which Ramón was seated.

Now he was isolated, there in the automobile, with no gas, with the worthless checks, as useless as the few coins in his pocket that seemed to be burning his body, as if the sun had penetrated his clothes and his flesh, while his feet and hands were like ice and his heart as heavy as lead. And back there was the body of Señor Reyes, on the upper level of the silo, within full view of any worker who might pass by.

He remembered the confused words about the fiesta that now whirled around in his exhausted memory, and accepted the fact that his time had finally come.

Richard Macker

A Deadly Joke

Translated from the Norwegian by Jorunn and Michael Fergus

The Richard Macker (a.k.a. Reidar Thomassen) story "A Deadly Joke" was first published as the title story in a collection that Norway's largest publishing house, Aschehoug, brought out in 1986 in honor of the author's fiftieth birthday. That same year, the story was filmed by NRK (Norway's premier TV station) and shown at the Easter holidays. Macker worked as a teacher and magazine editor before his first novel came out in 1969 and received a literary prize. In the 1970s, he penned his first novel in the crime genre and it was adapted for a series on Norwegian TV. He has been honored since with numerous awards for his short crime fiction. It is surprising that a writer who has enjoyed such phenomenal success in his own country has so far only seen print in English in the Passport to Crime series.

Karl Rynndal moved a black rook. Then he leaned back and stared at Olav Morvik with a triumphant expression on his grizzled, sunburnt face.

"Just put on your thinking cap, if you have one," he said with some irony. "It's checkmate again."

Olav Morvik was shorter and had a smaller build than Rynndal. His hair was thinner, his beard lighter and sparser. His glance remained fixed on the pieces on the board, as if he simply would not acknowledge yet one more defeat.

"Now you have just experienced an example of the Staunton attack," said Rynndal pedantically. "Named after the great English grand master Howard Staunton."

"He is of absolutely no interest to me," said Morvik with irritation.

"No, quite. You take no interest in the theory of the game or its history, so you are doomed to lose. You know nothing of Howard Staunton. Or of José Capablanca, Aron Nimzowitsch, Tigran Petrosjan, or any of the other great grand masters. But I have made an intense study of how they played. Maybe you knew that?"

"All I know is that you have a pretty big mouth," said Morvik in annoyance, as he swept the pieces from the board in one restless move. Then he added, "If you are so bloody good, why don't you enter the Norwegian championships, then?"

The question, and Morvik's irritation, seemed to amuse Rynndal.

"I'm afraid I regard myself as too good. All these competitions are like flypaper for the mediocre. Have you ever seen the most beautiful women entering a beauty competition? No, never. Have you ever seen the most intelligent and able people in this country taking part in politics or playing competition chess? No, never. Those who belong to the elite have enough to do manning the pumps and keeping the ship afloat, whilst the mediocrities do their best to sink it, or concern themselves with issues of no value to society."

A dark shadow crossed Olav Morvik's face.

"This megalomania is really beginning to get on my nerves, Karl. And you're becoming worse. I'm seriously concerned about how it is all going to end up for you."

Rynndal opened his mouth and uttered an almost soundless laugh. His light blue eyes shone.

"You're a bad loser, Olav," he said. "But let us have another game so that you get a chance to prove me wrong."

"No, thanks."

"Well, it's understandable. Anyone can give up after six defeats in a row."

Morvik said nothing. All that could be heard was the crackling from the fireplace and the howling of the wind outside. They had been confined to that little cabin by the weather for more than twenty-four hours and had long since begun to grate on each other's nerves.

They were clad in ski stockings, wind-proof trousers, and thick woollen sweaters. On the table between them stood coffee cups, a bottle of whiskey, and the chessboard. On a plate lay a pile of sliced lamb sausage and some slices of bread with a thick layer of butter. They had what they needed, and they still had another week of their Easter vacation. They had worked out that they could cover a distance of 300 kilometers on skis in the course of ten days. The trip had been well planned, and the cabin they were in now belonged to a colleague of Rynndal's. For the first few days, everything had gone as planned, but now it seemed as if the weather was going to stop them for good.

Morvik folded the chessboard and put it away. "We could take a round of hard poker," he said gruffly.

"We've played poker twice as long as we have played chess."

"Not hard poker."

Rynndal stared at Morvik with his shining eyes. And then he laughed again. "I don't play hard poker with civil servants of limited means," he said. "I don't have the heart to."

"No, indeed. You prefer to play when you are a hundred percent sure of winning, is that it?"

Morvik had placed all the chess pieces in the box and put the lid on and rattled it as if to emphasize his exasperation. Rynndal watched him with a smile. Then he yawned and drummed his fingers on the table. Suddenly he got up, went to a bookshelf, and leafed through some books that were there.

"Well, my goodness, what a collection of dirty books," he said after a while. "And I thought my colleague had at least a modicum of intellect. I see I am going to have to revise my opinion. There is absolutely nothing here with which to pass the time in a sensible fashion, apart from the chess set. Such a pity that you are so completely hopeless in that department, too, Olav."

Morvik still had that gruff expression on his face. "If you are so extremely bored," he said, "you could lie down in your sleeping bag and sing yourself a lullaby. In fact, the less I see of your arrogant face, the better it is for me."

Rynndal wasn't smiling anymore. He had unlocked a corner cupboard and was going through the shelves inside. Morvik got up and put some birch logs on the fire. When he had sat down again, Rynndal had positioned himself in the chair right opposite him. He was staring and his voice had taken on a brittle, metallic quality.

"I think it's time I made you aware of a couple of essential facts," he said. "First and foremost I want to emphasise that I left secondary school with absolutely top marks. You should also know that I then took my medical degree with honors and that my doctoral dissertation on hormonal functions in the adrenal glands brought me a research award which is very highly regarded. To put it briefly, as a person I count for a great deal. But what about you? Who are you? A typical mediocrity, with a pitiful degree in economics and some mindless function in the government bureaucracy."

Morvik's mouth fell open. A distinct reddening replaced the tan on his cheeks. "Things have really gone further than I had imagined, Karl," he said, slowly shaking his head. "Your conceit has completely gone to your head."

"It's not conceit but the truth."

Morvik was silent for a bit, and looked as if he wished himself a thousand miles away from this place. "That one should be subjected to this!" He sighed. "Here we set off on a trip in all friendliness, and then—"

Rynndal interrupted him in a cold, cutting voice. "Friendliness. Are you really using that word, Olav? You who from the very beginning have been planning to take my life?"

"Take your life? What is it you are saying, man?" Morvik had raised himself, shaking with irritation.

"Sit down," said Rynndal, without raising his voice. "Just take it completely easy. I know what you are hatching. But you will get nowhere, because I have this."

He stuck his hand into the pocket of his wind-proof trousers and fished out a pistol.

"I'm not stupid, Olav. I took my own precautions when I understood what you were planning."

Morvik sank slowly back into his chair, as if he was wanting to waken from a bad dream. "Your mind must be going. You must be raving mad."

"It's either you or me, Olav."

"Me or you—What sort of bullshit is this?"

"It's a matter of life. For me or you. It's as simple as that."

Morvik broke into a cold sweat. "Listen, Karl," he said hoarsely, "have you forgotten what we agreed on for this trip? We've been on many trips together, and we've discovered that we can test our powers against the elements. Yesterday we skied fifty kilometers in bad weather. You are still overtired, and you need a lot of sleep. Give me that toy gun, and I'll forget what you said."

Suddenly a deafening shot rang out from the pistol. The bullet went into the fireplace and ricocheted off the stone wall with a whine. Then came a laugh from Rynndal, dry and sarcastic. "Toy gun, did you say?"

Morvik sat bunched up in shock. And his breath began to heave. "You're completely crazy."

"I've never felt more sane."

They were silent for a bit. Then Morvik drew a quivering hand across his face. "And why would I want to kill you?"

"Because of Greta."

"Greta, your wife?!"

"Yes."

"What in God's name have I got to do with her?"

"You're having an affair with her."

"I'm having an affair with Greta? It's beyond me how you can come up with such a lunatic accusation. I've never been anywhere near her."

"Don't give me your lies."

Morvik sat open-mouthed. Then he laughed nervously. "But don't you hear what I say! I've never touched her. She's not my type. And I am definitely not hers, either. The fact that she married you reveals her dubious taste in men."

"Don't try to wriggle out of it with your untruths, Olav. Just sit quietly and listen to an interesting little story from life. About Otto Hall. Surely you remember him?"

Morvik didn't reply. He just sat there hunched up with anxiety and anger.

"Sure," continued Rynndal lingeringly. "Otto Hall is a mutual friend of ours from childhood. I know you remember him. Alas, he died twenty years ago. At that time, we were both studying medicine and he was going out with Greta Wikan, as she was called then. I was very much in love with her and their relationship was, to put it mildly, inconvenient for me. I had to do something."

"What do you mean, 'something' . . . ?"

"Yes, and as you will recall, Otto was a keen mountaineer. One day he was going to tackle a precipice on the training grounds at Bergkollen. Unfortunately he never made it to the top. But he came down, all right, twenty meters straight down. I knew that he was going to try this precipice, and I put a sedative in his thermos flask just before he was to set out."

"So you . . . murdered him," whispered Morvik.

"Rather we should say that I made my move in chess and defeated him."

Morvik leaned forward, his hands cupped over his knees. "And you sit there and admit it openly. What do you think Greta will say when she gets to know this? And what do you think the police will say?"

"Don't be funny, Olav. You know that neither Greta nor the police will get to know our little secret."

"So you are thinking of killing me, too?"

"Yes."

"Why?"

"I've already explained that."

"You've got no proof for your crazy accusations. I've already told you I've had nothing to do with Greta. Are you going to kill an innocent man in cold blood?"

"She has whispered your name in her sleep several times: 'Olav, oh, Olav,' she whispers. That is proof enough for me. That and this trip you convinced me to come on."

"Is that your only evidence? There are thousands of men called Olav."

"You are the only one in our circle of acquaintances with that name. That's enough for me."

"You're off your head."

"And you are repeating yourself."

Morvik's glance began to roam, and he seemed to be in a

panic. "Fair enough. You can shoot me. So go ahead and shoot me. You will have problems explaining everything to the police afterward when they find a bullet-riddled corpse. I can assure you that you will have problems."

Rynndal smiled. "Your thinking is as naive as ever, Olav. You are going to die, but afterward no one will suspect me of murder. I'll give you two choices. You can go out of the cabin as you are and start walking. If you go out you are not taking your rucksack, your skis, or the rest of your clothes. You'll manage for twenty minutes. Yes, maybe half an hour with your physique. And then that's it."

"And if I choose to remain here?"

"The result will be the same. First of all you will fall asleep. Then I can put you outside so that you freeze to death. Or I can put you in your sleeping bag in the room you sleep in and arrange for a fire in your sleeping bag. Everyone knows you are a heavy smoker. Either outcome will produce easily explainable results. No one will ever accuse me. We are known to be the best of friends."

"But why should I fall asleep? Maybe you will do so before me."

"No, because you have already taken a sleeping pill."

"What?"

"Yes, while you were stoking the fire, I put some easily dissolved sleeping pills into your coffee, and you have drunk it all up. Are you maybe beginning to feel a little drowsy?"

Morvik had gotten up. "You're . . . lying," he said inarticulately.

"Think what you like."

Beads of sweat ran down Morvik's face. "Listen, Karl," he said with a failing voice, "I've never had anything to do with Greta. I swear it."

"You are wasting your time."

Morvik crossed the floor slowly and went out into the

passageway. "I choose to die outdoors," he said hoarsely. "I refuse to stay one second more under the same roof as a mad executioner like you."

He hesitated a little before opening the door. The blizzard and the icy wind blew in over him from the darkness outside. He stood there a moment, pale and swaying. He took a step out into the deep snow, and at the same moment he heard Rynndal's sarcastic laughter right behind him.

"My dear Olav, you are taking me seriously. Don't you see that this was a joke? Close the door again before we both freeze to death."

Morvik turned round slowly. It looked as if he was going to faint. He stumbled in, pulled the door closed behind him, and sank down onto a stool.

"Joke," he muttered, half choking. "Do you call that a . . . joke?"

"Sure. Are you disappointed that it is not for real, maybe?"

"But what about the sleeping pills?"

"That was a mere bluff, of course."

"And the pistol?"

"I found it in the corner with a whole packet of ammunition. We can be sure that that colleague of mine is careless with his weapons. But he shoots in competitions, and usually trains up here in the mountains. Here is the pistol. I only put one cartridge in the barrel. The magazine is empty."

Morvik seemed still completely paralyzed. With a shaking hand he grasped the gun. Then he got up and took a step forward with raised fist. It seemed as if he was going to strike Rynndal a blow in the face. "This time you have gone too far," he said, blazing with anger.

"But I was provoked into doing it. You have repeatedly accused me of being a megalomaniac. And you know that is a form of madness. I had every reason to play a trick on you."

"Idiot!"

"But listen, Olav, why are you reacting in this way? If anyone here should be offended, it should be me. The fact that you fell for that spoof showed that you have a disappointing lack of confidence in me. You must have realized that it was one great bluff. Would I ever go round thinking that Greta, who loves me more than life itself, would betray me with you? And you actually thought that I had murdered my old friend Otto Hall. And that I would kill you? A murderer? Me? No, Olav, it is I who should be offended. You have wounded me deeply."

"Shut your mouth! I could have given you a real beating for that," said Morvik, quivering.

"That you could hardly have done. I'm bigger and stronger than you."

Morvik put the pistol on the table. "You can regard our friendship as finished as of tonight," he said bitterly.

"But my dear Olav. This was only a somewhat advanced form of party game. A bit rough at the edges, perhaps. But amusing to look back on, is it not? Our friendship can surely take a small knock?"

Morvik cast him a cool glance, and made his way to the room where he had his sleeping bag. But suddenly he stopped and pricked up his ears. Rynndal did the same.

There was something like a wail from outside, and it wasn't the wind, either. The sound grew louder and suddenly there was a fearsome banging on the door. Someone was screaming out there.

"What in God's name . . . Someone is coming." Morvik and Rynndal both started speaking at the same time. At the same instant the door burst open and in came a frozen figure covered in snow, with an anorak hood pulled down over the head. It was a man in his thirties.

"Help me," he groaned. "Help me before I freeze to death."
He sank where he was and lay still on the floor.

After half an hour, the frozen and exhausted man began to come
to. They had put him beside the fire and gotten some coffee into
him together with a sip of brandy. He said that he worked as a shop
assistant in the local village shop, and his job at Easter was to trans-
port goods by snow scooter to people vacationing in holiday cabins
in the mountains. But in the bad weather he had lost the track and
was literally out in the wilds. And then his snow scooter had failed.

"Ten minutes more out there and I'd have been a dead man,"
he muttered.

The three men sat and chatted. The newcomer was taciturn,
and stuttered in the beginning, but as time went by, the lively
Rynndal got him to thaw out. Morvik did not say much. Almost
all of the time Morvik sat and stared at Rynndal with a bitter
expression on his face, as if he would never forget the macabre
joke he had just been subjected to. Before he went to bed, he
took out his little pocket radio from his rucksack.

"The weather will have to get better for me to get away from
this place," he muttered to himself as he snuggled down into his
sleeping bag.

Reception was very poor, but not so bad that he could not
pick up the weather-forecast broadcast together with the midnight news. The weather would clear up soon.

"Excellent," muttered Morvik. Then he pricked up his ears as
the announcer read out a special news item. When Morvik had
heard it, he switched off the radio, sat up, and stared rigidly
ahead. Then he crept out of his sleeping bag again. He could still
hear the two men talking in there, and he gathered that Rynndal
had generously given his room to the newcomer.

When everything was still, Morvik carefully opened the

door. Rynndal was lying on a sofa in the living room, deep in his sleeping bag. He was already asleep. Morvik leant over him and wakened him. Rynndal blinked and wanted to say something, but Morvik told him to be quiet.

"Listen to me now," he whispered. "There was just an extra item on the news on the radio. The police are looking for a tall, fair, powerful man who beat to death the cashier at Åslien Mountain Hotel and disappeared with thirty thousand kroner,[1] and a snow scooter. The hotel is not far from here."

"My dear Olav," Rynndal said evenly, "you have a charmingly naive way of getting your own back! In fact, I really feel sorry for you."

"But don't you hear what I am saying? We must do something. Don't you get it?"

Rynndal shook his head and gave an ironic smile. Morvik shook him hard. "I've got a plan," he whispered. "I'll go for help whilst you hold the man here with the pistol."

Rynndal chuckled with laughter. "You're an idiot, Olav. If you had come up with this bluff a month or two ago I might have taken you seriously. But this is just too banal, my dear friend. I am really beginning to think seriously that your mental equipment is beginning to fail. Everything points to it."

Morvik was feverish. "The pistol," he whispered. "Where is it? I put it on the table and now it is no longer there."

He went to the corner cupboard and began rummaging about. "It's not here, either," he said. "And the package with cartridges has also gone. The killer has barricaded himself in there with the gun. Don't you see that we have got to get away from here, Karl?"

Rynndal's voice became irritated. "Obviously you have hidden the weapon and the ammunition yourself, Olav. And

1. five thousand dollars

you're pretending that you have not. Not really a bad piece of bluff for someone like you. I'll surely tell our shop-assistant friend about your fantasies when he wakes up early tomorrow. Until then, goodnight, Olav. I am going to sleep now."

Morvik had given up. He sneaked into his room again and put on all his clothes, put on his anorak, and packed his rucksack. He put on his ski boots in the hall, so as to make as little noise as possible. Then he opened the outside door carefully and went out into the icy, stormy darkness. *I've got to make it*, he thought.

He battled his way through the wind and the blizzard. The rucksack, a spade, and all his other equipment made him feel more secure. He could dig a hole in the snow to shelter in if worst came to worst. He knew the mountains, and he was in good physical shape. The weather had got a little better and he could soon glimpse a pale moon above the tattered clouds.

On the last few kilometers it felt as if his legs would give way under him, but when he at last reached the tree limit with the small, characteristic mountain pass, he knew he was going to make it.

It was half-past two in the morning when he tottered into the reception at Åslien Mountain Hotel. Guests in party dress came out from the bar and restaurant to stare at him as if he was the Man on the Moon himself as he staggered towards the reception counter.

At daylight, three snow scooters headed across the snowy, wind-blown mountain plateaux. In one of them sat Olav Morvik, well wrapped up in thick clothes. In the others were the local police chief and his men. They were armed, and they were in a hurry. The police chief, a gray-bearded man in his mid fifties, had a hard, clenched expression on his wrinkled face, and his glance swept searchingly across the barren landscape.

They found the snow scooter snowed-under, half a kilometer from the cabin. The police chief checked it over and nodded to the others.

"This is the one he stole, that scoundrel."

They approached the cabin, at a good distance from each other. "Now we'll have to move carefully forward, guys." The plan was to surround it, and for Morvik to make another try to get Rynndal out.

"Let's hope the scoundrel is a heavy sleeper," said the police chief.

At that moment a shot rang out from the cabin, and they stiffened. A moment later a tall, fair man emerged from the cabin door. He was red in the face and looked desperate.

"Drop your weapon!" shouted the police chief.

The fair-haired man stood stock-still. When he saw all the armed police he dropped the pistol and put his hands in the air.

Morvik went slowly towards the cabin door. He opened it. On the floor by the sofa lay Karl Rynndal. In the middle of his chest, the thick Icelandic sweater was red with blood.

"Too late," whispered Morvik.

The killer had a hysterical note in his voice when he screamed, "I had to do it. This guy was babbling on the whole time that it was all a joke that his mate had planned with me. And then he wanted to take the pistol from me. I couldn't let him fool me that way, for God's sake!"

Morvik couldn't take his eyes off the dead man.

"Karl, you idiot," he whispered. "You poor, damned naive idiot."

Mischa Bach

Full Moon

Translated from the German by Mary Tannert

German writer Dr. Michaela (a.k.a. Mischa) Bach began her career as a journalist in 1982, while also writing plays. She soon became a contributor of scripts to German national TV, and in 2000 she added novels and short stories to her repertoire. This story, first published in German, was nominated for the Friedrich Glauser Award for best short story. When the first Mischa Bach novel, Der Tod ist ein langer, *appeared in 2004, it too was nominated for a Glauser award.*

AUGUST

She moved in the day after the full moon. The apartment next-door had been empty for months. All that time, Sally and I were alone on the top floor of the old house and I'd had the rooftops to myself. So when the noise of the moving men woke me that morning, the first thing I did was curse. Sally lifted her head and looked at me, startled. I got out of bed, shuffled to the door—trying not to make any noise—and took a look through the spy hole. A broad back filled up the hallway, followed by a large desk moving across my field of view and then another broad shoulder. At least it wasn't a piano, I thought. Then Sally's cold doggy nose on my hand reminded me that it was time for breakfast and sent me into the kitchen.

While I waited for the coffee to drip through the filter—I

hate coffee machines as much as I hate electric stoves—and Sally fell on the contents of her dog dish, I went into the bathroom. Last night it had been too late to clean up by the time I got home, and the place was a pigsty. I muttered under my breath. Normally, after the night of the full moon I sleep until noon and have at least two cups of coffee and several cigarettes before going into the bathroom. But what can you do? You never know what new neighbors might need to drop by for.

Later, when the moving van had left, Sally and I went down to the street. I took the bus out of the city, out to an abandoned industrial area. The land there next to the old factories runs down to the river. Nobody bothers you there, nobody asks questions. You see a couple of punks, maybe, barely old enough to call themselves teenagers. Sally lets off steam running around with their dogs, and I sit and smoke. Without having to talk to anyone or take any grief about my fire. But today nobody else was there. Probably they'd gotten a party going somewhere or had gone to the quarry lake. No wonder, in the heat. But that was fine, too; the day after a full moon I'd rather be alone.

Dearest Helen,

You were right—an apartment that's been empty as long as this one smells like a grave. It took almost a week of airing to get the smell out. Right now I've got all the windows wide open, the birds are chirping, and I can hear the noise of children playing and rush-hour traffic, far away. It's all slowly becoming livable, almost pleasant.

You were also right about the sloping eaves being a problem up here under the roof. I underestimated the proportion of roof to wall, and my big wardrobe wouldn't fit in the bedroom at all! So I had the movers set it up in the hall, which is otherwise just wasted space, and that way my two rooms seem just a little bit larger.

When I read this, I can practically hear you saying that I'm just trying to make everything sound rosy again! Oh, Helen, the next time I start to leave a city because of some man, tie me down, put me in chains, don't let me go! I hate starting over from scratch—a new apartment, new people at work, new stores, new pubs. Nothing's right, nothing's the same, I'm alone in the world and don't even have a familiar home to go home to!

I know I always said I wanted to work for an alternative news-paper. And the rest of the staff is really nice, much nicer than my coworkers in the editor's office of the Daily News. *Plus, there's something to be said for having a monthly deadline instead of a daily one! It's just that I didn't expect to have to write about a serial killer. I never dreamed I'd get an assignment like that at a left-wing, basically culture-oriented publication. They call him the Werewolf, and he murders right on time for our copy deadline, according to the editor. I find it all gruesome. But never mind, no point in scaring you sleepless. . . .*

By the way, you'd really like the local culture factory. Lots of exotic creatures from the dance scene, and I get to write about them, too, which really beats the local garden club and the poodle-breeders' association!

I have to stop now; I'm really tired. Write back soon and let me know how you're doing and when you're coming to see me! Lizzy

Elisabeth's her name, Elisabeth Deutschmann. It says so on her nameplate. I've seen her a couple of times over the past two weeks since she moved in. From the window and the roof she looked like a little girl, a child, but she could be older than I am—late twenties or even early thirties.

She doesn't seem to know anyone here. I think she must be new in the city, no one ever comes to see her. That's fine with me. It's bad enough having someone next-door at all. Not that she's noisy or bothers me. It's not like my mother's house—nosy neighbors constantly poking their heads in, but then they never really saw anything. Elisabeth's not like that. What I mean is, she doesn't pester me. She really doesn't. It's . . . it's more that she invades my thoughts. Sometimes I'll be sitting in the kitchen and I'll hear just a little noise from next-door and ask myself what she's doing. Imagine how she moves through the apartment. She's got light feet—she moves like a cat, you could see that much even from the roof. I imagine her, imagine myself with her, and then I could just cry. Things were fine as long as I only shared this house with the people below me; they didn't want anything from me and I didn't want anything from them. I was alone and that was okay. I mean, I've always been alone, no matter how many men I . . . I was alone. Okay, I was lonely, too, but it wasn't so bad. There wasn't anyone I wanted around me, except for Sally—half wolf, half dog, and as white as my soul is black. Sally doesn't care when I go for days without saying a word. She doesn't want anything from me except for me to be there, and she's always there for me. But even Sally's noticed the difference. She's always taken the four steps all at once, together, not stopping until she reaches our door. But now she stops, her tail wagging, at the door across the hallway.

She doesn't make a sound, of course, not even yesterday. But Elisabeth knew we were there. She opened the door, looked at Sally, looked at me, reached out and ran a hand over Sally, just like that, and started talking to me as if it were the most ordinary thing in the world. And I stood there like an idiot and couldn't even open my mouth, just kept nodding and working the key, trying to get my apartment door open, to get away. And now I can't get her out of my mind. She's gotten into my blood, under my skin, she's like a thorn in my flesh and I could cry, I could just howl.

• • •

Dearest Helen,

No, I'm not mad because you couldn't come, and I'm especially not mad because you'd rather take pictures of exotic cultures than be here. It was the opportunity of a lifetime, and it would have been idiotic not to jump at the chance! But I am sad; I miss you. It's been four weeks, and I'm still a stranger here. I've gone out for coffee with the others at the paper, and now I know where the local supermarket keeps my favorite yogurt, and I've even found two pubs to eat in when I don't feel like cooking just for myself or I can't stand sitting at home alone anymore. And people here in the Rhinelands are nice; it's not hard to strike up a conversation. Yet somehow nothing matters very much yet.

But it's not what you think. Thomas can kiss my ass (but only from a distance). I don't regret leaving him for a second. Even the strange man next-door would be preferable to Mr. I'm-the-greatest, Mr. Let-me-tell-you-how-things-really-work, Mr. For-God's-sake-what-are-you-doing-at-your-desk-again? Oh, but I completely forgot to mention him—the man next-door, I mean! He doesn't have a nameplate, but his name, according to rumor, is Frank. The others in the building had already warned me about him: Picture, if you will, a woman, mid forties, curlers in her hair, looking around sur-reptitiously and whispering behind her hand, "He's crazy, not quite right in the head, he's been in the loony bin at least once, y'see. . . . And that dog! That a man like that should be allowed to have that kind of dog, well, it's just not right!" I just shrugged my shoulders and told her I hadn't seen or heard anything of either of them. "That's just it," said the neighbor, "they're like ghosts, it's just creepy how you never see the two of them!"

Anyway, last week I heard a soft noise at the door. I went and opened it, and there they were. The dog stood there, wagging its tail—snow-white, beautiful, half wolf. Frank—and that really is his name; I found that out the third time I ran into him in the hall—

Frank turned bright red and verily fled into his apartment. At first I thought he was mute, but now I know he's just horribly shy. It's true that he's a little strange, but even so, what people think up is absolutely incredible! I'm still shaking my head. Your Lizzy

SEPTEMBER

The years I was in the hospital, the night of the full moon was one of the easier nights to get through. They would have given me a night-light, but that didn't work out; the staff said it bothered the other patients. And by the time I finally got my own room, the dark was part of their "therapeutic approach." At least, that's what they said. I was supposed to get used to reality, and in reality sometimes it's dark. But my reality—practically my entire life—had consisted of darkness: sometimes absolute silence and loneliness, sometimes voices, touches, sweat, pain. But dark, always dark. They didn't want to believe that, though. Meanwhile, the dark really doesn't bother me. I spend lots of nights in my apartment, just sitting, Sally next to me, staring out the window, just like that. But the night of the full moon, I go out, for months now. It doesn't mean anything, really. Actually, a new moon's better if you want to move around and not be seen, but Sally loves the full moon, loves being out in the moonlight. My ghostly wolf and I. I don't think anyone's ever seen us during those nights. Not even during the full moon in September, not even then. Coming home, when I unlocked the door I thought, just for a second, that I heard something, but I was wrong. Lizzy—the name's better than Elisabeth, Elisabeth always reminds me of a queen, it's so formal, or distant maybe—Lizzy would have opened her door and looked out if she'd heard me. So I went in, got in the tub, and let Sally lick my hands clean. And just for a little while, I felt quiet inside. But then Sally'd had enough, and I turned the water on again, let it run cold over my body, then warm and then hotter and hotter. Except that this time I didn't just sink into my black soul, that exhausted peace inside of me. This time, a picture of Lizzy came into my head. I didn't even notice it at first; it seemed completely natural, just as natural as the hard-on I got when I started thinking of her. Then Sally went to work licking the tears that were running down my face and I realized that nothing was the same anymore. But one way or another I can handle the loneliness one more month, I'm sure of that.

Dearest Helen,

Photographing circumcision rituals, that sounds horrible! I'm sure you never imagined your travel job turning out like that! On the other hand, be glad you're not at this publication; you might end up doing scene-of-the-crime photos! Remember I told you I was supposed to look into that werewolf business? Well, I didn't get to it last month, I was new and there was so much to learn, but now he's struck again—and the blow landed on me, so to speak. That sounds terribly cynical, I know; I ought to feel sorry for the poor man who was murdered during the last full moon. "Bestially hacked apart" was the description in the news—the media are speculating like mad that it was a ritual murder. The police (who, I have discovered, are much more likely to grant an interview if I show up in a suit and heels, but who really let down their hair when the interviewer's wearing hippie overalls!) would only confirm that he ties up his victims and wounds them so that they bleed to death. And since they never find any physical remains of whatever he uses to tie them up, he must stay at the scene for hours, maybe even until his victims die. There's evidence of a break-in, but he never takes any money or valuables. And the television's always set to the video channel, but the VCR's empty; he must take the videos with him. Beyond the type of murder and the fingerprints, which the National Enquirer *keeps referring to as "not human" (that means the perp wore no gloves—I learned that much during my "date" with the detective), there's no connection between any of the six victims. I admit, it's all very puzzling and makes for great sales figures, but are they really ritual murders? And what on earth could I possibly write about them in a monthly publication?*

Changing the subject: No, I haven't fallen in love with my taciturn neighbor, whatever makes you think that? I just feel sorry for him; there's something vulnerable about him, as if no one's allowed to get too close. Granted, you'll probably think I'm nuts when I describe him—almost six feet tall, thin, always wears black sunglasses (quite a contrast to Sally, the white wolf dog!) and gloves with the fingers cut off. But nobody who can be so kind to that giant dog could be a bad person! You should do a series sometime on people like him— loners at the edge—and their animals. Love, Lizzy

The last few weeks I catch myself watching for her. At the same time, inside I'm running away. But that's normal, at least as far as the word "normal" could ever apply to me. I ran from all of them, even when it didn't even help to run away, when it just landed me in a mental hospital because no one wanted to believe what I said about my life with my mother. A nurse. So patient, so caring with her son and her old father. And when I realized that no one would believe me, that I was completely, utterly alone with everything that had happened, then I swore that never again would another living human being get close enough to hurt me.

But Lizzy is different. Lizzy came to me, chose my company, and that made my loneliness, my bad blood, and the emptiness inside me even more unbearable. Sometimes she just comes down to the river with us, and plays with Sally. Sally loves her, and Sally can't stand people as a rule any more than I can. I can sit there for hours, just watching them. And it never bothers Lizzy that I mostly don't say anything. I think she even knows that when she talks to me I don't understand a single word because the sound of her voice just hypnotizes me. It's like a caress, her voice . . . and I almost quit because of her, almost gave up everything I've started, but I can't, I can't.

Just when I was getting used to her being there, was starting to hope that she, that I . . . that with her I could get past the loneliness, just for a while, just this once in my godforsaken life, then her friend turned up. And that's when Lizzy, my "quiet like a cat" neighbor, turned out to be just the same as any other woman, just a reporter with a nosy photographer for a pal. They wanted me to come over, a little party, don't make such a fuss, they said, a little human company won't hurt you. I refused, but they wouldn't take no for an answer; they had to come over and ask again, and when I opened the door the second time, a camera flash went off in my face, just like that. I lost my cool, grabbed the camera from her friend and threw it down the stairs. The photographer started to yell and carry on and Sally growled like crazy; I'd never seen her like that before. Not with a stranger. And then I spent the night in my dark apartment, holding my ears shut against the noise and wishing it was all over.

Dear Helen,

Just get over it, will you?! It can't matter that much to you who replaces your damn camera. After all, I warned you Frank is shy—how did you expect he would react to your little blitzkrieg?!! Basically the whole thing is your fault, but since my insurance is willing to pay for a new camera, I can't see what the problem is. Frank probably wouldn't be able to pay for it anyway. He hasn't spoken to me since last weekend—your doing, Helen, thanks a lot!—but I've been checking up on him. If even half of what I found in the archives is true, I wouldn't want to be in his shoes for all the gold in China. He grew up with his mother and grandfather. Evidently the old man was mentally disturbed. Whenever the mother was away at work, he locked up the boy, presumably because he was afraid for him. Frank must have had a developmental disability; he'd hurt himself pretty badly a couple of times in accidents, and the old man went to drastic lengths to prevent another one. Since Frank barely talked, even then, his mother only discovered the truth on the day the old man died: He had a heart attack in the kitchen, and Frank, who was ten years old at the time, was found chained up in the basement in the dark. Obviously this deeply disturbed him, because years later he claimed it had been completely different, that his mother had not only knowingly left him to his grandfather's devices, but that the two of them had even "sold" him for any "service" people would pay for! It was an utterly fantastic story, with masked men, people rising from the dead, none of it provable, but everything completely imaginable in the soul of a child that had been tortured for years. There were plans to commit him, but he ran away, was later found on the street, working as a prostitute, and spent the years between seventeen and twenty-one in a psychiatric hospital, where he finally came to grips with his life. After that, the trail is cold. Until now, three years later. I assume he gets some kind of social assistance, because I can't imagine he can work or be around other people like a normal person. And you're upset about your stupid camera! I don't get it. Bewildered, Lizzy

OCTOBER

I don't know what I thought about how it all would end. In any case, I didn't imagine anything more concrete than the fuzzy images from the few pleasant dreams I've had—not the stinking, grimacing faces of the nightmares, the demons that haunt me. I simply knew, the whole time, that it would end, and that the end would come with the full moon in October.

Yet even the days right before the full moon were different than usual. I was in the grip of something besides my usual restlessness, that old familiar mixture of urgency and fear in the pit of my stomach. Sally wouldn't move from my side; the last two days she wouldn't even let me go to the bathroom alone. At some point, I stopped being able to eat anything at all. It was as if both dog and body knew that my time had come. But it also seemed right that Sally should start to cling to me so much, because every morning this last week when I woke I asked myself what would become of her. After all, it's not her fault. When I started, about six months ago, I didn't waste a thought on how it would end for Sally and me, even though it was obvious to me before the first of the seven full moons that the seventh would be my last. Celtic princes were always buried with their wolf hounds, but I think that's barbaric. Anyway, I'm a long way from being a prince and she's half wolf, and just as shy of people as I am, into the bargain. I was torn by the thought that she might have to spend years in a cage, but I knew I wouldn't be able to kill her. Anything, but not that.

So I pulled myself together and went over to see Lizzy. I even went into her apartment. Even though Sally started to glue herself to me. Still, it was clear that she didn't have anything against Lizzy and Lizzy didn't have anything against her; I was the one who had to face down his fears. So I stammered out an apology, saying how sorry I was about her friend's camera, and everything else. I got so worked up that it took me a long time to notice that Lizzy wanted to interrupt to tell me that that was all taken care of and anyway she had been really angry at her friend's behavior. Then I didn't know what to say, just stood there, embarrassed. Lizzy finally got her jacket—maybe she could sense that Sally was worried or she understood how hard it was for me to be in her apartment, a stranger's place—and we went out, down to the river.

I talked more that afternoon than in all the months before

added together, more even than during all the years in the hospital, I think. Mostly about dogs, about Sally. What she likes, what she needs, what she hates. I even told Lizzy how I'd gotten Sally: On the day they released me from the hospital, Sam, one of the staff, had pressed a tiny bundle of woolly dog into my arms. Because I had wanted nothing so much all those years as a dog. Because he had dogs himself, and he knew: Forget treatment plans, forget group, forget individual therapy, medication, the whole nine yards. Nothing pulls a soul back into the here and now like a dog. Nothing but an animal gives you such a strong feeling that there could be a future for you.

And Lizzy listened. She didn't just listen, she gave me the feeling that I was really there, that she saw me, all of me—and my life. It was wonderful and unbelievably painful at the same time, and for the second time I came close to changing my mind. It's impossible, I know, impossible just because she could be the one, because she *is* the one. I can't let her be poisoned by me and my life. She asked once about the hospital, whether it was awful, and looked right at me the whole time. After that, she didn't ask again, and I didn't care whether that meant that she had heard the rumors or read the newspapers, or maybe she didn't really know anything. Whatever she knew, she just let it be. As we headed for home, I knew she would take care of Sally, and that made things easier.

Dear Helen,

I said that when you'd calmed down and taken the money from the insurance, and when Frank would talk to me again, then we'd forget the whole stupid episode and pretend it never happened. And I meant that, even though I won't really be able to forget it. Not that it excuses your behavior, but Frank came over, appeared at my door with his dog and wanted to talk, seemed to think I was furious with him. I never heard him talk so much at one time as he has the last few days. And I would never have dreamed that he'd entrust Sally to me, ask me to look after her for a while. As I write, she's lying next to my desk. It's such a wonderful feeling! Thomas was so fussy, he didn't like animals, and my mother—well, I think she had a cleaning obsession, plain and simple. They have no idea what they're missing, what they deny themselves. Sally's only been here for a couple of hours and I can barely imagine letting her go. Frank didn't say why he had to go away, just that it was necessary and he didn't know exactly when he'd be back. But I've already decided: When he's back, I'm going to spend more time with the two of them. Maybe I can find out where he got Sally, and get a canine companion of my own. It makes a wonderful image, the two of us going for walks by the river, watching the dogs play. Hold on—Sally's just gotten restless, so I have to go—rather abruptly, I'm afraid, sorry about that. Your Lizzy.

The moon was already high in the sky when I set off for the seventh time, the last time, to do a job that would take me from a dark basement up into the light. It was awful and exactly right all at once, this last time, to go off alone, especially considering where I was going. This time, I didn't have to do anything special beforehand, like checking out the location during the light of day. Because I know this basement and this house like the back of my hand—almost better in the dark than in the light.

I wedged myself through the narrow basement window. It was hard work; I was glad I hadn't been able to eat anything the last few days. This hole, this window I'd tried to reach for so many years and had never gotten to, was like a symbol of the freedom they never let me have. And it was smaller than I remembered it. Or maybe I was just larger than my fear had ever allowed me to believe. I tore open the skin on my hands and knees, but I made it anyway, just barely. For a second I stood there motionless, trying not to smell the stale air, hoping that no one after me had had to breathe it in. Then I went upstairs, quietly.

She didn't hear me coming, but she knew both my hands and what they'd come for when I seized her from behind and held her mouth shut with the left. I tied her up without looking at her. It had been years. In the meantime she'd gotten to be an old woman and I was two heads taller. But still I knew that one look from those eyes, one word from that mouth before I was through with her, and fear would wash over me, make me blind to the many years that had passed and the reason I was here.

I didn't have to show her a video so that she knew who I was or what I wanted. After all, she'd made the videos. She was the one who'd burned my hands—and now she had to look at them again, and think about what they had come to do. I didn't expect her not to struggle against me, but maybe she thought that if she played the helpless old lady I would feel sorry for her. It only made the whole thing easier for me. And I didn't carry her into the bathroom like the others; instead, I took her down to the place where I had lost myself even before I knew I existed. And I didn't wait for the end, not in this basement. Before I left, I took off the gag. But I had to leave her tied up, the fear inside me was just too great.

"I gave you life," she said. Her voice already weak and thin from the loss of blood, but her tone was as bossy as ever. It chased the same old cold chills down my spine, and on the stairs I turned around one last time.

"You can't do this, and it won't help you, either," she went on, "because you carry me with you, and the bad blood, too, son!" That last part sounded like she thought she'd won some big argument, but even in the half-light that came through the open basement door, I could see that she was dying, just like the others had.

"I know," I answered.

Half an hour later I was back in my apartment up under the roof. I had always thought I would spend that last night outside with Sally, waiting until the moon was gone from the sky and saying goodbye, but Sally was already gone, and what had I ever had to say goodbye to? I'd never felt so completely alone as in that last night of the full moon. I hadn't counted on that. It should have been different, I should have felt different—better, or at least really and truly free, I thought, as I turned on the hot water in the tub. But there was nothing but emptiness inside me, not even anger, or the fear that had always been there. Just this emptiness and the well of loneliness.

And then someone knocked on the door and startled me back to the here and now. Without thinking, I turned off the water— the tub was threatening to overflow—and opened the door. Sally was glad to see me, wholehearted like dogs always are; she went to work right away, licking my left hand. Lizzy stared at me as if she had seen a ghost, and that's when I realized that I was covered in blood and still holding the knife in my right hand! Instinct took hold of me: I pulled Lizzy into my apartment, keeping the knife ready even if I didn't really hold it to her throat, and shut the door with my foot.

"What—what's the—what are you doing?" Lizzy gasped.

"You . . . you shouldn't have come, you shouldn't be here. I'm sorry," I said, without letting her go, while I looked around for something to use to tie her up. "I don't want to hurt you, but I . . . I have to do this!"

All of a sudden Sally was beside us, tail wagging, her leash in her mouth. I took it from her.

"Please, Lizzy, nothing will happen to you," I whispered, my voice begging her forgiveness as I tied her up, trying not to hurt her while I made the knots. "I have to do it, I have to make an end of it. And you have to look after Sally for me, afterward."

That's when she seemed to understand, because she stopped trying to wriggle free and started talking, and then she couldn't stop. I could get help, I was sick, I wasn't really a werewolf, and so on and so forth. I had to laugh, I just couldn't help it. Of course I'm not a werewolf, I don't even think I'm the Devil's child they always said I was, and probably my blood is just my blood and no worse or different from other people's. But there's just no going back, and even if someone else besides Lizzy would care enough to understand why those people all had to die, they'd just lock me up in a mental hospital for the rest of my life and leave me to the pain and the deep, deep well of loneliness that's always with me.

I didn't realize I'd been talking, that I'd taken off all my clothes down to the blood-covered jeans. I didn't even notice that Sally had begun to lick off the blood the way she always did. Then I stopped, and the silence seemed to take shape, like the moon shining between us, in the middle of the room—not a barrier, not a wall, but a bridge. And that's when I realized I'd told her everything.

"And what will you do now?" she asked. Her voice was kind and quiet in the stillness, and the words carried her to the middle of that bridge. I looked at her, at the knife in my hand, in the direction of the bathroom and the steaming tub, and then at the floor.

She said just two words: "Untie me." And I did.

And now I'm lying here. The water is warm like my blood, and getting redder and redder. Lizzy's sitting on the edge of the bathtub so that the water can't dirty her, holding my head in her lap. Sally's lying next to her on the floor, licking the fingers of my left hand, but I can scarcely feel the hand, not the scars from the stove or the cold. I'm getting tired, I know the end is coming, and for the first time in my life I don't feel so alone, I feel all gathered up and safe. Like a safe haven.

René Appel

Bloody Hot

Translated from the Dutch by Josh Pachter

Born in 1945, René Appel is a graduate of the University of Amsterdam, where he subsequently taught Dutch as a second language. His first crime novel, Handicap, *was published in 1987. Since then he has produced fourteen more thrillers, two collections of stories, two children's books, and a play, all published in Holland. He has twice won the Gouden Strop, Holland's prize for the year's best Dutch-language mystery. None of his books has yet appeared in the United States.*

I t was only nine-thirty, but the air in the living room was already heavy, hot, and humid. Kitty had opened the sliding balcony door, but the construction crew in the old office building beyond her back garden was hammering and sawing, and from somewhere in the neighborhood a stereo raised the decibel level even higher. They were turning the office building into apartments, and that meant that her peaceful mornings in the garden were a thing of the past—at least until the work was finished. Even thinking about it made her break out in a sweat, although she'd just stepped out of her second shower of the day after going out early to do some shopping.

She had the whole day to herself and no idea how to fill the time. Huib was at work and Jolie at school—wearing today a top even more revealing than usual. These fifteen- and sixteen-year-old girls must drive their teachers crazy with their low-cut belly shirts and low-rider jeans . . . especially whenever they bent over and showed their thong underwear to the world at large.

Kitty lay on the couch and let her gaze roam around the room. So this was it: her life, her world. Pretty, responsible, serene. What excitement there was came mostly from Jolie, with her unpredictable outbursts of inexplicable anger, her unreliability when it came to promises made, her adolescent laziness. The other day, Huib had actually offered her ten euros to straighten up the disaster area that was her room. "I'll do it for twenty," she'd said, the spoiled little brat. Thank goodness Huib hadn't given in to her.

Huib, her rock, her refuge. His job gave the family safety and security. He was a mid-level executive in the packaging industry, not exactly the sort of occupation she could brag about to her girlfriends at the tennis club, but that didn't bother her. Their house, the two cars, the expensive vacations, the lovely wardrobe from the chic boutiques of P.C. Hooft Street—that was more than enough compensation for the boring cardboard-box image her husband's profession called to mind.

Happily, they'd be able to have dinner out in the garden tonight, after the construction crew had silenced its hellish machines for the day. She'd bought what she needed for a refreshing avocado-and-shrimp salad. Hopefully Huib would make it home at a reasonable hour. He'd called around six o'clock yesterday: a meeting he had to attend, could turn out to be a long one. Wijnand, the CFO, ought to have handled it, but he'd unexpectedly had to cancel, which meant Huib had had to fill in for him. He hadn't slipped quietly between the sheets until almost two A.M. She'd pretended to be asleep—she didn't want to seem like a shrew, waiting up for him. She'd heard him in the shower before he came to bed, as if the meeting had somehow dirtied him. This morning, between quick bites of toast and sips of tea, he'd offered her an unclear report of a business deal closed over too many glasses of wine at an outdoor cafe overlooking the Amstel River.

She found herself realizing that, these last few months, he'd been delayed more and more often by meetings, visits from one of the firm's overseas representatives, or the need to finish up some rush assignment. She wondered why Wijnand didn't handle these matters himself.

The phone rang. "Kitty Schonerwoerd," she said.

"Hi, Kit! It's Leonie."

Kit. She'd always hated that childish nickname.

"It's such a gorgeous day," Leonie said. "I would *love* to go to the beach, but—wouldn't you know it?—my car's in the shop. Yours up and running?"

"Yes, of course, but—"

"Zandvoort won't be mobbed in the middle of the week, and at least there'll be a breeze by the sea." She blew out a breath. "It's so bloody hot here in town—just unbearable. Feel like joining me? It'd be so much cozier to go with a friend."

They settled themselves in a pair of beach chairs, as far as possible from the walkway up to the parking area. A deeply tanned beach god with a major tattoo on his right arm served them iced tea. They had brought their own beach towels, lotions, magazines, books.

Leonie pulled the current issue of *Elle* from her bag. The front cover promised a report on sexy summer fashions, Kitty noticed. Leonie herself was certainly sexy. She was topless, wore only a minuscule bikini bottom. Her breasts were large and full and well worth showing off. Kitty had begun to sag in recent years, so she'd kept her top on. Then again, Leonie was quite a bit younger. They'd met briefly at the tennis club several years earlier. Last month, Kitty had, to her surprise, reencountered Leonie, this time at an office party in honor of Huib's secretary Anna, a model of old-fashioned respectability, who was celebrating her twenty-fifth anniversary with the firm. Leonie's mother, it turned out, was Anna's best friend.

As Kitty gazed at Leonie, sitting there paging through her magazine with her proud breasts on display, a random memory from that party suddenly came back to her. She'd been walking down the corridor towards the ladies' room when she'd come across Huib and Leonie, huddled together, barely a few inches separating their faces. "Have you two met?" Huib had said, backing away a step. "Yes, just now," she'd said with a polite laugh. Huib had cleared his throat, and Leonie had begun to say something—Kitty couldn't remember now what it had been.

She set her book aside and closed her eyes and recalled the scene: Huib and Leonie looking shy and uncomfortable, as if they'd been caught with their hands in a cookie jar.

When she opened her eyes, a woman was settling in thirty feet away. She had two blond young children with her, a boy and a girl. As soon as she released his hand, the boy took off for the sea like a shot. "Jeremy," she shouted, "you come right back here!" The boy pretended not to hear her—he was already up to his knees in the water. The woman dropped her two heavy bags and chased after him. She dragged the frightened child back to their chairs, shaking him angrily by the arm. "Don't you *dare* go in the water by yourself!" she yelled. Jeremy burst into loud tears.

Leonie tossed down her magazine and stretched like a cat. "Late night," she yawned.

"Oh? Have a nice time?"

"Lovely."

Kitty tried to make her next questions sound casual. "What did you do? Or should I be asking *who* you did?"

Leonie smiled at her. A superior smile? "Oh, you know, just a nice night out."

"You don't want to talk about it?"

"Not really."

Around one, they had a sandwich and a glass of white wine in the pavilion. Kitty knew that it was dangerous for her to drink in the middle of the day, especially out in the hot sun, but she felt an irresistible compulsion to drown her suspicions. They talked about restaurants, food, recipes. Kitty described the class in Indonesian cooking she'd taken the previous winter.

Leonie set down her wineglass carefully. "Huib's a bit of a gourmet, isn't he?"

"Where did *that* come from? Did he tell you that?"

Leonie looked as if she'd let a secret escape her. "No, no, I'm just guessing. He looks like a man who enjoys a good meal." She laughed as if she'd said something amusing. "Shall we have another one?"

The woman had dug a deep hole in the sand for Jeremy and his sister, whose name seemed to be Viviane. The three of them sat in the hole together—one little blond head or the other peeked out occasionally over the edge. Kitty thought of beach times spent with Huib and Jolie. Huib would dig a hole and lie down in it, and Jolie would cover him with sand until only his head was visible. Buried in the sand, buried alive. She glanced at Leonie, who appeared to have dropped off to sleep and was beginning to show a sunburn.

Despite the two glasses of wine, Kitty was wide awake. Leonie and Huib? No, it was impossible—yet all the signs were pointing in that direction. After Anna's party, she'd actually brought Leonie's name into the conversation, but Huib had quickly changed the subject—perhaps, now that she thought about it, a little *too* quickly. Or was she letting her imagination run away with her?

A hole in the sand. She allowed herself to fantasize Leonie stretched out in such a hole. She saw herself piling sand onto the lush bronzed body. The skimpy bikini bottom disappeared, the ripe breasts were covered over, those breasts Huib had—

In Kitty's imagination, Leonie at last understood that it wasn't just a game and tried to rise out of the grave, but it was too late for her to free herself from the weight of the sand. And Kitty kept shoveling more sand onto the pile, more and more. Leonie tried to scream, but a scoop of sand in her mouth made that impossible. No one was watching them. They were, after all, just fooling around. Having fun on the beach.

Kitty's own throat was suddenly dry. She wanted another glass of wine, but knew better than to give in to the temptation. The avoidance of temptation, that was the key. If you always stayed in control of your actions, you would always remain in control of your life.

Jeremy threw a ball, which hit Leonie's right shoulder. She awoke with a little scream and sat up straight.

"I was asleep," she said. "What an awful dream I had!" She looked at her body, ran a hand across her flat stomach. "I'm burning," she said. "Why didn't you wake me?" She sounded reproachful.

"Didn't think of it," Kitty said. For at least a week, he wouldn't be able to touch her. No, nonsense. Huib and Leonie? Ridiculous. She had to stop tormenting herself with these absurd suspicions.

"I have to pee," Leonie said. She got to her feet and set off toward the pavilion.

Kitty watched her go, the sensual strut, the enticing sway of her hips.

Leonie's cell phone rang.

Kitty reached for her bag and found the phone. When she saw the number on the screen, her heart pounded in her chest like the waves on the sand. It wasn't until the third ring that she was able to answer it.

"Hello?" she said.

At the other end of the line, the connection was broken. She was absolutely positive: It had been Huib's office number on the screen. She dropped the phone back in Leonie's bag as if it had burned her fingers.

And then Leonie herself was back. "You look like you've seen a ghost," she said.

A ghost, yes, one ghost, but that was one too many. Kitty shook her head.

Leonie fished a towel from her bag, spread it carefully on the sand beside her chair, and lay on her stomach. "Will you do my back?"

Kitty tried to say something, but she couldn't form a coherent sentence. She kneeled beside Leonie, uncapped a bottle of sunscreen, and began to rub it in. Her mind swirled with unwanted images. Perhaps Huib had knelt beside her, just like this, his hands on her back, on her legs, between her thighs—no, no, no! She wanted to shriek, but forced herself to remain quiet.

They were together last night, she thought. There was no "meeting." They went out together, had a quiet little dinner, then back to her place, where they—

Leonie's back was so soft, so beautiful. Kitty rubbed the cream into her shoulder blades. The thoughtless brutality of inviting her to the beach today. The day after. Or perhaps it wasn't thoughtless, after all. Maybe it gave her an extra kick to adopt Kitty as a "friend," and this massage was Leonie's way of rubbing it in. Did she moan, just then, or was that the sound of the sea? Kitty watched her hands as they worked the lotion into Leonie's skin. Her nails were blood red and long, well cared for. Sharp. She envisioned herself digging her nails into Leonie's warm flesh with all the strength she could muster. Eight long stripes down Leonie's back, eight stripes which quickly welled with bright red blood.

To protect herself from losing control, Kitty jumped to her feet without a word and strode off down the sand. She saw nothing, heard nothing.

When she finally returned, Leonie suggested they go in for a swim. "A little break from this heat," she said.

They ran out into the water. Kitty dove into an oncoming breaker to wash the terrible thoughts out of her head. Leonie stumbled after her, was knocked off her feet by the wave.

Kitty swam out into deeper water, and Leonie followed her. Struggling for breath, she called out that she'd never really learned to swim.

The idea presented itself to Kitty as if a waiter had brought it to her on a serving dish.

She tapped Leonie's shoulder and asked, "Do you think Huib is handsome?"

Treading water clumsily, Leonie seemed surprised by the question. "Handsome? I suppose. Why?"

Kitty swam farther from shore with powerful strokes, then turned and watched Leonie dogpaddle towards her. This was her chance. There was no one within fifty yards of them. No one was paying the least attention to them. They were just two ordinary women enjoying a swim in the wonderfully cool sea.

When Leonie at last reached her, Kitty grabbed her by the shoulders.

"What are you doing?" Leonie demanded.

"Nothing," Kitty said. She stared deep into Leonie's eyes and tried to read fear in them.

Less than twenty feet away, a man's bald head broke the surface of the water. He saw them and looked embarrassed, as if he'd caught them in a secret embrace. "Afternoon, ladies," he said, with a note of irony in his voice, putting an odd emphasis on the word "ladies." He disappeared again beneath the surface.

Leonie paddled back to shore. Kitty stayed out a while longer, delaying as long as possible the moment when she would have to face Huib's mistress.

As she dried herself, she became aware that Leonie was staring at her.

"Why did you grab me like that?" she asked.

"I don't know."

Leonie examined her thoughtfully. "I guess that, sometimes, we all do things we don't understand."

"I suppose so." Kitty knew what Leonie was thinking. First the backrub, then the moment out in the water, now that strange look in her eyes.

Before they left the beach, they drank another glass of wine in the pavilion. Kitty was definitely tipsy when she slid behind the wheel of her Alfa Romeo. Another car had angled in so close beside her that there wasn't enough room to open the passenger door, so Leonie stood back and waited for her to pull out of the spot.

Kitty watched her rival standing there on those perfect legs. She had spread those legs for Huib, for her husband. The slut, the whore. And then she'd made nice-nice and asked the cuckolded wife out for a day at the beach, just to rub salt—no, *sand*—in the wound. She must be loving every second of this, the bitch.

Now, full throttle, right smack into her. She could crush the life out of her, smash her up against another car until every bone in her lovely body was broken.

Leonie winked at her.

She turned the key in the ignition. She could do it, right now—no one around to see except a couple a hundred feet away with their backs to her, loading bags and a cooler into the trunk of their car.

The motor caught. Leonie glanced apprehensively at the car, as if she didn't completely trust it. Kitty stepped on the clutch, shifted into first gear, eased off on the clutch, tapped the gas pedal.

The car shot forward—but then she stamped down hard on the brake, and the engine stalled.

No, she couldn't do it. She didn't dare.

Kitty drove in silence, her hands clamped tightly to the steering wheel. Leonie had no idea what was bothering her. Had something happened between her and her husband? Women who'd been married for fifteen years or more, who had kids to raise, whose husbands had well-paying jobs that kept them away from home a lot—sometimes they just went off the deep end. One would turn into a shopaholic, another would start taking ceramics classes, a third would suddenly convert herself to Buddhism. From what Wijnand had let slip about his Inge, Leonie had gradually built up a picture of the type. She'd seen it for herself at the tennis club, too. She'd even played against Inge a few times—of course, she'd let the older woman beat her. . . .

Kitty looked so *angry*. As if she had a score to settle with someone. Or was she just frustrated that her come-on out in the water hadn't been reciprocated? If that was really what she had in mind, she was seriously barking up the wrong tree—especially since Leonie had taken up with Wijnand. She wished she could confide in Kitty—about the affair, the passion—but Kitty would certainly spill the secret to Inge.

The car veered off the highway into a service plaza. "Gas," Kitty said abruptly.

"I'll run to the loo," Leonie said. She pulled her cell phone from her bag and headed over to the station. In a corner of the minimart, next to a pyramid of quarts of oil, she dialed Wijnand's private office number. There was no answer. She tried the other number he sometimes called from, and Wijnand picked up immediately, as if he'd been waiting for her to call.

"I'm in Huib's office," he said. "It's cooler in here than mine, and he's out of the building now, anyway. . . . No, I can't tonight, honey, I can't. . . . I'd love to, but I can't keep sticking Huib with all this extra work. The man needs time to have a home life."

"I understand," she said. "But I miss you terribly. At the beach today, I—"

"I tried to call you an hour or so ago," Wijnand said, "but someone else answered your phone."

"Someone—? Who?"

"I don't know. All she said was hello. I could hear it wasn't you, so, just to be safe, I hung up."

Kitty returned the pump handle to its hook and glanced toward the station. She thought she could see Leonie inside. Frankly, my dear, she didn't give a damn. She didn't want the woman in her car, never again. She slid behind the wheel, started the engine, and took off, tires screaming on the asphalt. In the rearview mirror, she saw Leonie come through the door, a puzzled expression on her face. Perfect. She let out a cry of triumph and took one last look over her shoulder.

Leonie stepped outside, the cell phone still pressed to her ear. What was Kitty doing? She was roaring off in a hell of a hurry, leaving Leonie behind, as if exacting vengeance for some imagined insult. Her purse—with her wallet and credit cards—was in the car, she suddenly realized. How was she supposed to get back to Amsterdam?

She watched Kitty careen from the ramp onto the highway, not even slowing down to gauge the traffic. Its horn blaring, an enormous semi swerved to avoid her, but there wasn't nearly enough time for it to get out of her way. It slammed into the Alfa Romeo and flung it with a terrible crash into the guardrail, where the little car burst instantly into flames.

Isaka Kōtaro

The Precision of the Agent of Death

Translated from the Japanese by Beth Cary

A lawyer by training, Isaka Kōtaro is also one of Japan's most promising young mystery writers. His debut novel, Prayer of Audupon *(2000), won the Shinchosha Mystery Club Award, and it was followed by two novels that were both short-listed for the Naoki Prize for popular fiction. For a subsequent novel,* Coin Locker of Ducks, *he won the Yoshikawa Eiji Literary Award. The following story took the Mystery Writers of Japan's prize for best short story in 2004.*

1.

A while back a barber told me, "I'm not interested in hair.

"You see," he said, "I go snip, snip with my scissors, without any break, from the time I open my shop in the morning until I close it at night. Of course it feels good to get my clients' hair tidied up, but it's not as if I really like handling hair."

He would die five days later, stabbed in the stomach by a passing stranger. Blind to his future, he sounded cheerful.

"Why are you a barber, then?" I asked.

He replied with a rueful smile, "Because it's my job."

I felt the same. To put it in more grandiose terms, this was my philosophy. I'm not that interested in people's deaths.

It means nothing to me if a young president riding eleven miles an hour in a convertible in a motorcade is shot by a sniper, or if a young boy and his beloved dog freeze to death in front of a painting by Rubens.

I remember that same barber once saying, "I'm afraid of dying."

And I asked him, "Do you remember the time before you were born?"

"No," he said, puzzled.

"Did you feel fear before you were born? Any pain?" I continued to press him.

"No."

"Isn't that what dying is about? You go back to the state before you were born. There's no fear or pain, you know."

There is no special meaning to a person's death. Everyone's death has the same value. That is why I have no interest in who dies or when. Yet, I go out again and again to investigate. Why? Because, just as the barber said, it's my job.

I stood in front of the twenty-story office building of an electronic-appliances manufacturer. It was about one hundred meters from the main street that led to the train station. The entire surface of the building shone like glass, reflecting the pedestrian bridge and emergency stairway across the way. It was an impressive facade. I stood to the side of the main entrance, self-consciously hanging on to my closed umbrella.

The clouds above my head were black, swollen, and muscular. Rain was falling. Not a driving rain, but tenacious. It seemed like it would never let up.

When I am on a job, I never have good luck with the weather. I used to think that bad weather came with the job because I dealt with death. But my colleagues have better luck. I guess it's merely coincidence.

I looked at my watch. It was just past six-thirty. According to the schedule the Information Department had given me, my target should be appearing any minute now. Just then she came out the automatic door.

I took my electronic organizer out of my coat pocket and checked her description. It said she was twenty-two years old—it wasn't a mistake—but she didn't look that age. I returned the organizer to my pocket and began to follow her.

She seemed unhappy beneath her transparent umbrella. She was tall enough and didn't seem overweight, but those were her only positive qualities. Her shoulders were stooped, she was bow-legged, and she stared down at the ground as she walked. She didn't appear to be healthy. Even her dark black hair wasn't sexy; she'd tied it plainly at the back of her neck. But the most depressing thing was the glum expression on her face. It was not just the rain that made her seem wrapped in gray.

I don't insist that a woman wear makeup, but she seemed to do nothing to adorn herself. The suit she wore was nondescript, certainly not a designer label.

I had to lengthen my stride to follow behind her. There should be a subway entrance about twenty meters ahead. That was where I had been directed to make contact.

As with all my jobs, I wanted to get this over with quickly; I do just what I need to do, nothing extra. That's my style.

2.

I closed my umbrella as I started down the subway stairs. I shook it a few times to get rid of the water. Since she happened to be standing right in front of me, mud from the umbrella splashed onto her slacks.

"Oops," I said, raising my voice. There was more water than I'd expected.

I ducked my head and looked down as she turned around. "I'm sorry," I said, "I splashed some mud on your slacks. . . ."

She twisted and tugged slightly at her slacks to survey the damage. She found a circle of mud the size of a quarter and looked up again with some confusion.

I thought she might be angry—of course, she had every right to be annoyed—but she only seemed bewildered. She turned to continue down the stairs. Flustered, I moved to block her way.

"Wait a minute." I offered, "I'd like to pay for the cleaning."

The Information Department had instructed that, on this assignment, I was to dress like a twenty-two-year-old male model. I was supposed to look attractive to young women, but I hadn't checked to see if I'd been successful. The department had selected me for this assignment because I fit the type that the target would find easy to work with. I was pretty sure that my appearance wasn't disagreeable, but my offer of money might have startled her.

She said something like "That's all right" or "It doesn't matter," but it was so soft and mumbled that I couldn't catch it all.

"Wait a minute," I said, and automatically reached for her arm. I stopped myself and pulled back immediately.

I had forgotten to wear gloves. We are not allowed to touch human bodies with our bare hands. It is forbidden except in emergencies. That's the regulation. Those who violate this rule are forced to do a stint of physical labor and undergo educational retraining.

I think this type of minor violation is about as dangerous as people scattering cigarette butts or crossing the street against traffic lights. The regulations shouldn't be so restrictive. But I have never said anything. Although I may disagree, I always follow the rules.

"I just can't let you go, after I've soiled your expensive suit," I said.

"You say it's expensive, but the whole outfit was only ten thousand yen." I could finally hear what she said. "Are you being sarcastic?"

"It doesn't look that inexpensive." Actually, it did look cheap. "If that's so, then even more, I can't let it go. You can't get such a good deal on a suit every day, can you?"

"The dirt doesn't matter," she said in a gloomy voice. "It's not going to change anything if I have a drop or two of mud on my suit."

That's true, I think to myself. *Your life won't change because of a spatter of mud on your clothes. You'll be dead a week from now, anyway.* Of course, I don't say this aloud.

"How about this, then? As an apology, will you let me take you to dinner?"

"What?" Her expression conveyed that she'd never had such an invitation before.

"I know a good restaurant. I couldn't go there alone, but I've always wanted to eat there. It would help me out if you'd come with me."

She stared at me, cautious. Human beings are extremely suspicious. They are so afraid of being tricked, and yet they are easily fooled. They are beyond saving. No, I don't even feel like saving them.

"Where are the others hiding?" she asked in a brittle way.

"What?"

"They're hiding somewhere, laughing at me, aren't they? I bet you're pretending to pick me up while they make fun of my reactions." She spoke in a monotone, as if reciting a mantra.

"Pick you up?" I hadn't expected this reaction.

"I may not be attractive, but I'm not bothering anyone, so please leave me alone."

She tried to move forward. At that moment, I inadvertently grabbed her shoulder, bare-handed. It was too late when I realized my mistake. She turned only her face toward me and, as if she had seen the agent of death—which in fact she had—she turned pale, the blood drained from her face, and she collapsed weakly to the ground.

Now I've done it, I thought. *It's too late for regrets.* I could only pray that no one from the Surveillance Department had seen me.

I took my gloves out of my pocket and slipped them on. Then I held on to her and lifted her up from the ground.

3.

"This really isn't a practical joke?" Sitting across the table from me, she was still half full of doubt.

Her voice was hard to hear, so I leaned toward her. We were at a table in a Russian restaurant. I had somehow managed to lift her out of her faint and had taken advantage of her semiconscious state to guide her into the restaurant.

"It's not a practical joke. I just wanted to apologize to you."

"Oh." Her expression softened, and she blushed. "Is that so?"

"I was surprised that you fainted so suddenly." I feigned ignorance as I couldn't possibly explain that she had fainted because I'd touched her with my bare hands.

It wasn't necessary for me to tell her the truth: When we touch you with our bare hands your life span shortens by one year. Still, since she was probably going to die soon, a long life span wasn't at issue.

"It's the first time I've fainted. I've always been physically tough."

I wished she would speak more clearly. Her soft, mournful voice put off the listener.

In a small voice, she asked, "Um, what is your name?"

"Chiba," I responded. When we're first sent out on a job, we're given a specific name. It's always the name of a city or town, and it stays with us, even though our appearance and age will differ for each assignment. It's like a code to make it easier to remember.

"What is your name?"

"Fujiki Kazue."

She explained that the characters for Kazue meant "one wish." I'd gotten her data from the Information Department when I received this assignment, so I already knew her name. But I pretended I was hearing it for the first time.

"My parents told me that they named me Kazue in the hope that I would have at least one talent. It's funny, isn't it?"

"Funny?"

"They must have had no idea that their daughter would grow up without any talents at all."

She said this not to generate sympathy but out of the resentment she felt.

"I'm not easy to look at," she said after taking a bite of the egg dish in front of her.

I misheard what she said. "Not easy to see?" I leaned back, squinted my eyes, and said, "No, you're easy to see. You're not hard to see."

At this, she burst out laughing. It was as if a spotlight had shone on her face for the first time. If only for an instant, she brightened up.

"That's not what I meant. I meant I'm not attractive."

"Oh, I see," I said, but I couldn't contradict her. Just as she said, she was homely.

She then asked me my age.

"Twenty-two," I replied. My age was fixed to be the same as hers.

"You seem mature for your age." She seemed admiring.

"I hear that often from people." This was actually true. Even my colleagues often said, "You seem mature" or "You're cold." In reality, I don't like to get excited unnecessarily, and I'm no good at expressing my emotional ups and downs. I also feel strongly that, when I'm on an assignment, I shouldn't speak informally.

She then began to talk about her work. Her voice was still hard to hear, but her tongue seemed to have become looser. It was due more to the beer she guzzled than to feeling more at ease with me.

She told me she worked at the headquarters of a large electronic-appliances manufacturer.

"That's first-rate. I'm impressed," I said as enviously as I could.

"But I'm in the complaints department." She frowned, and looked even more unattractive. "It's the kind of job no one wants."

"Complaints department?" I said.

"I get calls from customers. Their calls are first taken by the customer service department, but those with angry complaints are routed to me. I'm a specialist in dealing with difficult complaints, I suppose."

"It must be depressing."

"Yes, it is." Her shoulders slumped as she nodded. "It really gets me down. I only hear from people who have complaints. Some of them yell, others go on and on in a mean way, or they actually threaten me. I have to respond to those kinds of people. It nearly drives me crazy."

This is good, I said to myself. "Are your days tough?" I asked.

"No," she shook her head and said, "my days are more than tough."

"That bad?" I tried to look sympathetic.

"I may be like this now, but when I'm on the telephone at work I use a very cheerful voice. I feel bad for the person calling. But when the customer keeps attacking me, I get depressed."

Her voice sounded so damp, like mud bubbling on the surface of a swamp, that I couldn't imagine her speaking cheerfully on the telephone.

"Recently, an especially weird customer has been calling me."

"Really?"

"He asks for me specifically to complain."

"For you specifically?"

"There are five women in the complaints department, and the calls are routed randomly, but this person asks for me by name."

"How awful." I could imagine that a complaining customer with a stalkerlike mentality could be quite nasty.

"It's too awful." She hung her head as she gazed at me with lifeless eyes and smiled wanly. "I almost want to die."

That's good. Your wish is going to be granted. I nearly spoke out loud.

4.

"What do you enjoy doing when you're not working? Like on your days off?" I asked, even though I was not interested. I asked because it was my job to ask.

"On my days off?" she repeated, as if she had never heard such a silly question. "I don't do anything. Just housework. And maybe toss coins."

She seemed to be drunk. Her words were slurring, and her body slumped.

"Toss coins?"

"I think to myself, if it's heads I'll lead a happy life, and toss a ten-yen coin. It's a simple way of fortunetelling." She seemed to have gone beyond self-mockery and on to enlightenment. "But it usually comes up tails. Then I decide that on the next toss tails will bring happiness, and toss the coin."

"Then it comes up heads?"

"Right."

"Aren't you reading too much into it?"

"If one is forsaken by even a fifty-fifty chance, one must lose one's will to live, no?" She drank the last of her beer. "Things are the same whether I'm here or not, so it doesn't make any difference if I die, does it?"

"If you die, many people will be sad." I offered the first platitude that came to mind.

She slumped to one side and said, "There is one person. The guy who insists on picking me to complain to." Then she smiled and gave a shrill laugh.

"I see." I thought, *This is going well.*

"I really just want to die since I don't have anything good in my life."

Again, she spoke of death.

Even if we don't encourage them to, those we are assigned to often talk about death. They talk of feeling trepidation, or of longing, or as if they had a vast knowledge about death. They speak little by little as if they were looking out from the shadows into an ever deeper darkness.

This must be because people sense our real identity in a subconscious way. Anyway, that is what they taught us during training.

And in actuality, since ancient times there seem to have been people who sensed our true nature. Some have claimed, "I felt a chill down my spine"; and others have written of premonitions: "I have the feeling that I am going to die soon." Those rare people who sense our presence in an acute way sometimes use this ability to tell others' fortunes.

"You shouldn't speak so casually of your own death," I told her, though I didn't believe it.

"There's no reason to continue living when all I hear day after day are complaints, and I don't have anything positive in my life. I'm the one who would like to file a complaint about my own life." It was hardly an insightful comment.

I stifled what I would have liked to say, that there was no purpose to life in the first place.

"I wonder if there is such a thing as fate?" she asked. I thought that she couldn't hold her liquor well. She seemed even more depressed than when we'd sat down.

Based on the data I'd received, I thought that she had probably never had dinner alone with a man before. Perhaps her nervousness and excitement had made her drink too fast.

"Sure, there is fate," I responded. "But I guess we might not all die at the time fate demands."

She giggled at this. "That's nonsense. Fate determines when a person dies, doesn't it? It's strange to say that someone might die before fate demanded."

"It would be a big problem if everyone waited to die until fate took a hand."

I shouldn't have been giving out this much information, but knowing that she was on the way to becoming very drunk, I continued. "Things would get out of balance."

"What balance are you talking about?"

"The world's balance, like population and the environment."

"But don't people die when their time is up?"

"No. They may die before their time is up. A sudden accident or an unforeseen crime—in those cases it's usually not as fated. Like a fire, or earthquake, or drowning. Accidents are determined afterward, separate from personal fate."

"Who determines them?" Her eyelids were starting to droop.

I thought of answering truthfully, "The god of death," but I considered this to be too negative, so instead I answered, "Probably the gods." As the god of death was included in the term "gods," I hadn't lied completely.

"I don't believe it." She laughed merrily. "If there are gods, why don't they save me?" Her voice, louder now, was clear, and it surprised me. In that instant, her voice sounded beautiful. "What standards do the gods of death use to decide who will die?"

"That I don't know," I answered truthfully. I really had no idea what standards or policies were used to select our targets. Those decisions were handled by a different department. I merely did what the department told me to do.

"But it would be unbearable, wouldn't it, to meet with an accident or something based on an arbitrary decision?"

"I suppose so."

"It would be distressing if the decision wasn't made after a thorough investigation, wouldn't it?" she said in a singsong voice. Then, with a thud, her face dropped onto the table.

It's just as you say, I nodded vigorously to myself. *That is precisely why I have come to see you. I was sent to investigate you in order to determine and report on whether you are fit for the implementation of "death."* That was my job.

The investigation process wasn't that involved. I only had to contact the target a week before the termination date and listen two or three times to what the person had to say. Then I would note down whether the determination was "approve" or "pass over." Moreover, the criterion for either decision was left up to individual agent discretion, making this investigation pretty much pro forma. Unless there was something very unusual, we were expected to report "approve."

"Ahh, I just want to die," I could hear her mutter as if she were talking in her sleep, her cheek against the table.

5.

After I sent her home in a taxi, I walked through the shopping arcade late into the night. My steps were light because I felt that this assignment was going smoothly. My job was actually pretty carefree. As long as one didn't get tired of changing into human form and meeting with people, all one had to do was engage in a bit of conversation and fill out the report. Then it was over. It didn't require much involvement with colleagues, and once in the field, it was left up to me to do things my own way. So it suited me well.

I went into a CD shop. CD shops that were open late at night were a valuable resource, so I always located them in the neighborhood before I went out on a job.

It was past eleven P.M., but there were a few customers here and there in the shop. I glided past the shelves and moved toward the headphones. The greatest pleasure in doing this job was being able to listen to music. The melody flowing from the headphones into my ears was so fresh, so thrilling. It was quite wonderful.

I don't care about people dying, but it would be hard on me if people became extinct because there would be no more music to listen to.

I suddenly noticed someone—a middle-aged man already wearing headphones. It was a colleague.

I tapped his shoulder.

He had his eyes closed, as if enraptured by sound. He jerked and turned toward me. Then he took off his headphones and smiled. "Hey."

"Is your target in this area, too?" I asked.

"Yeah, though today is my last day."

"Have you finished your report? Or have you witnessed the end?"

"I witnessed the end," he said as he raised his shoulders. "He fell off the subway platform on his way home, drunk."

After our week-long investigation, we send our verdict to the department. If the verdict is "approve"—and most of them are— death occurs the following day. Once we witness the death, our job is over.

Incidentally, we are not informed beforehand how our target will die. We only find out the method when we see it happen.

"So this is your last chance to listen before you go back?" I said as I pointed to the headphones.

"I guess so. I don't know when my next time will be," he said as he smiled.

While we are on assignment, we go to listen to music at CD shops whenever we get the chance. If you ever see a customer under the headphones absorbed in listening, with no intention of leaving the shop, it might be me or one of my colleagues.

I had a chance to go to a movie once; it depicted angels as gathering in libraries. I was struck with admiration that, for angels, it was the library. For us it's the CD shop.

"This album is the greatest." He held out the headphones. I put them on. A pleasant-sounding female vocalist was singing a tune, something between pop and rock.

I agreed with him and handed back the headphones. We loved music so much, if we weren't careful, instead of enjoying music during work breaks, we'd be working only during music breaks.

In a slightly arrogant tone, my colleague began to talk about the music. "The producer of this album is someone you should pay attention to." He went on and on about how the producer was a genius.

"But isn't this music good because the singer's voice is good?" I responded. "It doesn't have anything to do with the producer."

"Sure, the voice has to be good. The producer knows that. It's natural aptitude and talent. That's exactly it."

"Exactly what?"

"The reason the producer who discovered the singer's voice is so great."

I responded vaguely that it might be so. Maybe my imagination was working overtime, but I wondered if my colleague identified with the producer, who works in the background, because his own jobs were always unexciting.

"And you?" He gestured toward me with his chin.

"I just started my investigation today. But, fortunately, it looks like a simple case," I said as I recalled Fujiki Kazue's face.

"Simple case or no, you've already decided to 'approve' from the beginning, I bet."

"I'm intending to give it serious thought before making my decision," I asserted. "I want to gather as much information as I can and make the correct determination." That is the way I am.

"But, in the end, it will be 'approve,' won't it?" He smiled.

"Well, I guess so," I acknowledged. That was the reality. "But I consider myself someone who takes his work fairly seriously."

"Fairly, right?"

"Yes, fairly." I nodded as I picked up the headphones next to him. I put them on and pressed the Play button.

The fellow raised his hand to say, "See you," and left the shop.

Whether it's jazz, rock, punk, or classical, music is the best. I get happy just listening to music. I expect my colleagues feel the same way. Just because we're agents of death doesn't mean that we like only heavy metal with a skull on the jacket cover.

6.

In the evening two days later I met Fujiki Kazue again. Of course, it was raining.

I waited for her outside her building, and I began following her as she walked out of the automatic door. A car splashed water from a puddle on the street. It sounded like a crashing wave.

She seemed to be in more of a hurry than before, making it hard for me to keep up with her. When I caught up, I stretched out my gloved hand and tapped her on her right shoulder.

Her body tensed as she turned around. Her response was so exaggerated—what one might expect if one spilled hot water on a cat—it was I who felt nonplussed.

Pressed against the wall, she looked at my face and let out a small "Oh," as her expression turned to one of relief.

It appeared she wasn't frightened of me.

"Actually," I said, taking her handkerchief from my pocket, "I wanted to return this."

"Oh, that's mine."

"Yes, you lent it to me when I spilled some beer the other day."

"Oh, really?" Her expression gloomy, she cocked her head.

It was a lie on my part. In reality, I had taken the handkerchief out of her pocket when I put her in the taxi.

"Oh, thank you for the other evening. I don't remember much of it." Her words were jumbled, and she nodded her head several times.

"Can we talk a bit?"

She glanced around and seemed more wary of something than concerned about being seen with me. So I hesitated a little and asked, "Maybe it's inconvenient for you?"

"N-No." She shook her head. "But he might be around."

"Who?"

"I may have told you before—the customer who makes the complaint calls."

I understood right away. "You mean the man who asks for you when he calls to complain?"

"Yes, him," she said in a faint voice. "He called again today, and asked to meet me."

"That's scary."

"I thought he might be nearby."

With this, I immediately hailed a taxi and we went to another part of town. I thought she might consider me too forward and refuse to come along, but fortunately she didn't resist. When we walked into a coffee shop neither of us had been in before, her shoulders relaxed and she said, "This place should be safe."

"That complaining customer is creepy." I followed her lead in conversation. It wasn't as if I really needed her to talk about it, but if I realized how burdened she felt every day, it would be helpful to me. It would give me some criteria for my decision, and, most of all, listening to her problems gave me a sense of satisfaction that I was getting work done.

"At first, it was a complaint that the Eject button on his video player was broken."

"You should speak up a little more," I said before I realized I had spoken aloud.

"What?"

"When you speak in such a faint voice, it sounds like you're depressed." She should at least try to speak in an upbeat way, I thought. Then her sense of darkness might lessen to dimness, at least.

"I force myself to speak in a cheerful way when I'm at work."

I would hope so, I thought. If she spoke in such a gloomy way, the customers might issue further complaints.

"The customers who get routed to me are usually those with minor complaints, so I listen to them attentively and just keep apologizing. All I say over and over again is 'We apologize,' 'We apologize.'"

"It makes me feel depressed just imagining that," I said.

"At first that customer was the same. But then he started saying weird things. He would suddenly say, 'Apologize again.'"

"Again?"

"Yes, 'Apologize again.' Of course I would apologize, but he would repeat his demand, insisting I apologize over and over. In the end, he would ask me to say something, and get angry if I didn't comply."

"He might get his sexual kicks from hearing a woman apologize," I said noncommittally.

Perhaps she was naive, because she blushed at the word "sexual." It was unfortunate that she was so unattractive.

"Finally, he hung up that day. But he called again the next day. This time it was about a television set."

"Television set?"

"He said the picture got narrower and narrower and faded away. I told him that we would send someone out to repair it, but he said that didn't matter, he wanted me to explain the cause of the problem."

"The cause of the problem?"

"There's no way that I could know the cause."

"That's not your job."

"Right, I'm in the complaints department. I've never even seen the television set. Then he insisted that I talk about anything, louder and clearer."

"It must be that it didn't matter what the topic was, he wanted to keep talking to you." When I said that, she looked disgusted.

"Next it was a radio-cassette player."

"Music!" I muttered, and realizing what I had said, I felt embarrassed. To cover up, I continued, "So his radio-cassette player broke?"

"That must have been a lie as well." Her face twisted in disbelief. "He said he couldn't get his CD out, and started singing the song."

"Sounds weird."

"Don't you think? Then he asked if I knew that song, and insisted that I sing it."

"It might be the customer's head that needs repairing."

"I got scared and kept apologizing. But he said I should obey him."

"That's vicious. Then, he said he wanted to meet you?"

"Yes," she said weakly, and looked down. "After he called to complain about his broken DVD player, he said he wanted to meet me somewhere."

"Maybe he took a liking to you."

"Me?" She seemed not to have considered that at all, and was quite surprised.

"He may have been completely taken by your response to his complaints." If so, would she not want to die? I worried.

"I can't imagine." She seemed a bit taken aback, and showed a bit of pleasure, but then regained her composure. "It doesn't make me feel good to be liked by such a weirdo."

"I guess not." I was relieved.

If she fell in love with a wonderful man, it seemed I would have to reconsider whether I would "approve" her. Whether or not I was going to recommend a "pass over," it seemed I needed to reconsider her case.

However, I was probably being overanxious. I couldn't imagine that a complaining customer who seemed like a pervert could make her happy, or that the future of a couple made up of a complainer and a depressed woman would be sunny.

She fell silent. Wondering if I should make conversation, I gazed out the window at a pedestrian frowning under an umbrella. The puddles in the sidewalk highlighted the uneven pavement.

"We've had a lot of rain lately," she said, seeming to follow my gaze.

"Whenever I'm working it rains," I confided.

"So you're a rain man." She smiled.

I couldn't tell what was so humorous. It brought to mind a question I had harbored for a long time.

"Is the abominable snowman the same thing?"

"What?"

"Is the abominable snowman a man who, whenever he does anything, it snows?"

She burst out laughing, clapped her hands, and said, "That's funny."

It wasn't funny to me. I was uncomfortable having my serious statement mistaken for humor. And, since I didn't understand why it was so funny, I didn't know how to continue the conversation. I often have this kind of experience, and it's annoying.

After a while, she murmured, "What is my life about, anyway?"

Whatever she had been holding back had boiled over.

This startled me. I saw the color of her eyes change. She was like a woman who had fallen down a hole and couldn't get out and was begging for someone to let down a rope.

I wondered if she was seeking my help. She seemed to hope that this man sitting in front of her could rescue her from her worthless life. I must have quite an attractive appearance on this job.

This was not a happy situation, unfortunately, because I could be of no help to her.

Some of my colleagues work so that their targets might have some happy feelings, even for a short time, since they are going to be dead in a week's time anyway. But that isn't my style.

That would be the same as adorning your hair just before a haircut. If it's going to be cut anyway, it is meaningless to do something with it.

The barber can't save people's hair, and I cannot save her. That's all there is to it.

7.

For four days after that, I hardly did anything that could be called work. I did not contact Fujiki Kazue until I received a telephone call from the Inspection Department. To be strictly accurate, I had done no work at all.

I had spent those four days listening to music at CD shops

until the staff looked at me with suspicion. Then I wandered the parks late at night and watched young thugs assault salary men. The rest of the time I spent reading music magazines at bookstores.

In one magazine I read an interview with the "genius" producer that my colleague had spoken of so enthusiastically the other day. I didn't know his name, but I'd listened to several of the CDs he had produced. As I recalled, all of them were masterpieces, and I wondered if he might be a genius after all.

One of his comments involved the word "death." The word caught my eye. "I am waiting to come across a true new talent before my death." I was envious of his vitality and what seemed to be an unshakable confidence. I had no plans to quit my job, but I did not have the kind of zeal that this producer had. It made me realize again that what I lacked was passion for my work.

The call from the Inspection Department came just as I had pressed the button on the listening station. I hurried out of the store to take the call.

"How is it going?" I was asked. Someone calls us at irregular intervals, as if randomly checking to see how hard we are working.

"I'm working on it," I replied vaguely. Even to me, my reply lacked enthusiasm.

"If you can already write up your report, get it done as soon as you can." This was the usual line they took.

"It might take until the last minute." This was also my usual reply. It was a lie, of course. I could submit my report right now. Whether it was Fujiki Kazue or anyone else, it was just a matter of filling in "approve" and submitting it. Yet, those of us in the Investigation Department didn't work that way. We walked around town as human beings until the very last minute. Why do we do this? Probably because we want to enjoy listening to music until our time is up.

"How does it look?" the caller asked.

"It's probably an 'approve.'"

As the conversation ended, I thought I should go see Fujiki Kazue again. It was not really a final confirmation, but it was customary in my work to say goodbye to the target just before writing the report. It was this convention that I was concerned to uphold.

She came out of the company building at her usual time. It might have been mere fancy on my part, but her shoulders seemed even more slumped than before, and she looked like someone who would soon die.

She held an umbrella against the drizzling rain as she hurried away.

Again, I followed her, and I wondered how I should approach her this time. It might be good to meet by coincidence in the subway. A crowded subway car would be a convenient stage to engage in casual conversation, and it would be easy to say goodbye when I left the train.

But, contrary to my expectation, she walked past the entrance to the subway and went on across the intersection.

Beyond the tree-lined avenue of famous brand-name stores was a run-down area, a covered street mall crowded with people. It was full of game centers and fast-food stores. The scrape of loud noises sullied the air.

She stopped at a small fountain set in the middle of the mall and sat on a nearby bench. Her head tucked down, she clutched a women's fashion magazine to her chest. She didn't read it. I guessed that she was waiting for someone. The magazine must be a signal to someone who didn't know her.

I was surprised that she was meeting someone. Who was it? It was unlikely to be a friend or acquaintance.

It occurred to me that it might be the complainer she had talked about. She may have gotten fed up with her dull routine and decided to take a chance on anything that might give her even a small possibility of change. Or, it might have been that she'd decided that even if it wasn't a change for the better, any change, no matter how painful, would be preferable to a boring life with no variation. So, she decided to meet the complainer even though he seemed to be a pervert. Yes, she could have decided that.

As I was mulling this over, a middle-aged man approached the bench where she sat. He was in his early forties. His hair was down to his shoulders and wavy from a permanent, and he wore tinted sunglasses. He was of average height and weight, dressed in black. Right away I could tell that he wasn't in a respectable business.

I walked quietly and leaned against the wall of a building so as not to be in the way of people passing by and watched what happened.

The man spoke to Fujiki Kazue. She looked up fearfully, but her expression instantly turned to one of disappointment.

Even seen in the most favorable light, the middle-aged man could not be classified as handsome. Neither did he appear to have enough of a fortune to make someone happy. He didn't seem to have sufficient charm to overcome the shortcoming of being a chronic complainer. She must have realized this as soon as she saw him.

I was thinking that the man might also feel disappointed in her, but I was wrong. He raised his voice and said, "Now I get it," but he didn't seem disillusioned.

He spoke to her and tried to get her to go with him further down the street. She hesitated for quite a while, but in the end started walking with him.

I began to give up hope that this meeting would lead to happiness.

I have witnessed many occasions when a naive woman is led into a different life by a cunning man. There were women who became sick from the tough work of the sex industry and there were some who went deep into debt and lost everything. I'm not interested in people's tragedies. I don't sympathize with them or feel sorry for them. But I could imagine that Fujiki Kazue was being dragged down that path.

This being so, there was no need for me to follow her any longer, but I did not turn back. I had not yet given her my goodbye.

They entered a side street. About twenty meters away I could see that the man was forcibly pulling her along.

He was pulling her by hand into a karaoke shop. A gaudy sign reading "Karaoke" was affixed to the building.

I don't like karaoke, despite the fact that I love to listen to music. I have gone into karaoke shops several times as part of my job, but they were so disagreeable that I wanted to rush out of them. I don't know why. But it seems that there is a deep, unbridgeable divide between music and karaoke. It wasn't a matter of which was better, it was that I could only enjoy one side of the divide and felt it was better not to get near the other.

I could guess why the man wanted to take her into the karaoke shop.

Such shops were set up with private rooms, and singing together often meant letting the other person hear one's carnal nature. This made it ideal for removing the distance between two people. It could be that he intended to seduce her as soon as they entered the room, or he may just want to release his stress by singing. In either case it was nothing out of the ordinary.

She appeared to be firmly resisting. She was pulling back,

nearly squatting down on the sidewalk, and was about to drop her umbrella.

It was not my place to get involved in whatever was to follow. It was not within the scope of my work to resolve problems between men and women. I decided to try another time. I turned away and shifted my umbrella to the other hand. At that instant, a voice flew toward me.

"Mr. Chiba! Help me, please!"

The voice was loud with a definite intonation. Fujiki Kazue was calling out the name just as a trumpet sounds out a note.

It took me awhile to register that it was my name she was calling.

8.

I tried to look as if I had just happened to come by. "What's the matter?" I said as I went to her.

The man standing next to her was clearly suspicious. He looked me over from head to toe and glared at me.

She stood up and tried to grab my arm, saying, "Mr. Chiba, please help me."

"What's the matter?" I asked again. It was difficult to ask convincingly when I already knew the circumstances.

"This person is the one I told you about," she said haltingly.

"The man on the telephone?"

"Yes."

"Who are you?" the man demanded. He seemed more decent close up than when I'd seen him from a distance. But he still didn't have the social skills of a polite company employee. His piercing gaze made me feel uncomfortable. He seemed unconcerned that the shoulder of his black jacket was getting wet in the rain.

"I'm just an acquaintance." When I said this, Fujiki Kazue's face turned sad and she looked away. "And you?" I asked in return.

"I have some business with her." His reply was mumbled, and he seemed not to want to explain the circumstances truthfully.

At that moment Fujiki Kazue began to run. She'd been standing like a wilted plant and had given no indication that she might move, and yet she suddenly tore away.

"Hey!" It was the man who raised his voice, not I.

Her coordination was awkward, but she ran with desperation, her arms flailing, her head down, and her handbag nearly dropping off her shoulder.

"Mr. Chiba, goodbye!" I could hear her shout from far away. Her clear, loud voice echoed throughout the arcade.

"What the hell do you mean, interfering?" the man accosted me. No doubt he was more upset than he himself realized, and he leaned forward, ready to charge.

At that instant, he lost his balance and fell toward me, and I felt afraid. Before I knew, I had rolled onto the ground with him on top of me. My rear end landed on a manhole cover filled with rain. The water seeped into my chinos and felt cold. I was dismayed to realize that I had touched him with bare hands.

I was disgusted that humans seemed so adept at creating problems for themselves. Then, when I took another look at the man's profile, I noticed something.

9.

The man came to, sat up and looked around him. Then he stood up, shamefaced, and slowly walked away.

I hid myself behind a vending machine and decided to follow him. Somehow, all I seemed to do on this job was tail people, as if I were a detective. This time, however, I was shadowing the man for personal reasons.

I knew this man. Well, no, if I said that, it might lead to a misunderstanding that I was acquainted with him. To be precise, I'd seen this man's photograph. Where? In a music magazine I'd recently read. He was the "genius" producer my colleague had told me about.

He walked unsteadily toward the side street, rubbing his backside. He took out his cell phone.

That was the perfect chance for me. I listened intently. We are able to hear voices on wireless frequencies even at some distance. Although it takes effort to single out the correct frequency from the numerous frequencies in use, it is not an impossible task. It is relatively easy as long as we know the location and time coordinates of the transmission source.

With his phone pressed against his ear, he scurried into a mixed-tenant building and entered the stairwell.

My ears caught the call signal.

"Yes," a woman's voice answered.

"It's me," I heard him say brusquely.

I couldn't tell if he didn't give his name because they were on intimate terms or because his number was known to the other party, and he could leave his name out.

"How was it?" She didn't sound annoyed, but neither did her voice emit any charm.

"Could you wait a little longer?"

"Things didn't go well? I really can't wait."

"Don't say that. I'm sure she's the real thing. I just heard it. That voice is for real." The man's voice was full of the same passion that came through in the magazine. "But I wasn't able to explain to her."

"Is there such a thing as a real voice?"

"Sure. Singing is a talent based on an appealing voice."

"No matter how nice her voice is, she could be tone-deaf."

"I tried to get her to sing karaoke, but she misunderstood my intentions."

"Are you sure it'll work?"

"Just trust my intuition."

"Why didn't you just explain to her? She'll only suspect you if you don't."

"Whenever anyone finds out that I'm a music producer and want to scout them, they end up with high expectations and become so nervous, their voice changes."

"Aren't you expecting too much from her?" The woman seemed to be an old colleague in the same field.

"She has such a great voice."

"Have you heard of Kathleen Ferrier?" she asked.

"Who is that?" he asked out loud.

Who is that? I echoed in my head.

"She's an opera singer. She was a telephone operator who was discovered by someone on a telephone call and ended up becoming a great opera star. That may only be a story that was made up after the fact. But you're doing the same thing, aren't you? You became infatuated with the voice of a girl in the complaints department who happened to take your call."

"That's right."

"Isn't that absurd? Besides, you called her over and over with complaints, didn't you?"

"Yes, in order to confirm my impression. The more I listened to her voice the better it sounded."

"How about her looks?"

"Not that great," he replied instantly. Then he laughed. His laughter was relaxed and warm. "It's all right. That's often the case in people whose talents aren't being used. Once their talents are recognized, they become attractive on the outside, like dead skin peeling away. That's what happens."

"Oh, all right," she said in a voice that did not indicate whether or not she believed him. "I'll wait just three more days for you to contact me."

The call ended. The man returned his phone to his pocket. He moved forward dragging his leg. His spine, however, was straight, stretched taut in the stance of a person who knows where he is headed.

He turned into a narrow street. Coming out of the covered arcade, he opened his umbrella with a light push of a button.

I didn't follow him any further. I stood still, wanting to think about what was happening.

The producer had fallen for the voice of Fujiki Kazue, an employee in the complaints department of an electronics manufacturer. Fujiki Kazue had said he once demanded that she sing when he called with a complaint. Was that because he wanted to hear her singing voice? I thought it was a reckless way to go about his business. But I didn't think it was objectionable.

I looked up at the sky, struck by a thought.

What was going to happen to her? Did she really have a talent for singing?

No matter how much the producer liked her voice, that didn't necessarily mean that she could sing. Even if she did have talent, the odds were against her that she would become a successful singer. And I didn't know if she would be happy being a singer.

What was I to do? If I put "approve" on my report, Fujiki Kazue would disappear from this world tomorrow. There would be no mistake, although I didn't know what kind of accident was being prepared for her.

I'm not curious at all about how humans die. I am only involved with them because of my job. It doesn't affect me much how my targets die.

If, however, out of one chance in ten thousand, that producer's intuition was correct, and if out of one chance in ten thousand my target succeeded in becoming a fabulous singer . . . Or, if a time came that I happened to hear her singing when I was listening to music in a CD shop, that might be pleasantly amusing, I thought.

I noticed that the rain was falling harder, causing the raindrops hitting the ground to splatter loudly. They seemed to be pressing me to make a decision.

Recalling Fujiki Kazue's face, I made up my mind. I took a ten-yen coin out of my wallet. Without hesitating, I flipped the coin in the air. I caught it on the back of my hand. It was wet with rain.

Was it heads or tails? That was the way I would decide whether I would "approve" or "pass over." Would she die tomorrow or would she live out her fate? As it didn't make much difference to me which it was, I would let a coin toss decide.

I looked at the coin. It was heads, but I'd forgotten whether I was going to "approve" or "pass over" for heads. The rain fell even harder. Urged on by the rain, I decided I had thought about it long enough. "Pass over" should do it.

Georgi Gospodinov

L.

Translated from the Bulgarian by Magdalena Levy and Alexis Levitin

Bulgarian Georgi Gospodinov began his writing career with two books of poetry, both of which won literary prizes. His debut novel, Natural Novel, *was published in Bulgaria in 1999, and later in France, the Czech Republic, Macedonia, Croatia, Serbia, Montenegro, and the United States (Dalkey Archive Press, 2004)—the latter resulting in reviews in* The New Yorker, *the* L.A. Times, Publishers Weekly, *and elsewhere.*

H e had it all in his pocket—the money, the cigarettes, the lighter . . . He looked around just once more, then carefully put on his bowler hat, took the bag, opened it for the third time that morning, and for the third time made sure the six densely printed pages were there. Then he fidgeted about the hallway, peeked into the kitchen and said a quick "Bye, Barbie" (even though there was obviously no one there), unlocked the door, and left.

There were two possibilities.

The first: It might well have come about as the newspaper stated when it announced the short-story contest—a contest for a crime story about a murder "for love." The newspaper explained: "The subject *Murder for Love* has been suggested by a contest with the same name carried out recently in the United States, based on an idea by Otto Penzler, owner of New York's Mysterious Bookshop."

It was logical for H. H., as a regular contributor—since he had made a name for himself (although in a limited circle) thanks to this newspaper, and the editors had praised him—to take part in the contest. Yes, it would even look suspicious if he didn't. That thought occupied him for no less than a hundred steps. Logic demanded that he go there and give them his story. At this point he stopped short, took out a Gitane—he usually got by with cheaper cigarettes like Melnik or Sredets, but the day demanded something better so he sheltered the Gitane between his palms and lit it. The harsh, pungent smoke put an end to this first, rosy version. He slowed down, partly because of the cigarette, and decided to think over the second possibility.

The contest had been announced three weeks after the case. The daily newspapers had run with that murder, "the most terrifying of the last 20 years," filling whole pages with speculation about it. Apparently, circulation had risen sharply. Even now, almost two months later, the event never left the front pages. People were hungry for a real thriller, for something unheard of. Not that there weren't the regular couple of murders a week, but they were banal—murders of money-exchange clerks; a shot in the head, some brains, the front of a skull missing, and that was it. But here the story was entirely different. A twelve-year-old girl, "beautiful as a Barbie doll," as one of the metropolitan newspapers put it, plunged alive into a boiling mixture of resin, wax, wolfram fibers, and lead-silver filings. "As if prepared for the Museum of Madame Tussaud," another newspaper said. A perfect silver-colored cast. An enormous balloon tied to her left hand, and a box of popcorn inserted between the right arm and the torso. The most terrifying thing about it was that this "doll" had waited six days—from December 29th to January 5th, the first working day after those long New Year's holidays—before it was removed as an illegal publicity toy, or for some other stupid reason. It had remained there for six days, placed on the rooftop of an apartment building right at the Eagles Bridge, in plain sight of the whole city, next to an illuminated Lucky Strike advertising billboard.

It looked spectacular up there, its lead-silver particles gleaming, the enormous balloon in hand and a sign on a long piece of cloth beneath that said, strangely enough: "Merry Christmas, Daddy!" It was impressive, like all new things, and people looked up and enjoyed it, although nobody knew for sure whom the doll was congratulating, or what exactly she was advertising. When the workers came to take it down, the cast broke and the decaying body of a young girl came tumbling out. A few days later the police sent all the newspapers a composite sketch of the murderer, supposedly seen by an old lady as he was carrying the doll up to the rooftop. H. H. was pleased to notice that the picture didn't look at all like him and was rather reminiscent of a Cro-Magnon man, with its low forehead, thick eyebrows, and solid jaw. It had obviously been dug out of some old manual on criminology. More recently a guard at the Japanese Embassy had been killed, and the man caught by the camera, with his rough face and long hair (bearing a striking resemblance to the Cro-Magnon, by the way) scared readers for a while, until the police caught two seventeen-year-old boys, both sporting cropped hair, in a train near Mezdra, covered with blood. Cheap cop tricks.

So—H. H. lit a second Gitane—three weeks after the live-doll story, the literary newspaper to which he contributed on a regular basis announced that crime-story contest. The prizes in the contest were suspiciously generous in light of the precariousness of the newspaper's financial condition. There was also a promise to publish a book of the best short stories. The bait was too loaded. The contest had been sponsored by some Crime-Story Lovers' Society that no one had ever heard of. He imagined them as a group hastily formed for the occasion—top cops shaven clean, plain clothes, jackets slightly bulging on the left. No jury was announced, but rumors mentioned the names of a few university instructors. It was quite possible that even if the contest was a setup, the jury and the newspaper's editors didn't know it, and did not at all suspect that the killer could be someone inside their literary circle, or a maniac who loved describing his deeds.

Were cops capable of understanding anything about fiction, or did they read everything as a confession, as a deposition? Could they ever have heard of Humbert Humbert?

H. H. stopped in front of the editorial offices, imagined (a third Gitane) the cops snatching out of the totally unsuspecting jury's hands his short story alone. The case spreading like wildfire all over the press, despite all efforts to suppress it; the newspaper editors, the jury taking the lead, discussing the admissibility of such methods, delving into the problem of fiction as court evidence. The media going crazy. H. H.'s name appearing in unimaginable numbers of newspapers. Enterprising publishers collecting all the stories he had published in periodicals. Intellectuals protesting the arrest. The World Court in the Hague . . . Salman Rushdie called to speak on the issue. H. H. caught himself thinking in titles. Enormous letters, boldface, stern print, and all of it on the front page. He felt buttressed by all of world literature, the whole world's fictional tradition, before which the cops, the prosecutors, the court, the state with all its institutions seemed miserable, like tin soldiers. No, like bugs scurrying around.

The metamorphosis was about to be accomplished. He took the six pages from his bag and read the end of the short story once again:

. . . soft-hearted, painfully sensitive, extremely cautious. Taking revenge for all the soft-hearted, the painfully sensitive, the extremely cautious.

Merry Christmas, Daddy!

And he opened the door to the editorial offices.

And he opened the door to the editorial offices.

Jutta Motz

With a Little Help From Your Friends

Translated from the German by Barbara Stiner

Jutta Motz has lived and worked in Switzerland for the past twenty-five years. She is, however, of German birth, and has a residence in Greece, too, where she spends her summers—and where this story is set. When asked about her nationality she says she prefers to simply be considered a European. She is an art historian and an archaeologist, and worked for many years in publishing in Zurich. In 1995 she wrote her first novel; she now has three novels and many stories in print from the German publisher Piper Verlag.

S iv had been dreading the day for a long time. But she still got a shock when Nonna Anna decided, a short while after the passing away of her husband, to move in with her grandson Kostas and his young wife.

In southern Europe it is quite common for surviving parents or grandparents to be accommodated and taken care of by the family rather than sent to a nursing home. Which means: The care is conveyed to daughters or daughters-in-law. Preferred are those members of the family who are homebound anyway because they are rearing offspring.

Nonna Anna's children and children-in-law were all middle-aged themselves, and all had jobs. So did Kostas, her eldest grandson. But his young wife promised to meet the requirements for nursing the old, since she was working at home. She did translations for some foreign newspaper nobody had ever heard of around here. Such may have been the old woman's reasoning when she packed her small suitcase and the nine family pictures.

Thus Nonna Anna moved into the little house of Kostas and Siv, into a small room on the ground floor, just to the left of the stairs, intended as a nursery sometime in the future. At present, Kostas and Siv were using the room as their study. They vacated the room without complaining, moving the heavy desk, the computer, and all the paper upstairs, to install their office in the open gallery of the upper floor. They would have had to move anyway once a little one was on the way.

Nonna Anna turned out to be a gentle, patient, and in no way demanding woman, even if she did need nursing. She also proved quite tough in her suffering. She never complained, never requested anything, never bickered or quarreled—she was just there. Also she never showed any disapproval of Siv's cooking, although most of it did not agree with her. Siv used many recipes she had learned from her mother, and these were Scandinavian specialties, all of which tasted horribly foreign to Nonna Anna. Bravely she sampled all that Siv put on her plate, but only small bits of everything. She understood that Siv was cooking the way she was used to from her mother, but it irritated her that her grandson Kostas seemed to like that strange fish food. Perhaps, Nonna Anna thought, this was because he had grown up near the sea, while she had remained in the interior of the country all her life, cultivating a small farm together with her beloved Vassilis.

In the course of the first year she continually lost weight, so that Siv began to get a local dish for lunch from the restaurant on the corner for her ward. With so much tender attention, and very proud of the special position she no doubt had in the house of her grandson, Nonna Anna recovered, and in spite of the hardship of having to move from her own home, and the stressful acclimation to the unfamiliar surroundings, she prospered. Sweetly smiling, she sat in her armchair every morning and, after an extended nap, in the late afternoon, of course supported by soft pillows. From the garden she watched what was going on in the village.

The villagers, who had in secret predicted only a short life for Nonna Anna in her new environment, noticed with amazement how the old woman, in spite of her eighty-two years, adjusted to her surroundings, and how lively and animated she was in responding to visits. Soon, one or the other of the neighbors came to keep her company when Siv was out shopping, discussing some translation with her editor, at the hairdresser's, or just swimming her daily round. When Siv returned, she quite often would find some tomatoes or fruit, a bar of homemade olive soap, or a piece of cake on the kitchen table, gifts the women of the village had brought for Nonna Anna. They used to deposit offerings for her in the kitchen so that they would not be nibbled by ants or stolen by cats.

The women of the village wondered how it was possible that Nonna Anna was living so long, in spite of her increasing fragility. They would utter sounds of pity for Siv and Kostas, who took on the heavy work without demurring, bathing the old woman or driving her to the doctor. And the burden this must be on the young marriage was not discussed in confidence, no, quite openly—but not in the presence of Nonna Anna, of course.

A year had passed already since Nonna Anna had moved in with her grandson and his wife. Her posture, or rather, her manner of sitting—for in the time that had passed she had become bound to a wheelchair—showed a newly acquired self-confidence, and one day she proclaimed: "I wish to duly celebrate my decision to come and live with you. I want to invite all my friends for coffee and cake."

All the women of the village showed up for this battle of the cakes, all those who were no longer or never had been working. Kostas had bought a number of colorful cakes and had them decorated as for a child's birthday party. For three hours, Siv was making coffee and serving sweet liqueur whose slight smell of anise made her feel sick. When she had to lean on the wall for a moment, the sympathetic and knowing looks of the women met her, intensely scrutinizing her waist.

"I was sick from the beginning," said seventy-four-year-old Maria, and the other women nodded, nudging each other and giving Siv an encouraging smile.

Before the situation became more embarrassing, Kostas came home. He had taken off a few hours from his job to bring a bouquet of flowers to his grandmother. The old woman had never received anything like this before. "I feel very comfortable here with you. I think I might live to be ninety," she said, proudly enjoying all the attention.

There was an awkward silence. The women were looking at each other; some were shaking their heads as if the old woman had made some indecent request, others just shrugged resignedly.

"We have to help Siv," Georgia suggested. Out of the whole group, only eight women were still sitting in the garden instead of having gone home to prepare supper for their families. They did not have to debate long to determine what this neighborly help should look like. They decided to bring a plate with food to Nonna Anna every day, for lunch and for supper—this would be no great effort, since all of them were cooking generous quantities anyway.

• • •

Nonna Anna eagerly accepted this suggestion and thanked her new friends, who returned to their own homes with packages of leftover cake.

Siv did not quite understand what this proposed help was supposed to mean, but Kostas explained it to her. While she had been occupied with the coffee machine in the kitchen, Nonna Anna had apparently told her visitors—very casually—how her stomach and digestion were suffering from all that Scandinavian cuisine. She was having regular stomach pains. Oh, she did not mean to criticize Siv, she pointed out immediately, no one should say a word against Siv and the care she took of her. She couldn't have it any better, really, there was no match in the world for this lovely young woman.

Siv's first impulse was to hit out at her husband, since he had had the nerve to repeat Nonna Anna's words with such obvious amusement. But then Siv decided it was not the messenger who should be punished for bringing bad tidings.

In the following days, Siv fantasized going for a walk with Nonna Anna in her wheelchair, to the high cliffs on the northwestern coast. When they got there, she would let the woman enjoy the grandiose view and then discharge her into the sea. This solution would have the indisputable advantage that the body would be carried out into the open water in the wake of the waves. There would be no burial, and Siv would not have to worry about having to clean the bones when after three years the remains were transferred to the ossuary—an honor bestowed for centuries on the women of the family, but which Siv would gladly forfeit.

Fed by the entire neighborhood, Nonna Anna visibly gained weight and strength. Siv's waist also grew round, and she got a lot of stupid and superstitious—as well as important—advice. But Georgia was the only one to ask the decisive question: "Where are you going to put the baby?"

Siv shrugged. She really didn't know. The nursery was occupied, and the gallery was used as their office. "In our bedroom," she decided, because she couldn't think of anything better.

"But that is no solution in the long term," Georgia declared wisely.

In the fall, when Nonna Anna was recovering from a bad cold, she said she would like to eat one of the simple dishes from Georgia's "witch's kitchen," as Georgia used to call her old-fashioned cooking area with the chimney above the stove. Here she roasted the meals that gave her a reputation as a chef far beyond the boundaries of her village. Probably the requested dish reminded the old woman of past, better times. Georgia hurried to comply. Siv set out a tray, put a nice placemat on it, got a new napkin from the cupboard—she wanted the old woman to enjoy her first meal after the high fever she had had.

"Feta Saganaki," Georgia announced when she carried, hands protected by potholders, the requested dish, in its pot, to the bed of her neighbor. Siv had opened a bottle of red wine, a mild 1998 from Nemea, ready to pour into the glasses. Georgia brought along an open bottle of red wine from Paros which would be better for Nonna Anna, she claimed. But she herself was curious to taste the wine from Nemea, new to her, and she praised its delicately sweet bouquet with a slight aftertaste of plums.

"Feta Saganaki and a glass of wine," Nonna Anna repeated with a yearning in her voice, looking forward to this tasty meal. While she was eating, she reminisced about the times when her own sheep and goats had been grazing around her little house. "Sheep and goat cheese, is there anything better in the world?"

The old woman ate slowly, tamping one mouthful after another of the melted cheese into her mouth, only a few teeth left sticking up like broken tree trunks after a fire. She mashed the soft pepper strips with her gums, making smacking noises as she moved the mild onions in position to be swallowed. Georgia and Siv sat by her side, each with a glass of red wine in her hand, and there were many toasts.

It was a very harmonious evening. The wine made Nonna Anna talk, and she was telling stories from way back. Every incident she could remember from the times of her youth and childhood was related.

Without anybody noticing, Nonna Anna had eaten up the contents of the bowl—of a size intended for two persons. She dipped up the spicy olive-oil sauce with fresh white bread before she allowed Georgia to take the bowl home. It may have been the wine that made Nonna Anna fall asleep almost immediately.

In the early morning hours, when the first light appeared behind the hills in the east, Siv woke up with a start. Was that not someone groaning in pain? She hurried downstairs to the room of the old woman, only to see blood running from her nose and mouth, the entire body writhing under the sheets. "Kosta! Kosta! A doctor!" Siv called.

The emergency doctor arrived forty minutes later and he, as was reported by the villagers later, ran from his car to the house of the patient with his heavy bag and an oxygen bottle.

Nonna Anna died before anybody could help her.

As soon as the news had gotten around, the neighbors came to help Siv with the preparations for the funeral. Georgia comforted the young woman, who was crying helplessly. She blamed herself when she saw that the linen of the old woman was soiled with bloodied feces. "She must have had a serious disease of the intestines," Siv lamented, guilt on her face. "Nonna Anna must have suffered horrible pain."

The emergency doctor passed by two more times that day to look after Siv; he was worried about the condition of the pregnant woman. He tried to calm her by saying, "She had a quick death."

But Siv would not be comforted. She was afraid the stomach cramps of Nonna Anna had been the consequence of the Scandinavian fish cuisine. Had Siv not mocked her complaints and considered them whims of an old woman?

The entire village came to the funeral, and in the tavern afterward everybody spoke well of the deceased. Her spirit and endurance in particular were emphasized. Siv felt more and more miserable.

A few days later, in the early evening, Siv went for a walk outside the village. She no longer had any obligations, she did not have to keep fixed times. She felt weary and full of guilt. She was walking through the meadows without any particular destination, without an eye for the beauty of the landscape. All of a sudden, an animal wail cut the quiet, where before there had been only birdsong and the chirping of crickets. Siv stood still and listened.

There, there it was again! That high-pitched, miserable sound. A few steps away, under a bush, lay a contorted cat, shivering on the ground. The animal was in a deplorable state. The fur was shaggy and wet, the eyes clouded and feverish. Siv bent down to pick up the cat to bring it to the vet, but the animal had one more convulsion, a gush of light red blood came from its nostrils, it released a thin bloody excrement, and died.

"Rat poison," a deep voice said behind her. Startled, Siv turned around. The old shepherd Anastasias was stepping beside her, looking down on the dead animal. He was reputed to know how to treat animals with natural medicine. "Rat poison—every household has some of that stuff in the basement."

Dominique Manotti

Zero Tolerance

Translated from the French by Peter Schulman

French novelist Dominique Manotti is also a professor of nineteenth-century economic history at St-Denis University in Paris. Her first novel, Rough Trade, *a late-twentieth-century morality tale set in the seedy underside of Paris, was awarded the prize for best thriller of the year by the French Crime Writers Association. Her other published novels are* Cop *and* Dead Horsemeat. *The latter was published by Arcadia Books in English translation in May 2006;* Rough Trade *appeared in English from the same publisher in September 2006.*

A man violently swings open the doors to police headquarters, bringing with him into the overheated room a sudden burst of cold air before he slams the door shut behind him in one fell swoop. The startled cop seated at the front desk jumps to attention, as the sleepy office again succumbs to the languor of the long afternoon calm. The fellow marching forward looks like a tough customer, a very ordinary-looking man in his early forties, with a thick face, brown eyes, and short, graying hair. Bundled up in a gray windbreaker that hides the lower part of his face, he wears black leather gloves—also thick—black corduroy pants, and construction-site shoes. Borderline worrisome, the cop thinks. The man puts his elbows on the counter, and says sullenly: "I've received a summons . . ."

"Very well. Show it to me. It's four o'clock, you're late."

He grumbles something under his breath: "You ought to be happy I came at all."

The cop picks up the phone before saying to him: "Captain Miette is waiting for you, ground floor next to the stairway, second door on the left."

" 'Miette,' that's not a serious name for a captain."[1]

"Well, you can tell him yourself." He glances briefly at the summons and reads: "Bouillon."[2]

The man drags himself away from the counter with a grunt, makes it to the hallway, barges in without knocking. It's a tiny room, badly lit by a condemned half of a window. A metal desk, file cabinets, two plastic chairs in front of the desk, a hinged ergonomic armchair behind it, and in the armchair, Captain Miette, who is older than the man who just walked in, but who also vaguely resembles him, as though they were related in some way. He is full without being very heavy, has sagging shoulders, wears a tweed jacket over a brown tieless shirt with an open collar. The room is poorly heated and smells slightly mildewy. Miette gets up courteously. "Do sit down, Mr. Bouillon."

"What do you want from me, exactly?"

"Nothing serious, nothing to get worked up about, just a few questions, that's all." Miette opens a pink file on the desk, which contains only two typed pieces of paper. "Three days ago, on January seventeenth at six-twenty in the evening, you were involved in an altercation with a taxi driver . . ."

"Oh, so that's what this is about."

". . . Mr. Muhammad Tahir."

"Mr. what?"

1. *miette*, "crumb"
2. *bouillon*, a bubble given off by boiling liquid

"Tahir."

"Where do you get a name like that?"

"Mr. Tahir is of Pakistani descent."

Bouillon takes off his gloves, which are enormous, places them on the desk, opens the zipper of his windbreaker, and snarls: "I'm not surprised. So it's Pakistan now."

"Mr. Tahir's papers are completely in order."

"That doesn't surprise me." (He snickers.)

"So, according to Mr. Tahir, you were picked up at the Montparnasse train station . . ."

"That's right."

" . . . You gave him an address, 130 rue de Crimée."

"Still right."

"Approaching the Bastille . . ."

"Off the bat, that ain't the way he should have gone, taking Bastille like that. Would you have gone that way?"

Miette reads from the papers that have been placed before him, without lifting his head for a second. " 'He then proceeded to take the Boulevard Richard Lenoir, and stopped at the first red light.' You allegedly punched him violently in the head, his forehead smashed into the steering wheel, causing a gash that would require five different sutures. The hospital spoke about some cranial trauma as well. During the time it took him to regain his senses, you allegedly ran away . . ."

"That's a good one. I didn't *run*. I left calmly, and I took the metro. I had had enough of that cabbie. But I don't know how that guy could have tracked me down."

"It's not rocket science, Mr. Bouillon. You gave him your address, he went there, he chatted with a few of your neighbors who gave him your name . . ."

"The silly buggers!"

" . . . and he came to police headquarters to lodge a formal complaint. Now, I would like to hear your version of the events. Do you admit to having punched him?"

"More or less."

"What could have provoked such an action on your part?"

"He didn't tell you? His taxi reeked of patchouli oil, or something like that. It made me sick to my stomach. And then it sticks to your clothes, a stench like that. What will the neighbors think of me if I walk around stinking of patchouli oil? Well, I lit myself a little cigar, just so I could breathe a little." As he utters his last word, Bouillon puts his hand on his windbreaker, searches for an ashtray with his eyes, but is unable to find one on Miette's desk. "You don't smoke?"

"No, Mr. Bouillon, and I would urge you to refrain from smoking in my office."

"That's why it smells so moldy around here. Tobacco kills the moldy smell. Okay, so to get back to my Paki, he points to a sign hanging from the dashboard: 'No smoking.' I get all riled up. I tell him that asphyxiating passengers with the odors of savages and hookers should also be prohibited; he tells me he doesn't smell a thing, and repeats that I have to put out my cigar. Well, we weren't going to go on like that forever. I punched him, nice and hard, to put an end to the discussion, you see, and then I left. But punches like that, they're no big deal. I've given 'em and I've received some that were a lot worse, and nobody made any fuss over them."

"I'm going to take your deposition."

Miette sits down in front of the computer, starts typing rather quickly; his eyes go from the keyboard to his screen, which allows him to avoid making eye contact with Bouillon, who makes him feel uneasy. "So, allow me to sum things up: 'I admit to having struck Mr. Tahir in the head, because he asked me not to smoke in his cab.'"

Miette lets a moment of silence go by. No denial.

" 'And to having left the cab without paying the fare.' "

Bouillon raises his hand. "Wait a minute, not the full fare, just a part of it, up until we got to the Bastille, and I don't owe him a thing, since he didn't take me all the way home."

Miette stops looking at his computer to get back to Bouillon.

"If I have one piece of advice to give you, it is to reconcile amicably with Mr. Tahir. Try to see if he'll accept your apologies and some financial compensation for withdrawing his complaint. He is completely in the right, and you have everything to lose by going to court. You might very well be convicted."

"In court!!! Convicted!!! For a measly, harmless little punch? You've got to be kidding. You don't think you're blowing things out of proportion, Lieutenant? All this just for a Paki. With the Duchesne widow, who, by the way, was at least a good French woman, there wasn't all this commotion over everything."

"It's 'Captain,' Mr. Bouillon, 'Captain.' Who is the Duchesne widow?"

"She was my neighbor, for about four to five years."

"And you struck her like you did the taxi driver?"

"More or less."

Bouillon quiets down and starts playing with his gloves without looking up at Miette.

"What were the circumstances? Do you remember?"

"Of course I remember."

"All right then, tell me all about it." (Pause.) "It will enable me to learn a little bit more about your personality."

"Personality." Bouillon snorts.

"The widow was very deaf. She lived on the same floor as me, and she played these records all night to keep herself company, full blast. And I have an aversion to noise. She listened to Tino Rossi, and a lot of crap like that, Luis Mariano, operettas. Apparently she had been an usher at the Mogador Music Hall, but that wasn't exactly yesterday, if you get my drift. Anyhow, that high-society bugger music really got on my nerves. I couldn't take it anymore. I told her to turn it down ten times. Nobody could say that I wasn't patient. The eleventh time, I went into her apartment and I gave her a whack. More of a slap than a punch. To put an end to the discussion, like with the Paki. Once you get to a certain point, that's the only thing left to do."

"And then?"

"She fell backward onto the floor, and when I leaned over toward her, to help her up, she was dead."

"And what happened next?"

"There is no next. I went back home, and I could read my paper very peacefully, without all that ridiculous cooing."

"Mr. Bouillon, let's be clear here. You're in the process of explaining to me that Madame Duchesne, your neighbor, died as a result of blows that you gave her."

"That's not right at all. The day after, it was a Saturday, I wasn't working, there was a rumbling on the floor, policemen, a doctor. The concierge told me that they agreed that she died as a result of an accident. The widow died as a result of falling accidentally in her home, and hitting her head against a piece of furniture as she slipped. I had nothing to do with it. I'm telling you this just to point out to you that the old lady's fall was completely different from the Paki's five sutures, and no one made a big deal out of it. But of course, that old Duchesne widow was a nice old lady from our own country, which interests the police a lot less than Mr. Tahir who comes from God-knows-where and who's got his papers in order."

Miette focuses on the telephone. "Stéphanie, could you pull out the Duchesne file for me?" He spells out the name. Bouillon nods. "130 rue de Crimée. An accidental death. Bring it to me as soon as you find it. And right away. Hurry."

He closes the file, places it on the left-hand side of the desk, folds his hands in front of him, and, with a broad smile, remarks: "To put it bluntly, you're in the habit of punching people, aren't you?"

"No. Not at all." (Some time elapses.) "I'm a hard worker, I have a tough job. I'm a mason, working for the same boss for almost ten years now, never missed a day. And a good citizen to boot. I vote. I never get in trouble with the police." (Some more time elapses.) "But you have to admit that there are some moments in life when you can't extend a conversation forever. One sees black, the other white, no one makes any headway, so you just have to give up after a while."

Stéphanie knocks on the door, comes in, drops off a very thin file on Miette's desk. Miette scribbles a note: "Bouillon, 130 rue de Crimée, police records registry? Urgent. Send reply by e-mail." He hands it to Stéphanie, and delves into the Duchesne file:

" 'Madame Duchesne, widow, seventy-nine years old. Her daughter visited her on Saturday July sixth at ten o'clock, as she does every Saturday, but found her dead this time, stretched out on her back in the living room. She immediately called the police, who brought in the forensic pathologist. Conclusion: Large temporal hematoma; in all probability the old lady hit her temple against the corner of her table as she was falling. The death, which occurred the night before, is the result of an accident. Permission to bury. No investigation. Signed: Lieutenant Carvoux.'"

He's not much of a workaholic, that Carvoux. No neighborhood investigation, nothing. A rather botched job. Mind you, you wouldn't have done any better; who knows, it seemed so simple. In any case, it jibes with everything that loony's been telling you. What else does he have down that trap of his? I'll make him talk.

"Have you lived on the rue de Crimée for a while, Mr. Bouillon?"

"About fifteen years. Always at the same address. I hate changes. I hope you noticed that the neighborhood is changing, however."

"And you live alone?"

Bouillon tightens up. "Yes. It's not against the law, is it?"

Do your job, Captain, scratch around there where it hurts.

"Have you always lived alone?"

"No. I was married once."

Miette looks him over. *Keep going, there's something else. I can feel it.*

"Is she deceased?"

"Not her, the kid."

There is a deadly silence in the room, and Miette is afraid. But he's got to dig deeper.

"Your son?"

"Yes, my son." Suddenly, as if to explain himself: "It was three or four months ago and she claimed I killed him. Of course, it wasn't true."

"Of course. But why would she come up with a thing like that?"

"That baby, it was crying a lot, and I have an aversion to noise. I've already told you that. I can't stand repeating things."

"And then?"

"She thought I was shaking him too much. To make him shut up. She didn't want to leave me alone with him, and then, one day, she had to go to the dentist. A Saturday afternoon. She was working. Like any other day. When she came back, the baby was dead. She made a big stink out of it. What could I have done, I tell you? I just sat there reading my paper in the next room. I simply noticed that he wasn't crying, for once. Needless to say, he was dead."

"What happened next?"

"We buried the little guy."

"Where?"

"Let's see now . . . the cemetery. You really ask the craziest questions."

"Was an autopsy performed, an investigation of any kind?"

"Nothing like that. Why should there have been? The baby's pediatrician came over, and he said that it was a sudden infant death."

Miette gets up.

"A cup of coffee, Mr. Bouillon?"

"With pleasure. Black and hot, if you don't mind."

Miette walks out of his office and takes a few steps towards the coffee machine. There is a maelstrom of activity in his head. *This guy might well have killed the old lady, his baby. And what about his wife? What did he do with her? This is a guy who's as dangerous as a loaded gun in the middle of a crowded theater. I might really be on to a major case here. This could be my chance to make commissioner right at the tail end of my career. Or maybe he's a compulsive liar. I better not let myself be jerked around by him.* He returns, places a cup of coffee in front of Bouillon.

"After the burial, what did your wife do?"

"She left."

"Left?"

"Yes. Left. Here one day, gone the next, without a word of warning. Everyone has the right to do what they want, but it still caused me pain. I really liked her, my good wife, and the baby, too."

"She didn't leave out of the blue like that because your baby died of infant crib disease. What did your wife have to say about all this?"

"She criticized me for hitting her."

"And was that true?"

"No."

"Come on. It was the same with the taxi driver or the old lady, your way of putting an end to the discussion."

"Sometimes, a few whacks, when I had a little too much to drink, nothing really serious. All men drink, isn't that right, Lieutenant?"

"More or less, Mr. Bouillon, more or less. Let's get back to your wife. She criticized you for beating her, and for shaking the baby, and she never lodged a complaint?"

"That's all I needed. If anyone was going to do the complaining, it should have been me, you would think. Correct me if I'm wrong, but abandoning a home . . . that's illegal, isn't it?"

"You never tried to see her again?"

"No. I've got my pride. I went back to my old café habits, before coming home to sleep, that's all."

Café habits. Investigate.

"Which café?"

"The Bar des Sports, it's only a hundred meters from where I live."

Miette sinks into his chair, finishes his coffee, stretches his legs. Ah, the Bar des Sports. That small square, a stone's throw from the canal, the tiny church, the manicured trees, the *pétanque*[3] area, and the children's sandbox. The Bar des Sports and its loyal alcoholic clientele, its unending fights between drunks. Bouillon, of course, fits the bill to a tee. And then there was that accident, someone got killed in a brawl that was a bit rougher than usual. Miette himself was working full-time at police headquarters, just starting out, in fact, and right then and there, with a flair for authority, he starts interrogating this one,

---

3. a French form of boccie ball

that one, and latches on to an individual named Lambert, who was in a quasi ethyl-induced coma at the time, but who, after twenty-four hours in police custody, ended up confessing. A case that was promptly taken care of before the golden boys of the Crime Unit could put their hands on it. It was an easy opportunity for a promotion, that would surely come in handy around retirement time. That Lambert fellow got himself five years in the slammer. A nice memory, that Bar des Sports.

"I know the Bar des Sports."

"They respect me over there." Bouillon's face lights up with an intense self-satisfaction. "The boss trusts me. I'm the one who keeps everyone in line when things get too hot."

You should have stayed there. You shouldn't have tried to be such a smart ass.

"Were you there when Chevrier was killed by Lambert?"

"Yeah, I was there when Chevrier kicked the bucket."

"I'm the one who led the investigation."

"Oh yeah?"

"Perhaps I even interrogated you?"

"No, not at that time. I had to leave before you arrived."

"Why?"

That was one question too many.

"Chevrier had a big mouth and was constantly causing trouble, and he never paid for his round. The boss told me: When you get a chance, give him a nice roughing up, so he can take his business elsewhere. Well, on that day I got my chance. . . He started to push Lambert around. That Lambert was a good bloke that everyone liked. I caught Chevrier, and gave him a nice beating. Maybe a bit too nice. That explains why I might not have been so eager to meet with any cops that day. But everything worked out in the end, since Lambert's the guy who took the rap."

Miette starts to sweat buckets. Pictures Lambert in his office, so drunk that he had to be held up lest he fall from his chair. He was terrified, submissive. He couldn't remember a thing, but wanted to say whatever "Monsieur le Commissaire" wanted to hear.

"Bouillon, you've just told me, calmly and to my face, that you beat Chevrier to death, even though Lambert got five years in jail for his murder?"

"That's the point. The case has already been tried. You never go back to a case that's already been tried. I'm telling you all this just so you understand that in my neighborhood, I'm the one who gets respect, and it's not some Paki cab driver who's going to—"

Livid, Miette stands up. *Promotion, career, retirement, the gossip from colleagues. I have no choice:*

"Get the hell out of here, Bouillon. You're a deranged, pathological liar. I don't want to see you around here ever again. And I'll take care of your Pakistani, I will. Beat it."

Frauke Schuster

German Summer

German writer Frauke Schuster was raised in Egypt. Her experi-ence growing up in a foreign country explains, in part, why she likes to write (as she does in the following story) about people who have to deal with cultures that aren't originally their own. The author had written short stories for many years before her first crime novel, Atemlos, *was published by KBV in Germany in 2002. She has now sold a fourth novel in Germany but has yet to be translated into English at book length.*

When Moustafa woke, he heard his wife crying. At once he knew: It had happened again. His stomach tight with that strange mixture of anger and fear, he scrambled out of bed and grabbed for his pants and worn-out T-shirt.

Downstairs, in the poky little shop where he tried to eke out a living selling fruit and vegetables, his wife sat on the sole chair, right hand frantically wiping streaming eyes, plump body rocking back and forth. Helplessly Moustafa looked at the big hole in the windowpane, at the grey, round stone on the floor.

"We should have stayed at home," his wife wailed. He said nothing.

Only minutes later Moustafa spotted five-year-old Aysha,

crouching under the wooden table laden with an enormous heap of big red apples. The little girl was sobbing, too, though she didn't really know why.

But Moustafa knew. He knew who the man was who'd done it all. That bald guy in his military-looking outfit. The one who had beat Moustafa up two months ago, shortly after his twenty-seventh birthday. At home, Moustafa had tried to explain away his bruises and his missing tooth by muttering something about a fall. His wife had pretended to believe him, hadn't dared to question him. In Turkey once, the police had beaten up her brother. She had no experience with authorities here in Germany and she didn't want any. . . .

Feet dragging like an old man, Moustafa went out on the sidewalk to scrub off the words that had been sprayed on the windowpane: *Bugger off, Turk!* Big, bold letters in garish red, burning the glass like undying fire and burning even fiercer in Moustafa's soul. When he returned inside, his wife still sat on the chair, unable to rise. Talking gently, Moustafa coaxed small Aysha upstairs, poured milk over a bowl of cereal, and gave it to her. When the little girl had finished and settled down to play with her fairhaired doll, the man went down again to do his work in the shop.

Stacking boxes with peas, eggplants, potatoes on the stands outside, he suddenly got the eerie feeling of being watched. Suspiciously he straightened up, looked around. No one behind him, but—His stomach turned to an icy lump when he saw him, on the opposite side of the street. That bald guy, about his own age, in his usual military boots, camouflage shirt, but no camouflage to cover up his menacing stare. He was smoking a cigarette, watching the shop with malevolent, piercing eyes.

Moustafa wanted to run, to hide in the house, like a frightened kid. But he was too old to play the kid any longer—and too frightened to move. Besides—the smell of the tobacco smoke drifting lazily through the summer morning made him dizzy. In Turkey, Moustafa had always smoked, but after three months in this small town in Southern Germany he had abandoned the habit. Cigarettes cost dearly here, and he needed to save up. For his wife, for young Aysha, for the self-esteem a man couldn't live without. So Moustafa remained fixed to the spot, fearful and yet with a dim longing, even when the guy slowly crossed the street and came over to the fruit shop, cigarette dangling in his hand.

Only when the bald guy's lips parted to speak, Moustafa came to life again, fled into the shop, saw that his wife wasn't there. Probably she had gone upstairs for her own breakfast or to check on frightened little Aysha.

A dark shadow fell through the door, and there the bald guy stood, dusty boots planted firmly on the threshold, eyes narrowed to slits while he looked at Moustafa, took in the shabby room, the raw wooden shelves and tables Moustafa had laboriously built with his own hands.

"Lots of wood," he said in a hoarse voice Moustafa would never forget. "Should be afraid of fires, shouldn't you?" The gaze of his pale blue eyes wandered lazily to the back of the room, came to rest on the stairs. "You live up there? Might be dangerous." Slowly, slowly he raised his hand, let his cigarette stub drop onto the floor. "Would be terrible if something got on fire in here . . ."

The moment the guy turned to leave, Moustafa stomped his foot on the remnants of the cigarette, swallowing hard, partly in anger, partly in his craving for nicotine.

He didn't turn to the police, in spite of the broken window, in spite of the threats, being nearly as distrustful of police officers as his wife. Instead he worked mechanically, in a daze, shouting angrily at his young daughter when she came downstairs to play in the shop as she often did on normal days. He didn't want her there today, didn't want the bald guy to see the girl if he should come back. His wife looked at him with an odd expression on her round face when he shouted at the kid to get upstairs and stay there for the rest of the day, but she didn't rebuke him. Only Aysha cried fretfully, because she loved the shop, and the customers loved her. Some of the old women, buying daily what little fruit and vegetables they needed, used to give her candy regularly, delighting in the small black-haired girl with her delicate features, her huge, shy eyes.

All through the endless morning Moustafa stayed tense and alert, attending to the patrons as usual, twisting his reluctant face into a grimace of a smile, though deep inside his soul wept with fear and frustration. Three times his window had been shattered, three times those ugly words had been written on the glass, for everyone to read . . .

"Where's Aysha today?"

She was one of the most regular customers, this tiny old woman, hands shaking from Parkinson's disease when she fumbled for the money to pay for the two bananas and three of the cheapest apples he offered. "Would you give her this?" A small bar of chocolate in trembling spindly fingers, the skin shriveled with age. Skin and fingers like those of his mother, when Moustafa had seen her for the last time before he left for Germany and the fortune that would provide for them all. When Moustafa took the gift from the old woman's hand, hot tears welled up in his eyes. Embarrassedly he bent his head, pretending to have a problem with the cashbox.

Noon came hot and still on that August day. Moustafa closed the shop for two hours, ate the stew of potatoes, mutton, and beans his wife had prepared. Little Aysha was still angry with him, but her looks softened considerably when he showed her the chocolate. For the first time on that dreadful day Moustafa dared to relax.

When he opened the door of the shop again, the bald guy was sitting at the curb on the opposite side of the street, smoking again. He didn't seem to have a regular job, often turned up unexpectedly, sometimes hung around for hours watching Moustafa and his shop with an evil eye. Moustafa's hands shook like that of the woman with Parkinson's, and nowadays it wasn't only the want of nicotine that made him tremble while he arranged boxes with raspberries and peaches on the table outside. Though he was working in the shade, and though he normally would bask in the heat of a summer's day, he felt a surge of sweat soaking his shirt.

He had known the bald guy would return once more. He knew the guy satisfied his perverted mind seeing Moustafa's nervous movements, his anxious looks. Determined to lessen the triumph of the other as best as he could, he went inside and busied himself with dusting, with no eye for the dust.

Then the guy stood in the door again. He never went into the shop, never even pretended to be interested in buying anything. He stood there, his tall frame nearly too big for the door, and while he stood in silence, staring, Moustafa suddenly heard fairy-light steps on the stairs. His heart started to race, the beatings hammering in his ears.

"Aysha! Upstairs!" He bellowed the words, but the little girl didn't obey, came dancing into the room, laughing her childish, silvery laugh, black hair flying around her tiny face.

"Go upstairs!"

She paused in her dance, looked up at him with dark eyes whose innocence wrung his heart.

"Please, *sevgili!* Darling! Go to your mother!" His words now were barely audible, more a wish than a whisper. The little girl stuck her thumb in her mouth, slowly retreated towards the stairs, finally sensing something was frighteningly, horribly wrong.

When Aysha had gone, the bald guy spoke in his hoarse, harsh tones. "Cute girlie, your kid! What a pity if she got hurt." Again he dropped his cigarette end where he stood, and Moustafa didn't dare to rush forward to pick it up. "Things burn that quickly these days, what with the heat and all . . ." His voice trailed off.

Moustafa's head swam; he couldn't see the guy clearly. The guy who threatened his daughter, his precious little Aysha, named after his mother and even dearer than her. He wanted to scream, to shout, to hit the guy's face, to run a knife into the broad chest, into that evil heart that talked of murdering a child! But once more, he couldn't even move, much less think clearly, frozen to the floor with fear, confusion, hatred. A hatred that grew so intense that by and by it extinguished every other feeling, till his whole lean body was filled with this hatred, till the hatred started to show in his eyes, and he lowered his head quickly, not knowing what to do. He had never killed even so much as a chicken with his own hands, but there he stood, longing to stab a man. . . .

He blinked rapidly, trying to clear his vision. When he finally succeeded, the bald guy had vanished. Slowly, feet leaden, Moustafa picked up the cigarette butt, threw it out on the pavement as if it could burn his fingers. Far down the street he could see the bald guy leisurely walking away.

In a sudden impulse, Moustafa called upstairs for his wife to handle the shop for a while. Still soaked in the sweat of fear and hatred, he followed the man, deliberately staying far enough behind that he wouldn't be noticed.

Twenty minutes later they had left the small town, wandering now through rich cornfields, the stalks tall enough for Moustafa to hide easily if the man should look back, but he didn't. In a flash-back Moustafa remembered his own country, the stony, barren soil he worked with his brothers and father. This new country he had come to looked like paradise in comparison, but earthly paradises never seemed to be without a flaw.... At least out here in the open country, the heat wasn't quite as stifling as in the streets of the town, but Moustafa's sweat nevertheless continued to trickle down his back, down his forehead, burning his eyes like acid.

Finally the bald guy reached a wooden barn, a big one, boards gray and black with age. Motorbikes were parked outside, three or four battered cars. For the first time, the guy looked over his shoulder, and Moustafa had to jump between the cornstalks. He waited long, anxious minutes till he dared to venture back onto the path.

All of a sudden, deafening sounds of music rose from the barn, while Moustafa watched the old building from behind a couple of thorny bushes. Sometimes young men stepped out to pee in the grass, and sometimes a couple would walk out for fresh air, the men all strangely alike with their shaven heads, the girls in miniskirts, giggling and drinking. Moustafa felt pretty sure the party would last till late into the night.... Thoughtfully he went back to town.

Far away a clock struck midnight, as he returned under a pale, full moon, equipped with a kitchen knife. Yes, he had been right! The party was still in full swing, and Moustafa settled down behind his bushes, from where he could watch the door unseen.

His heart beat faster when once he saw the bald guy step out with some others, laughing in his hoarse, croaky voice. The men talked awhile, then the guy left his companions and staggered to the bushes. For a second Moustafa's heart stopped beating; he pressed his body flat to the ground, didn't dare to catch his breath. The bald guy opened his fly, urinated, walked back. Moustafa nearly fainted with relief.

He waited patiently, saw the first of them leaving at two in the morning, dead drunk, singing, joking coarsely. Cars roared off, motorcycles left, sending pebbles flying in all directions. Moustafa didn't know what he was waiting for exactly, what he would do, but he held on to his knife, and whenever he let his fingers run over the blade, he thought of little Aysha in the frilly pink dress he had given her for her birthday, and of the menacing words the bald guy had spoken when he saw the girl.

The music had long since stopped. Everything had gone quiet around the barn. Moustafa hadn't seen the bald guy leave, though the moon was shedding its silvery light amply over the fields. Slowly Moustafa rose from his cover, crept over to the barn. He jumped with fright when he heard the noise, till he realized that inside someone was snoring.

Hands clammy with fear, knife in shaking fingers, Moustafa sneaked up to the heavy door that no one had bothered to close. His eyes needed some time till they adapted to the dimmer light inside the wooden building, then he saw the guy. He lay sprawled on the floor, snoring loudly, reeking of stale beer and gin. Through a small window a beam of moonlight illuminated his bald head in a ghastly white light, and it gleamed like a skull.

Throat dry as the desert, stomach churning, Moustafa cautiously glanced around. Broken bottles, deformed beer cans everywhere on the earthen floor, sad remnants of the day's party. To the left, where the bald guy lay in his stupor, huge stacks of hay. On one of these, the guy's cigarettes and matches.

Not really knowing what he did, Moustafa crept closer. Terrified by the situation, the physical nearness of the man who had threatened his child, he wasn't able to control his craving for nicotine any longer.

Without letting go of the knife, he fumbled one of the cigarettes out of the pack, lit it, inhaled deeply, and would have closed his eyes with satisfaction and the sweet soothing of the smoke if he hadn't been so afraid that the bald guy would wake up.

Cigarette in his left hand, knife in his right, his mind finally seemed to calm down. The blade of the weapon reflected the moon's cold light, and Moustafa shivered at the thought of running it into this man's warm, living flesh. At this moment he realized he couldn't do it. He couldn't bend down and kill the guy in his sleep even if he deserved to be dead. . . .

Moustafa walked back to town as if recovering from a nightmare. He didn't want to think about what he would do should the bald guy show up at the shop again. He didn't want to think about what might happen to little Aysha or his wife. He didn't want to think at all, just wanted to lie down and sleep, he felt so drained.

When he reached the first houses, dark in their peaceful slumber, a siren started to wail. Automatically, Moustafa turned in his steps. The night sky glowed in a strange, fiery red, back where the barn stood.

Aware that he was still clutching the knife, Moustafa tried to remember what had become of the cigarette he had smoked while watching the bald guy sleep.

Stacks of hay, all dry. *Things burn quickly these days . . .*

His whole body started to shake.

Had his fingers betrayed him, had they done of their own accord what his soul, his mind, his religion had forbidden him to do?

As he crept into his bedroom he could hear the fire engines pass through the street. "We should have stayed at home," his wife mumbled, only half awake. "At home in Turkey." Moustafa said nothing.

Norizuki Rintarō

An Urban Legend Puzzle

Translated from the Japanese by Beth Cary

The following co-winner of the 55th Mystery Writers of Japan Award in the short story category is an homage to Ellery Queen. We close this volume with it because it demonstrates so clearly the power of fiction in translation. While the character Ellery Queen and the books and stories that bore the Ellery Queen byline have gradually faded from consciousness in English, even in the United States, they remain in print in Japanese translation and they have recently given rise to a whole new movement in Japanese crime writing called "new traditionalism," in which puzzle construction is key. Norizuki Rintarō is part of that movement, and in "An Urban Legend Puzzle" he makes his inspiration clear by mirroring all of the elements of an Ellery Queen mystery: a complex puzzle, a father-son/police inspector-mystery writer detecting team, and use of the writer-sleuth's name as byline for the story. The pseudonymous author has several novels and a story collection in print. Who knows, perhaps as he and his fellow "new traditionalists" return the American-inspired form to us via such translations as the following, they'll generate a return of interest in the traditional mystery in the West.

1.

"What would you think of a message that said, 'Aren't you glad you didn't turn on the light?' This wasn't spoken, but a sentence written by hand."

" '. . . didn't turn on the light' . . . ?" Rintarō cocked his head. "I've heard that phrase somewhere. Is this a quiz or something?"

"No, it concerns a homicide I'm investigating. Late Monday night, a university student was stabbed to death in a one-room apartment in Matsubara, Setagaya Ward. Those words were inscribed in blood, in an unsteady hand, on the wall of the crime scene. Of course it was the victim's blood."

"Letters in blood on the wall of the crime scene?"

Inspector Norizuki nodded, his expression serious. It was a weekend night and he'd changed into his pajamas and was enjoying his after-dinner cigarette.

Rintarō shook his head. "Come on! You can't fool me that that's a case you're working on now. It's a famous urban legend."

"A famous what?"

"Urban legend. That's what sensational rumors that are spread by word of mouth are called. People claim that they're true stories heard from a friend of a friend. Some of these are standard occult or ghost stories, while others have their roots in celebrity scandals or strange cases involving vicious crimes. The story you've heard is one of the more popular ones, Father."

"Wait a second." Inspector Norizuki looked bewildered. "You've actually heard tell of such a case before this?"

"Yes, I have. And when you say 'actually,' I think you're just trying to pretend innocence because I've blown your cover."

"This isn't one of your novels, Rintarō. I wouldn't do something so roundabout. Tell me about this rumor."

"You're a harsh critic, Father. All right, then. The story I've heard goes like this:

Ms. A, a college student, went to a party at B's apartment with other members of her club. B was a year ahead of her at college. They had a good time drinking. A little after midnight, the party ended, and A left the apartment along with a friend.

After walking for a while, A realized that she had left her handbag at the apartment and decided to part with her friend and go back to retrieve her bag. When she returned to the apartment, the lights were already out and there was no response when she rang the doorbell. It appeared that B had already gone to bed. Feeling dejected, A tried turning the doorknob and it opened. B must have forgotten to lock the door.

The apartment's one room was pitch dark. But she remembered where she had left her bag and felt bad about waking the soundly sleeping B. Without turning on the light, A whispered, 'I came to pick up what I forgot,' as she groped for her bag. She left the apartment as she had entered it."

"Hmm, that's very interesting," Inspector Norizuki mused. The expression on his face was deadly serious, in contrast to the seeming nonchalance of the statement. Unaware that the lengthening ashes of his cigarette were about to drop onto the table, he asked, "And then?"

"The next day, A, concerned that she hadn't seen B on campus, went to his apartment. When she arrived, a police car was parked in front of the building, and the street was filled with policemen and onlookers.

'Did something happen here?' A asked one of the neighbors clustering around.

'There was a murder here last night. Mr. B in Apartment X was killed.'

It seemed that after A and the others had departed, someone had entered through the unlocked door and stabbed B to death as he was sleeping.

I should have woken him and told him to lock his door when I came back to retrieve my bag, A thought. She was filled with remorse, but no matter how much she regretted her actions, B would not return to life. Nothing could be done for him now.

Starting the next day, the club members who had been drinking with B just before he was killed were called in by the police to give their statements. Feeling somewhat responsible for B's death, A went voluntarily to give her statement to the detective in charge, offering as much detail as she could about the events of the night of the crime. When she'd finished, the detective took out a photograph. Prefacing his question by saying the picture might shock her, he asked, 'This message was left at the scene of the crime. Does it mean anything to you?'

The photograph was of the wall in B's apartment. Smeared on the wall in blood were these words:

'Aren't you glad you didn't turn on the light?'

Upon seeing the photograph, A turned pale and fainted. When A had returned to B's room that night, he had already been killed! If she had turned on the light to try to wake B, she would have come face to face with the killer and A would most certainly also have been killed."

Inspector Norizuki folded his arms across his chest and groaned. "You said it was a popular urban legend. Does that mean quite a large percentage of young people have heard it?"

"I suppose so. Nowadays there are many sites on the Internet dealing with urban legends. Leaving aside whether one believes it to be a true story, it's likely most young people have come across it at least once. There was even a movie last year that dealt with a similar tale."

The inspector opened his eyes wide in wonder. "Even a movie?"

"An American film that was given the title *Rules* in Japan. The original title was *Urban Legend.* It was a horror-suspense B-movie on the subject of urban legends—just as it says. It should be out now on video. The plot sounded interesting—a series of murders made to look like popular urban legends in America, like 'The Backseat Murderer,' 'The Boyfriend's Death,' or 'The Babysitter and the Man Upstairs'—but it wasn't really very good as a mystery movie. A different version of the story we've been talking about was used."

"By 'a different version' you mean . . . ?"

"It's a type known as 'The Roommate's Death.' And it might be closer to the original. The version we were just talking about didn't arise spontaneously. The core of the story must have been translated from an earlier American version. After all, the recent boom in urban legends started in America. What kicked it off was the book *The Vanishing Hitchhiker,* written by the folklore scholar Jan Harold Brunvand, which came out in nineteen eighty-one."

The inspector snorted impatiently and said, "Quit showing off your knowledge. What was the version of the story in the movie *Rules?*"

"I'm sorry, sir," Rintarō apologized. "Details of 'The Roommate's Death' can vary, but in the movie, it goes like this. It's set in a dormitory of a college far from any major city. The heroine's roommate is a dissolute female college student. One night, she enters the room to hear moans from her roommate's bed. Assuming, mistakenly, that her roommate is in the midst of a tryst with her boyfriend, the heroine doesn't turn on the light, but goes directly to her own bed and falls asleep listening to music through her earphones. Waking up the next morning, she discovers her roommate's butchered body in the bed next to hers. On the wall, written in the blood of the victim, are the words, 'AREN'T YOU GLAD YOU DIDN'T TURN ON THE LIGHT?'"

"So again, by not turning on the light, she saved her own life.

I see. It's a valuable piece of information. The fact that the film was shown in Japan means that it is possible the murderer may have seen it. If it's out on video, then we should check the video rental shops. If we're lucky, this could help us narrow down the suspects." Inspector Norizuki took out his pocket notebook and jotted down the movie title. He seemed to be serious.

Wondering if he could really be in earnest, Rintarō said, "This isn't just an after-dinner entertainment? Don't tell me that such a strange case has actually occurred?"

"Yes, it has, actually. I've been saying so from the beginning, haven't I? But it's not the movie version. This case is just like the first story of Ms. A that you related. We've kept the message written in blood from the media, so it hasn't become a news item."

Rintarō stared wide-eyed at his father. "A copycat murder of an urban legend?"

Frowning deeply, the inspector replied, "It seems like it, from what you have to say."

"Then, please," Rintarō said eagerly, "give me the details and circumstances of the case."

2.

"The victim, or student B," Inspector Norizuki explained, "is Matsunaga Toshiki, a second-year student in the Sciences Department at M—— University. He lived in Room 206 of the Belle Maison Matsubara apartment building at Matsubara 1-chōme. This is a building for students a five-minute walk from Meidaimae Station on the Keiō Line. The name of the building is fancy, but the one-room units are just one rank above low-end apartments. Apparently the soundproofing is thorough, but as the front entrance has no auto-lock system, anyone can freely enter the building, even those who do not live there.

Matsunaga's body was found lying on the floor of his room on Tuesday afternoon."

"Who found it?"

"A deliveryman from Yamaneko Delivery Company. It just happened that on Monday, the day before, a package was sent from Matsunaga's family in Shizuoka. The deliveryman rang the doorbell for Room 206, but there was no response. Noticing that the door was unlocked, the deliveryman suspected that Matsunaga was actually there but pretending not to be. It does seem a waste of gasoline to go repeatedly to the same address to try to deliver a package to a student who might be sleeping in until the sun is high in the sky," the inspector said, seeming to sympathize with the deliveryman. "Just to make sure, he opened the door and peeked into the room to discover the victim lying in a pool of blood on the floor of the 8-tatami-mat-sized[1] room. In a panic, the deliveryman tried to raise him up, but it was obvious that hours had passed since the victim had died. It was one forty-five P.M. when he called the police emergency number, 110, from the scene on his cell phone."

"It is fortunate that he gave priority to contacting the police over fulfilling his delivery quotas. What was the method used in the crime and the cause of death?"

"Matsunaga died almost immediately from loss of blood, having been stabbed in the chest with a sharply pointed object like a pick. But it wasn't that he was suddenly attacked while he was asleep in his bed. There were signs that he struggled with the assailant. So we should take it that the victim woke up and resisted."

"You say 'a sharply pointed object like a pick.' Could it have been something like a screwdriver?"

"No, we discovered an ice pick left in the sink with blood on

1. 140-odd square feet. Tatami mats are used for flooring. They are approximately 6' by 3'. Japanese room measurements are often given in terms of them.

the tip that matched the victim's blood. We found out that this ice pick wasn't brought in from elsewhere. It was one that Matsunaga, who liked to drink, frequently used. As the handle had been washed clean with water, we couldn't lift any fingerprints that might have been those of the murderer. According to the Identification Section, the murderer must have washed off most of the victim's blood at the same time."

"I see. The fact that there were signs of struggle and that the ice pick from the crime scene was used seems to indicate that it was an unpremeditated crime. What about the estimated time of death?"

"According to the medical examiner and the results of the autopsy, Matsunaga was killed between eleven P.M. on Monday and one A.M. on Tuesday. But we ascertained from the statements taken from those associated with the victim that he was already dead by about eleven-thirty P.M."

"Whom do you mean by 'those associated with the victim'?" Rintarō cut in.

Inspector Norizuki did not respond right away; he appeared to want to tell his story at his own pace. Only after he had reached for a cigarette and taken his time lighting it did he continue.

"Those who were in the same club at the university, of course. I told you it was exactly like the story of Ms. A, didn't I? Matsunaga Toshiki was a member of the university Bowling Club. He often invited other members of the club to drinking parties in his apartment. The solid soundproofing had the advantage that even if they became drunk and boisterous, his neighbors would not complain."

"Hmm, and that's why Matsunaga had his own ice pick?"

"Right. Monday, when the crime occurred, was the last day of first-term exams at the university. The Bowling Club members had gathered early in the evening at a pub in Shimokitazawa to celebrate the end of their exams. When that initial party at the

pub broke up, the seven members of the club who were an especially close group repaired, as usual, to Belle Maison Matsubara
to continue to drink. They said they bought some drinks and
snacks at a convenience store on the way and began the second
party just after nine P.M."

"Who was at the second party?"

"Four male students, including Matsunaga, and three female
students. Here's the list of them."

So saying, the inspector opened to a page in his notebook. The
list noted each member's name, major department, university
year, gender, and the train station closest to his or her residence.

Matsunaga Toshiki	Sciences	2nd year	male	(Meidaimae)
Nozaki Tetsu	Sciences	2nd year	male	(Machida)
Miyoshi Nobuhiko	Law	2nd year	male	(Yōga)
Nagashima Yurika	Literature	2nd year	female	(Kichijōji)
Endō Fumiaki	Economics	1st year	male	(Tsutsujigaoka)
Hirotani Aki	Literature	1st year	female	(Yoyogi Hachiman)
Sekiguchi Reiko	Economics	1st year	female	(Umegaoka)

"There are two first-year female students, aren't there? Which
one played the part of Ms. A?" Rintarō asked as he attempted to
commit the names on the list to memory.

"It was Hirotani Aki of the Literature Department. But let me
tell you the facts in order. At first, the drinking party on Monday
night was friendly and lively. But then it veers from your story.
Partway through, there was quite a disagreement. Matsunaga
and Miyoshi Nobuhiko, also a second-year student, started
arguing over some small matter. Disregarding the efforts of the
others to calm them down, they continued to revile each other."

"I thought you said it was a close-knit group? Did they dislike each other?"

"Apparently not normally. And though they insulted each other, they didn't actually come to blows. Matsunaga, who was the calmer of them, seemed to enjoy dishing out a string of insults that angered Miyoshi. Since he was drinking, Miyoshi must have overreacted to comments he would have let slide if he had been sober. Isn't that what student gatherings have always been like? Nevertheless, Miyoshi apparently did have a reason to dislike Matsunaga."

"Would that be related to this?" Rintarō extended his little finger, indicating girlfriend problems.[2]

The inspector made a sour face and nodded. "Exactly. What they call a love triangle."

"Did it involve one of the three women there?"

"No, that's not it. It all happened in the past. There was a girl named Sasaki Megumi who had been a member of the Bowling Club. She was in the same year as Matsunaga and Miyoshi and was going out with Miyoshi. Then Matsunaga seduced her. With the trouble that created among the threesome, it became uncomfortable for her and she stopped attending club gatherings. She dropped out of the club, and ultimately her relationship with Miyoshi fell apart."

"I see. It's the kind of story you hear quite often."

"Well, yes. There's a bit more to it, but for now let's go on with the case. The two young men started quarreling shortly after ten P.M. At ten-thirty, Miyoshi said he had drunk too much and didn't feel well, so he would go home. I don't think he was really drunk. He probably felt uncomfortable. No one attempted to keep him there, so he left alone."

"The party didn't break up when Miyoshi left?"

"Not right away," the inspector replied. "But a pall was cast

2. Raising the pinky while making a fist with the other fingers is a Japanese slang gesture for "woman." Raising a thumb is the corresponding gesture for "man."

over the party, and those who remained started squirming. For about half an hour they continued with some desultory conversation until they decided to break it up. Matsunaga, the host, had stayed up all night the night before to study for his exam that day, so apparently he was having a hard time keeping his eyes open by then."

"Then perhaps his taunting Miyoshi wasn't out of spite but partly to keep himself awake."

"I wonder about that. In any event, shortly after eleven P.M., after cleaning up the cigarette butts, empty bottles, and trash, the five remaining club members (other than Matsunaga) left Belle Maison Matsubara. They divided into two groups. Nozaki Tetsu and Nagashima Yurika, along with Endō Fumiaki, headed for Meidaimae Station. Hirotani Aki and Sekiguchi Reiko, the two first-year coeds, went in the opposite direction to Umegaoka Station on the Odakyū Odawara Line."

"Just a moment, Father." Rintarō broke in. " . . . I can understand why Nagashima Yurika, who lives in Kichijōji, and Endō Fumiaki, who was going to Tsutsujigaoka, would go to Meidaimae on the Keiō Line. But Nozaki Tetsu lives in Machida, doesn't he? Why didn't he go to Umegaoka Station on the Odakyū Line with the two first-year coeds?"

"That's because instead of going home to Machida, Nozaki went to spend the night at Yurika's apartment in Kichijōji," Inspector Norizuki said. "I should have explained earlier that Nozaki and Yurika were an accepted couple within the club. But Yurika asked me to keep this secret from her parents."

"So that's the deal. Sorry I keep interrupting your story. The point isn't that group but the two who headed for Umegaoka, isn't it?"

"Right you are." The inspector cleared his throat and wet his lips. It was his signal that the story was entering its key stage.

"The distance from Belle Maison Matsubara to Umegaoka Station takes about fifteen minutes on foot. When the two women reached the station, Hirotani Aki noticed that she didn't have her cell phone with her. She had received a call during the party, had taken her phone out of her bag then, and had forgotten it in Matsunaga's room. If it had been a different item that she had left, it would not have mattered much. But she couldn't go home without her cell phone, which to her is more valuable than her life. Flustered, Aki decided to go back to Belle Maison Matsubara."

"Did she go alone?"

"That's right. Sekiguchi Reiko did not go with her."

"That's strange. Even though the trains were still running, it was late for a young woman of nineteen to be walking the dark streets alone. That's not safe. Why didn't Sekiguchi Reiko go along with her? Perhaps the two of them weren't such good friends after all?"

Inspector Norizuki shook his head. "No, Aki and Reiko were the best of friends even within the group. This is unmistakable. Your doubts are justified, but there was a valid reason why Aki returned to Matsunaga's apartment alone. Aki borrowed Reiko's bicycle."

"Her bicycle?"

"Yup. Reiko lives in an apartment at Umegaoka 2-chōme, south of Umegaoka Station. She rides her bicycle to the station, where she takes the train. That's why Reiko's bicycle was at the station's bicycle parking lot that day. A distance that takes fifteen minutes to walk one way can be covered in a ten-minute round trip by bicycle. It's practical, isn't it? Reiko handed her bicycle key to Aki and went to the late-night donut shop facing the station to wait for her."

"I see. This is more involved than the urban legend. What happened then?"

"Aki pedaled to Belle Maison Matsubara on the borrowed bicycle. The party had let out after eleven P.M., and they had taken fifteen minutes to walk to Umegaoka Station. Let's say it took a few minutes to arrange to borrow the bicycle and five minutes to bike to Matsunaga's apartment. Aki would have reached the door of Room 206 around eleven-thirty P.M. The highlight of the case starts here. Aki rang the doorbell of Matsunaga's apartment, but there was no answer. The light was off as well. As I said before, Matsunaga had stayed up all night the night before the drinking party and seemed quite sleepy by the time everyone left. It would not have been strange if he had turned off the light and crawled into bed as soon as he was alone. Wondering what she should do as she stood outside the door, Aki tried turning the doorknob. Matsunaga must have forgotten to lock his door before he went to bed. The door opened. The room was pitch dark. . . ."

"This is just like the story of Ms. A. But listening to you, it does sound like a plausible turn of events."

"That may be. After opening the door, Aki hesitated at the entryway. She felt she shouldn't wake the soundly sleeping Matsunaga just for her convenience. Besides, in the worst case, a groggy Matsunaga might mistake her appearance for a seduction and suddenly come at her. So, without turning on the light, she whispered softly, 'It's Aki, I've forgotten my cell phone, so I've come to pick it up.' She crawled on her knees so as not to have to take off her shoes and proceeded into the pitch-dark room. Having been there many times, she remembered the layout. She said she found her cell phone right off when she felt around on the floor where she had been sitting. She backed out the way she had come in without making a sound, quietly closed the door, and quickly left Matsunaga's room. She said it crossed her mind that it was unsafe to leave the door unlocked, but she told herself he would be all right because he was a man. Aki then jumped onto Reiko's bicycle and returned to the station to meet up with Reiko, who was waiting at the donut shop."

"Didn't she notice anything unusual when she entered Matsunaga's room?"

"No, nothing. Her mind must have been taken up with collecting her cell phone. She was convinced that Matsunaga was fast asleep in his bed, and apparently she didn't sense anything or hear any sounds that were eerie."

"I suppose she can't be faulted for that. Say she stayed in Matsunaga's apartment for a few minutes, then it took her about five minutes to return to the station by bicycle, the same amount of time as getting there. In that case, it must have been about eleven-forty when she met up with Reiko at the donut shop."

"Right. During our questioning I had them show me their receipts for the drinks they had ordered. They showed 11:26 for Reiko and 11:41 for Aki, who entered the shop later. The two of them chatted for a while at the donut shop, sobering up. They said they talked about their reactions to the argument between Matsunaga and Miyoshi. As Aki was returning to Yoyogi Hachiman, they left the shop a few minutes before 12:33 A.M., the departure time for the last train toward Shinjuku, and parted at the ticket gate."

3.

While Inspector Norizuki went to the toilet, Rintarō prepared some cold drinks in the kitchen. The night was deepening, but the discussion about the case was only now entering its crucial phase. His father would be wanting a drink about now.

"Hey, that's considerate." Returning to the living room, Inspector Norizuki took a sip.

Rintarō joined him, just to wet his throat.

Bending his neck sideways to give it a stretch, the inspector continued, "I got as far as telling you that Hirotani Aki and Sekiguchi Reiko had parted at Umegaoka Station. I don't have to tell you what happened next. It's almost the same end as Ms. A's story."

"Almost?"

"There are a few differences. For example, Aki didn't drop by Belle Maison Matsubara the following day, and during her questioning she didn't faint when she found out about the message written in blood. But she turned pale when she heard about it and couldn't stop shaking. It will affect her for quite a while."

"It must have been quite a shock."

"Of course it was. It wasn't only Matsunaga's dead body that was right in front of her eyes in that pitch-dark room but also someone who had just committed murder. She must have been in mortal fear. I sent her home with an officer for protection in case of the worst. I've had her watched ever since. It would be good if she could recall something that might be a clue to identifying the murderer, but I don't have much hope of that. After all, the phrase 'Aren't you glad you didn't turn on the light?' was also a warning aimed at her."

"Can that message be used as physical evidence? The trace of the finger or the handwriting?"

"No, the murderer is quite clever." His expression glum, Inspector Norizuki turned his eyes to the ashtray on the table. "According to the Identification Section, the words in blood were written with a cigarette butt left in the room, by soaking the filter in blood. The victim was a chain smoker. We haven't found the blood-soaked cigarette butt. It must have been flushed down the toilet. We can't rely on the handwriting, either. It is unnaturally faltering, almost as if it were written by a child."

"Does it look as if it was written with the nondominant hand to hide the penmanship?"

"Yes, that's about it. And now I'd like to have your thoughts. You said there were many versions to the story of Ms. A. Are there any that deal with the murderer's character?"

Since his father had chided him earlier for showing off, Rintarō took care not to be pretentious when he answered, "Even if there were some, it probably wouldn't be of any use. In these kinds of rumors, the murders usually end up being committed by an escaped convict or a crazed killer with a screw loose."

"I thought as much. Just for the record, there's been no report of any prison escapes this month," the inspector said.

Nodding, Rintarō continued, "There's probably influence from an actual crime committed in America in the motif of a psychotic killer leaving a crime-scene message written in blood. For example, in the nineteen sixty-nine Sharon Tate mass murder, where five people including the actress were butchered by the Charles Manson Family, the word 'Pig' was inscribed with the victims' blood on the wall of the crime scene, and at the scene of another murder they committed that same day, the words 'Helter Skelter' were used."

"I've heard of that one. Weren't those words from a Beatles song?"

"Yes. And even further back, from nineteen forty-five to the following year, there was the case of William Heirens, a murderer who killed three females, including a six-year-old girl, for the fun of it. A seventeen-year-old student at the University of Chicago at the time, Heirens left a message written with the victim's lipstick at the crime scene. It said, 'For heaven's sake catch me before I kill more. I cannot control myself.'"

"Hmm. He must have been completely crazy."

"In Heirens's case, it wasn't written in blood, but the memory of these kinds of shocking crimes works on the public's subconscious. And you can see why the 'message written in blood' was made into a symbol of the indiscriminate psychotic murderer. But this is just to say that this was the case for the original urban legend. It doesn't prove definitively that the actual murder at Belle Maison Matsubara was committed by a psychotic, or in the manner of a killer who wantonly knifes passersby."

Inspector Norizuki rubbed his chin and nodded his satisfaction. "I agree with you on that. As a practical matter, even if we consider just the time factor, I can't conceive that a psychotic with no past connection to the victim would enter Matsunaga's room and kill the occupant."

"What do you mean 'the time factor'?"

"As I explained to you, it was just past eleven P.M. when the club members departed Belle Maison Matsubara. And it was eleven-thirty when Aki, having returned to pick up her cell phone, nearly ran into the murderer in the pitch-dark room. It is much too preposterous to suppose that a total stranger would break into Matsunaga's room and kill him in the span of those thirty minutes, even if he had forgotten to lock his door. I just can't believe that such a thing could happen."

"That is true. In that case, do you think that the message 'Aren't you glad you didn't turn on the light?' was an elaborate trick to make it look as if a wanton psychotic killer was the culprit?"

"Yes. But rather than say it was an elaborate setup, I would say it was done on the spur of the moment. I wasn't sure until I talked to you, but hearing that the phrase is straight out of a popular urban legend, I'm able to have conviction about my theory. That's not all." The inspector set his glass on the table to stress his next point. "When we consider what went on before and after, there's a high probability that Matsunaga's murderer was one of the members of the drinking party on Monday night."

"The way you say that, it sounds as if you already have an idea who the killer is. Is it because of an alibi?"

At Rintarō's anticipation of the next step, the inspector grinned.

"That's about it. From Aki's statement and the content of the message in blood, there can be no mistake that the murderer was in Matsunaga's room around eleven-thirty. Now, turning to everyone's alibi. We've already discussed Hirotani Aki and Sekiguchi Reiko. I can add that not only do we have the times stamped on the receipts, we also have backing for their statements from an attendant at the donut shop. During the fifteen minutes or so before she met with Aki, Reiko occupied a seat within sight of the shop attendant and did not leave the shop. It was about twelve twenty-five when the two of them left the donut shop."

"Seems airtight. Next?"

"The couple, Nozaki Tetsu and Nagashima Yurika, I just told you about. After they parted from Endō Fumiaki, who was going home to Tsutsujigaoka, on the platform at Meidaimae Station, they went toward Kichijōji on the Inogashira Line, and then to her apartment. They were together until morning, and provide alibis for each other."

"Hmm. We can't discard the possibility that they were accomplices, but . . . What about Endō Fumiaki after he left the other two?"

"He stated that he went home directly, without stopping off anywhere. There isn't any direct proof to back up his statement, but we found out that just at that time a classmate, also in the Economics Department, called Endō's cell phone. According to that classmate's statement, he talked continuously with Endō for about ten minutes from eleven twenty-five."

"I see." Rintarō started and slapped his knee. "That was when Aki was in Matsunaga's room. At that moment, the killer must have been hiding in the dark room after killing Matsunaga. So, regardless of where he was, Endō, who was talking on his cell phone with his classmate, couldn't have been the killer."

"Exactly. As for the last one left, Miyoshi Nobuhiko, he doesn't have a definite alibi. According to his statement, after he left Belle Maison Matsubara alone at ten-thirty, he went to several video-game centers in the area, still in a foul mood from his argument with Matsunaga. He played games for about an hour, and then took the train home to Yō ̄ga. He lives with his parents and siblings. The family stated that he returned home shortly after midnight."

"So he got home shortly after midnight. Say he left Matsunaga's apartment after eleven-thirty. If he walked to Matsubara Station, took a train on the Tōkyū Setagaya Line, and changed to the Denentoshi Line at Sangenjaya, he would have had time to reach home by then."

"Right. We're looking for witnesses around the game centers, but so far we have no reports of anyone seeing someone fitting Miyoshi's description around that time. Not only doesn't he have an alibi, but also in terms of motive, since he had an intense argument with the victim during the drinking party, Miyoshi seems suspicious to me," Inspector Norizuki stated emphatically.

It was perfectly natural to suspect Miyoshi from what had been discussed so far. Yet, as he sifted through the alibis, Rintarō felt a slight doubt. Since he couldn't put his finger on what specifically was bothering him, he decided to go along for a while longer with his father's theory.

"We were still in the middle of the story with regard to motive, weren't we? You said that there was a story behind the trouble between Matsunaga and Miyoshi—concerning the former club member Sasaki Megumi. What's that all about?"

"It relates to the victim's conduct. And it's typical of young people these days in that drugs were involved."

Inspector Norizuki let the implication hang and reached for another cigarette.

"One of Matsunaga's relatives is a cousin eight years older than he who is an internist with a psychiatric specialty. Apparently Matsunaga had something on this cousin. It's probably a trite thing, like he knew of the cousin's extramarital affair or something. In exchange for keeping quiet about this secret, Matsunaga hit his cousin up for drugs that are ordinarily hard to get."

"Were they illegal drugs?"

"No. Only Prozac, an antidepressant put out by an American pharmaceutical company. It's not a crime just to possess it. The victim had some fifty green-and-white capsules hidden away. When the crime scene was investigated, the search of Matsunaga's room revealed the pills in a cardboard box in his closet."

"Prozac is a drug said to promote the production of seratonin in the brain and to be very effective in treating depression. I hear that since it came on the market in America, it's sometimes used as a legal 'happy drug' even by healthy people. . . . Does that mean Matsunaga had a tendency toward depression?"

"No, he himself was quite healthy. He may have tried it once or twice, but there's no indication that he was a regular user. It seems Matsunaga was selling the Prozac he got from his cousin to people he knew as a way to earn some spending money."

Rintarō furrowed his brow at this piece of unexpected information. "Just a minute. If the victim was selling drugs, the motive for the crime could have been trouble related to a drug deal. I don't mean to say a drug user is necessarily a psychotic, but doesn't this completely change the nature of the case?"

"I don't think so. We checked into that possibility, but Matsunaga wasn't selling enough to make him a drug dealer. And he didn't have any drugs other than Prozac." He added that Matsunaga used a rough count, and appeared not to have a ledger or list of buyers, either. Having struck down Rintarō's suspicion with one blow, Inspector Norizuki exhaled smoke and continued, "It's also called SSRI—Selective Seratonin Re-uptake Inhibitor—and there is a similar domestic drug on the market. Insurance will cover that one. Prozac hasn't been approved by the Health and Labor Ministry yet. But it's all right for qualified physicians to prescribe it to patients, and it's no longer rare for people to use the Internet to import it on an individual basis."

"You mean it's rather widely available, so selling it can only bring in enough for spending money?"

"Exactly. If he did it too openly, he would be targeted, and if he approached someone in the know he would be taken advantage of. After all, there are plenty of other routes to get hold of it. Unless he was using it as a way to pick up girls, about all he could do was to sell small amounts to naive, earnest coeds as a cure for May depression.[3]"

"May depression isn't so prevalent anymore. But are you suggesting that Sasaki Megumi is one of those who bought Prozac from Matsunaga?"

"Yes. Megumi was an intense, introverted type from the start, so she must have been an easy mark for Matsunaga. She regularly bought the drug from him without letting her boyfriend Miyoshi know about it. If that was all, it would have been one thing, but Matsunaga apparently pressed for a physical relationship in exchange for giving her the drug. He probably didn't actually succeed, but this caused Megumi to become deeply neurotic. She couldn't face Miyoshi, and she may also have suffered a reaction to having become dependent on Prozac. Not only did she stop showing up at the Bowling Club, she also

3. That syndrome that follows relief at entering university in April after studying so hard for the entrance exams.

stopped attending her classes. Now she is on leave and recuperating at home."

Disheartened, Rintarō said, "That's abominable. I can't blame Miyoshi for holding that against Matsunaga."

"See? There's no doubting that he had a motive. And as to opportunity, if we consider the crime to have been committed by Miyoshi, the time factor that has been the bottleneck for the case will fit exactly."

"How so?"

"It would go like this. Having had a verbal fight full of recriminations with Matsunaga, Miyoshi left Belle Maison Matsubara at ten-thirty. But instead of going to the game center as he claimed in his statement, he could have wandered around nearby, intending to cool his head. He did this for thirty or forty minutes, but he was still angry, so he went back to the party intending to settle the argument. But when he returned to Belle Maison Matsubara, the party had ended, and Room 206 was quiet. He rang the doorbell, but there was no answer, and it appeared that Matsunaga had already gone to bed. Just as he was about to give up and head home, Miyoshi noticed that the door was unlocked."

Folding his arms across his chest, Rintarō uttered without much enthusiasm, "I see. And then?"

"Miyoshi stole into the room without turning on the light, roused the sleeping Matsunaga, and let loose a string of abuse. The time was between eleven-fifteen and eleven-twenty. At this stage I don't think Miyoshi had any clear intent to kill. But having been woken from his sleep, Matsunaga could hardly have stood for this. Mistaking the intruder for a burglar, he may have swung at Miyoshi without first questioning him. The two of them scuffled, and after several rounds, one of them took hold of the ice pick left in the room. As they grappled for it in the dark, Miyoshi's hand faltered and the stainless-steel tip ended up stabbing Matsunaga's chest. The hands of the clock showed half-past eleven. It was then, as Miyoshi was standing in a daze over Matsunaga's dead body in the darkened room, that Hirotani Aki, who knew nothing of this, came to retrieve what she had forgotten."

Having recreated the crime as if he had seen it happen, Inspector Norizuki jerked his chin up and sought his son's reaction.

Arms still folded, Rintarō absent-mindedly gazed at the ceiling. Finally he said, "You certainly make the time factor fit. Your theory gives a logical explanation for the victim having been killed in less than thirty minutes after he was left alone. However . . ."

Peering at Rintarō dubiously, the inspector said, "What do you mean, 'However'? Is there something that is unconvincing to you?"

"Yes, a major something. If that were the end of the story, then your theory would hold up. But the problem lies in what comes after that. If we consider Miyoshi to be the murderer, it is inconceivable that he would have written the message in blood. The message 'Aren't you glad you didn't turn on the light?' was not left by Miyoshi."

4.

"I started thinking something was off as I reviewed the alibis of those at the drinking party," Rintarō explained to his father as he unfolded his arms. "I should have realized what it was earlier. Namely, that if Miyoshi were the murderer, then the disadvantage to him of leaving the message in blood far outweighs the advantage of making the crime appear to be like the urban legend."

Inspector Norizuki cocked his head. "Disadvantage?"

"Yes. Let's first look at the advantage. We've been thinking that the message 'Aren't you glad you didn't turn on the light?' was a deliberate trick to make Matsunaga's murder look like a crime committed randomly by a psychotic. However, if you think it over a bit, it's obvious that one couldn't hope to alter the focus of the investigation with such a childish trick. As the phrase is copied straight from a popular urban legend, even if I hadn't told you, sooner or later someone would have noted that fact. Once the message was discovered to be a fake, it is clear that suspicion would fall on whoever harbored hatred toward the victim. The killer would have been able to foresee that much. And even more so from Miyoshi's standpoint, as he had had a confrontation with the victim over a love triangle. To put it another way, there is hardly any advantage for Miyoshi to have left the message in blood."

"What you say makes sense, but isn't it merely a theory born of hindsight?"

"You could say that if we look only at the advantage side. But the disadvantages that come about from leaving the bloody message are even more critical. Can you see? Let's say that, just as you imagined, Miyoshi killed Matsunaga at eleven-thirty P.M., and was nearly bumped into by Aki at the crime scene. Under cover of darkness, he succeeded in not being seen by her. In that case, why would he purposely leave a message saying 'Aren't you glad you didn't turn on the light?' which would tell not only Aki but also the police that he had been there at that time?"

The inspector sucked in air in surprise.

Rintarō continued: "According to your story, Father, Aki wasn't aware that the murderer was hiding in Matsunaga's room until she was told about the bloody message. That means that if the message hadn't been left, no one would have found out that the murderer was at the crime scene at eleven-thirty. The same can be said for the estimated time of death. Without the bloody message, it would have been impossible to specify the time when the crime was committed."

"Yes, what you say is true, but . . ."

"Let's keep this in mind and review the theory that Miyoshi committed the crime. If, as in the initial supposition, he killed Matsunaga at eleven-thirty P.M., he should have been the one to most dislike having the time the crime was committed narrowed down. This was because he had no definite alibi from the time he left Matsunaga's apartment at ten-thirty. As he had no way of establishing an alibi after the fact, all Miyoshi could hope for was that suspicion be deflected from him onto others who had attended the party due to there being no precisely estimated time of death. That is, the wider the range of the estimated time of death, the greater the benefit to him. Though he may have been upset immediately after killing Matsunaga, when he calmed down and became more rational, he would have been able to make such a calculation. That is why I wonder about Miyoshi having left the message written in blood. . . ."

"Just a minute. Isn't it dangerous to jump to such a conclusion?" Recovering a little, Inspector Norizuki attempted to put the brakes on Rintarō's deduction. "We can't assume that Miyoshi assessed the advantages and disadvantages and acted rationally. It is possible that he may have had his attention only on the less likely advantages and impulsively wrote the message."

"I can't see that happening. After all, you yourself said the killer was exceedingly clever. And if Miyoshi had lost his cool, could he have held his breath in the dark and refrained from killing Aki as well?"

The inspector's face betrayed acknowledgment of his weak point. Yet he seemed not to be entirely convinced, and said, as if he were poking at the crumbs left in a lunchbox, "Your argument certainly makes sense, but to me it is, after all, founded on extremely passive grounds."

"What do you mean?"

"The reasoning your theory attributes to Miyoshi is entirely passive. For no matter how much the estimated time of death is broadened, it doesn't change Miyoshi's not having an alibi, does it? Wouldn't he be pushing his luck to sit back and do nothing and expect to avoid being suspected?"

Nodding at this commendable objection, Rintarō replied, "Naturally, you would have such a rebuttal. But go back to what you said about passive grounds. If Miyoshi were the culprit, he would also have had an active reason for leaving the scene without writing the message in blood."

"And what would that be?"

"As I said before, if there had been no message in blood, when Aki returned at eleven-thirty to pick up what she had forgotten, no one would have found out that the killer, that is, a third person other than Aki and the victim, had been there. In fact, she had visited the victim's apartment entirely alone within the limits of the estimated time of death. This meant that the first person to be suspected would be none other than Aki herself. If the message hadn't existed, would the police have taken her statement as the truth? I can't think that would be the case. If Miyoshi had been there, I'm sure he would have thought the same way—that he had motive and no alibi. And that by quitting the scene without leaving evidence that someone else had been there he would be helping to shift the suspicion of murder to Aki, who had the misfortune to have shown up at the scene of the crime. This wouldn't at all be an unnatural way to think."

Rintarō stopped to wait for his father's response. The theory of Miyoshi Nobuhiko as murder suspect was about to go under.

Still, the inspector seemed to persist in promoting his own theory. With a jut of his chin he said, "It might be that Miyoshi was in love with Aki. Weighing the fact that Aki would be suspected versus the fact that his crime would be exposed, what if he deliberately chose to leave a message that would be disadvantageous to himself?"

Shaking his head firmly, Rintaro⁻ countered, "That is an impossibility. If Miyoshi loved Aki, he wouldn't have left a message written in blood that would frighten her. It could result in her becoming deeply traumatized, just like Sasaki Megumi. I'm sorry, Father, but you have no more escape routes. The Miyoshi-as-culprit theory is now completely disproved. He is not the one who killed Matsunaga."

"Mmm." Letting out a moan of defeat, the inspector, having nothing else to do, lit a cigarette. He smoked it wordlessly for a while, but then he slapped himself on the forehead. "All right. I agree. I'll take back my suspicions about Miyoshi. But this means the investigation is back to square one. If it wasn't Miyoshi, then who the hell killed Matsunaga?"

"There's no need to go back to square one."

The inspector raised his eyebrows. "Does that mean you have an idea who the real murderer is?"

"Yes. All we have to do is to look at our argument from the opposite direction. We should ask what conditions would allow for the disadvantage of leaving the message in blood to work contrarily, to favor the killer. In other words, who would gain the most from the existence of the message 'Aren't you glad you didn't turn on the light?' That's what we need to look at."

His cigarette still at his lips, Inspector Norizuki suddenly glared.

"Do you mean Hirotani Aki? You just said that if there had been no message in blood, she would undoubtedly have been the first to be suspected."

"Just as you say. The reason Aki's statement was recognized as being true to fact was due to the message in blood. What if, though, her statement was a boldfaced lie? What if, when she went back to Belle Maison Matsubara to retrieve her cell phone, Matsunaga was still alive, and no one was hiding in the darkened room?"

"Then the message saying 'Aren't you glad you didn't turn on the light?' was . . ."

"Of course, Aki herself wrote it."

"What?! I can't buy that."

But Rintarō persisted. "Let's start from where her story begins. When Aki went back to Matsunaga's apartment, did she really not turn on the light? Her own statement is the only thing to back this up. You mentioned that in her statement she said one of the reasons she didn't turn on the light was that in the worst case, a groggy Matsunaga might mistake her appearance for a seduction and suddenly attack her. What if this statement wasn't hypothetical but what actually happened, and Aki let it slip out?"

"What actually happened? You mean Matsunaga tried to assault Aki?"

"It's not impossible. After all, Matsunaga had made a prior attempt at seducing a friend's girlfriend. Returning to Matsunaga's apartment to retrieve her cell phone after the party, Aki entered the unlocked room and turned on the light, waking the soundly sleeping Matsunaga. Drunk and half-asleep, Matsunaga seized the chance of Aki having come back alone and tried to take advantage of her. Of course Aki resisted. Desperate to protect herself, Aki grabbed the ice pick used during the party, which was within reach, and stabbed Matsunaga in the chest. I doubt she had any intention to kill him, but that one stab was fatal, and he slumped to his death."

"That section is similar to the Miyoshi-as-murderer theory."

"Is that sour grapes?" Rintarō grinned. "It goes without

saying that Aki was shaken up. Coming to her senses with difficulty, she considered how she might conceal her crime. Her problem was Sekiguchi Reiko, who was waiting for her return at the donut shop. The police would eventually find out from Reiko that Aki had returned alone to Matsunaga's apartment to reclaim what she had forgotten. At that point, she would be the first to be suspected. Was there some way she could avoid this predicament? At that moment, what flashed across her mind like a revelation was the story she had heard from someone of Ms. A and the murderer who had left a message written in blood. She might be able to thwart the police investigation if she acted the part of Ms. A, who narrowly evaded becoming a second victim of the person who had just killed a fellow university student in the dark. Having thought this up on the spot, Aki copied the urban legend and left the message 'Aren't you glad you didn't turn on the light?' Then she turned off the light, left the apartment, and rode the bicycle she had borrowed from Reiko back to the donut shop as though nothing had happened."

"If that were the case," said Inspector Norizuki doubtfully, "what about her reaction when she saw the message during her questioning?"

"Of course that was an act."

"But I can't believe it was."

"That's likely because you had a preconception as to what her reaction would be."

"I wonder. It's not as though I've learned nothing during the many years I've spent in the interrogation room. If she had fainted on the spot like Ms. A did, I would admit that Aki had faked it. But her reaction was the real stuff. And even if my perception is wrong, your theory has holes in it."

Rintarō sat up so as to squarely face his father's counterattack. "What holes?"

"It's a time problem. As the donut-shop receipts show, there were at most fifteen minutes when Aki was alone after she parted from Reiko. And ten of those minutes were taken up bicycling round-trip between Umegaoka Station and Belle Maison Matsubara. Even with a liberal estimate, Aki could have been in Matsunaga's room for only five minutes. Just think about it: Five minutes is only three hundred seconds. On your theory, in just that short amount of time, Aki began to struggle with Matsunaga, who tried to take advantage of her," as he continued, the inspector counted the points off on his fingers, "stabbed him with the ice pick, then, barely recovering from the shock of killing someone from over-defensiveness, she immediately thought up the brilliant idea to make it seem like a copycat of the urban legend, wrote the message in blood with a cigarette filter, flushed the filter down the toilet, washed the blood from the ice pick and her hands at the sink, made certain she left nothing, and quickly left the scene of the crime. And that's not all. She would have needed time to straighten out her appearance, which must have become disheveled during her struggle with the victim, so that Reiko wouldn't suspect anything. This might be possible in one of your novels, but in actuality, do you think she had enough time to do all of that in just five minutes? What's more, Aki is a nineteen-year-old college student, not a professional killer. She couldn't possibly have remained calm enough to complete all that so quickly and efficiently immediately after she had unexpectedly killed someone."

The tables had turned. Uncharacteristically red-faced, Rintarō dejectedly scratched his head. "I have to admit that the time factor is rather difficult. . . . But what if Aki used an illusion as a trick, causing Reiko's sense of time to be off, and was able to squeeze out more than five minutes?"

"Hardly. What about the times stamped on the donut-shop receipts?"

"Maybe she pilfered another customer's receipt and switched it with hers or Reiko's receipt?"

Inspector Norizuki gave a snort. "Now you're forcing an improbability. I told you we have corroboration from the donut-shop attendant regarding the alibis for Hirotani Aki and Sekiguchi Reiko. There are no holes in their statements. I say there is no chance that Aki killed Matsunaga."

5.

Still, Rintarō was unable to give up on his theory that Aki had committed the crime. Various possibilities branched out in his head. Somewhere there must be a shortcut that would clear the time obstacle. . . .

After a while, he spoke. "What if we look at it this way? The crime committed on Monday night wasn't spontaneous, but planned out to the smallest detail."

"You mean Aki planned it? But Aki had no reason for killing Matsunaga, did she?"

"Maybe she did. Just as with Sasaki Megumi, drugs may have been involved. Aki may have regularly obtained Prozac from Matsunaga, but there was some trouble over the deal. When that became a big problem, Aki decided to kill Matsunaga."

"Hmm. Trouble regarding Prozac deals," Inspector Norizuki said, without much enthusiasm. "But I wouldn't think that would lead to murder—though it can't be ruled out completely. Well, what then?"

"In her murder plan, Aki decided to use the rumor about the murderer leaving a message written in blood at the crime scene. It goes without saying that her objective was to deflect suspicion by playing the role of Ms. A. So, on Monday night, she didn't happen to forget her cell phone in Matsunaga's room; she had planned it. This was to create a natural reason for returning

to Belle Maison Matsubara after the drinking party was over—
she may have already taken the ice pick with her at that time.
And it was probably Aki who suggested that she borrow Reiko's
bicycle in front of Umegaoka Station. If Reiko had gone back
with her, she would have hindered Aki's committing the crime.
At the same time, arranging to meet her at the donut shop must
have been done with the purpose of creating an alibi."

"Why was the door to Matsunaga's apartment unlocked
when Aki returned to Belle Maison Matsubara? It's too convenient to have been a coincidence."

"Of course, it wasn't a coincidence. She must have secretly
told the victim before the party that she would return alone
later. I don't know what kind of reason she gave, but Matsunaga
was waiting for her without going to sleep, unaware that she had
murderous intentions. Aki pedaled the bicycle as fast as she
could back to Belle Maison Matsubara. As soon as she entered
Room 206, she stabbed Matsunaga in the chest with the ice pick
when he welcomed her—with no hesitation."

"Wait. There was evidence on Matsunaga's body that indicated he had struggled with his assailant."

"Aki faked the evidence afterward. As she had planned, after
she dipped the cigarette filter in his blood, wrote the message
'Aren't you glad you didn't turn on the light?' and quickly took
care of all those things that you just counted off, Aki hurriedly
left the room. With a plan firmly in place, it wouldn't be impossible to complete all of these steps within five minutes. In actuality, there was no grappling with the victim, so her hair and
clothes were not messed up. After this, Aki again pedaled full
speed to the station and met up with Reiko at the donut shop as
if nothing had happened. How about that, Father? I would
think that it was quite possible for Aki to kill Matsunaga even
if she only had about five minutes."

The response from the inspector was not favorable. Blowing a lungful of smoke at Rintarō's face, he retorted, "It might be possible—as a desktop plan. But your theory has a fatal flaw."

"Oh?"

"Let's say she did plan Matsunaga's murder," the inspector said cuttingly. "Why would she need to fake it as an urban legend in order to accomplish it? If it were a spontaneously committed crime, I could understand—Aki's random behavior happened to coincide with the story of Ms. A and became the impetus for leaving the bloody-lettered message. But if the murder was premeditated, nowhere is there a reason to embellish it with the urban legend motif. There are many other ways to set it up, so why would she have concocted such a convoluted, intricate plan? Such a plan, which mistakes the means for the end, could only be entertained in the abstract by someone lacking a real necessity for committing the crime."

Rintarō was forced into silence. He had to admit it was exactly as his father said.

6.

"This makes it a draw between us in terms of injuries." Inspector Norizuki spoke as if to encourage the despondent Rintarō. He had just returned from the kitchen, fresh drinks in hand. He set the glasses on the table and sat down heavily.

"Don't be so discouraged. The night is still young. Let's rethink the case one more time, going back to our first assumptions. I don't buy your identifying Hirotani Aki as the murderer, but I don't think the direction of your reasoning was wrong. As you suggested, Matsunaga's killer was someone who would benefit from leaving the message 'Aren't you glad you didn't turn on the light?'"

Sighing deeply as he reached for his glass, Rintarō said, "The problem then becomes the nature of the benefit, doesn't it?"

"Yeah. But I don't have any bright ideas on that. Shall we go over the list of those at the party one more time? It's not unusual in a race in which the front-runner and its rival horse fall for a dark horse that no one had paid attention to to carry off the victory."

So saying, the inspector drew lines through the names listed in his notebook.

~~Matsunaga Toshiki~~	~~Sciences~~	~~2nd year~~	~~male~~	~~(Meidaimae)~~
Nozaki Tetsu	Sciences	2nd year	male	(Machida)
~~Miyoshi Nobuhiko~~	~~Law~~	~~2nd year~~	~~male~~	~~(Yōga)~~
Nagashima Yurika	Literature	2nd year	female	(Kichijōji)
Endō Fumiaki	Economics	1st year	male	(Tsutsujigaoka)
~~Hirotani Aki~~	~~Literature~~	~~1st year~~	~~female~~	~~(Yoyogi Hachiman)~~
Sekiguchi Reiko	Economics	1st year	female	(Umegaoka)

"Of the four remaining, can we exclude the two who have solid alibis for eleven-thirty P.M.—Endō Fumiaki and Sekiguchi Reiko? If so, we can look at the couple—Nozaki Tetsu and Nagashima Yurika. As you pointed out before, if these two had colluded and concocted a false alibi . . . Huh? What is it, Rintarō?"

While the inspector was speaking, Rintarō suddenly looked up at the ceiling, his jaw dropping open. From his lips escaped the whisper, ". . . a solid alibi."

He did not stir at all for a time, until eventually his eyes began to shine brightly. All of a sudden, he slammed both of his hands on the table.

"That's it! That's the only possibility! I've been blind!"

Inspector Norizuki was dumbfounded at this turnaround. "Hey, are you all right?"

"Sure I am, Father. Actually I should say I've finally come to my senses. The answer has been right in front of our noses all along, and I didn't even notice it."

"In front of our noses?"

"Yes. The clue to the truth was something I said when we were discussing the Miyoshi-as-killer theory. Didn't I say that if there had been no message in blood, it would have been impossible to pin down the time the crime was committed?"

"Yeah, I remember hearing something like that."

"That's exactly the advantage gained by leaving the message in blood. It's a simple but extremely effective alibi trick. Can I explain? The medical examiner estimated the victim's time of death to be between eleven P.M. on Monday and one A.M. the following day at its broadest. This means that the actual crime could have been committed before eleven-thirty or after that time. But the murderer used Aki's statement and left the message 'Aren't you glad you didn't turn on the light?' to plant the impression that the crime was committed at eleven-thirty—despite the fact that the murderer was not in Matsunaga's room at that time. To put it another way, the person who benefited from the existence of this message, that is, the real killer of Matsunaga, had to be someone who had a solid alibi for eleven-thirty P.M."

Rintarō had rushed on without pausing for breath. As if his son's excitement had transferred to him, Inspector Norizuki was now on the edge of his seat. "I see. The trick of using preconception as a counterattack. In that case, the couple Nozaki Tetsu and Nagashima Yurika, whose alibi isn't limited to eleven-thirty don't fit the criterion. The ones who have a solid alibi for eleven-thirty P.M. are Endō Fumiaki and Sekiguchi Reiko, but—"

"Endō isn't the killer. I can say that because he doesn't meet the other criterion necessary for leaving the message in blood."

"What other criterion?"

"In order to leave that message in blood, the person had to know not only that Aki went back to Matsunaga's apartment to retrieve what she had forgotten, but also the fact that she left the room *without ever having turned on the light*. Without knowing that, it would be meaningless, impossible, really, to leave the message 'Aren't you glad you didn't turn on the light?' Endō was not in a position to have known in advance about the details of Aki's actions. Therefore, he is not the killer."

Solemn-faced, Inspector Norizuki said, "That leaves one person . . ."

"Sekiguchi Reiko. She meets both criteria that I just set out. One: At eleven-thirty P.M. Reiko was at the donut shop at Umegaoka Station and had a solid alibi. Two: Reiko met up at the donut shop with Aki, who had returned from Matsunaga's apartment, and had the chance to hear from her the details of what happened in his room."

"Hmm. Most likely Aki told her about it right off. The two of them left the donut shop around twelve twenty-five A.M. That means that after parting with Aki at the station's ticket gate, Reiko went back to Belle Maison Matsubara. What was her reason for that?"

"This is just my supposition, but I think it involves the Prozac that Matsunaga had. Let's say Reiko purchased the drug periodically from Matsunaga. He may have charged more than the normal rate, and Reiko may have had difficulty paying up. But that night, Reiko heard from Aki about Matsunaga's room—that he was fast asleep with the door unlocked."

Stroking his chin, Inspector Norizuki said, deep in thought, "I get it. And I wouldn't be surprised, from the impression I got talking to her, if she were taking Prozac. She seemed to be kind of a highly-strung type, one of the best students from the countryside. That's the type who sometimes do bad things on the spur of the moment, though they don't look like they would. On your supposition, then, Reiko crept into Matsunaga's apartment while he was asleep and tried to steal some Prozac, which was put away somewhere."

"When we look at it that way, everything fits into place. It took five minutes for her to return to Belle Maison Matsubara from the station on her own bicycle. She entered Room 206 just after twelve-thirty. Leaving the room dark so she wouldn't wake the sleeping Matsunaga, Reiko began to search the apartment, feeling around with her hands. But she must have tripped on something in the dark, making a loud noise. Woken up by the noise, Matsunaga noticed Reiko's presence. He must have realized right away that she had come for the Prozac. Angered, Matsunaga hurled himself onto Reiko and grappled with her. Here our familiar ice pick comes into play and Reiko stabs Matsunaga dead. . . . At the latest, this all happened before twelve forty-five."

"That's just barely within the range of the estimated time of death. Then what?"

"With Matsunaga's body in front of her, Reiko probably couldn't think of anything for a while. Her initial aim of stealing the Prozac must have flown out of her mind. But she had plenty of time to come to her senses and devise a coverup. She could bicycle back to her place in Umegaoka, so she didn't need to be concerned about the time of the last train. As her breathing returned to normal in the dark, while she gazed at Matsunaga's dead body, Reiko remembered that Aki had returned to Matsunaga's apartment to retrieve what she had forgotten. That led quite naturally to her recalling the rumor of the message in blood that she had heard from someone. If she set it up so that it seemed Aki had narrowly avoided bumping into the murderer . . . Of course, at the time that Aki actually went back to Matsunaga's apartment, he was still alive, fast asleep, unaware of her presence. But, if Reiko created conditions in which it would appear that Matsunaga had already been killed and the killer was hiding in the room, her alibi of being at the donut shop in front of the station at that time would clear her of suspicion. Reiko must have smiled slightly at her idea. She stood up and found Matsunaga's cigarette lighter to use for a light. Then, picking up a cigarette butt, she dipped it into the blood flowing from the victim's wound. Holding this in her nondominant hand, she wrote the message on the wall—'Aren't you glad you didn't turn on the light?'"

Awhile later, postcards, always with the same message, began arriving once a week for Ms. A. They were sent by Ms. C, who had been her best friend and a member of the same club. The sender's address was the medical correctional institution in Hachiōji. When Ms. A moved, the deliveries would stop for a while, but someone must have been secretly looking up her address, for soon the postcards, with the same message, would start arriving at the new address. Written on the back of the postcard, always in red pencil, in an unsteady scrawl, were the words, "Why didn't you turn on the light?"

Every time she read these words, Ms. A felt a chill go up her spine. She also felt that she could never get rid of her regret—if, that night when she had returned to his room, she had turned on the light and woken B, then he would not have been killed! And her best friend, Ms. C, would not have been so burdened by her guilt that she went insane.

ACKNOWLEDGMENTS

Special thanks to Mary Frisque of the International Association of Crime Writers for leads pertaining to authors in the Passport series, and to Lauren Kuczala of *Ellery Queen's Mystery Magazine* for help in preparing the manuscript.

We are grateful to the following for permission to use their copyrighted material:

"Ramon Acuña's Time" by Isaac Aisemberg, translated by Donald A. Yates. First published in Spanish. Copyright ©1994 by Isaac Aisemberg; translation copyright ©2004 by Donald A. Yates. Reprinted by permission of the translator and the author's estate.

"Table Talk, 1882" by Boris Akunin, translated by Anthony Olcott. First published in Russian. Copyright ©2000 by B. Akunin; translation copyright ©2003 by Anthony Olcott. Reprinted by permission of the translator and Linda Michaels Ltd.

"Bloody Hot" by René Appel, translated by Josh Pachter. First published in Dutch. Copyright ©2004 by René Appel; translation copyright ©2006 by Josh Pachter. Reprinted by permission of the author and translator.

"DeKok and the Hammer Blow" by Baantjer, translated by H. G. Smittenaar. First published in Dutch. Copyright ©1996 by Uitgeverij De Fontein, Baarn, Netherlands; translation copyright ©2004 by *EQMM*. Reprinted by permission of the author, Uitgeverij De Fontein, and *EQMM*.

"Full Moon" by Mischa Bach, translated by Mary Tannert. First published in German. Copyright ©2000 by Mischa Bach; translation copyright ©2005 by Mary Tannert. Reprinted by permission of the author and translator.